4/10/06

You're convinced you have only two weeks left to live.
What do you do?

    A. Lie on your bed and cry.
    B. Calculate exactly how many hours you have left and
       graph the most efficient way to spend them.
    C. Fall in love ASAP because you just have to know
       what love is really like!

You're a mild-mannered accountant whose irrepressible
secretary is determined to fall in love—with the wrong
man. What do you do?

    A. Stay out of it. It's none of your business.
    B. Protect her from her own folly, because the guy
       could be a complete maniac, and you're terrified she
       might get hurt.
    C. Get her to fall in love with YOU!

If you picked A, Madison O'Donnell has a few lessons for
you on seeing the brighter side of life.

If you picked B, you might be a kindred spirit to certified
public accountant T. Laurence Hobbs.

But if you chose C, then you're ready to join Madison
and T. Larry for a ride on the road to love—where a fun-
loving free spirit teaches a by-the-numbers accountant that
there's more to life than tax codes and that love doesn't
work on a plan.

Jennifer
Skully

DROP
DEAD
GORGEOUS

HQN™

ISBN 0-373-77104-5

DROP DEAD GORGEOUS

Copyright © 2006 by Jennifer Skullestad

This edition published by arrangement with Harlequin Books S.A.

® and TM are trademarks of the publisher. Trademarks indicated with ® are registered in the United States Patent and Trademark Office, the Canadian Trade Marks Office and in other countries.

www.HQNBooks.com

Printed in U.S.A.

Dear Reader,

I love names. When I hear a fantastic name, I get chills. I share this in common with Barbara, my hairdresser. She comes up with the greatest names and passes them on. And that's how *Drop Dead Gorgeous* was born! See, I was having my hair done, which is a long process, and Barbara whispered, "What about Madison O'Donnell?" Ooh! Right before our eyes, Madison came to life. I saw a second-generation Irish Episcopalian free spirit with lots of gorgeous red hair who loved shopping at garage sales with her mother and had lots of loving, overprotective brothers. But who to pair her with? Barbara to the rescue! T. Laurence Hobbs. He just sounded so completely opposite to Madison. And Madison was dying to know what the *T* stood for, but he wouldn't tell (okay, Barbara and I were dying to know, too, but Laurence was keeping that a secret). And Madison called him all sorts of iterations, T. Larry being her favorite, but never ever Laurence. Madison and T. Larry came to life that day in Barbara's shop, and I just had to tell their story. So thanks to Barbara for loving names as much as I do. And, dear reader, Barbara does make a special guest appearance in *Drop Dead Gorgeous*. Now, here's the question—since I plotted a whole book while having my hair done, does that make my hair expense tax deductible? I'm sure T. Larry will know!

Jennifer Skully

To Jon Skullestad
For being my inspiration
You have my total admiration

Acknowledgements

Thanks to all the special people in my life!

Barbara Berens for helping me envision
Madison and T. Larry.
The characters came to life that day!

Jenn Cummings, Dee Knight, Rose Lerma,
Pamela Britton, Moni Draper and
Cheryl Clark for all their input. And Lucienne Diver
for setting me on the right track.

My editor, Ann Leslie Tuttle.

And lastly, to my entire family
for all their wonderful support.
You guys make me cry!

DROP
DEAD
GORGEOUS

CHAPTER ONE

MADISON O'DONNELL loved a lot of things. Chocolate peanut butter cups and hot dogs with extra mustard. The treasures she found on her once-a-month rounds of the Saturday garage sales with her mother. A good mystery, a great romance and erotic videos. She loved telling clients she'd cut her boss into pieces and stuffed his body parts into the bottom drawer of her filing cabinet. It made them smile, and goodness knew people needed a smile when faced with a tax consultation early in the morning. Madison loved to make people smile. She loved her wavy titian hair—the word red would simply never do. She loved her three older brothers, her mother and her mother's sugar-n-lemon pancakes.

Yes, Madison "loved," but she'd never been "in love," and falling in love was something she absolutely had to do before she turned twenty-eight. Which meant she had only fifteen days left to achieve that nearly impossible goal before it was too late.

But fall in love with whom? After pondering the question the entire day, Madison still hadn't a clue.

T. Laurence Hobbs, her staid yet adorable boss, entered her cube, and blew her musings to the winds. On the other side of her cubicle, fingers tapped ditties on keyboards and ten-key adding machines and the low rumble of voices drifted through the six-foot partitions. The phone rang on the desk in front of her. T. Larry— a nickname she loved and he'd endured with long-suffering sighs over the seven years he'd employed her—harrumphed when her hand went automatically to the receiver. Choosing the phone over him, Madison swung her chair, put her back to him and answered with a chipper smile.

"Carpal, Tunnel and Syndrome. Mr. Hobbs's office." Spoken fast and slurred, the client wouldn't understand the play on words, which should have been Carp, Alta and Hobbs, CPAs. T. Larry would know, though. His frown jabbed her between the shoulder blades, and her smile widened. She loved teasing him.

"Hey, beautiful, what are you doing?"

She didn't recognize the voice on the other end, but hanging up on anyone calling her beautiful was incon-ceivable. A nice voice, sexy, deep. The perfect voice for phone sex lite. Who was it? She could have asked, but relished figuring out his identity on her own.

Hoping for a clue, she said, "Just waiting for your call."

At her back, T. Larry puffed like a fire-breathing dragon.

"What are you wearing?"

Jim? He'd always wanted to know the color of her panties. Though he'd never asked over the phone. Ooh. "Something red and lacy."

T. Larry broke into a spasm of coughing, recovering before she had to turn around and pound his back.

"You're driving me crazy, how was your day, did you think of me?" was said as one purring sentence, as if her mystery man had only one thought on his mind.

Not Jim, the voice was too tempting. Not Matthew, either, since he'd broken it off at the beginning of May, over a month ago. Unless he'd decided he'd made a mistake. She was willing to forgive just to find out if she could have fallen in love with him given more time. Hmm, what was the best way to play this? "I can't say I did think of you today."

"I'm wounded. Make it up to me by having dinner with me." A touch of laughter laced the deep voice. Matthew, for sure. He had a quirky sense of humor, a thick skin, and it was just like him to forget he'd snapped her in two like a twig.

It had taken her a whole day to get over it. Still, "Don't you think we ought to talk about what happened first?"

T. Larry cleared his throat, then his arm slid into her line of sight, the finger of his other hand tapping the face of his watch. Five minutes to five, she was still on *his* time.

Matthew went on. "Let's talk about it over champagne and veal picatta."

Veal? She couldn't bear to think about those poor calves stuck in pens and slaughtered like... Madison shoved T. Larry's arm away. "I'd love to have dinner, but I've got to catch the 5:20 train home, and my brother Patrick's picking me up—"

"Your brother?"

"—and it's too late to tell him I won't be on it." Besides, she shouldn't have dinner with her former beau at all without first discussing that goodbye. "So call me tonight, Matthew."

"Matthew?" A quizzical tone, probably raised eyebrows, too. Oops, she'd put her foot in it. She was always doing that.

"My name's not Matthew. Is this Kim?"

With only fifteen days left until her birthday, she was beyond the usual embarrassment. "I'm Madison."

He laughed, a lovely full laugh that must have come straight from his belly. "I'm really sorry. I thought—"

"And I thought—"

"So what are you doing tonight?" A deep breath, a smile still in his wonderful voice. "How about dinner?"

Madison laughed with him. "You don't even know me."

"You're Madison. I'm Richard."

"Nice to meet you, Richard, but I still can't have dinner with you tonight."

"I know. Your brother's picking you up from the 5:20 train."

T. Larry knocked the back of her chair with his knee. She waved a dismissive hand and plugged a finger in her ear.

"How about tomorrow?" Richard pushed.

Friday. She was free. He really did have an amazing voice. Madison was never one to dismiss coincidence. Coincidence was destiny patting you on the back. Especially with her birthday bearing down like an avalanche. Twenty-eight. What if she never knew what it was like to fall in love? What if Richard was *The One,* her destiny?

"Okay, I'll have dinner with you tomorrow." She bit her lip to keep the excitement from bubbling over. "But no veal." Then she told him what she looked like so the man of her dreams could recognize her across a crowded restaurant.

GOOD GOD. Laurence adjusted his glasses. Madison O'Donnell had just told a complete stranger the color and texture of her underwear. With the whole office listening on the other side of her cubicle walls. Then she'd made a date with the man.

Unbelievable. Unimaginable. But then Madison always did and said the unthinkable. She wasn't quite…normal.

Yet T. Laurence Hobbs found himself hopelessly fascinated.

Of course, he'd never act on it. She was his secretary, and as such, she deserved better than office ogling or unwanted advances. Besides, he was ten years her senior in actual years and probably twenty in demeanor. No one had ever called Laurence young at heart. Not even when he was young. On the other hand, the term had been coined for Madison. He couldn't hope to keep up with a woman like her. She would exhaust an Olympiad.

She smiled sweetly then, replaced the receiver and turned to him, all even white teeth and red lips. "That wasn't Matthew."

"I gathered." He'd heard about Matthew, who'd dumped her for a blonde with at least six inches on Madison's five-foot-two and two additional letters in bra size. He'd seen the woman, and Madison was mouthwatering in comparison.

He caught himself before he accidentally ogled and steamed up his glasses or offended Madison.

She began shutting down her computer. Two minutes to five, she always left on the dot, her train wouldn't wait. She was ever conscientious about not keeping her brothers waiting, a trait Laurence admired.

"His name is Richard," Madison said, flipping off the desk lamp. "He mistook my voice for someone named Kim."

"I gathered that, too."

She stopped in mid-mouse stroke and settled her brilliant green gaze on him. "Is that a note of displeasure? I'll stay five minutes extra tomorrow night to make up for the call."

She'd have time, too, since she was meeting *Richard* at six o'clock in a nearby restaurant—Laurence had eavesdropped on the entire call. It wasn't the five minutes that bothered him. "What would your brothers say if they knew you were having dinner with a man you've never met? Not to mention your mother?"

"They'd say I was sensible for choosing a public place." Madison always had an answer.

"They'd be appalled you didn't even ask his last name."

She tilted her head, giving his comment consideration. "I suppose I should have asked. I could have Googled him." Then she flashed a smile. "But a little mystery is much more exciting."

"It's foolhardy."

She turned back to the computer. "Girls just want to have fun, T. Larry."

He'd realized one month after hiring her that she'd never call him Laurence like a normal person. He'd gotten over it. He hadn't, however, gotten over her perky attitude that never wore down. Someone had probably gotten the idea for the Energizer Bunny Rabbit while observing Madison.

"You can't go out with strangers just because it's fun." The thought of Madison alone at the mercy of some maniac parched his throat.

The men she chose to date—which she was never shy to talk about—were frightful. Fickle Matthew, interested-in-only-one-thing Jim and a host of others with equally unappealing qualities, none of whom were worthy of her radiance. She needed someone stable, responsible, someone older, with worldly experience. *Fun* should be the lowest on the list of traits one looked for.

She pointed her mechanical pencil at him. "You need to learn how to *have* fun. Maybe along the way, you'll even find the future Mrs. Hobbs."

He was abruptly aware of thin cubicle walls. They didn't dampen an iota of sound. No one, except Madison, left Carp, Alta and Hobbs at five o'clock. There were always audits to perform, tax forms to prepare and clients to advise. That meant every one of his thirteen staff members not at a client's—he hoped they were all creating billable hours—could hear this suddenly delicate conversation.

The inside office area was one large space separated into smaller cubes by the cloth and pressboard dividers while the manager and partner offices ringed the bull pen. Laurence considered directing Madison into his office a few short paces along the hall as around them collective breaths held and ears tensed. Phone ringers went dead and cell phone chatter ceased.

Dragging his secretary into his office at the end of the workday was not an option. Madison's reputation was of the utmost importance.

Laurence lowered his voice. "I know how to have fun. And I'm doing quite well in my search for the future Mrs. Hobbs, thank you very much."

Opening the bottom drawer of her desk, Madison hauled out an immense purse, perched it on her lap and rummaged. "If you're doing so well, why hasn't Alison called for two weeks?"

"Alison didn't—" Why was he letting her get away with an invasion of his private life? He didn't need to explain that Alison was consistently tardy for dates by at least half an hour. He wanted a wife who would teach his children good manners. He'd dated semi-regularly, looking for the right woman. He'd even had a few fairly serious relationships, but for some reason, he hadn't been quite ready for marriage to any of them. Maybe Madison was on to something. He wasn't searching as earnestly as he should be. There was always one more step in his career to take or one trait he couldn't accept in a woman. But those musings were for another time.

"We were talking about you and…Richard." The man should shorten it to Dick. That would suit him better. "Meeting someone like this is dangerous."

Hands still inside the purse, Madison cocked her head to stare up at him. "It's not like I'm going to sleep with him."

Thank God, he thought, until her next revelation.

"I'm going to marry him."

Blood rushed to his brain and his face, boiling one and burning the other. He spluttered, but nothing came out.

"Lighten up, T. Larry. That was a joke." She wagged her finger at him. "You're never going to find the perfect wife if you don't develop a sense of humor."

His breath came back, but the head rush left him dizzy. "I know how to laugh."

She put a finger to her full lips to shush him. "Come to think of it, you should get rid of that Plan of yours. It's inflexible and passionless."

What was wrong with his Plan? It was failure-proof, consisting of subplans. First, the Financial Plan leading naturally into the Family Plan where he'd settle down with a charming wife who watched FOX News Network while knitting booties for the three children they'd have in two-year intervals. Laurence straightened his already straight tie. "A man has to have financial security before considering a family. Passion gets in the way of good decision making."

"T. Larry, don't you realize you'll never have Total Financial Security?" She curled her bright, red-nailed fingers in double quotes and rolled her lovely green eyes. "Love doesn't work on a plan. Take my advice, find someone before you're too old to catch a woman whose biological clock hasn't gone into overdrive."

She didn't seem aware of her mixed metaphor or the profundity of her words. Still, he wasn't worried. His plan wouldn't fail. He'd covered every foreseeable outcome and adjusted for it. This discussion, however, wasn't about him. It was about her.

"What if Mr. Right doesn't fall in love with *you?*" The moment the insensitive words were out of his mouth, Laurence regretted them. An apology lay on the tip of his tongue.

Madison, unoffended, smoothed her splendid yet unruly curls behind her ears and smiled. That smile never failed to knock him senseless.

"Don't you see?" she said. "It's more perfect if he doesn't love me back."

At that moment, Laurence wasn't sure of his own sanity, let alone hers. "Aren't you missing half the *fun* that way? Love isn't supposed to be one-sided."

She tapped her temple. "It's all up here. I can believe anything I want to believe. Women are excellent at deluding themselves. If he isn't really in love with me, I won't worry about hurting him, when—" she shrugged "—I die."

His chest tightened just contemplating that word and Madison in one sentence.

Madison thought her death imminent because her father had died of a stroke when he was twenty-eight. It had been his second, the first striking him when he was in his teens. Just as Madison had had her stroke when she was fifteen. Like father like daughter, that's what Madison believed. Which explained her zest for life. Almost dying when you'd barely begun to live would make anyone view every moment that came after as precious. Madison went further. She'd convinced herself she would suffer her father's fate at twenty-eight, though as far as Laurence knew, there wasn't a shred of medical evidence indicating that outcome. *I just know it, T. Larry.* If he'd heard it once, he'd heard the phrase a thousand times. And she didn't intend to leave behind any motherless children, widowed husbands or tearful lovers. Therefore, in her mind, it was better if her chosen one didn't love her back.

Laurence narrowed his eyes. "Somehow, somewhere, I know there's a fault in your logic."

Madison grinned, the endearing lopsided quirk a remnant from her brush with death. "Maybe. But you can't find it."

She was right; he couldn't, so he turned things on her again. "This Richard could be a serial killer looking for a next victim."

She snorted. On anyone else, it would have been graceless. With Madison, it was as infectious as her laughter. "God already has big plans for how I'm going to die. He wouldn't add a serial killer in there to complicate things."

"Madison, you've gone crazy this time." Scheduling a date with a man whose name she didn't know was over the top, even for Madison. And a first, as far as he knew.

"It was just a wrong number, T. Larry, nothing alarming." She followed that up with a soft, sad smile indicating her immense pity for his suspicious mind.

He couldn't define why this incident bothered him more than a myriad others. Like the time she'd let it slip to Zach, one of his senior accountants, that she'd watched a porn flick. Porn, for God's sake. Laurence didn't think himself a prude, but weren't women genetically programmed to abhor pornography?

She'd never fit in anyone's neat little box, so he pushed the ridiculous. "I suggest you ask your perfect Richard about the Terrible Triad."

Her eyes widened, question enough.

"Bed-wetting, fire setting and cruelty to animals. It's indicative of a potential serial killer."

She flashed a smile that had brought lesser men to their knees. "Sometimes I wonder if you have a much bigger sense of humor than you let on."

"I must have to allow you to keep working here."

She rose, smoothed her short black skirt over her tummy, then her thighs. Laurence lost his voice.

"Seriously, T. Larry." With a step forward, she raised her emerald-isle eyes to his. Her voice dropped to an intimate note. "What if he's the one? *The* one, I mean? I have to find out."

Then she was gone, leaving behind the soft scent of flowery perfume to fog his mind.

"*The* one, my ass," Laurence whispered to the now-closed front entrance. She'd told some stranger what she looked like and the exact length of her gorgeous red hair, just so he'd recognize her the next night. She'd even told him where she worked. All right, not the firm's name, but the building address. She was crazy. She was a menace to herself.

She was Madison. That said it all.

Voices buzzed beyond the cubicle walls, a burst of laughter, a dampened snort. The sounds always followed Madison. After seven years of the woman, Laurence could no longer be completely shocked.

He turned abruptly and almost smacked into Harriet Hartman.

"T. Larry, I mean Laurence, can I speak to you a minute?"

"Tomorrow, Harriet. I have a meeting."

Madison had nicknames for all the accountants in the office—even for Harriet. Despite the fact that the young woman was as bad tempered as Madison was good, as negative as Madison was positive. Madison called her Chicken Little—to her face, of course, since Madison never meant anything in a nasty way— because, for Harriet, the sky was always falling. Due to his upcoming budget review, Laurence wasn't equipped to hold up Harriet's sky tonight.

"But, Laurence—"

"Tomorrow. Come see me first thing, and we'll sort out whatever issue you have." He closed his office door in Harriet's face. Madison would have read him the riot act over that action. An excellent accountant who could find several thousand dollars of tax deductions in a shoe box of coffee-stained receipts, Harriet had a problem with taking no for an answer. Good for his clients most times, not good for Laurence right now.

He had a dinner scheduled at five-thirty with the senior partners, Carp and Alta, to discuss the quarterly budget and the signing of Stephen Tortelli as a client. Alta insisted the man was legit, but Laurence felt him to be, at best, a tax evader, at worst, a Mafia crime boss—and that wasn't because of the Italian-American name. The man was slime. Laurence wanted no dealings with him. The three-week-old argument was becoming heated, but tedious.

Crossing the plush beige carpet, Laurence entered his executive washroom. He'd worked hard for the office with its mahogany desk, black leather sofa and view of San Francisco from his twenty-second-floor window near the end of Market Street. Yet did it all signify Total Financial Security, with Madison's double quotes?

Over the years, she'd labeled him a variety of things, staid and humorless among them. Now she'd implied he was getting too old to attain his marital goals. Too old at thirty-eight?

It was the hair, or rather his lack of it. Laurence put a hand to his bald spot, not actually a spot but the whole top of his head. He always thought it lent him a distinguished air, as any good tax accountant should have. He wasn't too old to attract a wife, to have children.

Was he actually too old for Madison herself? Exhaustion factor aside.

Dear God. He'd lost his mind to even consider it. Madison dating *him?* Her latest and most outrageous act to date had addled his brain. That could be the only explanation for the idea to even occur. It hadn't before. At least not in serious contemplation. After all, he was her boss.

Besides, Madison was light-years beyond him.

He needed to stop thinking about those red lace panties.

HARRIET STARED at the closed door. *Goddamn him.* Well, she'd given him his chance. Now T. Larry was going to pay for ignoring her. And Zachary would pay for what *he'd* done, even if T. Larry refused to fire him. Madison was on the list, too, with her sympathetic looks and annoying pity. What did she know about being the office joke? Harriet hated being one of Madison's pity projects, a problem that had to be fixed. As if she were a dog to be neutered. Oh no. When Harriet got done with her, Madison would be the one who needed pity.

Harriet would get her turn. She'd make them all pay.

MADISON HAD TO FIND T. Larry a wife. He needed one so badly.

The train, packed to capacity as it left the city, lulled her. She'd nearly ruined her favorite black suede high heels in her dash to make the 5:20, but still managed to snag a window seat next to an elderly lady with painfully swollen legs. Poor dear.

And poor T. Larry. He'd somehow come to the conclusion that he was getting old. It was his baldness. In a way, he was kind of sexy, like Yul Brynner or Director Skinner on the *X-Files,* glasses and all. He had the nicest gray eyes, even when he was yelling at her. She'd find him a nice girl who wanted to settle down, get married and have babies. Someone like herself—except for the marriage and babies part—who knew how to have fun, who'd mess up his routines, teach him the word spontaneity and make him forget all about his silly Plan.

The train car smelled of bubble gum, melting chocolate and overtaxed deodorant. The little girl opposite, on the aisle side, mouth covered with the remains of a Hershey's bar, swung her feet in time to the clack of the train wheels. A cute tyke with Shirley Temple curls and pinafore dress, she couldn't be more than five. Chocolate handprints marred the white material and pink lace.

T. Larry would have been appalled. All the more reason to find him a wife ASAP, before he forgot what little kids were like.

Madison was sure T. Larry's stuffiness problem stemmed from an inability to create nicknames. Take herself, for example. He unerringly, even when pissed as a hornet, called her Madison. Never Maddie, which was okay with her since she sort of hated that rendition. How about Mad? Or there was Madison Square Gardens, President Madison, Madison Avenue. Even Oscar Madison, for her perpetually messy desk. *Anything,* she wasn't picky.

Something caressed the back of her neck. Madison jumped, turned, then realized it was the breeze from the open window behind her. People read books, rustled newspapers as they turned the pages, or cranked up the volume on their iPods, all to pass the time until they reached their stop. No one had touched her. Of course not. Madison's seat companion dozed. The little girl, mother staring out the window beside her, swung her feet in an ever widening arc toward the old woman's legs.

Okay, stuffiness. T. Larry had too much starch in his shorts. He couldn't even buy a car just for fun. He'd purchased the white Camry, which was nothing bad in and of itself. But it was the reason he bought it, claiming white didn't retain heat as much nor show the dirt as easily. How about a black Porsche Boxster, T. Larry? Now *that* was fun.

There. Madison felt it again. Nothing so tangible as a hand on her, more of a sensation, of eyes staring at her. She turned quickly. All the same people with all the same reading material. So why did she get the creepy feeling she was being watched? Darn T. Larry anyway, putting thoughts of serial killers in her head.

Next to Madison, the old woman's eyes snapped open as an oomph burst from her lips. She looked down at her legs, then at the little girl's patent leather shoes which had just kicked her.

"Excuse me." The lady's voice crackled with age and disuse as she called softly to the mother seated opposite Madison.

No response. Guilt flickered in Madison. She should have seen the child's accident coming and put a stop to it.

"Excuse me," the elderly lady said again.

This time the mother turned, her lids sleepy and her mouth set in a straight line. One dark chocolate print hardened on the sleeve of her dress. "Yes?"

"I'm sorry, but my legs hurt. Could you please ask your daughter not to kick me?" The old woman's eyes, rheumy and glazed with advancing cataracts, watered.

"I'm sorry, I follow the rule of free discipline. You'll have to ask her yourself. It teaches her to learn on her own."

"Free discipline?" Madison echoed the old lady. What silly thing was that?

The old lady sighed and turned a kind smile on the girl. "Could you please stop kicking me, dear?"

The child stuck out her tongue. Her mother

shrugged and turned back to the buildings flashing by outside her window.

Free discipline obviously meant *no* discipline. Madison turned a sympathetic glance to her seatmate just as another oomph issued from her lips.

Of all the cheeky things. "Knock it off, sweetheart." Madison added her best stern look.

The brat stuck out her tongue at Madison. T. Larry would have freaked if he'd witnessed the display. Madison crossed her legs, mouth pursed, eyes narrowed, foot swinging.

This was ridiculous.

Madison's foot swung harder, connecting with a whack against the mother's shin bone.

The little bugger stopped swinging her feet, her mouth hanging open. The mother rubbed her shin and stared speechless at Madison.

"Why'd you kick my mommy?"

Her gaze fixed on the mother, Madison explained. "Because *my* mother believed in free discipline, and consequently, I learned extremely bad manners." She then turned to the child, who remained wide-eyed but immobile in her seat. "Keep your feet to yourself."

If she'd only imagined it before, eyes were certainly on her now. The old lady's, mother's and child's, an elegantly suited woman's seated behind the girl, two men's standing in the aisle, their knees bending in rhythm with the movement of the train.

The old woman's hand crept across the seat and settled on Madison's, giving it a squeeze.

She wondered if T. Larry would approve of her unconventional yet effective strategy. Nope. He'd cross her off his list, as he'd crossed off Alison. Not that

Madison would make his list in the first place. Not even if she were the last woman on earth of childbearing age.

Busy cataloging her friends for potential T. Larry material, by the time the train arrived at her station, Madison forgot all about that strange sensation of being watched.

CHAPTER TWO

"T. LARRY, ARE YOU DONE checking yourself out in the bathroom mirror?" Madison's voice jumped through the speaker phone, interrupting Laurence's routine.

Laurence rolled his eyes. It had never been Madison's way to give a normal morning greeting. "What is it, Madison?"

"I've penned in Amy Kermit for seven-thirty on Monday."

He moved to the side of his desk so he didn't have to shout. "Madison, I don't finish my workout until eight."

"I said *penned* in, T. Rex. It can't be changed."

She'd thought up a new name. God save him. "And it's Miss Kermeth, not Kermit."

"Oh." A pause. He was sure she was laughing. "She always answers to Kermit. Maybe you're wrong."

"Madison—"

"Gotta run," she cut him off. "By the way, does the *T* stand for Tax Crusader?"

She was forever trying to figure out his first name. He enjoyed the game too much to tell her. She sweet talked, he never relented. A subtle battle of the sexes.

"And Harriet wants to see you."

Harriet Hartman. Damn, he'd forgotten. As hard as Harriet was to forget.

"She's mad." Madison's voice dropped. "As mad as the time I accidentally flushed her diamond ring down the toilet."

"That wasn't an accident."

"I wanted her to see what a toad that guy was."

Harriet had. The hard way. When her fiancé demanded she reimburse him for the lost ring, he took her to small claims court because she refused.

Sometimes Madison's meddling took a circuitous route to eventually working out for the best. Harriet had finally recognized the man for the toad he was. Though in the ensuing three years she'd never had another fiancé, either, as far as Laurence knew.

Laurence opened his office door just as Harriet beat on it with her fist. The blow landed on his chest, and damn if it didn't almost knock him off his feet with its unexpectedness.

She'd moved beyond Chicken Little and wore her Harriet the Harridan face. He was sure Madison hadn't used that name within earshot. Then again, Madison hadn't been the one to make it up.

"I demand an apology." Harriet stormed past him like a hurricane and threw herself into the chair opposite his desk. Anger rose off her shoulders like heat off summer concrete. Laurence closed the door.

"What did I do?" he asked solicitously.

"It's not you."

Laurence half turned the black leather chair that matched his couch and sat beside her. "Then who?"

"Zachary." A bead of spittle spoiled her bottom lip.

Harriet Hartman had blue eyes and an abundance of blond hair. At least she had until she'd dyed it a ghastly shade of red a few months ago. She also had a pretty face and quite an attractive smile. When she did smile. Which was rare.

Unfortunately, in her own mind, Harriet had four strikes against her. She was a professional woman in a workplace dominated by men, she was five-foot-one, twenty pounds overweight, and she was three years past the age of thirty. Harriet hated being thirty-something and didn't take her weight, her height, her age or her gender with cheer. She took it out on everyone, especially Zachary Zenker.

Zach, on the other hand, had only one strike against him, if you didn't count his initials, which Madison had transformed to ZZ Top. Zach was excessively shy. He was also tall, well over Laurence's own six-foot-one, reasonably good-looking in an ordinary way and of moderately good build though on the thin side. He had all his brown hair, too, a fact Laurence had never held against him. He kept the length short, his shirts neatly pressed and all in all gave the impression of a good solid accountant. Even if he did stoop a bit to compensate for his height.

Harriet despised Zach, for reasons Laurence had never understood and thus didn't know how to combat.

"What did Zach do this time?"

"He said my dress was pretty."

Laurence couldn't help it. He looked her up and down. The dress in question was neon pink and two inches too short for the workplace. Neon pink was probably not her best color.

"Not *this* one." Two dots of spittle now clung to Harriet's lower lip.

"Oh." Laurence didn't have an intelligent word to say.

"It was yesterday."

For the life of him, he couldn't remember what she'd been wearing the day before and therefore couldn't reassure her. Morning sun slanted across a quarter of his office. Damn, it was getting hot in here, but he contained the desire to run his finger around the inside of his collar.

"Hmm. Yes. Well." Words this time, but certainly nothing intelligent. Finally, he managed to get to his point. "I'm not sure I see the problem with that. If I'm not mistaken, it sounds almost like…yes, I'm sure it sounds just like…a compliment."

Her lips pinched into a perfect round O which thinned her cheeks unflatteringly. Harriet was not a happy person, not now, and unfortunately, maybe not ever.

"Are you making fun of me?"

Laurence held out his hands. "No, no, no." He searched for a way to handle this volatile situation.

"Zachary was making fun of me. That's why he did it. In front of Mike, Anthony and Bill."

Mike, Anthony and Bill. That explained everything. They didn't like Harriet, and, Laurence suspected, made her life miserable on a job, despite the fact that she was the senior and they were only staff accountants. As Senior, Harriet had had the dubious honor of supervising them. A macho-thinking bunch, they didn't appreciate a woman being smarter than they were. And Harriet could be—what was the least derogatory word?—snippy if she caught the same mistake twice.

"I'm sure Zach didn't mean any harm."

"They snickered. All of them."

Why couldn't he remember what she'd been wearing? He was sure there was a clue there.

"I want an apology," Harriet went on when Laurence failed to provide an immediate response. "It's sexual harassment."

For Christ's sake. "He said he liked your dress."

"He made a personal comment concerning my attire, and I was intimidated."

Harriet intimidated? By ZZ Top? "You've got to be joking."

Her eyes narrowed like the harridan she'd been nicknamed for. He'd said the wrong thing. He was a tax accountant. He knew numbers, rules and regulations. He hadn't the faintest idea how to defuse the situation. However, he did know she'd judged Zach unfairly. If Mike, Anthony or Bill had said her dress was pretty, then yes, the so-called compliment might well have been demeaning. Zach Zenker was a completely different page in the ledger, and Laurence felt honor-bound to stick up for him. God knew Zach wouldn't do it for himself.

Laurence stood, then launched into his unrehearsed speech. "He said your dress was pretty, Harridan, I mean, Harriet." Damn. Bad slipup, he knew by the flare of her nostrils, but he forged on stoically. "He didn't ask you to go to bed with him. It was a compliment. You should thank Zach. You should be glad—" A little too much said. Christ, a lot too much said, nor did it come across in the benign way he'd meant it. He needed to be beaten upside the head.

Harriet rose, the top of her hair reaching to the second button of his shirt, but the flames in her eyes leaped six inches above his head.

His goose was cooked.

Harriet the Militant Feminist stomped from his office.

Laurence opened the door Harriet had just slammed, crooked his finger at Madison, then moved to sit behind his desk.

"You should have warned me," he told her, though there was no use blaming Madison for his idiotic handling of the delicate meeting.

"I didn't know."

It was a small office. Friction traveled fast. Everyone would know soon. "Tell Zach I want to see him." Then he stopped, dumbfounded. "What are you wearing?"

Madison looked down at her outfit, arms spread.

She towered in spike-heeled pumps, a snug black skirt and formfitting red jacket that made her waist seem impossibly small. He shouldn't be noticing at a time like this. He shouldn't be noticing at all.

"What's wrong with what I'm wearing?"

"I didn't say anything was wrong." Everything was too right.

"I have a date tonight, remember?"

That damn Dick person. "You dressed like that for a stranger?" His voice rose. "Close the door."

She did, her backside swaying. It needed a good spanking. This thing with Dick had to be stopped. "Sit down."

She did, her skirt riding up to reveal too much leg for his well-being. To his dismay, he couldn't stop himself from looking. What was happening to him? This date episode had somehow thrown him into a downward spiral of salacious thoughts.

"T. Larry, I think I understand what happened with Harriet."

"Right now, I don't give a da—" After a deep breath, he started again. "Harriet's problem is not the issue at this moment. I want to reiterate our discussion of last night." Good, he came off sounding like a concerned relative.

"Why don't you like Richard?"

His teeth ground. "I don't know the man. My point is that neither do you."

She waved a hand. "If it will make you happy, I promise to be very, very careful."

"I'll call you tonight. What time will you be home?"

Her eyes widened and her lips parted, luscious red lips. He had to stop noticing her physical attributes, at least not all the time. He was worse than Mike, Bill or Anthony.

"T. Larry, what's wrong with you?"

Yes, Laurence, what's wrong with you? "I feel protective. You've worked for me for seven years." In all that time she'd never noticed him as a man. Not that he'd wanted her to. It was simply that she'd gone too far out on a limb with this *date* thing for his peace of mind. "You can't meet a stranger in a bar."

"It's a restaurant."

He sighed. She was a menace to herself. As her boss, it was his duty to protect her. "You're twenty-seven—"

"Almost twenty-eight." She pointed to his desk calendar. "In fourteen days. I have to fall in love before I die."

He winced, but didn't comment on the reference. "If you want to meet him, I can't stop you. But I *can* at least make sure you get home safely. I'll call you."

"How sweet." She meant it. Madison didn't have a sarcastic bone in her body. "Now about Harriet. What did you say to her?"

At the reminder, he wanted to smack his head at

what he'd let dribble out of his mouth. "I told her she should thank Zach." He didn't tell her the worst, what he'd *almost* said, but which Harriet most assuredly grasped, that she should be glad a man had complimented her, which made it sound as if he thought Harriet didn't deserve admiration. His lapse was unforgivable.

Madison groaned. *He* almost groaned, for several reasons, most of which were highly inappropriate.

"I think perhaps you should have told her you thought her dress was pretty, and that you were sure ZZ Top meant it, too."

"I did tell her Zach meant it. But I couldn't remember what it looked like."

"You should have lied."

"I don't lie."

She rolled her eyes and pleaded. "It's a white lie to preserve someone's feelings. There's a difference. Complete honesty is *not* always the best policy."

Good point, he hated to admit. "I'll have Zach apologize."

She pursed her red lips. "It's too late for that."

She was probably right. She was right about what he should have said, too, but there came a time when a boss—or a man—simply didn't know how to handle the delicate workings of the female mind. It took another woman to understand.

"I suppose at this point there's nothing else to do," she went on. "I'll get ZZ Top." She rose, smoothing her skirt down. He did *not* look. At least not for long. She was at the door when she turned, nearly catching him in the despicable act of observing her delicious backside. "By the way, I have someone I want you to meet."

"Who? What are their qualifications? We don't have any openings at the moment." She constantly recommended friends for jobs. To date, he'd hired—and fired—exactly two. He wasn't up to a third.

"This isn't for a job. It's a date."

Laurence almost choked on his own tongue. "A date? With one of your friends?" Lord help him, now she was trying to set him up. "No," he said before she had a chance to open her mouth.

"But Lila's a sweetie."

"Didn't you tell me she was a pathological liar?"

"No. She doesn't tell lies. She just makes up stories."

"Like the one about writing her memoirs."

"She *is* writing them."

"She said she had a million-dollar book deal."

"Wishful thinking."

"Except that she had a champagne party to celebrate."

"Lila resonates to the reality she wants to create."

Madison's friends knew a soft touch when they saw it, though trying to get her to see that was impossible. Still, Laurence tried. "That's why she charged the caterer to your Visa account?"

"She didn't have her glasses, and she picked up the wrong card." Madison believed in unconditional acceptance.

"From *your* purse?"

Madison shrugged. "She paid it all back. Then she moved out. You'd really like her if you just gave her a chance."

He couldn't think of a worse match. "I don't need you making dates for me. Handling my work calendar is enough."

"I'm just trying to help you with your Family Plan."

Here she was, dressed to kill, her jacket unzipped to reveal enough cleavage to scramble his laptop's motherboard, all for another man. Topping that, she had the temerity to try setting him up with one of her irresponsible friends. He was looking at her and thinking about her too much. All because of that damn phone call yesterday. It shouldn't affect him this way—none of her other dates had to this extent—yet still, it did. "The answer is no, Madison."

"But—"

He held up his hand.

"You'd re—"

"Zzzp." He cut her off with the sound. He'd take *her* over any of her kooky friends. In his present state of mind, most definitely.

"But you—"

"Zzp." He made the noise between gritted teeth.

Madison shut her mouth.

Was he so pathetic in her eyes? She rhapsodized about a voice over the phone, wore an outfit to knock a man's eyes out and tried to pawn Laurence off on her far-from-reliable ex-roommate.

Damn. It had nothing to do with jealousy. It was an affront to good manners, to his manhood even. He almost sighed. All right, he had to admit there was a part of him, a very small part, mind you, that loathed the idea that she lusted after a man she'd never met when Laurence himself had been standing in front of her for seven years. Though he'd always found her appealing—who in his right mind wouldn't?—this wasn't jealousy per se, just that she'd never seen him as a man who possessed attractive qualities beyond fun-loving and mysterious. He'd listened to her prattle, handed her a tissue when a relationship ended, done what a boss should do for a distressed employee. But this phone date was more than any self-respecting man could abide.

"I'll find ZZ Top," she said again.

It was what she should have done before opening her mouth about Lila. She closed the door with the softest of clicks. Very good idea. Before he humiliated himself by showing her he was a man and he wasn't too old.

He turned in his chair to stare out the window, all the while drumming his fingers on the armrests. What was happening here? He'd put a match to Harriet's flame instead of dousing it. He'd become overly obsessed with Madison's assets. He was jealous of a voice on the phone. That damn phone call.

Or maybe it was hearing Madison declare twice in less than twenty-four hours that she only had a few days left to live.

Laurence stilled, a cold spot spreading from his chest to his extremities. She was not going to die. The idea was ludicrous, but his heart beat erratically and sweat popped out on his brow. She was on a quest to live life to its fullest, but God only knew what trouble that could bring her. She might want to fall in love, but what she really needed was shielding, from Richard and from roommates who accidentally stole her credit cards.

Madison needed saving from herself, at least until she turned twenty-eight and realized she wasn't going to die.

ZACH WOULD APOLOGIZE, just like T. Larry had told him to. He owed Harriet that. Not for the dress incident—

he'd meant every one of those four words—but for the other thing he'd done to her, the thing they hadn't talked about since that night all those months ago.

Zachary Zenker slipped into the coffee room, got himself a soda and slipped back out. No one saw him, not Madison where she stood at the coffee machine making T. Larry a fresh pot and not Mr. Carp who'd nabbed T. Larry's pot right out of Madison's fingers. Sometimes Zach felt like little more than a ghost in their midst. He longed to be noticed, longed to be a part of them, longed to speak his mind the way everyone else did.

As it was, he never got a word in edgewise.

He'd tried to talk to Madison about his problem yesterday, but she'd been on the phone. With nothing more than his daily peanut butter cup for his efforts, he'd left like a dog with his tail between his legs, or worse, a wraith no one even knew was there.

He hunkered down in his cubicle before the digital glare of his portable PC and comforted himself with his spreadsheets, his numbers and his accounts. They didn't offer the usual solace. He kept remembering that T. Larry had never even looked up from the contract on his desk as he issued that apology instruction.

Someday, somehow, he'd do *something* to make them notice him.

"YOUR TIRES ARE SLASHED." Mid-afternoon, Harriet stood in Madison's cubicle opening.

"My tires?"

"On your car. In the garage." There was just enough venom in Harriet's voice to make Madison wish she didn't always have to look for the best in *every* person.

"I forgot I drove today." She'd driven her sporty little

compact this morning because she was having dinner with Richard the Lionhearted. Sometime in the middle of the night, she'd dubbed him with the name. Her Richard. Suddenly she didn't feel the bite of Harriet's tone as much.

"Aren't you going to check it out?"

"Yeah. Thanks for telling me." Madison tried to smile brightly in appreciation.

"Well, don't sound so cheerful about it. Someone did a really nasty job." Harriet seemed to relish the idea.

An unpleasant tingle nipped her neck. "Where have you been?"

Harriet glared as if Madison had accused her of something. "At a client's. I'd have told you when I left if you'd been at your desk."

Cheeks flushed, eyes a glittering blue that didn't quite match the orange-red of her dyed hair, and her dress a bright pink, Harriet glowed with color. And animosity.

If you can't find anything nice to say, don't say anything at all. That being one of her mother's favorite axioms Madison had taken to heart, she said nothing. Harriet wouldn't have grabbed an olive branch anyway. Madison had tried often enough to know what to expect. Harriet simply didn't want her advice or her help and, in recent months, had seemed downright hostile.

"Aren't you going to call triple A or the cops?" Harriet pushed and shoved.

"Yes. Thanks for letting me know." That was pleasant enough. Madison tried for a little bit more. "I wouldn't have found it until I left for home." After her date with Richard. It would have made for an unpleasant ending to a pleasurable evening.

Harriet made a noise of disgust, shrugged her shoulders and walked away, the nylons on her inner thighs rasping with her angry stride.

Madison breathed a sigh of relief. Harriet was her greatest disappointment, the one person in all the world Madison couldn't seem to like no matter how hard she tried. Nor had she been successful in getting others to like Harriet. When Madison suggested Harriet lighten up, Harriet had adjusted her attire rather than her demeanor, abandoning her black, gray and navy-blue suits for more colorful dresses and skirts. With disastrous results. The girl had become the office laughingstock, and her attitude took a dive. Madison had tried to extol her virtues to others at every opportunity, but she'd found little to draw from. If only Bill hadn't overhead that "Chicken Little" comment she'd made to Harriet and turned the nickname into yet another curse. Madison had racked her brain for a solution to the Harriet problem but nothing worked.

Right now, however, she had her tires to worry about.

She couldn't call her brothers. They'd freak like loving but overprotective mother hens. They'd been that way since her stroke. Not that she blamed them. She figured that worrying about *her* allowed them *not* to worry about the possibility of having a stroke themselves. She was sure that wouldn't happen, but the thought must have occured to them. So she let them worry about her to their hearts' content. Except for now, when she couldn't let them interfere with her date with Richard.

She whirled the Rolodex, stopping at the *C*s. Dialing, she leaned her elbow on the desk to stop the tremble in her hand. The shakiness in that hand and the fact that one corner of her mouth wasn't quite as high as the other were the only noticeable effects of her stroke. The doctors attributed her miraculous recovery to her youth. Madison just said a prayer of thanks to God and counted every minute of her life as more wonderful than the one before.

Then the ring was answered and Madison asked for her favorite tow truck guy.

"WHAT DO YOU MEAN you're not calling the police?"

"Calm down, T. Rex."

Laurence didn't feel like a dinosaur. He felt like the fire-breathing dragon Madison sometimes called him. She would have gone to the garage alone if he hadn't heard about her tires through the office grapevine and insisted upon escorting her. "Have you no sense, woman?"

Madison merely smiled and craned her neck to once more look for the tow truck she thought would bring her four new tires. How had the culprit managed to find adequate time and privacy to do that much damage? In the five minutes they'd been down here, no fewer than eight cars had passed on their way in or out. This was one of the more popular garages in the city, mostly due to its reasonable rates and excellent location, but there were no security cameras and inadequate, even faulty lighting. Laurence had previously encouraged all his employees to use the lot.

He squatted for a better look. On the level below, tires squealed like a banshee wail. Gas fumes and the scent of burning oil suffocated him. The sight of Madison's tires wrapped around his vocal cords and stole the air from his lungs.

The perpetrator had plunged the weapon into the sidewall, à la *Psycho*'s Norman Bates. Not one thrust to expel the air, but again and again, reducing the rubber to mincemeat. The act had taken time, power and a vengeful rage.

What if Madison had surprised the perpetrator in the act? Laurence's blood raced in his veins and throbbed through his temples.

"If you don't call the police, I will."

Madison finally deigned to answer him. "It was just a couple of kids making mischief."

"That—" he rose, moved to within a foot of her, then pointed to the tires "—is the work of a maniac."

"It doesn't mean it was directed specifically at me."

"Then why did they single out your car?" He waved an arm indicating the rest of the packed underground garage. "Of all the cars here." He folded his arms and waited.

She looked up at the missing bulbs above her car. "The lights were out?"

"They could have broken them when they got here."

By her hesitant glance, he knew she couldn't remember the condition of the lights when she'd arrived that morning. He still expected her to argue.

Then Madison did the most amazing thing. Without even a blithe contradiction to his statement, she gave him a direct answer. "I don't want to cause trouble for someone I might know."

She almost robbed him of his next question. Almost. "You think you know who did this?"

"Harriet isn't too pleased with any of us. She was the one to discover what happened to my car."

A first. In seven years, he'd never heard Madison say

anything bad about anyone, not even a hint. "*Our* Harriet?"

She shook her head, her earrings swinging with vehemence. "Of course I don't think she did it. Nobody *I* know could be responsible for this." Laurence didn't have the same faith she did, but he let her go on uninterrupted. "But you know how Mike and Anthony and Bill make mountains out of molehills where Harriet's concerned, and if the police ask what *they* think…" She spread her hands in a draw-your-own-conclusion gesture.

Mike, Anthony and Bill, the instigators of yesterday's dress incident, would certainly love an opportunity to bring Harriet down yet another peg. He should fire the lot of them, but while Harriet bemoaned the trio's existence, she'd also done a bang-up job passing on her expertise to them. They would be difficult to replace.

Firing them didn't resolve the immediate issue. "Give the police more credit. They'll probably look at the ones talking *about* Harriet. Blaming someone else is always suspicious."

Madison's eyes widened, one not quite as much as the other, another of Madison's endearing features. "I wasn't—"

"I didn't mean you said anything bad about her, Madison."

"I still don't want to get the police involved." She stared up at him with a faint glimmer of moisture in her eyes, put her hand on his arm and squeezed gently. "Please, T. Larry."

Sure he'd do anything she wanted at that moment, right down to running naked along Market Street with only his Florsheim shoes on, Laurence changed the subject before he actually gave in. "Tow truck drivers do not bring a new set of four tires with them. He's going to have to tow you. Which means you'll have to cancel your date tonight." Her date, which was the reason she'd driven the damn car, which made it Dick's fault that her tires were slashed. "You can't get this fixed in less than two hours."

She smiled, the glint of tears vanishing. A woman of wiles when she needed them, she thought he'd succumbed to her wishes and given up on calling the police. Not the slightest bit concerned that someone had annihilated the tires on her yellow compact car, she chattered happily. "Yes, tow truck drivers do, T. Larry. When they're your oldest brother's best friend's cousin."

Date cancellation had been wishful thinking on his part, but perhaps he'd found an ally against Madison's silly notions. "Your brother isn't going to let you get away with not calling the—"

"And sworn to secrecy. Not a word will reach James's ears," she finished up, neatly cutting him off with a zip of her lips, pursing them almost into a kiss.

He was a horse's ass, because he had the irresistible urge to kiss her senseless. Maybe it would convince her to let him do what he knew was best for her.

Not. Once Madison got something in her head, it took an act of Congress to get it out. Tire slashing wasn't enough. She wasn't even willing to take the incident seriously.

Madison needed someone to shake a little sense into her and at that moment, Laurence was the only man around for the job.

Furthermore, in order to safeguard her in the future, he had to be more than just her boss. He needed to make

her think he was—yes, yes, a plan was forming—
T. Laurence Hobbs needed to convince Madison *he*
was The One. The plan fit perfectly with his recent
chaotic thoughts concerning her.

The first step was to take charge. Madison would
soon see that's what the *T* stood for. Laurence whipped
out his cell phone to call the police. Whether she wanted
him to or not.

CHAPTER THREE

MADISON HADN'T really expected T. Larry to leave the police out of it, not after he'd seen her tires. She suppressed a shudder. It had appeared vicious, but directed at her? Another shudder threatened. What if Harriet really had…no, no. Madison couldn't allow anyone to even think the half question had crossed her mind. Down deep, Harriet wasn't a bad person, and Madison would *not* cause her unnecessary trouble. Mischievous kids were responsible. Why, even the police had said so.

What other boss would have supervised the cops, demanded they act on her behalf—though they insisted such a thing was an everyday occurrence in big cities—berated the tow truck driver for being late and still gotten her to her date with Richard on time? Though she couldn't say the same for her date. Richard was late.

She did wish T. Larry hadn't seated himself on the other side of the crowded restaurant. At a lonely table at the edge of the bar, next to a wooden railing separating drinkers from diners, T. Larry nursed a sparkling cocktail. Ginger ale, most likely. He wasn't a big drinker, and not at all when he had to drive.

Madison raised her glass of ice water and lemon to him. He raised his in return. Maybe she should go over there and tell him about the two women at the bar checking him out. Women were suckers for bald guys.

Music blared above her, though indecipherable over the rising tide of voices and laughter. The floor was concrete, the ceilings high, and the noise thunderous. Perhaps Richard, when he arrived, could procure them a better table, something at the back in a quiet intimate corner. The bar was crammed, a baseball game playing on three TVs in the corners. Whoops and hollers went up every time a white-suited player did something, dispersing not only throughout the bar but also into the dining area. Madison didn't understand baseball, or more correctly, she didn't grasp the fascination. It was a slow, boring game interrupted by brief moments of pure delirium when someone struck a home run.

T. Larry wasn't facing any of the TVs. He was watching her, elbows on the lacquered table, hands clasped, fingers laced.

She shouldn't let him stay, but T. Larry needed to play the hero tonight; he'd looked positively haggard in the garage. She needed to do something for him, something that would—

Goodness. Richard had arrived, and he took her breath away. She could almost believe she'd seen him before, his handsome face familiar, his features Prince Charming perfect. That was it. She *had* seen him before. In her fantasies. Richard was her dream come true.

Fourteen days until her birthday, surely she could fall in love with him by then.

RICHARD THE LIONHEARTED, she'd called him. Madison's eyes shone with that emerald glow, her mouth opening in succulent glossy surprise, and Laurence knew the great man had stepped through the doorway into Madison's fantasy. How had she recognized him? Must be the corny rose stuck in the black lapel of his polished three-piece suit.

Somewhere in his early thirties—very early—the man was movie-star handsome, spit-shined to the luster of vinyl. All surface polish with no substance. But he had hair. Loads of it, thick, wavy brown stuff the likes of which Laurence had seen women drive their hands through up on the big screen. Women loved hair, especially a misbehaving lock like the one that fell effortlessly over the guy's forehead. It took a man to see beyond a few elegant curls. Women didn't know when they were being had.

Of course, the same could be said about men drooling over a woman's breasts. Laurence sipped his drink.

Richard the Lionhearted. My God. More like Dick the Prick. Why was he sitting here bearing witness to Dick's attempted seduction? Because Laurence had sworn to himself he'd look after Madison. With the slashing of her tires, he simply couldn't allow her out with a stranger at night all by herself. He was acting like a father, like a big brother.

Oh Christ, now the man was bending over her hand, almost touching his mouth to her delicate skin. Laurence was sure he'd lose his lunch. Madison's lips curled with a sublime smile, then she murmured something in the ear bent close to her. Dick straightened, flicked a wrist and snapped two fingers at a passing waiter. Damned rude. He spoke, never taking his eyes from Madison's face, then dismissed the apron-clad man with another twist of his wrist. Laurence's mouth tightened and his nostrils flared as he inhaled sharply. Moments later, Tricky Dick whisked Madison away to a secluded table in the back.

Laurence stood and muscled his way to an empty seat at the bar where he could once more watch over Madison from a slightly elevated position. Of course, the only stool available necessitated him leaning out into the aisle to see properly.

"Hi."

Was someone talking to him? He looked right to two baseball-capped heads. Not that way. A blonde sat to his left, her body angled toward him, her black nylon-covered leg swinging back and forth.

"Hi," she said again. He looked over his shoulder, but the bartender was at the other end of the bar.

She nodded. "Yes, I was saying hi to you."

"Hi." What a great conversationalist he was. He'd never known he had it in him. Wouldn't Madison be pleased?

The woman smiled, a nice white-toothed smile, but it didn't have that endearing tilt to one side as Madison's did. Madison, however, was on the other side of the room drinking champagne and probably ordering some ridiculously expensive meal.

"Can I buy you a fresh one?" the woman said, pointing at his glass.

Laurence's drink consisted of shrunken ice cubes and the dregs of once-sizzling ginger ale. He knew he wasn't unattractive to women, but usually they needed to get to know him a little first.

"Shouldn't I be offering you a drink instead?" It was the polite thing to do. Besides, talking to her gave him the perfect method to keep an eye on Madison over the woman's shoulder.

"You could, but mine's full and yours is empty." The woman tilted her wine to him as proof.

"Well, then, uh…" He couldn't think of a courteous reason for refusing. "I'd like that."

She signaled the bartender, then dipped her finger, indicating Laurence's glass. "What's your name?"

He almost told her, then stopped. For the first time he wondered what it would feel like to be something other than Laurence. "Larry." He left off the Hobbs which seemed to go so much better with Laurence and not at all with Larry. "Thanks for the drink."

The smile never left the woman's unlined face. He glanced at Madison. She was enthralled, her red hair all wispy about her temples, the glow of candlelight on her flushed cheeks, her upper body tilting toward Dick. Damn. Madison liked Larry much better than Laurence. Maybe he should consider going by the nickname full-time.

"I'm Veronica. But you can call me Ronnie."

Laurence dragged his attention back. Ronnie tugged on the hem of her short plum leather skirt. It rode right back up to midthigh when she crossed her legs. Madison's legs were more sumptuous, though right now he couldn't see them through the sea of diners.

"What do you do, Larry?"

He almost looked to his right again, then remembered *he* was Larry. It didn't have the right ring without the *T* and without Madison's musical voice around it.

"I'm a tax accountant." Definitely a showstopper. If he were actually trying to secure a date with Ronnie, Madison would have advised him to beef up his profession a bit. Tax Avoidance Specialist, perhaps. Ahh, how about Tax Crusader? He chanced another glance in Madison's direction. Their waiter gone, her hand now lay suspiciously close to Dick's. If that man tried to take advantage of her—

"Oh, I love taxes."

He felt his eyes widen involuntarily. Only an IRS agent loved taxes. Or another accountant. He struggled for continuing pleasant conversation. After all, Ronnie was being kind enough to allow him to peruse Madison over her shoulder, not that either of them knew it. "What do *you* do?" he asked for lack of something more intriguing.

"I'm in investments." With a practiced gesture, she flipped her long hair over her shoulder, straight silky strands. Whereas Madison's hair was a riot of tangled curls that seemed to fascinate her date. Christ, was Dick the Prick actually reaching out to touch those locks? No, no. He stopped midgesture. Laurence's heart slowed its furious pace.

Investments? Isn't that what Ronnie said? By all rights, she should hate taxes. Investors disliked parting with a dime, especially to the government. "What do you do in investments?"

She flashed him an odd look, as if no one ever got that precise. Maybe they didn't, in a bar. She certainly didn't wear that skirt or those high heels—four inches at least—to any investment firm. Even Madison had never worn a leather skirt to work. It might be very nice indeed if she did. But he was talking to someone named Ronnie. Maybe the woman had changed before her evening out. Always magnanimous, Laurence gave her the benefit of the doubt. "I mean what do you do specifically?"

She paused, worked her jaw. "I invest."

Okay, *definitely* not used to details in this atmosphere. He strove for cordial discourse, but what came out was rather inane and probably inappropriate. "Are you punctual for appointments?"

With his recent Alison dating debacle, tardiness had been on his mind, but still, a topic of conversation in a bar? Madison would have rolled her eyes at him.

Ronnie leaned back three inches, tilting her chin. "Excuse me?"

It was safe to admit that he wasn't particularly good at idle chitchat. He invariably said the wrong thing, as evidenced by his handling of Harriet's interview that morning. Madison had never held his ineptitude against him, but after Ronnie's reaction, Madison would advise him to change the subject yet again.

But to what? Taxes. Stick close to what he knew. "Have you ever cheated on your taxes?"

He saw it for the asinine question it was the moment the last syllable left his mouth. He should have asked what cash flow method she used to project income. Or something.

Instead of being offended, Ronnie laughed. "You have the most amazing sense of humor, Larry."

Madison didn't think he had any at all, though she certainly thought Dick the Prick was funny. The tinkle of her laughter carried into the bar, even over the screech of the TV and the lament of a female vocalist who was either stretching too far for the high note or killing a cat.

Ronnie thought Larry had a sense of humor, an amazing one at that. Just wait until he told Madison.

T. LARRY SEEMED to be having the best of times. With a tall, big-breasted, flawless creature. Maybe it was just the bar stools they sat on that gave the woman the appearance of above-average height. Those breasts were no illusion, though, and perfect for T. Larry. He wanted a wife who could breast-feed. Would wonders never cease? Madison would swear on the picture Bible her mother gave her when she was eight that T. Larry had laughed out loud.

Good for him. Maybe she wouldn't have to set him up after all. As long as he didn't ask the woman how often she shaved her legs until at least the second date.

No longer feeling the need to worry about T. Larry, Madison concentrated on Richard. The table he'd gotten them, though not exactly quiet, was in a corner, and the blast of voices from the bar and the too-loud music cocooned them in intimacy. She leaned close with her mouth to his ear, felt his breath on her nape and his leg only millimeters away when he moved his chair.

He really was magnificent. With dark, wavy brown hair, the most amazing chocolate-colored eyes, endearing almost dimples when he smiled and a body as well exercised as T. Larry's. Charming and suave, not to mention fairy-tale gorgeous. He was all that and more, the best part being that he didn't seem to know these things about himself. He didn't exactly stutter, but while asking her what she liked to do, what she did for a living and if she had any pets, he not so casually managed to tell her he was a lawyer and had just bought a house, a really nice house, in a suburb south of San Francisco, with a big backyard, a tree swing and a white picket fence. Vital statistics slipped in with little finesse, as if he were advertising himself on a billboard.

Richard Lyons was a bit unsure of himself. She'd been worried when he'd snapped his fingers at the waiter, but she realized now that had a been a show of bravado for her benefit. He couldn't sustain it. She hadn't wanted him to. She much preferred the Richard seated at the table with her now. Madison adored a shy man, someone she could help. Like ZZ Top. Like T. Larry himself, who, despite all his confidence in the tax arena, was out of his depth in social situations.

Except tonight. He was exhibiting newly acquired skills. T. Larry actually made the big-busted blonde laugh. What had he said that was so funny?

Back to Richard and the small problem Madison had with him.

"Is Kim your girlfriend?"

"Kim?" Richard looked blank.

"The girl you thought I was when you called."

"Oh, Kim." He laughed, lackluster, almost nervous, and his gaze centered on his plate rather than her eyes. "No, she's just a friend."

She smelled a rat. Though Madison liked to believe the best about people, she was neither gullible nor stupid. All she did was look for motivation as to why a person might be compelled to lie or treat someone badly. She might stretch a bit to find a reason if she had to, but she did need some explanation for bad behavior in order to forgive it.

She speared a piece of lettuce. "*Kim* thinks you're her boyfriend, doesn't she?"

T. Larry would have been proud of her for pushing the issue. Speaking of T. Larry, he was taking that woman's card. She wondered how smart it was to move this fast, the evening wasn't half over. T. Larry was a bit of a babe in the woods when it came to dating. And bars. You just never knew what you got.

Not like Richard, of course. She hadn't met him in

a bar. Their meeting had been a fluke, an accident, a slipped digit when he punched in a phone number, which surely meant heavenly tampering.

She'd almost forgotten the question when Richard finally answered. "Not exactly."

Oh yeah, about Kim not giving up on him yet. "Could you define not exactly?"

"Kim sort of dumped me, not the other way around."

It was the last thing she expected to hear, but confession was good for the soul, both for the confessor and the confessee. Madison put her fork down, lacing her fingers beneath her chin. Richard toyed with his salad. He needed a little push. "And?"

"When I called you, I was hoping Kim hadn't really meant it."

Using a burst of laughter from a nearby table as cover, she said, "So you asked her what color underwear she was wearing?" Which was not a particularly sterling lead-in to asking a woman if she was sure she wanted to dump him.

It was something Madison might have said in similar circumstances, however, if for nothing other than the shock value.

"I didn't ask that. Did I?" Just enough pause to show he wasn't certain.

"When a man asks a woman what she's wearing, she doesn't immediately think he's referring to the cut of her business suit."

"Oh."

Waiting for more, she buttered a small piece of sourdough bread.

When Richard didn't offer further explanation for questioning her attire on the phone, Madison offered a reasonable excuse with a sympathetic smile. "You wanted to know if she was dressed for a night on the town with a man or just a movie with girlfriends."

"You were right the first time." His head down, but his eyes raised to hers, his mouth crooked on one side with a faintly bad-boy smile. "Well, Kim sort of liked phone…" He cleared his throat instead of using the word.

"So you thought you'd change her mind if you started a little phone…" Madison cleared her throat delicately.

Richard busied himself with his own piece of bread, then finally gave her the answer she'd been waiting for. "Yes."

God, she loved honesty in a man. He'd just bared his soul, revealed his insecurities and let her see the real Richard Lyons.

He also liked phone sex.

She cocked her head. "I'd have changed my mind if I were her."

"You would?"

Building his confidence before their main course even arrived was the least Madison could do. "Especially with your voice."

"You like my voice?"

She adored his voice. Deep, but not too deep, with a hint of mischief over the phone. Most of all, it was that tinge of uncertainty he had right now. "Kim's going to figure out she made a really big mistake."

He pushed his salad away. "Maybe there's something wrong with me."

Nothing Madison couldn't fix.

LAURENCE REALIZED with a jolt that he had Ronnie's card in his jacket pocket and her hand on his thigh. High on his thigh. Damn close to his… Conversation hummed pleasantly around them, the baseball game was over and the music no longer split his head in two, but Ronnie's hand made him extremely uncomfortable. After all, they'd merely exchanged idle chitchat while he kept an eye on Madison.

He looked pointedly down at her long pale fingers tipped in crimson. "I don't think I know you well enough for that."

Her jaw dropped open in a very unfeminine gape. "Excuse me?"

"Your hand. On my thigh. I don't think that's appropriate at this stage of our acquaintance."

She snatched her hand back as though he'd touched it with a cattle prod.

"I realize that I must seem like some Neanderthal, but I just don't think I'm up on this new dating protocol. How old are you?"

"Twenty-seven."

"When will you be twenty-eight?"

Eyeing him warily, she answered. "At the end of the month."

God, Madison's age to a tee. Did that mean Madison would soon be putting her hand on Dick the Prick? She'd better not. Laurence wouldn't be answerable for his actions. "I'm a good ten years older than you, and when I was your age, it was the man who put his hand on a girl's thigh." He thinned his lips. "Then the girl was supposed to slap him."

Something feral flickered in her eyes, and her nose tipped to a haughty angle. "Are you going to slap me?"

He had the oddest feeling this wasn't going his way. "That wasn't what I meant. I just meant that ladies used to possess a certain decorum that *some* women seem to have lost these days."

She put a hand to her mouth, the same one that had recently been on him, but something nasty had happened to her eyes. "Oh, you mean that in your day, women weren't the aggressors."

In *his* day? Didn't she know it was *still* his day? He was only thirty-eight, for God's sake. "Men *are* the aggressors." *Was* that what most women believed? Surely not Madison.

Obviously Ronnie did have a prejudice. "Who says they're the ones who get to decide when a sexual move will be made?" She had daggers in her eyes just for him.

He tried to clarify. "It's as inappropriate for a woman to put her hand on a man's thigh as it is for a man to do it to a woman."

"Men are chauvinists. Men are pigs. Women have just as much right to make the first move."

Perhaps it was the uncalled-for attack when he'd only been trying to explain to her a little about how men felt. Perhaps it was the snarl disfiguring her lips. Perhaps it was Harriet's harangue earlier in the day. Or maybe it was the fact that Madison's hand *had* disappeared beneath the white linen tablecloth. Whatever it was, Laurence suddenly lost control.

His eyes never leaving Ronnie's twisted face, Laurence reached into his jacket pocket and pulled out her card. "I'm sure I won't be needing this." Then he ripped it in half.

He saw it coming and didn't flinch.

Her hand smacked his jaw with a slap that cut through every word, every voice, every snippet of conversation, every peal of laughter and even the music blaring overhead. Silence.

Then she threw her drink in his face, and the entire place erupted. Or maybe it was just Madison coming like a whirlwind to his rescue.

He thanked God Ronnie had already grabbed her purse from the bartop and stormed from the raging bar in staccato-heeled fury.

Madison's touch on his arm was heaven. He didn't like scenes, couldn't believe he'd participated in this one, had actually encouraged it.

"Are you all right, T. Larry?" She dabbed a napkin at the wine on his face, his cheeks and his lips. He closed his eyes.

Voices buzzing around them became a din. He hated being the center of attention. "I didn't handle the situation well."

"T. Larry, you're a wonder of understatement. I knew letting you sit by yourself in a bar was a bad idea. I should have sent you home immediately."

"Is this your brother?" Dick the Prick was on her heels, his face a ghastly shade of white.

Laurence put one foot to the floor and came half off his seat, fists clenched. "No, I'm not her brother—"

Madison didn't let him finish. "He's my boss. He's had a bad experience. We'd better walk him to his car."

"We?" he chorused with Dick, then slumped back onto the stool.

She put a perfect little hand on the bastard's sleeve. "We were just finishing, weren't we, Richard?"

"Uh, uh, yeah," Dick stuttered, presumably because they clearly couldn't have finished.

Madison went on. "We'll drop off T. Larry, then you can walk me to my car."

Laurence saw red. "I'll walk you to your car, and Dick here can find his way to his own vehicle."

"He goes by Richard, not Dick."

Laurence took a deep breath. He wasn't jealous. The ginger ale had gone to his head. Or he'd lost his mind. There was no other explanation, not for this incredible need he had to smash every bone in Dick's face, nor for the earlier embarrassing scene with Ronnie. "I think I'm having a nervous breakdown."

Madison patted his arm. "You'll feel better after a nice hot shower."

Only if she were in it with him. And *not* near Dick the Prick in any way, shape or form.

Laurence rose, holding his head in his hand, Madison's soft, perfumed touch doing yet another number on his brain. Pulling out his wallet, he yanked out two twenties, enough to cover Ronnie's tab as well as his.

The bartender held up his hand. "It's on me, bud."

"But…"

The man leaned his belly against the bar. "You said it for us all, man. Did us guys proud. You never gotta pay for another drink inside these doors as long as I'm here."

Madison gripped his arm, her breath sweet with champagne. "What did you *say,* T. Larry?"

The bartender slicked back his thinning hair, puffed out his chest, then put his hand to his heart. "He upheld male honor everywhere."

Laurence grabbed Madison's hand and made a dash for the exit amidst a deafening roar of applause, slamming the door on a refrain of "Way to go, dude," which almost drowned out the female answer of "Lynch the dirty bastard."

Too bad they hadn't managed to leave Dick on the inside.

Seemed Madison hadn't forgotten her date, either. "Oh, Richard, I left my purse at the table. Will you get it?"

"Of course." The pompous bastard oozed charm.

"Did he pay the bill?" Laurence wanted to know as soon as the door closed after him.

"I didn't notice since I was rushing over to you."

Ah, she hadn't noticed Richard the Lionhearted in the dash to be at *his* side. Good, very good. He'd have dragged her away right now if she hadn't left her purse behind.

"How old is he?" Laurence indicated the door with a thumb over his shoulder.

"Thirty-three."

"I'm five years older."

"Yes, I know." She put a hand to his forehead. "Did she scramble your brain when she hit you?"

"It was only a slap, not a hit." What the hell was taking Dick so long? Throw some bills on the table, get the purse and leave.

The door burst open once more, and there the Prick was, all flushed, Madison's huge purse under his arm. She took it with a grateful smile. Laurence growled, grabbed her arm and pulled her along with him.

"T. Larry," she said, while his feet ate up the concrete. She tugged on his hand to slow him down, touching the still-burning mark on his face. "What did you say to her?"

He looked back at Dick the Prick. The creep was following them. He thought about where Madison's hand *might* have been. "She put her hand on my crotch, and I told her to remove it." The slight exaggeration didn't bother him in the least. Madison would have done the same to make a point. Just today she'd told him little white lies for a good cause were acceptable.

"You told her to what?" That was Dick.

Laurence had eyes for only Madison. Hers were deeper than green, as fathomless as the sea. "I told her to take her hand off my crotch."

He'd left off the other bits because the end had really come about when he hadn't responded the way Ronnie wanted him to. Madison understood. "You insulted her woman power."

He'd do it again. "What should I have done, Madison?"

Madison beamed at him. "I think you did just the right thing, T. Larry."

All he could think was that if it had been Madison's hand…

Well, there it was, plain and simple, with Dick standing sentinel. Laurence wouldn't have told Madison to take her hand away, instead he would have moved it right onto his very important and most private part. He might even have begged.

He couldn't quite say when the terrible thing had happened, but he knew for sure he wanted Madison O'Donnell. He wanted her hands on the rest of his anatomy.

She needed a man, not some thirty-three-year-old boy with too much hair.

He didn't want to just pretend he was The One, he wanted to *be* The One.

At least for as long as it took to convince her she wasn't going to die.

CHAPTER FOUR

"I'LL WALK MADISON to her car."

"No, I'll walk Madison to her car."

Madison put one hand on each of their chests and pushed them apart. "If you two don't cut it out, I'll walk myself to my car."

That stopped them.

T. Larry's eyes glittered with manic fervor, probably the aftereffects of his altercation. Who'd have thought? She was proud of him. He'd put himself out on a limb in a public forum rife with opportunities for humiliation, and he hadn't lost sight of who he was or what he believed in. Later, she'd ask him what he'd said to make the woman laugh before she slapped him and threw her drink in his face. First, though, there was Richard.

"Richard is my date," she told T. Larry, "and he'll walk me to my car."

T. Larry balled his fists. "Madison."

"T. Larry." She prepared for a Mexican standoff.

Despite the warmth of the June day, the night had turned cool. Madison hugged her jacket tighter. Exhaust stung her nostrils. Taking up the middle of the sidewalk in front of Cruzio's Grand Café, they'd attracted attention. A man pulled his wife close to his side, then inched past them as if he expected a fight. Another couple stopped for the impending fireworks. Richard's gaze switched from her to T. Larry and back like a tennis match.

"I'm not going to stand out here forever."

T. Larry's fists relaxed. "He can walk you."

"Thank you."

"I'll walk ten paces behind, since we're going the same way."

She almost smiled. This time Richard clenched his fists, but she took his hand, pried his fingers loose and slipped her palm against his. "Make it twenty."

T. Larry growled as she pulled Richard through the small throng that had gathered. She loved the city. True, nooks and crannies emitted unpleasant odors and panhandlers begged on most corners, but bright neon signs lit the night and the enticing scent of garlic laced with voices and laughter floated on the air. Her black skirt swished around her thighs, her feet tingled inside her high-heeled pumps, and her hand tucked in Richard's perspired lightly with excitement. On nights like this, she thanked God she was alive. She didn't worry about dying. Especially not with Richard's cologne wafting around her and T. Larry's hot, protective glare on her back.

"Is there something I should know about…that man?" Richard glanced over his shoulder.

"T. Larry?"

Richard sighed with irritation. Ooh, he was jealous.

"He's my boss."

"I know." Richard paused, pulling her hand through his arm. His silk suit jacket caressed her knuckles. "He's the first boss I've ever seen follow his employ-

ees around for their—" he looked down, a puff of breath
ruffling her hair "—protection."

"He's not usually like this, but today's a special day."

"Special how?"

They turned in at the garage before she could answer.
Madison dropped his arm to fish in her purse for her
ticket and some cash. She hadn't bought the monthly
pass since she preferred the train and rarely drove her car.

Richard reached reflexively into his back pocket for
his wallet. "I'll get that for you."

How sweet. "I've got it." She fed the bill into the
machine along with her ticket. T. Larry waited a short
distance away by the street opening. Was that twenty
paces using his feet or twenty paces using mousesize
feet? Close enough to overhear Richard, T. Larry rolled
his eyes. Taking Richard's arm, she steered him away
before he saw.

They waited by the elevator. "Now about why today
is special…"

The elevator came, they stepped inside, then just as
the doors were about to close, T. Larry pushed through.
Richard's lips thinned. T. Larry's mouth split in the
biggest grin she'd ever seen him wear.

"You jumped in here on purpose." She should have
been mad, but Madison hadn't been mad about
anything in so long she'd sort of forgotten how. Besides,
that grin was infectious, though she managed to hide
her own for Richard's benefit.

"I didn't want to miss this one," T. Larry explained
without necessity, and Madison was sure he meant more
than the elevator. "Sometimes, these things take forever."

Which was true, but Madison knew that wasn't the
only reason. T. Larry didn't trust Richard. And he didn't

intend to let them out of his sight for a moment. Testosterone battled in the small lift. She was thankful when the doors finally opened on her floor.

They spilled out into the gloomy parking garage.

"My car's this way," she told Richard.

"Mine is, too," T. Larry answered.

She jabbed a finger in his chest. "Thirty paces."

Beneath the silk suit, tension transformed Richard's arm to rock. The heels of her shoes echoed off the walls. An engine rumbled to life on the floor below. A quick glance told her T. Larry kept his position by the elevator, his lips moving as he counted. Thirty, then he started to follow.

The ridiculous turn of the situation made Madison want to laugh. Badly. Almost uncontrollably. What *had* gotten into T. Larry? Merely the state of her tires that afternoon?

Her yellow coupe was parked five stalls down from his Camry. His keys jingled loudly in his pocket as he fished them out.

Richard bent to her ear. "Are you going to tell me what's so special about today and why your boss is breathing down your neck?"

"It started with my tires." Actually it started with Richard's phone call. They neared her car.

Richard stopped, almost tugging Madison off her feet when she blithely kept going. "Your tires?"

She pulled him the extra steps to her bumper. Whatever was wrong? His face had gone deathly white.

"Some kids slashed my tires this afternoon as a practical joke. It wasn't any big deal." Thank God T. Larry had climbed in his own car. He'd have strangled her for saying that, especially for believing it.

Richard's hand kneaded her fingers where he'd grabbed her. His knuckles cracked. "You got them fixed."

"Well, yeah. How else was I supposed to drive home?"

He stared at her brand-spanking-new and absolutely gorgeous tires. "I would have driven you home."

"You're sweet. But T. Larry would have done that."

Five spaces away from them, T. Larry's car roared to life. He gunned the engine.

"Did T. Larry get the tires fixed, too?"

"Oh, no. I did that." Richard's hand relaxed on her arm. "T. Larry just called the cops for me."

All sorts of things happened to Richard's face then. His nostrils worked air in and out, his lips tensed, and tiny lines shot from the corners of his mouth. "Seems like T. Larry does an awful lot of things for you."

Goodness, an honest-to-God spark of jealousy. She couldn't mistake that. No one had ever been jealous before. It was nice. But she couldn't let it get out of hand. "Oh, he's just a big protective teddy bear. Like my brothers."

T. Larry chose that moment to cruise by. He did look like a bear, teeth bared, eyes narrowed. His tires squeaked on the concrete as he pulled away, slowly, his gaze on them in his rearview mirror.

And then Richard said the most amazing thing. "Madison, you're not like anyone I've ever known before."

Well, she hoped not, but that odd note of reverence sent a little thrill straight through her body. "Thank you."

He took a step closer, dropped his voice low, intimate. "I wish I could have been there for you when you found your tires vandalized. It must have frightened you so."

Of course, she'd told him it had been no big thing, but that tone, that caring... "Kids," she murmured as if she were saying something completely different. "It wasn't like it was personal."

"I can't help but worry when something bad happens to you."

Boy, this was nice. If only it could go on forever. Like a fairy tale. "I wish you'd been there, too."

He looked at her mouth. "I'll be there next time, I promise."

She leaned forward an inch, then two, parting her lips. Yes, his eyes were the loveliest shade of brown and his breath caressed her ear.

T. Larry's tread squealed on the concrete as he circled again. Madison jumped back as if he'd caught them in the act.

With a quick cryptic glance at the receding lights, Richard said, "I better let you go."

"It's getting late," she agreed. She reached, almost reluctantly, into her purse. Where were those keys? She usually put them in the side pocket. She found them under her wallet.

Richard stared at them dangling from her fingers almost sadly, as if they were the symbol of their date's end. She strained toward him once more. *Kiss me, kiss me.* Normally she didn't on the first date, but time was running out. Her birthday was just around the corner.

Richard edged away from the plea in her eyes. "Can I call you at home to make sure you're safe?"

"Yes. My number's—" She snapped out of her mesmerizing need, T. Larry's admonitions sounding in her head. No kisses and no giving out her phone number, not on the first date. "I mean, why don't I call you?"

"You're afraid to give me your number." Hurt glazed his eyes.

Afraid wouldn't be the right word. Cautious. T. Larry's anxiety *had* rubbed off on her. She hoped it didn't put her off her schedule completely. She only had two weeks to fall in love.

"I know, I'm sorry," he said before she could answer. "I'm rushing you." He reached to his inside breast pocket, the back of his hand brushing her hair. Writing on a card, he handed it to her. "Please call me."

Oh, she would. She really, really would. Because when she looked into those sad brown eyes, she was sure she could make him into *The One*.

"IT'S MADISON." It came out huskier than she'd intended, a tad too sexual, maybe even too pushy. But time was running out, and she'd decided to call Richard once she got home.

Richard sighed. "I'm glad you're safe."

She'd washed her face, brushed her teeth, put her silkiest nightgown on, then jumped into bed to call. It wasn't as if he'd see the filmy garment. But Madison felt it as she slipped down beneath the covers and nestled into the pillows.

"You didn't block the call."

"Hmm." She stretched, then what he said hit her. "Huh?"

"I've got caller ID. You should have blocked your number, Madison."

"I didn't think about it."

"I thought of it for you. So don't worry, I'm not memorizing it until you give it to me for real."

He was so thoughtful. She curled her knees to her

chest, then stretched them out again. The lingering scent of cinnamon-and-almond treats drifted up from the Danish bakery below her apartment, making her mouth water.

"What are you wearing?"

She laughed softly. "Now what did I tell you asking that kind of question really means?"

"I admit I'm really asking *that*."

She couldn't find an answer for the moment. Hadn't she always wanted to try phone sex? Just a hint of it, starting small, like the lace on her bra or the texture of her nightie, a subtle sexual innuendo.

"I'm sorry. I'm rushing you again."

Yes, he was, but she felt the same rush. And the apology endeared him. "I'm wearing a very short silk nightgown, and I had a wonderful time tonight."

"Me, too. Can I see you again?" He didn't mention the nightie.

His eagerness turned her knees to Jell-O. She fingered the silk hem, and debated telling him about the plunging neck. Too soon, really too soon. There was rushing, and then there was *rushing*. One suited "Falling In Love," the other was just plain risky. She needed to know him better. And there was only one way. "I'd love to go out again."

"Without your boss?"

She laughed at his insistent tone. "Yes, without T. Larry."

"When?"

The weekend was shot, her nephew's birthday party was tomorrow, and she still had to shop for his present. Then church on Sunday morning and Sunday supper at her mother's. She wished for once she could cancel, but Ma would be heartbroken. "Monday?"

"Monday night?"

"For dinner." And that was all. She didn't want him to think she was easy. What a short timeline she'd drawn for herself. But she didn't have to have sex to fall in love with him. Maybe guys thought that way, but she didn't.

"Dinner's all I really want right now." He read her thoughts, her fears. Oh, he had such possibilities.

The phone clicked in her ear. "Wait a minute, I've got another call." She switched over.

"Are you home? Are you safe?"

"T. Larry, how could I be answering the phone if I wasn't?"

"Just checking."

"I'm on the other line. Hold on a minute."

She switched back over to Richard without asking herself why she wasn't just hanging up on T. Larry. "I have to go."

His frown came through in the silence.

"So Monday then?" she checked.

"Yes. Six o'clock. Is that okay? We can meet somewhere if that makes you feel more comfortable."

Madison smiled and burrowed deeper into the covers. "You're really so considerate, Richard." A fact which would make T. Larry puke if she told him. "Six is fine. Where shall I meet you?"

"Golden Gate Park. Outside the arboretum."

"The park?" The Japanese tea garden was near there. Oh, how fun.

"I'll bring the food. We're going to have a picnic."

Better than fun, a picnic was oh-so-romantic. "Oh, Richard," she said on a breath.

A beat of silence, then, "Sweet dreams, Madison."

With a click, he was gone, and T. Larry's snort sounded in her ear.

"Was that him?"

"Him who?"

"Dick the—I mean, Richard."

"Yes." She sighed with just a hint of the music she felt singing through her body. "Wasn't he wonderful?"

T. Larry said nothing, his answer in his harshly expelled breath.

"Richard said that exact same thing about you." She rolled to her side, tucking the phone between her ear and the pillow. "He's taking me on a picnic. In Golden Gate Park. Monday night. Isn't that romantic?"

His sigh indicated he didn't see the same romance in it that she did. "Madison, you're driving me crazy with this."

She lived in a second-floor apartment just off University Avenue in the heart of Palo Alto, only minutes from Stanford University. The relative quiet in her room suddenly enveloped her, the soft almost melodic shush of tires on the road outside her window, the gentle laughter of a couple walking in the night and T. Larry's whisper.

She'd never heard quite that quality in his voice, perhaps because it was the first time she'd listened without the accompaniment of phones ringing, cell phone static, traffic, voices, horns, et cetera, et cetera, ad nauseum.

"Why am I driving you crazy?"

"Is he the one?"

The quiet was thick, the low hum of his voice new and almost tantalizing with her bedclothes pulled to her chin and her nightie riding her thighs.

"Is he?" His tone lowered, deepened, became a touch more intimate.

Madison didn't dare analyze how his timbre made her feel. "I don't know yet."

"I don't trust him."

"You don't trust anyone."

"I'm only looking out for you."

"And I really appreciate it."

The silence was long. Her toes tingled with the sound of his breath so close to her ear.

"What are you wear—" He cut himself off. "I mean, what are you doing tomorrow?"

The oddest question. "You need me to work, on a Saturday?"

"No."

"Then why are you asking what I'm doing?"

"I thought we could have lunch."

"To talk about Richard and how I'm driving you crazy?"

"Just to have lunch."

"Whatever for?"

The soft, quiet, intimate T. Larry disappeared. "Do I have to have a reason?"

"Yes."

"Well, I don't. I just want...lunch."

Stretching out on her back, she held the phone away, looked at it, brow furrowed, then put it back to her ear. "Are you asking me for a date, T. Larry?"

"I'm trying to show you I can be just as impulsive as you."

"I like the word spontaneous better. Impulsive has a negative connotation."

"Then I'm spontaneous."

She sat up and switched on the bedside lamp, as if that would somehow shed light on T. Larry's brain. "I can't. I have a birthday party to go to."

"Why didn't you tell me that in the first place and save me fifteen minutes of irritation?"

"It wasn't fifteen minutes." She hugged her knees to her chest. She kind of felt bad for him when he was only trying to break out of his prudent, well-thought-out plans—something she'd always wanted him to do. "Would you like to go to the birthday party with me? It's for my nephew, Thomas."

A thoughtful pause. "How old is he?"

"Five."

"Too young. I don't do well with children."

"You'd better start unless you're giving up the Family Plan."

"All right, I'll go."

Easy capitulation. It robbed her of a pithy response. "You will?"

"Yes. What time?"

"The party's at one. Can you pick me up at a quarter to?"

"I can do that."

She gave him directions after which he seemed ready to hang up. For some inexplicable reason, she wasn't ready to let him go. "Why'd you laugh tonight?"

"Laugh?"

"With that woman. Before she smacked you."

Music tinkled faintly. He'd turned on the radio. She held her breath waiting for his answer.

"She said I had an amazing sense of humor."

Madison's eyes widened involuntarily. "She did?"

"After I asked her if she cheated on her taxes."

She gasped. "You didn't."

"She thought I was joking."

"You weren't?"

His voice dipped, melting her. "Do you think I have an amazing sense of humor, Madison?"

Amazing? She couldn't exactly lie about it. He'd know. But she didn't want to spoil his strange mood. Mostly, she couldn't believe she was having this conversation with T. Larry at all.

"Do you think I have an amazing *anything?*"

There *was* something she'd wondered about. "Well, you do wear a very small watch, T. Larry, and they say the size of a man's...you know..." She cleared her throat. "Well, the size of *that* is inversely proportional to the size of his watch. So I'm being led to believe that you have an amazing...you know."

He sputtered, coughed, then started to laugh. He was still laughing when he hung up on her. He certainly did amaze her.

It wasn't until she'd turned off the light and snuggled back beneath the covers with a smile on her lips that she thought to wonder why she hadn't extended the birthday party invitation to Richard instead.

THE SCENT OF PINE-SOL swept in from the bathroom, furniture polish lingered on the dusted tabletops, and her dishwasher swished in the kitchen. Harriet had scrubbed, scoured and washed from the moment she'd gotten home to her two-bedroom, one-bath apartment. Exhaustion rested pleasantly in her arms, her flannel pj's caressed her limbs, and Errol purred against her belly as she fed him fish-shaped treats. Fuzzy slippers warmed her feet. The 1938 movie *The Adventures of*

Robin Hood, the only decent version of the story, starring Errol Flynn, seduced her on her thirty-two-inch TV.

Harriet mellowed with the gratifying fatigue and a movie she knew ended happily. As Robin kissed Maid Marion, Harriet began to consider if she'd been too harsh over Zachary's comment, maybe even overreacted. Zachary had actually offered the compliment in the wake of Bill's complaint that the color of her dress resembled puke after a two-kegger night.

Zachary said her dress was pretty. Then he'd smiled, his gaze roaming to her legs.

Maybe that's what bothered her. His smile. Was it your garden variety gee-you-have-sweet-thighs smile? Or was it the nasty damn-I-can't-believe-you'd-show-those-thighs smile?

That was the trouble. She could never tell with Zachary. He wasn't quick to smile, and when he did, one couldn't tell if someone had forced it out of him. If he even had emotions, he held them so tightly to his chest that he seemed little more than an automaton. Except when he was slinking over to Madison's desk, ostensibly for one of her Reese's. Then, he resembled Tarzan drooling over Jane.

Madison called Zachary shy. She always searched for the nicest word possible to cover a person's idiosyncrasies. She said Harriet herself was misunderstood. Misunderstood? That was the nicest thing Madison could come up with? The worst part was that Madison was right about Timothy. A ring, even an engagement ring, was a gift and nonrefundable. He'd asked for its return when he realized Harriet would forever remain the soot-covered chimney sweep in her pumpkin instead of miraculously blossoming into Cinderella, the beautiful princess with tiny glass-slippered feet and narrow waist. "See what I've done for her. See how great I am." He wasn't a prince but a jerk with a bad case of Cinderella Syndrome. What was there about her that everyone seemed to think needed changing? At first, she'd found his suggestions charming. A man really *looked* at her and seemed to have her best interests at heart. Until Harriet recognized that his main concern had been about how her appearance reflected on him. She'd been nothing more than a pity project to him, too. And wham, bam, thank you ma'am, he'd dumped her when his pity didn't generate the desired alterations.

Errol nudged her hand for another salmon treat. She smoothed his silky fur, willing her tension to fade away. She shouldn't think of Timothy. Timothy made her think of pity projects, and pity projects made her think of Madison, and thoughts of Madison always upset her. Harriet wasn't jealous. Rather, she was defeated. Her expensive perm, highlight and cut had failed to resemble Madison's. Her more colorful attire had been met with derision. And if she offered a good-natured compliment, everyone asked if she'd been possessed by Casper the Friendly Ghost. She couldn't compete with Madison. Madison the perfect. Madison the Paragon. Madison the...

Her doorbell chimed.

Harriet looked down the length of her pajamas, the nap worn off with loving overuse. It was probably Mrs. Murphy from next door wanting a cup of sugar. The lady always baked when she couldn't sleep. The mouthwatering aroma of fresh chocolate chip cookies often followed Harriet into her dreams.

Bag of sugar in her hand, Harriet opened the door.

And dropped the five pounds on Zachary's foot.

"Oh my God, I'm so sorry."

He hopped on one foot. "When you get pissed, Harriet, you really get pissed."

Funny that he could string together sentences extremely well when she was the only one around. Was that a good or a bad thing? "It was an accident."

They didn't move for a moment, he on the outside, his face red, she on the inside, biting her lip.

Then she saw the way his gaze skimmed her pajamas. His eyes reflected the distorted image of Miss Piggy. Harriet wanted to cry. "What do you want?"

His Adam's apple bobbed. "I came to apologize."

"Because T. Larry told you to?"

He straightened his shoulders, his polo shirt stretching over his chest. She gave him an A for effort. "I'm not sorry I said your dress was pretty, Harriet."

"Then what do you want to apologize for?" She hated the nasty tone, wishing she could have asked him if he'd meant it, if he'd been trying to protect her from those three bullies at work. But she couldn't.

"Can I come in?"

Yes. Please. "No."

He stuck his hands in the front pockets of his jeans, then quickly pulled them out. "I wanted to say I'm sorry about what happened...." He faltered, started again. "I'm sorry that I..."

God, he couldn't even get the words out. This wasn't about her dress. "What, Zachary? Sorry that you dumped me after one night? Or sorry that you screwed me in the first place."

"I…I…"

She really would like to cry. But not in front of him. "You never used to be a stutterer, Zachary. What's wrong now?" She took a step closer. "Afraid I'm going to tell everyone? Afraid they'll all find out you had sex with Harriet the Harridan?"

"No…" His mouth worked, but nothing else came out.

It was all so clear. It had been eight months since that night, since they'd worked late on the AMI account, when he kissed her, and she'd put her hand on him, and they'd made love.

Then the next morning he'd pretended as if it never happened. Pretended for eight long months.

"Bet you would have crowed like a rooster if it was Madison." Why oh why did it seem Madison always stood in her way?

"Harriet, I—"

She cut him off. "You're a pig. Get out." She didn't slam the door, merely closed it in deference to Mrs. Murphy, who might have fallen asleep.

Harriet was proud of herself. She hadn't screamed, hadn't even raised her voice. Albeit, she wasn't very nice, but if she hadn't said those things, she might have asked him why he ignored her. She might have invited him inside. She might have cried in front of him, begged him to touch her again, sweetly, gently, devoutly, the way he had that night.

And none of that would do.

ZACH HAD BLOWN IT AGAIN. As always, when it came to Harriet.

Slunk down in his seat, he stared up at her window. Street light beat down on the hood of his car. Cool night air breezed over his face through the open window. A dog barked, and a van drove by in the otherwise quiet neighborhood. His long legs hit the steering wheel, and he shoved the seat back for extra room.

Sometimes Zach wished he'd never touched her. That had been the start of all his troubles. They used to be able to talk. He'd even made Harriet laugh. She'd helped him out on that AMI account, given him the credit and stood back while T. Larry slapped him on the back for a job well done. Then later, Zach had kissed her the way he'd been thinking about doing for months.

And life went to hell.

He'd tried to tell her that he wasn't ashamed of what they'd done. He just wanted to keep it private. He didn't want it dissected over the watercooler in the copy room. He didn't want to fend off the guy jokes.

Harriet deliberately misinterpreted everything he said and did. Like that comment about her dress. Then again, maybe she'd seen right through it. Puke green best described the color. The harsh fluorescent lights turned her skin a shade to match. But he'd seen the tilt of her chin, and he'd felt her pain. Was it really such a bad thing to want to stand up for her?

But no one defended Harriet except Harriet.

She'd boss a man to an early grave. She'd abrade the skin off an armadillo. She'd stick her head in the sand until her ass turned blue and never acknowledge a word he said. But she could be so damn sweet when she wasn't worried someone had demeaned her.

Why didn't he admit the truth? He'd once again picked a woman just like dear old mom, and he was dear old dad, destined to be henpecked to death. And he didn't want it. Harriet wouldn't listen to him because she knew he *did* regret their one fantastic, unforgettable night. No matter what he said, no matter how he pleaded, she saw right through to that layer of self-reproach.

She saw him wishing she was more like Madison, a woman he could never aspire to date and Harriet could never aspire to be.

CHAPTER FIVE

HOW HAD HE GOTTEN himself into this? Laurence wondered.

He'd been seduced with his own fantasies.

He clung to the corner chair on Dorie O'Donnell's huge covered back porch. The house itself was two-story with white shutters against a blue exterior. Madison's mother plied him with iced tea; her two cats did figure eights around his legs; and Thomas, the birthday boy, had taken ownership of his lap.

Madison sat to his left, rocking the youngest O'Donnell against her shoulder. Pudgy fingers kneaded the swell of her breast like a newborn kitten, bubbles popping from its mouth as it slept—a boy or a girl, Laurence couldn't decide. The breeze wafting gently over Madison carried the scent of formula and baby powder. She managed to talk and eat without disturbing the baby as naturally as if she were its mother.

The other six children—Laurence's critical accounting mind calculated frantically—splashed in a hopelessly small plastic pool in the center of a plush green lawn trimmed with late blooming camellia bushes all around. All under the age of ten, their aggregate vocal cords created a cacophony loud enough to wake the dead. On another continent. Or another planet.

No one seemed to notice but Laurence.

"Have another cupcake."

Dorie, as she insisted he call her, offered him a chocolate confection topped with two inches of cream icing. With the last one she'd given him, all that icing had found its way up his nose. Every aroma drifting his way now came laced with the syrupy sugar.

"No, thank you, wonderful as they are."

She tut-tutted like a grandmother of seventy, though she could only have been in her midfifties with a smattering of gray in her dark hair. Obviously Madison's red hair didn't come from her mother, though Laurence suspected Madison's trim figure was from Dorie's gene pool. She was a handsome lady with a well-kept shape. The woman had been feeding him constantly since he'd arrived two hours ago. The center table overflowed with chips, salsa, crackers, cheese, spinach dip, and the "boys" hadn't even started the barbecue yet. Laurence issued a soundless groan.

"I want one, Gramma." The cake disappeared into Thomas's mouth, frosting splattering his cheeks and chocolate crumbs sprinkling Laurence's khaki slacks.

"Thomas," someone admonished.

The child swallowed, belched loudly, smiled and wiped his icing-covered fingers on Laurence's shirt.

Dorie handed him a napkin to wipe off the mess.

"You wanna see my Yu-Go cards?" Thomas held a grimy stack aloft, the stack Laurence had already been through. Four times.

"Sure."

"Children seem to love you." That came from Carol, blond, late twenties, a pretty smile in a round face, Sean's wife. Or did she belong to Patrick? All red-haired, with the developed muscles and tanned faces of hardworking outdoor men, the brothers were James, Patrick and Sean. That much Laurence had gleaned during the time Madison had worked for him, though he had to admit he'd never memorized the relationships, and thus today he'd lost track of which man, woman and child went with whom.

Except Madison. She was with him.

"They do like him, don't they?" Madison winked at him over the baby-soft hair nestled beneath her chin. The tip of her sandaled foot swung lazily, brushing his shoe. He'd been watching that bare, tanned leg until he was afraid he'd start to drool.

What was she saying? Something about children. She'd explained it all on the short walk over from her apartment. He needed to be around children, large groups and small, needed to talk with them, read to them and cuddle them on his lap. Hence, the placement of Thomas. Laurence thought children couldn't sit still, especially under the age of five. But Thomas had been content on his lap for well over forty-five minutes. Laurence's left leg had numbed as the boy chattered, scattered his playing cards, waited patiently while his mother picked them up, then started all over again.

"He's going to make a perfect Daddy." Madison beamed.

Sean—or was that James—choked momentarily on a cherry pit, then spat it out in his hand. Somewhere in his midthirties, lines fanned out from the corners of his eyes as if he laughed a lot. He wasn't laughing now.

"What the hell are you saying, Madison?"

"James, don't swear." Carol and Madison's mom spoke concurrently.

Ah, James was the husband, not Sean or Patrick. James and Carol, parents of the birthday boy. Laurence cataloged the relationship.

"I asked her what she was saying, Ma. I think we deserve an answer." James spoke to his mother about his sister, while his eyes bored two holes right through Laurence's forehead.

"I'm not pregnant," Madison said, "if that's what you mean."

"Then what? Are you planning to marry him?" This from…Sean, who had lighter colored hair than the rest, but no fewer laugh lines though he was the youngest son. James being the oldest. Patrick, the middle one. Three sets of male eyes fixed on him. They were all hopping mad.

Per Madison, the only things Dorie O'Donnell had intended to keep of her children's Irish-Catholic heritage were their names and the red hair on each of their four heads. But Irish-Catholic genes couldn't be buried, not even under the Protestant mantle she'd foisted on them, as evidenced by the protectiveness of Madison's three brothers and the number of young redheads dotting the yard—something to do with the rhythm method, he was sure.

Laurence should have been horrified by the marriage comment and the ecstatic glow in Dorie's eyes, not to mention the fight on the faces of Madison's brothers. But two hours of O'Donnells had polished the edges of his nerves until he felt absolutely nothing.

Except the caress of Madison's arm against his as she rocked the little one, or her pinkie against his chest when she straightened Thomas's cards, her foot along his calf…

Did she know what she was doing to him?

"What about Yu-Go?"

"Yu-Gi-Oh! has to wait until your aunt answers the question." Patrick, the largest of the three brothers in height and breadth but by no means fat, narrowed his eyes on his nephew, and Thomas's lips clamped. Discipline in this family was meted out by whatever adult was closest.

The only sound was the screeching laughter of children, and below that, the insistent buzz of summertime flies.

Laurence decided to rescue them all. "What Madison means is that though I plan on having a family someday, I've never been around children, and she wanted to help me get my feet wet."

A multitude of eyes turned to Laurence. He hadn't explained well enough. Electricity crackled in the two inches that separated Madison's shoulder from his.

"We're not talking about our children *together.* Just children in general."

It still wasn't enough. Sweat gathered in his armpits. He was out of his depth. He had been from the moment Madison dragged him through the front screen door. He was an only child from an orderly household run by a very sweet June Cleaver look-alike who'd insisted on spotless clothing at all times.

This was bedlam.

"Stop embarrassing T. Larry." Madison patted his arm. "I'm never getting married, and we aren't having children, so shut up."

Just like that, they did. Miracle of miracles. Or maybe it was that everyone thought suddenly of *why* she believed she'd never get married. Yet, he didn't get the hint that her family held the same fatalistic view of her life. For long moments there, Dorie's eyes had definitely glazed over with matrimonial hope, and her brothers had defended her virtue—or something. Those were not the actions of a family who thought they were going to bury her in less than a month.

Odd that they let her fantasy—or whatever the hell it was—continue. Then again, Madison herself was odd, so what else did he expect?

The conversation turned elsewhere, people broke into groups of two or three, while Madison's mother rose to bring out yet another tray of food. Laurence couldn't stand to look at it.

"Yu-Go," Thomas whispered.

"Yu-Gi-Oh!" Laurence whispered back, aware of Madison's knowing smile and the scent of her flowery perfume somewhere beneath the sugary icing in his nose.

With remarkable comprehension for a child of five, Thomas explained each card, delighting in describing the different monsters. Of course, since Thomas had a problem getting the name of the game correct, Laurence was dubious that the rules he outlined were the actual rules of the game. He had a feeling the child made them up as he went along. Laurence leaned back in his chair, one hand securely on Thomas's bottom so the boy didn't fall, and his arm on the rest, next to Madison's, close enough to feel the vibration of her laughter.

"How big is your penis?"

His heart stopped right in his chest. Heat burned in his cheeks. Blood vessels popped in his head. How could one little boy have that much volume?

Laurence did the only thing a sane man could do.

Making sure Thomas was securely balanced, Laurence held up his hands, spaced them a little more than twelve inches apart and said, "About this big." Then added, to accommodate Thomas's saucerlike gaze that moved from Laurence's face down to the crotch of his own denim pants, "Don't worry. You've got plenty of time to grow."

"WELL, YOU SAID you wanted to know." T. Larry spread his hands in a what-gives gesture.

"Know what?" Madison pretended she didn't understand.

"If the size of a man's…you know…is inversely proportional to the size of his watch." T. Larry held out his thin, plain, unassuming watch for her perusal.

"I never said I *wanted* to know the size of your…you know. I merely said a watch could be an indication."

T. Larry had only made his outrageous comment in front of her family because she'd impugned his spontaneity. And boy, had he come back with a whopper, so to speak. She'd never challenge him again, at least not on that issue. Once again, she was proud of him. She'd make him spontaneous if it killed her.

As he walked her the six blocks back to her apartment through her mother's well-tended neighborhood, T. Larry commandeered her hand, tucking it through his arm and pulling her close, their bodies touching as they moved. Strange. Pleasant. Safe. Her fingers tingled with the sensation of masculine skin against hers. Tall, leafy trees covered the sidewalk and street like an arbor. Huge, trimmed hedgerows separated green, immaculate lawns. The last of the spring flowers faded on the shrubs. The setting sun had cooled off the early summer day, but the mouthwatering bouquet of steaks on barbecues hung in the air like fog.

Next to her, T. Larry smelled sugar-frosted.

She didn't really want to know the size of his "you know." At least she *shouldn't*. But… She needed something to take her mind off it. "Do you sunburn on the top of your head?"

His muscles tensed beneath her hand, his eyes lost their twinkle, and the teasing smile on his lips got stomped by a frown.

"It was just a question, T. Larry. Nobody cares about your hair but you."

"You mean my lack of hair."

She pulled on his arm to stop him. Street light reflected on his glasses, obscuring his eyes, but she knew he needed a verbal stroke. "Women think bald is sexy."

"That's if the man is completely bald." He was referring to the fringe of hair on the sides.

"No. Skinner on the *X-Files* is—"

"I never watched the *X-Files*."

"Well, you should. They play reruns all the time on the cable channels. But anyway—"

"Do you think it's sexy?"

"This isn't about me, T. Larry."

Not a muscle of his face moved, then he started off again in the direction of her apartment. "I didn't think it was."

Crickets chirped in the silence that fell. Madison tugged on the hem of her skirt where it had ridden up to within an inch of her butt. A breeze blew through the street, kicking up the few leaves that had died in the summer sun, whisking them across the pavement and leaving in its wake the echo of footsteps behind them.

She turned, her cheek to T. Larry's shoulder. They were the only ones on the street.

It reminded her of the train. That sensation of being watched, eyes on her back, but when she looked, no one paid her the least attention.

"What is it?"

"Nothing." No one was following them. She'd merely felt footsteps walking over her grave, suggesting how close her birthday was, whispering to her not to waste a moment, not a single moment. She left the niggling fear behind and hugged close to T. Larry's arm. "And I do love your bald head."

"Will you drop the bald references? Let's talk about your brothers instead."

"Let's talk about Thomas. He adores you."

But T. Larry was on a mission, and nothing was going to stop him from completing his thought. "James thanked me for taking care of your tires."

She yanked his arm. "You promised you wouldn't tell."

He yanked her forward. "I didn't tell. He knew. I think it was your tow truck pal."

"That rat. See if I ever bake him double-dipped chocolate fudge cookies again."

"All you did was bake him cookies?"

That earned him a narrow-eyed glare. "How else did you think I got my new tires?"

He raised a brow.

"You dirty rat." She punched his arm.

"I thought *he* was the rat."

"You're both part of the same rat colony."

Ahead, tiny outdoor Christmas lights glowed, lighting the way up her stairs. She left them on all the time. Amazing how long those things lasted.

It didn't bother her that T. Larry thought she might sleep her way to the things she wanted. She probably would. If the thing was important enough. It was just that nothing ever had been.

What about falling in love? And being loved in return. Seemed to Madison you *couldn't* sleep your way into that.

"I wasn't finished telling you what your brother said."

"Well, go on, seeing that you're dying to tell me."

"He wanted to make sure we weren't sleeping together."

She stifled a giggle. She and T. Larry?

"But if we were, he wanted to be sure I used a condom."

She laughed aloud. "Where does James come up with this?"

"And then he offered me two he had in his pocket, just in case I wasn't prepared for tonight."

She screamed. Not loudly, just vehemently. "What was James doing with condoms in his pocket?"

"What the hell was he doing offering them to me? And I thought your brothers were overprotective."

"They are. Sex just isn't one of the things they feel the need to protect me from."

They'd reached her apartment. She went up on one step. His hand slid down to her arm to capture her fingers.

She looked at her hand in his, the long, blunt fingers of a big, masculine hand. "Did you tell him you wouldn't dream of sleeping with me in, oh, say, this millennium?"

"No." He shook his head. "I didn't tell him that."

"Did you take the condoms?"

"No." He shook his head again. "I didn't do that, either."

Madison, who was never at a loss for words, was…at a loss for the *right* words. "Do you want to come up for coffee?"

"Yes."

Her head blocked the light so she could see his eyes clearly through his glasses. What was written in them wasn't quite so clear. But her heart began to beat just a little faster, and she felt hot all over. *All* over. She must have had too much sun.

"I've got regular coffee or decaf. Or I can make a mocha. Or a cappuccino. Or—"

His eyes smoked. "I'll take whatever you're offering."

That didn't mean what it sounded like it meant. Did it? Her body, right down to her toes, tingled.

"Espresso." She turned and practically ran the rest of the way up the stairs, glancing over her shoulder to find him staring at her bare legs. Her bad hand shook more than usual, and her breath came in little pants by the time she got to the top.

Flowers blossomed on the landing. Daisies and carnations and blooms she didn't know the name of dripped from a vase set by the door. The stems were a tad wilted and the petals browned around the edges as if they'd sat in the afternoon sun. A card peeked from the leaves.

T. Larry breathed down her neck.

Why was he standing so close all of a sudden, all day and yesterday, as well, in fact? T. Larry didn't like his space invaded. He didn't like invading others' space, either. Unless he felt the need to intimidate. Which sometimes, as the boss, he did.

"Who are they from?"

She grabbed the card and turned so he couldn't read over her shoulder, her arm brushing the cloth of his shirt.

"Dick?"

"Richard." He'd signed with a red heart, nothing more, but she knew it was him. Oh, how romantic and sweet.

"Too cheap to buy you roses?" T. Larry's brows knit over the rim of his glasses.

She hugged the card to her breast and stared at the beautiful, if faded, spray. "I don't need roses."

"You deserve roses."

She cocked her head. "Do serial killers send flowers?"

She thought she saw one corner of his mouth lift in a hint of a smile that vanished before she could be sure.

"Yes. They send something exactly like that." He pointed at the vase. "Decayed around the edges. Serial killers are masters of symbolism. Should I throw them out for you?" He looked over the banister to the Dumpster at the end of the alley.

"Don't you touch them." She bent to gather the bouquet in her arms, a draft sneaking up her skirt.

"Are you wearing underwear?"

She slapped a hand beneath her bottom, almost dropping the vase. This time, she found him smiling.

"Were you looking?"

"Is that a no?"

T. Larry flustered her. The queen of shock, she hadn't been flustered since she'd recovered from her stroke at fifteen. But T. Larry had discovered the knack somewhere.

She fumbled her keys near the lock. He took them out of her hand, crowded her against the wood and unlocked the door for her.

He *was* trying to intimidate her. But why?

Both her hands shook now. If she had espresso at this

time of night, she'd turn into a jumping bean. "How about some Baileys Irish Cream instead?"

"Whatever you want, Madison."

He watched her with smoky gray eyes. Her throat went dry. Whatever was wrong with her? She thought about those eyes. She thought about drinking Baileys from small snifters, about the taste on her tongue, about the feel of it in her blood. "No, I think we'll stick with the espresso."

"As I said, it's all up to you, Madison."

Oh goodness.

Flipping on a light, she eyed the room, the sofa no bigger than a love seat, filled with a jumble of stuffed animals her mother knit to sell at the church bazaar—a pink pig, the Cowardly Lion, a white rabbit. And the mess of magazines, newspapers and yesterday's blouse covering the top of her coffee table.

She'd forgotten the state the apartment was in. Panty hose peeked from beneath the chair she'd sat in last night to peel them off. Her high heels tipped over by the leg of that same chair. At least he hadn't seen her kitchen yet. She really had meant to wash those dishes.

She heard his voice and smelled his frosting first, and when she looked up, he was a hairbreadth from her face. She looked at him cross-eyed.

"Do you want me to help clean up?" Miraculously, the panty hose dangled from his fingers.

She grabbed and stuffed them beneath a cushion, then fanned herself with her hand. "Gosh, the place hasn't cooled down."

With a dash, she opened the front window, then pulled the filmy curtain closed. A soft breeze blew the lace in and out. Once again, T. Larry was right there when she turned around.

She backed away, her buns pressed to the window-sill. She wasn't nervous. She didn't know what she was. Besides overheated. Or embarrassed.

Embarrassed? Nothing she'd ever said or done around T. Larry embarrassed her before. So what was this feeling?

She had a plan for T. Larry. All she had to do was stick to it and the strange tingling would go away. What was the plan? *Come on, Madison.* Oh yeah, a wife. What about BeeBee Barton, her best friend in the whole world? Of course, BeeBee. She was wonderful. Madison bit her lip. Not BeeBee. She didn't analyze that uncomfortable prickle that couldn't possibly be jealousy.

Who then? "I know the perfect woman for you. I've been thinking about it all the way home."

"And?" His voice was suspiciously low, deceptively calm.

"Barbie Doll."

Deadpan, he answered, "She's made of plastic."

"Not *that* Barbie Doll. This one is a friend of mine. Who was unfortunate enough to be born to parents with the last name of Doll. And they thought it would be such fun to name her Barbie. But she's completely done with therapy now, and she doesn't hold an ounce of anger toward them, and she'd be perfect for you."

He was a step closer, though she hadn't seen him move. "You're babbling."

"No, I'm not. I'm explaining quickly so you don't have time to shoot down my idea."

"It was shot down before it even went up. I'm not dating someone named Barbie Doll."

"You can't hold her name against her. It wasn't her choice."

"Does she look like a Barbie Doll?"

"Which one? The new version or the sixties version?"

He closed in, giving her heart palpitations. "Aren't they all impossibly large breasted, thin waisted, and perfect hipped?" he said, his gaze traveling to each of the mentioned parts of her body.

Her voice squeaked on the first syllable. "Yes."

"Not interested."

"You answered too fast."

He put a hand to his chin, pursed his lips and tilted his head this way, then that. "After careful consideration, I've decided I'm not interested."

"But T. Larry—"

"Shh."

"You should give her—"

He put a finger to her lips "—I said—" and raised a brow "—shh."

No finger was going to stop her saying something this important. "But—"

He clamped his hand over her mouth, pinned her there with his other hand on the nape of her neck. "Don't you ever be quiet?"

Not if she could help it. And then she became aware of the fact that somehow, in the process of shutting her up, he'd managed to plaster his body the length of hers, front to front, chest to breasts, thighs to thighs, and everything in between. Everything.

Oh my God.

She opened her mouth and licked his palm. Salty. Sort of delicious actually.

He jumped back, let go of her imprisoned lips and cradled his hand as if she'd thrown acid on it.

"What did you do that for?"

"So you'd let me finish what I was saying."

"Not on your life."

She put a hand to her mouth. "Did you smudge my lipstick?"

"You lost it with the potato salad."

He'd been watching? "Why didn't you tell me? How awful to be walking around without lipstick. It's unwomanly. It's—"

This time he used his mouth on her. Madison shut up. He tasted of the chocolate cream mousse her mother made for dessert and smelled of Thomas's cupcake. Sugar and spice and everything nice. That was little girls. T. Larry was all man. His hands dropped from the back of her head to her waist, pulling her against him.

Oh my God. T. Larry wanted her. Impossible. Incredible. Irresistible.

She went up on her tiptoes and wound her arms around his neck. Her nose bumped his glasses. He didn't stop kissing her, touched his tongue to hers and then he was inside. Oh my. His shoulders were muscled from that daily workout—thank God for T. Larry's routines—his chest hard against her breasts. He was hard everywhere. Really hard. Goodness. She eased back a fraction, rubbed lightly against him. T. Larry groaned and deepened the kiss, an arm across her back, fingers in her hair.

The phone rang.

She pushed at his shoulders.

"Don't answer it." He didn't allow an inch between them.

"It'll be my brother checking to see I got home."

He brushed his lips across hers. "James wouldn't be calling at a time like this."

"Oh." Yes, they'd already covered the condom issue. "One of the others then." It rang a third time. "They'll wonder what I'm doing."

"Christ." He stepped back, running a hand over his head. "I'm wondering the same thing. Answer it."

She caught it just before the machine picked up. "Hello."

Nothing. She hadn't gotten it in time. No. There was the slight sound of breathing. "Hello?"

Someone was breathing in her ear. And something else. A faint buzz, then what sounded like a dog barking. Definitely, a dog. Someone on a cell phone. "Hello?"

"Who is it?"

She gave T. Larry a that-is-the-dumbest-question look.

"Hang up if you don't know who it is."

She tried one more time. "Hello?"

T. Larry held out his hand. She gave the receiver over without a protest. "Who's there?"

He hung up, having no better luck than she had. "You did that on purpose," he accused.

"Did what?"

"Had someone call right in the middle of my kiss."

"Your kiss? It was mine, too."

"I forced you. So technically it was mine."

"You didn't force me. I wanted to kiss you."

A smile grew on his face. Her knees almost melted. What had she just said? "Glad to hear that, Madison." He backed away from her, smiling like a cat that lapped up a whole saucer of cream and wasn't lactose intolerant. "I'll see you Monday morning."

He was out the door when she remembered. She ran to the top of her stairs. "What about the espresso?"

He stopped at the bottom, one hand on the banister, light shining on his glasses. A cat screeched, a trash can fell over. And T. Larry still smiled. "Oh, I think you've had enough stimulation for one night, don't you?"

HER NIPPLES SHOWED in her nightie. Cheeks flushed, lips full, Madison looked as though she'd been kissed. Long and hard. She put her fingers to her lips and stared into the vanity mirror.

Who would have guessed? She'd known T. Larry had a tongue—he yelled at her enough—but that he knew how to use it like *that?*

She put her hand automatically to the dresser top, searching for her hairbrush. Her fingers didn't find it. When she looked, it wasn't there.

She rose, the nightie swishing down her thighs to the tops of her knees. She must have left the brush in the bathroom.

What had possessed him? That comment about his lack of hair. Or the way she'd offered him Barbie. Madison understood now. She'd put a challenge out there. He'd taken her up on it.

Poor T. Larry. He didn't get it. She wasn't right for him. She was flighty, which had never been a bad thing in her book. She said whatever came into her head, and she'd never do a single thing he told her to. T. Larry craved complacency. She'd die if she was nothing more than content. He'd try to mold her into something she could never be. She'd stifle with his routines.

She'd have to slash her wrists. Of course, that wouldn't be necessary when she had a stroke after her twenty-eighth birthday.

Goodness, it was just a kiss, not a marriage proposal.

She found herself in the small bathroom, in front of the mirror, touching her lips. She didn't look merely kissed, but divinely kissed. There was only one way to view the situation.

If T. Larry's kiss took her breath away, Richard's had to ring bells.

Where was that brush? She opened the drawers and lifted the towels on the shelf above the toilet. In the front room, she looked in the side table drawer, then on the countertop that separated the kitchen. She searched everywhere, keeping her back to the window over the street, where she'd stood as T. Larry kissed her.

A nice kiss. But just a kiss. Really nothing divine about it, even if she *looked* that way in the mirror.

Back in the bedroom, she looked under the bed, finding nothing but a discarded bra—she'd been looking for that—and a few dust bunnies clinging to the carpet.

Darn. Her hairbrush was nowhere to be found.

CHAPTER SIX

WHAT HAD Laurence been thinking kissing Madison like that? He'd lost his mind. Some sort of mental fugue had overtaken him. He'd had an out-of-body experience.

The truth was much less palatable. Laurence had simply given in to the intoxicating scent of her and his irritation over her desire to see him date a Barbie Doll.

Still, his actions were unacceptable. He was supposed to protect her, not seduce her. However, if he didn't seduce her, how would she come to believe he was The One? That was mere rationalization for bad behavior. He'd wanted her. He'd acted on it. Kissing her had nothing to do with helping her get over her unnatural notion that she was going to die.

That kiss had disturbed Laurence's sleep and troubled his mind from the moment he'd succumbed to it. It fogged his brain when he'd sat in front of his home computer on Sunday. It made him fifteen minutes late leaving Monday morning, which caused him an extra half hour in traffic. He'd forgotten his appointment with Amy Kermeth, hadn't gotten his workout and had discovered the coffee machine was broken when he finally reached the office. The rest of the morning was no better. He couldn't forget Madison's filmy blouse draped across the coffee table or her panty hose and high heels on the carpet.

The three times he'd called her into his office, his mind's eye had stripped her naked, imagined the scent at the base of her throat, the color of her nipples...

He hadn't a clue what she was actually wearing.

The worst part was that he hadn't needed anything when he buzzed her, at least not anything work related. He'd gone insane. He'd lost control of his libido. He'd forgotten the Family Plan.

This was bad, very bad. A boss should never, under any circumstances, notice such intimate details about his employee. Madison deserved far more respect.

He'd unequivocally and irrevocably fallen in lust with Madison O'Donnell.

So, what could a fourth visitation really hurt? He was already doomed as it was.

He pushed his intercom button. "Madison, a minute, please."

He'd need her for a lot longer than that, considering everything he wanted to do to her. But this time, he'd note her attire, and he wouldn't even think about the silky texture of her panty hose against his fingers.

"Draft a letter to..." He couldn't remember the name of the client, any client.

Her gauzy skirt, wrinkled by design, wrapped around her calves. Black nylon hugged her ankles. Suede pumps caressed her feet. His heart stopped when his gaze rose to her face. Actually it never made it to her face. It didn't get past her shoulders, her throat bared by the cut of her lacy black vest, not to mention the swell of breast above the plunging neckline. Or that tight choker around her neck.

He was unreasonably incensed despite himself. "You dressed for him, didn't you?"

Her pen and pad bobbed in one hand while the other fiddled with the rainbow-colored necklace at her throat. "Him who?"

She'd left the door open behind her. Laurence tried not to yell. "Dic—"

She glowered, a look less than intimidating when you took in the whole petite package.

Laurence gave in anyway. "Richard."

"Yes."

"You'll freeze in that skimpy vest." Or she was going to incite Dick the Prick to lust.

"It's summer."

Beneath the desk, Laurence clenched his fists on his thighs. "You drove your car again?"

"Squeaky's watching it for me to make sure nothing happens."

"Squeaky?"

"Our attendant."

Laurence couldn't even remember the man's face, yet Madison had learned his name. Then he noticed the almost nervous way she fingered her rainbow necklace. What was the thing made of anyway? "What?"

Her eyes shifted to the left. "What do you mean, what?"

"You're twitching. You only do that when you want something." Maybe he should tell her what she wanted. Then he could give it to her. Gladly.

"It's about my picnic."

Thank you, God, she wanted to cancel it. "I can tell you to work late if you need an excuse."

"No." The purse of her lips didn't last long. "I just want to ask you not to follow me to Golden Gate Park tonight."

"I wasn't going to follow, but there's nothing wrong with a man taking a stroll through the park."

"You don't stroll." She fluttered her eyelashes and puckered her lips. "Please, T. Larry."

He would look a little ridiculous watching them from a park bench. Not to mention obsessive and compulsive. "All right, but you have to sit out in the open where everyone can see you. No dreamy little clearings amidst a lot of trees."

"Okay."

"And you have to promise to park in plain sight and leave before it gets dark." He'd called the police several times since the tire incident. They'd tried reassuring him by saying that there'd been similar occurrences in three other garages that same day. So reassuring. Not. Changing garages wouldn't help, either. Damn.

"Promise?" he repeated when she pressed her lips together, fingering that damn necklace again.

"All right, all right."

"And—"

"Isn't that enough?"

He tapped his finger against his lips. She shut up easily this time as if afraid he'd use his mouth on her again, a method he would have preferred. He made up his mind before he could consider the wisdom of his decision. "You have to give me Tuesday night."

"Tuesday night?"

He raised a brow. "Do I hear an echo in here?"

"But what do you mean you want Tuesday night?"

He enunciated clearly. "If he gets tonight with you, then I get tomorrow night."

"Whatever for?" She stared at him as if he'd sprouted a thousand snakes from his bald head.

He wagged his finger at her. "Or I can just follow you through the park."

"All right. But this won't be a date or anything, will it? It'll just be an outing."

She could call it whatever she wanted, but she'd kissed him back, and she'd liked it. He hadn't a doubt about that. "Deal. An outing."

"Why do I think I just got suckered?"

He smiled. She was going to get a helluva lot more than suckered, though that was a good place to start.

She tipped her head. "Where are you taking me?"

Ah, that was the question, how did he top a picnic in the park, romantically speaking? He hadn't a clue. "It's a surprise."

Her eyes sparkled. *Gotcha.* Madison loved surprises. "Oh come on, tell me. How will I know what to wear?"

Anything she wore would do just fine. "Let's worry about that later."

Madison tapped her shoe. "All right. Did you call me in for something else?"

Foiled. He'd called her in simply to see her. "Pull the file for," and he threw off a garbled name she wouldn't understand while he cleared his thoughts.

"Who?" Her thumb worked its way beneath the beads around her neck, pulling as if the baubles were strung on elastic, then let it snap back in place.

"The file for…" He stared at the hollow of her throat. "What's that thing you're wearing?"

She tilted her chin back and pulled on the necklace until she could see it. "It's candy."

"Candy?" His voice rose like an adolescent boy's.

"Yeah. You eat it like this." She tugged a bead into her mouth, bit it off, sucked on it, then licked her lips. Her cherry-red lipstick somehow managed to stay in place.

His head would surely explode. "And you wore *that* for him?"

"No, I wore it for Kirsten."

"Kirsten?"

"My niece. You remember, at the party, she gave it to me?"

All he remembered was that kiss at the end of the night. "You can't wear that at work."

"It'll be gone before the end of the day."

It would be gone before he let her out of his office. He half rose from his chair with the psychotic idea of chewing the thing right off her neck. And he wouldn't stop there.

He might have done it, too, if Jeremiah Carp hadn't rapped on his open door. "I need Harriet."

Harriet who?

"She called in sick today," Madison supplied.

"The girl's never sick." Jeremiah sucked in his big belly, pursed his fleshy lips and puffed out his cheeks in a very good imitation of the fish he was named for.

"She is today."

Laurence had yet to find his voice when Jeremiah lumbered from the doorway, but at least he was in his chair, his demented urges in check. Momentarily. Unless he didn't get Madison out of his office. "That's all for now."

"But you never even told me what you wanted me to do."

His thoughts about her were plainly wrong. At least in the confines of the workplace. They were, in fact, unjustified at any time. Laurence couldn't help himself, but he could spare her any more embarrassing ogling today.

"Close the door on your way out."

She stood and backed away from him, her brow creased with worry lines. "Should I call a doctor, T. Larry?"

A psychiatrist. "No."

She pursed her pretty lips. "I'll check on you later then."

God forbid.

She closed the door.

Laurence beat his head on his desk three times.

MAYBE SHE SHOULD HAVE given T. Larry a bead to chew on. Candy medicine, Madison thought as she heard him start banging his head again. She looked at her calendar to check if it was a full moon. Nope, but marked clearly was the fact that only ten days remained until her birthday. Ten and a half, if she counted today. Then her phone chirped.

"You better get out here right away. There's someone—" Rhonda Templin in reception said, panic vibrating in her voice.

"Who is it?"

"It's someone for T. Larry."

Madison wasted no time in coming to Rhonda's rescue. The reception area being small and enclosed and the man being so large, Madison couldn't miss him. They should provide bigger chairs, or ones without arms. The poor man overflowed the tastefully pastel seat, sweat beading his upper lip and forehead.

Madison leaned over Rhonda's desk to whisper. "Turn up the air-conditioning."

Rhonda's eyes protruded in her thin face, as if she'd never seen a person of such large proportions. "Here's his card." She gulped air down her windpipe. "He's a lawyer."

The card trembled in her hand. Once relieved of its burden, the appendage shot beneath the desk.

"Don't tell him my name." Lawyers terrified Rhonda. Once a hairdresser, she'd been sued by a client when the woman's hair fell out after a perm. Rhonda swore the hair had been falling out in clumps before the perm, which was why the hapless woman wanted it done in the first place.

Rhonda lost, vowing never again to touch another person's hair. Not even her own. Which was obvious. Her dark roots had grown out down to her ear lobes, and from there her hair was a faded platinum blond in varying choppy lengths. On the up side, she was under thirty, favored black clothes and nail polish and could say she'd purposely chosen a punk-rock hairstyle.

Madison looked at the business card, then the man and back to the card again. What a wonderful name, such a delightful rhythm to it. Harold. Or Harry. "Mr. Dump, how can I help you?"

"It's pronounced Doomp," he said, "as in oom-pah-pah. The first name is Harold." With a hand on the armrest to the right, then the left, he rose with a rolling motion and an effort that sent droplets of perspiration hurtling into his too-tight collar.

Harry Dump's oversize briefcase pulled his arm down almost to the floor, giving him the appearance of a listing barge. Extending his other hand, he wagged Madison's arm until the bones in her neck jarred. The scent of shoe polish rose from his plump, greasy fingers.

Stepping back, she could now see the scars in his battered briefcase had been blacked with shoe polish. His bulk stretched the repaired seams of his blue suit jacket and a fresh pink carnation covered the lapel shiny with overuse. Laundry soap lingered beneath the odor of polish.

"You don't look like a T. Laurence Hobbs." Dimples bracketed his mouth.

His smile infected her. Madison laughed. "I'm his secretary. Madison O'Donnell."

The dimples turned into exclamation points, and his blue eyes glowed. "My dear, secretary is a term from the pre-female-emancipation days, and it's demeaning. Your job description should be Executive Assistant," he said with capital letters.

She took his game one step further to see his reaction. "But the term Secretary oozes sex appeal."

He sighed, his chest puffing up impossibly. With sleight of hand, another business card appeared in his palm. "Take this, my dear. Women don't have to use sex appeal to get ahead these days. Your boss is obviously living in the dark ages."

Madison got a very bad feeling about the reason for Harry Dump's visit. "Mr. Hobbs is very busy right now. Perhaps we can schedule an appointment." Say for next year.

"Oh, I think he'll want to see me."

"Can I tell him what this is about?" Madison was dying to know.

"Tell him I've been retained on behalf of Harriet Hartman."

Rhonda gasped, and Madison thanked God for the enclosed reception area.

If T. Larry hadn't already given himself a concussion, Mr. Dump would give him a coronary.

Especially after Rhonda broadcast the news to the whole firm.

"I'll be right back." She beat it out of there, hoping Harry Dump didn't take a seat again. Getting up had seemed such a painful process.

Hopefully T. Larry would refuse to see him, she thought as she knocked on his office door.

"I COULD TELL HIM you're indisposed."

Madison's worry disturbed him, but Laurence didn't push off bad situations, especially not ones which involved Harriet. Not after last Friday. "I'm not indisposed."

"Then I'll tell him you're busy."

"Madison—"

"It's a secretary's responsibility to fob off people her boss doesn't want to see." She twisted her finger in the candy necklace.

"You're a wonderful secretary. But fobbing off people isn't in your job description."

"But he said you should call me your Executive Assistant. He said the word secretary is demeaning." Her hand quivered.

His head ached. Pounding his forehead against the desk again didn't seem propitious. "Have I ever demeaned you?"

In his fantasies, he'd demeaned her all morning. Like sugarplum fairies dancing through a child's dream, the feel of her lips beneath his and the phantom taste of candy necklaces had irreverently flitted through his mind. Much to his chagrin.

Madison leaned on his desk, the scoop neckline falling away to reveal a deadly amount of cleavage. "There was that birthday when you smirked because I dropped a strawberry down my shirt."

He did his level best to keep his gaze on hers. Unfortunately, the emerald sparkle in her eyes entranced him. He kept himself on track. Barely.

"I didn't smirk." At the time, he'd been too busy thinking about how he'd help her clean up the whipped cream that had fallen along with the strawberry. "I told everyone to *stop* smirking."

Damn. He hadn't merely "noticed" Madison. He'd been having salacious, demeaning thoughts about her. This was not a new phenomenon. They'd paved the way for these uncontrollable lustful urges he now harbored towards her.

"Send him in, Madison." Things couldn't get much worse anyway. He was guilty of sexual harassment, even if he'd never acted on it prior to Saturday night.

Madison's eyes, with their lovely shade of green, widened with unease. "Remember his name is Doomp."

Laurence glanced at the card. "It looks like Dump."

"It's not pronounced that way. And don't call him Harry."

"You did."

"Not to his face."

"Get him." He waved her off with a negligent hand, but his gaze when she turned was anything but. Her hips swayed, the skirt swished, and Laurence almost groaned aloud.

Maybe he should fire her. For her own good. She desperately needed protection from him.

Then Harry Dump could file a suit on her behalf. The lawyer would definitely have a case.

"How many times on the morning in question did you visualize your Executive Assistant in the nude, Mr. Hobbs?"

"At least every eight seconds. And do you want to know the things I visualized during the other seven seconds?"

A collective gasp from the courtroom, his fantasies showing above his head like a cartoon bubble.

"Your Honor, this man is guilty."

To his discredit, he smelled her return before he saw her, flowers and strawberries with whipped cream.

Guilty, guilty, guilty.

Harry Dump followed, turning sideways to fit through the door. Creaking like an old shoe, he smelled like leather polish.

"Please make yourself comfortable on the sofa, Mr. Doomp."

Obviously Madison realized the man would never fit the chair opposite Laurence's desk.

Awestruck, Laurence didn't offer him coffee. So Madison did. Harry Dump refused.

"You can go now, Madison."

She raised a hopeful brow. "I could take dictation."

Which she couldn't, never having learned shorthand. She was, however, excellent at a computer, with good command of grammar and vocabulary. She could also charm his clients, make them laugh and put them at ease. In his line, that was her most important quality.

His current visitor, however, didn't need charming. Laurence pointed at the door.

Harry Dump avidly followed her exit, eyes on her shapely bottom, then her spiked shoes.

"Hot little number, isn't she?"

Laurence's stomach burned hearing the words on Harry Dump's lips. "Her name is Madison O'Donnell. That's the only way you'll refer to her in my presence, Dump."

"Doomp." Harry raised a surrendering hand surrounded by a frayed cuff. "I was testing. Hostile work environment, you know, fostered by the employer. Have to have verification of our claim." Harry smiled. A dimple appeared. "You passed, by the way. This time."

Laurence didn't believe the excuse for a moment. Harry had enjoyed ogling Madison's rear view. That fact only served to spike Laurence's guilt, and with it, his politeness quotient dropped. He *would* protect Madison, from tire slashers, ogling attorneys and most especially himself. Not another salacious thought would cross his mind.

The devil on his shoulder snickered.

Harry stroked a hand down his massive front. The faded tie had seen too many washings that failed to completely expunge a tenacious gravy stain.

"What is it you want, Dump?"

"Doomp." He set his briefcase on legs splayed to provide a table. Snap, snap, the latches unlocked, the abused lid rose, held open by Harry's ringless left hand as his head disappeared from the eyes down. Papers shuffled; he coughed, shuffled again.

Harriet had found an ambulance chaser, a lawyer thin in the pockets. The irony of his name wasn't wasted on Laurence, either. Harriet and Harold, an unbeatable combination. The band of his wristwatch had been stapled together, and his head sprouted an abominable comb-over shellacked in place with a bottle of dime-store hair gel.

Have some respect for yourself, Laurence wanted to say. Cut off that ridiculous hair and be proud of your bald head.

"Here it is." As if Harry Dump had so many cases and so many papers. Snap, snap, the top of his brief-case closed again, and a thick folder Laurence was sure could only be filled with blank pages flopped atop the lid. "As your assistant informed you, I'm here on behalf of Miss Harriet Hartman who has come forward with a complaint against—"

"So Harriet lied about being sick."

"Are you calling my client a liar?"

"I would never call Harriet a liar." Especially not to her lawyer. "I merely wanted to point out that while she was seeing you this morning, she claimed to be sick."

"First, I don't believe I said *when* I had discussions with my client, and secondly, your company accounts for 'personal' time, not sick time. 'Personal' time can be used for—" Harry spread his hands eloquently "—anything an employee deems...personal."

Damn, how had Madison talked him into that termi-nology?

It became clear Harriet had been harboring resent-ment far longer than last week's incident. Laurence realized he had done little to defuse it, though, in his defense, he'd had the terrible trio, Mike, Anthony and Bill, in his office more than once for a good dressing-down. Had he adequately documented those stern talks?

"Now, as I was saying, our suit is against the

employer, that being you, due to a failure on your part to effectively discipline the employees, those being specifically one Zachary Eric Zenker and one Madison O'Donnell, and thus allowing the hostile work environment to breed." He put emphasis on the word as if to indicate the sexual nature of the situation.

"Why Madison?" What on earth did Harriet have against her?

"In more than one instance, Ms. Hartman has told you that Ms. O'Donnell's attire is inappropriate and fosters a negative work environment."

Harriet complained bitterly about the length of Madison's skirts and the tightness of her sweaters. She complained at the Christmas party and the company picnic. She'd cornered him in his office. Somehow, Harriet had developed a profound jealousy over the fact that Madison's breasts and legs looked better than hers.

Laurence had the good sense not to voice that thought aloud. He'd instead extolled Harriet's accounting virtues, each and every one of which he'd appreciated wholeheartedly.

She had becoming attributes, such as her intelligence, her ability to find every loophole the tax laws allowed, her exemplary number of billable hours. As opposed to a woman like Madison, who, no matter how nice her legs might be—he hadn't said that part aloud— was strictly overhead. Harriet had not appreciated the comparison despite his best efforts. Laurence, in a word, had failed. He hated failure.

Yet he had one trump card Harry obviously knew nothing about. "Harriet has, on occasion, worn skirts of equal brevity as compared to Miss O'Donnell's. I can provide several witnesses to that fact, which, I'm afraid, nullifies her complaint."

Harry smiled. "My dear Mr. Hobbs, it is not the garb itself, but the unequal treatment based upon the garb which has created the hostile environment. Ms. Hartman is a very sensitive young woman." The lawyer was a master of understatement. "My client's physical assets have been reduced to office targets. Unable to cite names due to the fact that most comments are made behind her back, Ms. Hartman has nevertheless been subjected to profoundly cruel harassment on the part of her coworkers."

Bill, Anthony and Mike had belittled Harriet one too many times, damn them. He couldn't blame Harriet for her anger. God. He'd gotten his MBA so he could become a babysitter. Didn't they teach the ills of harassment in grammar school? He suddenly thought of the bully of his class tearing into a poor overweight kid. Children could be a vicious lot. The terrible trio obviously hadn't learned anything in the ensuing twenty years since they'd left their elementary days behind.

Harry pulled a handkerchief from his jacket pocket, held it poised in one hand. "I can only begin to imagine the damage to Ms. Hartman's psyche."

He stopped, blew his nose. His eyes sparkled with—God forbid—moisture. Tears. Emotion. Pain. Empathy?

The man seemed to believe everything he was saying on Harriet's behalf. He hadn't taken the case for the money. Well, he probably had, but he also believed in Harriet's pain. He held himself aloft as a champion of the underdog. Or the overendowed.

Laurence suddenly liked him, and his respect jumped a notch.

That didn't mean the case had any real validity. Harriet had chosen to wear the "garb" despite knowing the reaction she might garner. It certainly wasn't Madison's fault or Madison's doing.

"And Zach? What is her complaint against him?" The latest dress comment, of course. Laurence wanted to hear Harriet's version expounded upon in Harry's words.

"Ms. Hartman states that due to your lack of understanding concerning the hostile work environment, she was unable to get reparation through you after she was accosted by Mr. Zenker."

"Accosted?" he parroted, not quite sure how Harriet could skew complimenting into accosting.

"The night of last October fourteenth, while working excessively late, Mr. Zenker coerced Ms. Hartman into having sex on the table in Conference Room B." Pause, smile. "Which, I believe, is two doors down from *your* office."

ZZ Top? On top of Harriet the Harridan? In *his* conference room?

Absurdly, his next thought was of Madison perched on the conference table, index finger beckoning him closer as *he* locked the door.

What was happening to his heretofore normal, hardworking flock? What was happening to him?

God Almighty. Were salacious fantasies and scandalous behavior contagious?

CHAPTER SEVEN

SOMETHING WAS VERY WRONG, Madison thought. T. Larry didn't smile as he escorted Harry Dump out of the suite. He didn't smile when he came back, either. Passing his own open office, he stopped two doors down at Conference Room B. There wasn't an accompanying Conference Room A. Jeremiah Carp had converted it into his own office two years ago.

Madison, following close on T. Larry's heels, almost rear-ended his back when he stopped just inside the door.

All talk ceased in the surrounding cubicles, the incessant click of computer keys hushed. Pens and mechanical pencils snapped down onto desks. A phone rang, followed by a slam of the receiver to shut it up.

"What is it?" she whispered.

T. Larry stared at the twelve-man oak table, then shook it. Solid as a rock, it didn't move. It didn't even shudder. He rubbed his forehead, then his hand slid down to cover his eyes.

"Are you all right?" He'd given himself a concussion from all that head banging, she was sure.

With a deep breath and a long exhale, he turned. His eyes, almost blue like a sunset sky, moved from her lips to her breasts to her shoes. If it was anyone else, she'd have said sexual thoughts paraded through his mind.

This was T. Larry. Though he'd kissed her thoroughly, T. Larry just wouldn't have sexual thoughts about her. He couldn't. He was her boss.

What about how he'd *felt* against her? The *physical* evidence?

Madison lobbed that thought aside and had the good sense to move out of the way as T. Larry headed back out the door and down to his own office. She made it in before he slammed the door in her face.

"What did Mr. Dump want?"

One hand stroking his chin, T. Larry ignored her question. "How long have you worked for me?"

Maybe he was having a midlife crisis. He was a little young, but… "Seven years."

"How often have you worked late in all those seven years?"

"Umm…there was that time…but no, I still got out by five." She chewed her lip. "Oh, I know…but no, I had to catch the train so I couldn't stay."

Another of his deep belly breaths, a long exhale, then his glance flashed down her body. "You need to do more overtime."

"Harriet's suing you over my not doing equal overtime?"

"No." That's all he said. He didn't deny that there *was* a suit, but he offered no explanation.

Poor T. Larry. She stepped forward and, without thought, put a hand to his forehead. Her palm cool, his skin hot. Heat radiated off his body. "Are you sick or something, T. Larry?"

"Or something." He looked at her with that steely gaze. She'd never quite noticed how expressive his eye color was—maybe it was the glasses. He regarded her with a definitely stormy gaze. She dropped her hand and half stepped back.

His eyes shot to something way over her head. "I'm going to work out."

"But it's—" she glanced at her watch "—two o'clock. You never work out in the afternoon."

Something was terribly wrong. She had no idea how to help.

He countered her half step with a full one of his own. He felt tall. She'd never quite noticed that, either, how tall he was, how imposing, how broad.

"Someone made me miss my morning workout."

A queer sensation filled the bottom of her tummy, and warmth streaked to her fingers and toes. She backed up, then backed up again. "You've still never made up for it in the afternoon."

He shook his head slowly. "Ah, Madison. I have a lot to make up for. And starting this afternoon would be just fine."

He advanced. Her back hit the door. Heat was everywhere, her cheeks, her ears and parts unmentionable in front of T. Larry, even in thought.

"Okay. I'll tell anyone who asks that you're working out."

He reached out, fingers flexing, closing on the doorknob just to the right of her hip. Blue flecked his gray eyes like the hottest part of a flame. He smelled like man, a hint of cologne, but something more, something that turned her knees to rubber.

She sucked in a breath.

Then he backed off, just like that, heading toward his workout bag down by the side of his leather sofa. She couldn't be sure he'd been that close at all. Except for his oddly enticing scent still lingering in her head.

"It's two. Find Zach and tell him to meet me in the steam room at three."

"You want to see him in the steam room?"

His lips flattened. "Most important business is conducted in the steam room," he said as if she didn't get it. "Then set up an appointment with Jeremiah and Ryman at four-thirty. Tell them I'll brief them, and that there's no problem I can't handle. After that, call a company meeting for eleven tomorrow in Conference Room B. Mandatory. Even if they have to drive in from a client. I have a memo to distribute. New workplace rules. I'll write the text tonight. You can type it up in the morning."

Now this was the T. Larry she knew, with the added bonus that she'd finally gotten him to break out of a routine by doing his workout in the afternoon. Which was kind of a contrary thought, but... Punching a fist in the air, she cheered him on. "Go T. Rex."

Then she opened the door for him.

"Tomorrow we'll talk about your overtime. Plan on staying late some evenings. Very late."

Hmm, he still needed her help with this whole Harriet thing. She just had to figure out a way to fix it. It didn't, however, seem that overtime was the answer.

OVERTIME. YES. On that big table in Conference Room B. Laurence would start with her bared throat above that lacy black vest. She'd forget all about Dick with his perfect hair.

Steam hot enough to sear his lungs pumped into the small room. Sweat covered the top of his head and dripped down his face. His muscles ached with the ag-

gressiveness of his workout. With the faint scent of eucalyptus in his nostrils, Laurence should have felt
relaxed and pleasantly exhausted. Close to physical
nirvana. Instead, the small white towel failed to hide the
erection he hadn't managed to get rid of.

He should have locked himself in his office with her
when the urge gripped him.

Christ. He was losing control of himself. He'd long
since lost control of his staff. He was being sued. He'd
probably be excommunicated from the company when
Jeremiah and Ryman found out. Harry Dump had the
temerity to ask him if he needed any legal work done.
He might even be forced to fire Zach, who had the
makings of a damn fine accountant. And, he'd succumbed to Secretary Lust, the dread disease he'd
hitherto managed to avoid. Right now, Laurence should
have been worrying about the deterioration of his Financial Plan, which then put his Family Plan in
jeopardy. The specter of failure loomed on the horizon.
He should plan damage control. He should apologize
to Madison for his disrespectful thoughts.

Instead he imagined her on the sturdy table in Conference Room B.

That's what worried him the most. He wasn't a sex-
in-the-office man. Especially not when the ceiling-high
twenty-second-floor windows faced other twenty-
second-floor windows. And never with an employee. He
maintained a professional demeanor. He liked sex simple
and quick, no hot sweaty bodies, no muss, no fuss. In and
out, so to speak, fresh sheets, a comfortable mattress.

He had the terrible notion making love to Madison
would be very messy. The idea raised the tented towel
another notch.

The door opened with a rush of escaping steam just as Laurence was enjoying the memory of her strawberry taste.

Zachary Zenker, a towel held snug around his narrow hips, stood in the open doorway.

"Don't let all the steam out." At least the vapor might hide the embarrassing fact that Laurence was stiff as a post. Not that Zach was likely to look. The Steam Room Code imitated the Men's Room Code. Gaze on the wall or eye level at all times except when zipping, and then you only looked at your own zipper.

The boy was thin, his muscles unworked and his flesh overly white, not a hint of tan, as if he spent too many hours over a ledger. Actually not a boy, Zach was over thirty, but his very paleness, his shyness, made him seem a boy to Laurence. Which made it harder to understand why he'd turned to Harriet, of all people. What had possessed the boy?

Zach sat on the bench three feet from Laurence.

Laurence closed his eyes again. "I suppose you think my invitation is a bit unusual." More than an invitation, it had been an edict.

"Yes, sir."

He used to be Laurence, or T. Larry when Zach sometimes forgot. Now he was a sir. Someone had warned the boy. "Harriet's hired a lawyer. She's suing us for sexual harassment."

"I apologized for the dress comment, like you told me, sir."

"It isn't the dress comment, Zach. It's what happened when you were working on the AMI account back in October." Laurence had pulled both their files to check the *reported* goings-on for the night in question.

He opened one eye to see what little color Zach did own drain from his face. "The AMI account?" The boy's voice cracked.

Laurence settled himself again, clasping his hands over his stomach. The steam room had been a perfect idea. The eucalyptus vapors were doing the trick, filling him with an agreeable lassitude. Even on the lower half of his body.

"Don't stall, Zach. You know what we're talking about."

Zach cleared his throat, but words failed him.

"You had sex with Harriet in the office." Laurence's mouth tightened as he fought an unbidden image of Madison.

"Sir, I didn't—"

"Harriet says you did." He paused for dramatic effect. "I believe her."

Something changed in the boy's voice. An infinitesimal amount of backbone crept in. "I wasn't going to deny it, sir. I was going to say that I didn't mean for it to happen. At least, not where it did."

"Did you do the deed during work hours?"

"It was after everyone left. It just sort of happened."

"Did you bill the client for the time?"

Zach hesitated.

"Don't make me check the billing hours to verify."

"No. We finished the return at ten. It was after that."

"Thank God you didn't do it at a client's." Laurence leaned forward and cracked one eye open again. "Have you done it again?" He held his hand up when Zach wanted to jump. "I mean have you done it at the office or during work hours? The rest is your business."

"No, sir, we haven't."

"Was it consensual?"

"Yes, sir, I believed it was. I still do."

"She said you coerced her."

"Harriet's angry."

Laurence raised a brow.

"I...we...we haven't discussed it again, and..."

Laurence filled in the rest. "You ignored her."

Zach hung his head, nodding slightly.

That explained it. Harriet's anger was understandable. A man couldn't play with a coworker's feelings for one night, then walk away. Harriet was sensitive. Women were sensitive. Which was why Laurence needed to be careful with Madison's feelings in carrying out his own plans to save her from Dick.

Still, one thing wasn't clear. "Why is Harriet suing eight months later?"

"I don't know."

Laurence gave Zach the eye again.

"I really don't know what happened to make her so upset right now. I complimented her dress, and she went postal."

The steam valve shut off. Laurence reached down to turn it back on. Deep breath again. Ah, calming eucalyptus.

"She's suing, Zach, claiming that you coerced her and that I didn't provide an adequate environment to stop it or a shoulder for her to cry on. What are we going to do about it?"

"I don't know, sir."

"That's one too many I-don't-knows."

"I tried to talk to her, but she just got more angry."

"Why is she so angry?" Laurence had already drawn

his obvious conclusion, but he wanted to hear it from Zach. "And 'I don't know' isn't going to cut it."

Zach took so long answering that another thought surfaced in Laurence's Madison-drugged mind. Harriet was angry, Harriet was suing, Madison's tires had been slashed. His blood chilled. He admired Harriet for a variety of reasons. Though he couldn't go so far as to say he liked her, he'd never considered her capable of something so vicious. He couldn't believe it of her now. Shades of Madison, with her blinders on. Yet even Madison had said she didn't want to cause trouble for Harriet, so obviously the ugly possibility had crossed her mind. If there was the slightest chance she was a physical threat to Madison, he'd watch Harriet as he watched the bottom line, focused, no-nonsense. For now, he had to solve the Harriet-Zach problem.

So, Laurence pushed. "I'm waiting, Zach."

"I think she expected something more."

Laurence slapped his hand to his forehead. "My God. Do you really think so?"

The corner of Zach's mouth lifted. "Yes, sir, I do."

"You don't have relations once with a coworker, then run and hide, Zach."

"No, sir, I didn't want it to be just once."

Laurence opened his mouth to speak.

"Don't knock her." Aggression entered Zach's tone before he added another *Sir.* "That's how all this trouble started."

"I wouldn't dream of disparaging her."

"She's a very generous and caring person," Zach went on.

Laurence wondered if the boy had moved from healthy respect and desire into delusion, but quashed the uncharitable thought. "Then where did everything go wrong?"

"I didn't want to be part of the office gossip mill, but I don't think Harriet wanted to keep it a secret."

They hadn't actually talked about it, Laurence surmised. Another part of the problem. "You were embarrassed?"

Zach shook his head vehemently. "No, no, that wasn't it."

Laurence sighed. "Then what kept you silent?"

"All right. That was part of it. The guys would have made my life miserable. You know how they are."

Laurence knew. Did "the guys" look at Madison's legs, eye her breasts and drool over her pretty little derriere when Laurence wasn't watching them? He'd damn well put a stop to it.

Perhaps a dress code change was needed. Harriet had specifically cited Madison's attire, which translated to short skirts and tight sweaters. A change of dress code would bring office harmony.

Yet a policy change would require Madison to purchase an entire wardrobe. That would constitute a hardship. He couldn't, in good conscience, tell Madison what she could or couldn't wear. Even if his career went down in flames.

Which it most certainly would now that he'd contracted Secretary Lust.

And that was the gist of his quandary. Secretary Lust. His own predilection was the basis for not instituting an office apparel policy. He wanted Madison in short skirts and tight sweaters, but his desire to see her in them was demeaning to her as well as Harriet. He admitted to himself that he was the worst of a bad lot.

Madison's attire in the workplace had to change. He'd have to add "garb" to the memo he planned to write tonight concerning office conduct.

That difficult decision made, Laurence turned back to Zach's problem with Harriet. "Do you want a relationship with her?"

"I've been thinking about that for eight months, and I'm still not sure." Zach chewed on the inside of his lip. "She's a lot of work."

"But do you care about her?"

"I guess I do. I can't seem to get her out of my mind."

"If you feel that way about her, you'll just have to be a man, Zach, and take the heat from the guys."

Zach nodded. "But I've screwed up things so badly now, I don't think there's any hope."

Laurence smiled the smile of experience. "Let me tell you what you're going to do to fix this mess."

"WHEN WAS THE LAST TIME you tried on my wedding dress?"

Madison rolled her eyes, glad her mother, being on the other end of the phone, couldn't see.

"When I get married, Ma—" which would be never, though she avoided saying anything like that flat out to her mother who frowned on Madison's self-diagnosis of her condition "—I want to pick out my own wedding dress." Sentimentality was great, but Madison's mother got married in the late sixties, and the dress she'd worn looked as if it would go with one of Jackie Kennedy's pillbox hats.

T. Larry had closeted himself with Jeremiah and Alta. He had to get out of there before five. He just had to. Because she had to know how things went with

Zach. She'd chewed the lipstick from her lips and bitten her nails to the quick, or would have, if her manicure hadn't cost so much.

"And don't think I didn't recognize that subtle reference to marriage, Ma."

"It wasn't subtle at all. But that nice Laurence—"

"His name is T. Larry."

"Then why did he introduce himself as Laurence?"

"It doesn't matter, because I'm not marrying him."

"Do you know how much he makes a year?"

"I'm his secretary, not his accountant. And money isn't important."

"Then it's true love."

Madison thought about banging her head against her desk, just like T. Larry, but tried to think of her end of the conversation. Gauging what Bill, Anthony and Mike thought about it from their vantage point on the other side of her cubicle wall seemed quite important. Of course, then she couldn't remember exactly what she'd said. "I told you yesterday after church—"

"Does he attend church regularly?"

"I have no idea."

The conference room door stayed tight as a vacuum-packed seal. What was going on in there?

"James thinks he's marvelous."

"James offered him condoms."

"Madison."

"He did, Ma. You've got a big problem brewing in that household of his. I think it's called birth control."

Another shocked exclamation, then, "In my day people didn't dream of talking about that kind of thing."

Her mother's day had been smack-dab in the middle of the sexual revolution, though it somehow managed to roll over Ma and leave her untouched. "Are we referring to sex or birth control?"

"I know what you're doing."

"What?"

"You're trying to deflect the subject. Now about marriage and that nice Laurence—"

"I'm not marrying T. Larry." Taking T. Larry to her nephew's birthday party might not have been one of her brighter impulsive decisions. Had she said that too loudly? The guys were being awfully quiet on the other side of the wall.

"What does Laurence have to say about that?"

"He doesn't want to marry me, either." It became difficult to lower the decibel of her voice when the level of her ire was rising. Then she sucked in a breath. Why was she angry? She never got angry. It must be her upset over Harriet and the suit. "Ma, can we talk about this later?"

"But we need to start planning..."

"Ma."

"All right. I just called to tell you your brother would be by tomorrow to fix the disposal. So leave a key under the mat."

"I always leave a key under the mat." Because one of her brothers was always coming over to fix something for her, the big sweeties.

"And for goodness sake, clean up the kitchen a little. You know he hates to work in a mess."

She didn't have time to clean up. She had her picnic with Richard. "Sean already told me."

"I don't know where you get your messiness from."

She got it from having too many better things to do. "Bye, Ma. I love you."

"One more thing, Madison dear. I'm Episcopalian,

and I've always believed in birth control. Except for that brief stint where your father corrupted me into being a Catholic." A pause, her lips would be pursed. "So take your brother's condoms just to be sure."

Oh. My. God. Her mother had succeeded in shocking her.

Madison put the phone down, then shrieked, suddenly seeing ZZ Top standing right in front of her desk.

"How did you get there?" And how long had he been listening? What embarrassing things had she said? Not that it mattered. Except to T. Larry, of course. T. Larry hated to be embarrassed.

ZZ didn't answer her question. "Mr. Hobbs told me to tell you not to leave until he's done with his meeting."

"Mr. Hobbs?"

"T. Larry."

"I know who he is. I just can't figure out why you're calling him Mister." She cocked her head. "Are you all right, ZZ?"

Something flickered in his somber eyes. "Do you believe in ghosts, Madison?"

She let her eyes wander left to right, then back to him. "Uh…yes."

"Can you see them?"

She quirked her mouth to the side. "Uh…no."

"Well, I think you're gonna start seeing them real soon." He blinked. "Do you have any Reese's cups?"

"Uh…yes." Whatever was going on in that man's head? She pulled a bag from her drawer and held it out to him.

Taking one, he undid the wrapper, sucked the chocolate thoughtfully, rolled the foil into a ball and handed it to Madison. Then he walked away.

FIVE MINUTES TO FIVE. If he didn't cut off Jeremiah's fourth refrain on the theme of we-won't-pay-a-dime-and-don't-involve-our-lawyers-until-absolutely-necessary, Madison would be gone despite the message he'd sent through Zach.

He wouldn't be able to tell her about his decision on the new dress code. On second thought, if he didn't tell her until tomorrow, that would be one more day of short skirts.

Unfortunately, some things just couldn't be put off. The firm's reputation—not to mention his own—was at stake. "The problem's taken care of, gentlemen. By this time tomorrow, Harriet will have withdrawn her suit."

Zach would be punching Bill, Anthony and Mike's collective lights out for numerous ribald remarks made at Harriet's expense. It would be an object lesson in becoming men for them all, Zach included.

The boy had failed with Harriet the first time because he hadn't developed a plan. Laurence had now supplied him with a foolproof one.

Enough patting himself on the back. He had to see Madison before she left. Despite the pleasant thought of one more day regarding her tight sweaters, he had a company responsibility to carry out. He rose and turned, stopped by Ryman Alta's hand on his shoulder.

Ryman's face resembled a wizened old apple. Many a client, auditor, employee or partner had confused his slow, quiet, thoughtful manner for Alzheimer's. That's when Ryman went for the bare throat. The man was a pit bull, and Laurence felt the bite of his bony fingers.

"Get rid of the two of them as expeditiously and quickly as possible. I don't like troublemakers."

"It will be difficult and extremely unwise to terminate Harriet. It will only give grounds to her suit."

"Then make sure she doesn't have a leg to stand on. Make sure neither of them do."

He didn't like what lay sunk in Ryman's dark eyes. "How do you propose I do that?"

"If you'd covered your watch a little more closely the first time…" Ryman let Laurence draw his own conclusion. "Perhaps you'll be more vigilant a second time."

"A second time? Are you saying I should encourage them to have sex in the office so I can catch them at it, then fire them?"

"I'm suggesting you get rid of them with the least backlash against the partnership. If you value your voting status in this partnership, that is."

"I don't like to be threatened, Ryman."

"And I don't like a mess."

Neither did Laurence, and Ryman was only adding to it.

"And while you're at it, get rid of that sexpot secretary of yours, too. We don't want any more suits due to her attire."

Now that made his blood boil. "Madison isn't a sexpot." And that fantasy about the conference table was really only a fantasy. He'd *never* act on it. "I'm not firing her."

"Then at least get her to stop wearing those clothes."

As much as he would miss those skirts, Laurence had already made that decision. "I'm handling all the issues, Ryman."

"See that you do."

The "or else" was in there. But Carp and Alta

wouldn't vote him out of the partnership. They needed him. He managed the office, the audits, the staff, and took care of a plethora of small details they couldn't be bothered with. Laurence washed his hands of the threat as Ryman shuffled down the hall to his office.

Then Ryman turned back. "Laurence."

Damn, he didn't have time for this. Almost five o'clock, he didn't want to miss Madison. "Ryman?"

"Have you looked at Stephen's file?"

Tortelli. Laurence kept his voice low for the sake of the hallway conversation. "I looked at it, and I put it aside."

"What did you think?"

"It's all very neat and squeaky clean." Too clean, every line item complete with explanation. Clients just weren't that well documented. It wasn't in their nature. Unless, at one point, they'd come under close governmental agency scrutiny. With the recent rash of accounting scandals, which were due not only to negligence and fraud, but, in his opinion, an overcomplicated rules base, the firm couldn't afford even the slightest hint of impropriety. He couldn't put his finger on it, but something about Tortelli screamed misconduct.

"He appears to have a perfectly adequate accountant, Ryman. Why would he want to change?"

"It's our job to get him to change. It's called courting. That's how we grow the business, Laurence, by bringing in new clients with large holdings who need *your* amazing expertise."

Was that Ryman sucking up to him, flattering him? Laurence generally disregarded the idea of gut instinct, but his gut had been prodding him ever since Tortelli had first appeared on the scene. It went into overdrive with Ryman's flattery. "I'm not prepared to take him on without further extensive investigation."

"Why?"

Laurence, not one to use his size to intimidate, took a step closer to Ryman's shrunken form. "I don't trust him."

Ryman narrowed his gaze. "He's legitimate, Laurence."

"You're seeing billable hours, Ryman, nothing more."

They didn't need questionable clients. They weren't a large firm, but they were by no means straddling the edge, either. Ryman's net earnings alone were in the mid-six-figure range last year. As a partnership, they were comfortable, secure and very clean. Laurence didn't intend to jeopardize their reputation. Yet the older Ryman got, the less he cared about reputation and the more about money. Carp just went along.

Somehow reading the determination in Laurence's stance, Ryman put a fatherly hand on his arm. "Take another look. I'll answer any questions you have, reassure you."

Laurence was about to tell him to stuff his Tortelli file and remove his goddamn hand, but they were still in the hallway, separated from staff by mere cubicle walling. It wouldn't do for the partners to be heard arguing. "I'm late for an appointment."

"We'll talk at the end of the week then."

He gave neither a yes or no answer, simply turned his back to Ryman and set off for Madison's desk.

One minute to five. Madison's desk drawers slid open and closed. Her papers rustled. Her computer beeped. He rounded the end of her cubicle to find her purse already out on the desk.

Her fingers stilled on the mouse. "How did it go? With Zach? With the partners?"

"Fine." Residual anger with Ryman made the word sharper than he intended.

Madison, however, didn't notice. "Just fine? Give me details. I'll find them out later anyway when you ask me to type up your meeting notes."

"There will be no meeting notes." His teeth clamped down on the sentence.

"All right, fine. You don't want to tell me…" She spread her hands, raised a pretty brow and twitched her lips.

That's when Laurence noted her lips and forgot all about Harriet, Zach, Ryman, dress codes and Tortelli. "Where's your lipstick?"

"I just put a little lip gloss on instead."

Panic seized his heart, sending its beat into triple time. "But you always wear lipstick. It's unwomanly not to, you said."

"It's okay as long as you've got lip gloss. Now, since you're refusing to tell me anything about your mysterious afternoon meetings, I've got to go or I'll be late."

Screw Zach. Screw the partners. "You're only half-dressed without lipstick." She'd had it on all day. Until now. Because she'd wiped it off.

"You had something you wanted to say to me, T. Larry?"

He couldn't quite remember and didn't care. Only one thing careened through his boggled mind. Madison without lipstick.

"Well, then, if the cat's got your tongue, I really do have to go." She brightened. "We can talk tomorrow morning. First thing." She backed away from him, turned and skedaddled through the front door, her gauzy skirt swishing about her calves and highlighting her strikingly petite ankles.

Damn. The dress code. *That's* what he'd wanted to tell her.

Today's skirt had an appropriate length, but her vest revealed too much delicious skin. At least she'd taken off the damn candy necklace. Or eaten it. The idea of Dick getting a taste of her candy was unthinkable. As it was, Laurence decided he'd have to kill someone because, Christ Almighty, Madison had wiped off her lipstick because she was planning on kissing Dick the Prick.

The image burned low in Laurence's belly long after Madison left. It ate a hole through his stomach lining as the traffic piled up in front of him. He leaned on the horn with a vengeance only to realize *he* was the one who'd done the cutting off.

Really, what was he worried about? He could compete with a man five years younger even if the wimp did have a full head of hair and twenty-twenty vision. He sure as hell knew he kissed better than a puppy like that.

Trapped in another staggering image, this one of Madison on a soft blanket, her hair all around her, and that bastard leaning over her, Laurence slammed on his brakes when the bumper in front suddenly loomed too close.

But it wasn't the kiss. It was the date Laurence wasn't sure he could compete with. How was he supposed to do a one-up on a picnic in Golden Gate Park? It was romantic, it was impetuous, and while Laurence was a whiz with numbers and tax codes, he didn't have a romantic bone in his body. He didn't even know what women really wanted on the romantic level.

What would it mean if she wore lipstick for him tomorrow night? He wouldn't worry about it now. He'd worry about his driving instead, sliding into the slow lane. There were road sharks out tonight.

To the task at hand. Think romantic. Five-star restaurant? Too ordinary. A show at one of San Francisco's premiere theaters? Was *Beauty and the Beast* still playing? He didn't keep up on these things, the last time he looked having been…five years ago? Besides, the romantic *Beauty and the Beast* wouldn't work. She'd think he was auditioning for the role of the Beast. He'd already lost the hair on the top of his head, and he wasn't about to turn into a prince at the end of the night.

Then Laurence saw it on the left-hand side of the freeway, rising like a phoenix in the suburban landscape. It was perfect, inspirational. It would show her he wasn't a stick-in-the-mud.

He'd take her miniature golfing.

CHAPTER EIGHT

POOR T. LARRY. Things were bad.

"Have a chicken wing?" Richard offered.

And poor Richard. All Madison had done since she'd met him at the arboretum entrance was moan about T. Larry. Richard had provided such a beautiful meal, too. He'd smoothed a soft blanket over the grass in a spot resplendent with the last of the afternoon sun. They'd watched Frisbee throwers, joggers and two old women scattering birdseed to the pigeons, whose iridescent feathers caught the sun's rays. He'd served her on bone china with real silver and poured champagne into crystal glasses. They'd dined on roasted chicken. Then he'd tantalized her taste buds with white chocolate mousse. She'd do just about anything for white chocolate mousse. This was a fairy tale and Richard was Prince Charming.

Except that Madison couldn't stop thinking about T. Larry. About his problem.

"I don't know what to do to help him."

"Help who?"

"T. Larry. I should have a talk with Harriet, see if I can fix this whole thing." A perfect idea. Woman to woman. Except that she wasn't quite clear on what "this whole thing" was, and she hadn't been victorious helping Harriet in the past. No matter. For T. Larry's sake, she had to give it another try.

"Is there something I should know about your boss?" Richard pushed a lock of gorgeous thick hair from his forehead.

"Like what?"

"Are you in love with him?"

She choked on her mousse and forgot Harriet. "T. Larry?"

Richard's lips thinned.

The sun dipped below the trees. She pulled her sweater over her shoulders. "It's hard to explain about T. Larry—"

"Then you *are* in love with him."

"T. Larry's a lost soul who needs my help." She'd never said it that way, but as the words came out, she knew it was true. "I'm like his fairy godmother, shocking him out of his safe, secure little plans."

Richard's eyes darkened. "I thought you were his secretary."

"That's such a label, Richard. I'm more than that."

The lines of his face softened. "You're very special."

Her heart fluttered. "And so is T. Larry. Which is why I have to help him. He thinks he's old—"

The softness vanished. "He's bald."

"That doesn't mean he's old. But if I don't help him, he's just going to slip right into this awful mold he's picked out for himself. I can't let that happen to him."

"But he's just your boss."

She cocked her head, closing her eyes to savor the scent of freshly mowed grass. "Sometimes people forget life is about touching people along the way."

Richard turned her hand over in his and squeezed. "That's so profound."

She laughed. "T. Larry would puke if he heard me say that." Her own mother would puke. But Richard brought the profundity out in her with his sympathy, his empathy and his romantic dinner.

"More champagne?" He held up the bottle.

Another glass and the bubbles would be coming out her ears. "No, thank you, I have to drive."

"I can drive you."

"But I've got my car."

"I know. But your car was vandalized. It's such a dangerous place out there. I worry about you."

Oh, how sweet he was. "I'm just fine. I've got three big brothers to look after me. Not to mention T. Larry."

The twinkle in his eye winked out. She had been talking too much about T. Larry. "Enough about my car and my boss and stuff."

Richard hadn't let go of her hand. Oh, he was so wonderfully earnest.

He leaned forward. "Did you like the dinner?"

"I'm dazzled."

"I wanted to dazzle you."

She strained closer. "I've never had a more romantic picnic."

"Madison, may I kiss you?"

Such a gentleman. But she had the feeling their dialogue sounded like something out of a badly written Victorian novel. So what. "Yes, Richard, I'd love for you to kiss me."

His mouth descended. Soft lips, white chocolate mousse and champagne sizzle. But no bells. Her hands pushed awkwardly against the blanket for balance. She couldn't touch him. He didn't open his mouth. But that could have been out of respect for her, for their first kiss.

He pulled back. "Oh, Madison."

"Oh, Richard." *Very* bad dialogue. Maybe she'd wanted the fantasy to come true so badly, she was rushing things.

But Richard's kiss paled in comparison to T. Larry's.

Maybe she wasn't rushing things enough.

Madison rose to her knees, threw her arms around Richard's neck and attacked, parting her lips. He groaned. She gave him her tongue. Grabbing her around the waist, he crushed her to him. His body warmed her thighs and breasts, his mouth turned hot, and his hair fell like silk through her fingers.

A small child giggled nearby. Madison stopped to catch her breath and open her eyes. The young mother tugged on her little girl's hand. Madison pulled away from Richard, then leaned to the side, supporting herself with her hand.

"Madison."

"Richard." She'd mussed his hair. His lips were wet. A glaze clouded his eyes. But she still hadn't heard bells. "I'm sorry, that was forward." She spread a hand, cocked her head. "But I'm always forward."

"Don't apologize. You're charming."

And disappointed. Like champagne gone flat. Where were the bells? She looked at her watch. "It's late. I have to go."

She helped Richard pack up the food, then ran to the trash can to throw out the garbage. Maybe it was the unexpectedness of T. Larry's kiss that had made the difference. She'd prepared too much for Richard, built him up in her mind. How could reality compare?

Whereas with T. Larry, just the surprise had made it exciting. That's all it was. She needed more time with Richard. The bells would come.

Richard closed the lid on the wicker basket he'd brought, his rich brown hair falling across his forehead. Goodness, he was handsome. The bells deserved another chance. She plopped down on the blanket beside him.

"Can I see you tomorrow night, Madison?"

Well, *he* must have liked the kiss. "I'll be with T. Larry tomorrow. How about Wednesday?" Her social calendar had never been so full.

"He's making you work tomorrow night?" He raised his eyebrows, and his smile faded.

Maybe she shouldn't have blurted it out like that. She couldn't lie now that she had. Now just wasn't the right time for one of those little white lies. "It's not really work. It's more like an outing."

"A work outing? With everyone from the office?"

Goodness, this was getting difficult. "Not exactly."

"What do you mean *not exactly?*"

His voice had grown sharp. She tried to put herself in his shoes and decided to tell the absolute truth. "I made a deal with him so he wouldn't follow us to the park tonight."

Richard scowled until his eyebrows became one long line. "Maybe you ought to explain this deal."

She pulled her purse closer to her leg for comfort. "He gave me tonight with you in exchange for tomorrow night with him."

"I thought you weren't dating him."

"I'm not. It's an outing."

"Where are you going with him?"

"I don't know. It's a surprise." She barely managed to keep excitement out of her voice.

"That sounds like a date."

"But it's T. Larry. He's just flexing his muscles. He's like one of my brothers. Overprotective and—"

"I don't like it."

She wasn't sure she liked his tone. "Are you jealous?"

He dropped his gaze, plucking at the filmy folds of her skirt where they'd swirled around her legs. "I guess I am. I'm not usually like this." His eyes were puppy-dog soft when he looked at her again. "I don't think I know how to compete with the guy."

Goodness. Her legs felt all weak, and her heart melted. This was so romantic. "I can't explain about T. Larry. He's just…" She looked off into the leaves sparkling in the sun's final rays. "He's just been there forever. Like a big brother." Except for the kiss part. "But you don't have to worry about competing." She looked Richard square in the eye then. "I'm not like that. I don't play guys against each other. That's not me."

He took her hand. "I'm sorry. I didn't mean it like that."

"Good. Then it's settled. You have nothing to worry about. Wednesday I'm all yours." She fluttered her eyelashes. "And thank you for the best picnic I've ever had."

He beamed.

She decided against another kiss. She'd save it for the next date. Something to look forward to. Something to make the bells ring.

Something that would outshine T. Larry's kiss.

THE PHONE RANG a third time in the last half hour. Not another hang up, Madison hoped. It was late, she was tired, and at this rate, she'd sleep through her alarm and be late for work. T. Larry hated tardiness. She gotten the first call when T. Larry was there on Saturday. Then another last night. And all the caller did was breathe. At least he could have uttered a few obscene remarks to make her feel special.

She picked up before the machine did. "Are you going to say something this time?"

"I'll say whatever you want me to say."

"T. Larry." Her voice squeaked.

"How was your date?"

She usually had just the right comeback to whatever T. Larry said. Now all she could manage was an ineffectual chirrup. "My date was fine, thanks." Dull answer, very dull. She pulled the covers to her chin as if she were hiding.

"Did you kiss him?"

Her baby doll pajamas, short, and soft against her skin, sexy in an odd sort of way, made her think of T. Larry, not Richard.

"A girl doesn't kiss and tell." There, that was better, a little mysterious. Maybe even a little flirtatious.

T. Larry growled with that faintly erotic, extremely intimate note he'd used with her Friday night. "Then you *did* kiss him."

A car honked down the street. The neon sign for the hair salon across the way cast a pink-and-blue glow across her ceiling as she lay in the dark. A gentle, familiar yet exotic dark with T. Larry on the other end of the line. Since she didn't know his game, Madison decided to play one of her own. "Yes, I did. And it was wonderful."

"Liar."

"It was stupendous."

"Tease."

Yes, and she liked teasing him. She was a hypocrite, of course, because she'd told Richard she didn't play guys against each other. She'd never done it before. But there was something about the darkness, and T. Larry's voice on the phone that made her want to push him. "It was hot."

He sucked in a breath. "How hot?"

"Sizzling." She wondered if this could be considered phone sex, then set the line on fire. "I used my tongue."

Silence dropped like a bang in the middle of the room. Then he said, "Let me come over."

"T. Larry," she squeaked again. "It's just a joke. We're playing a game." She didn't even want to think about why he wanted to come over.

He breathed with a hint of acceleration. "A game. You're right." He paused as if he expected her to say something, then went on. "I called—"

"To make sure I didn't become serial killer Richard's next victim." In his own way, T. Larry was as sweet as Richard. Which is why she wouldn't tell him about those breather calls. He'd worry. Then she might start worrying. And really, they meant nothing at all, especially after today's visit from Harry Dump. Now she knew that interview was much more important than any silly phone breather, especially since that's all he'd done, breathe.

"Actually, I called to tell you what to wear tomorrow night."

"What to wear?" Her fingers flirted with the hem of her baby dolls.

"Since where I'm taking you is a surprise, I thought you'd at least want some idea of what to wear so you won't feel out of place."

"Oh." It wasn't like T. Larry to be so thoughtful.

"Remember that dress you wore to last year's company picnic?"

She remembered his glower. "Yes."

"Wear that one."

"You said I couldn't wear that to work anymore after Bill got distracted and missed a nineteen-thousand-dollar deduction."

"Bring it with you, and change before we leave."

It seemed highly inappropriate. And suspect. "What are you planning, T. Larry? I don't think I trust you."

He sighed, almost groaned. "Just bring that dress."

Whatever. He was acting so oddly. "Sure."

"And next time, call me as soon as you get home so I know you're safe."

The phone clicked in her ear. She hugged the gadget to her chest. She hadn't even asked him about Harriet, about how he was feeling, how she could help. She felt so odd, her heart thrumming, a strange little tingle all over.

Boy. Richard's champagne must have affected her more than she thought. A lot more.

SITTING ON HER COUCH, a bowl of popcorn on the coffee table, Harriet wasn't just sick anymore. She wanted to die. Her mother always said she acted before she thought. Well, this one was a doozy. She didn't know how to undo it. She couldn't crawl to T. Larry and say it had all been a mistake. She couldn't admit she was jealous because no one laughed at Madison's short skirts, yet harangued Harriet for her new dress. Oh, but it was so much more than skirt length. Harriet hated, just hated being one of Madison's pet projects. She couldn't, without sounding whiny and pathetic, explain to T. Larry how much she loathed Madison's be-nice-to-Harriet moments, as if Harriet was a charity case. She couldn't even ask Harry Dump for her retainer back. That would be even more humiliating than what she'd already done to herself.

Okay, so the morning with Harry had been cathartic. She'd raged about Madison. She'd cried about Zachary. She'd hurled the blame at T. Larry. She'd felt wonderful. Liberated. Vindicated.

Until Harry called to say he'd talked to T. Larry, and she realized everyone, absolutely everyone would know Zachary had porked her—porked as in poked a pig—then dumped her.

Harriet wiped the tears from her cheeks, blew her nose and fed Errol another kitty treat.

She was so stupid. Harry had said T. Larry would keep it all "strictly confidential," but by the end of the day, they'd all know. Carp, Alta and Hobbs had info leaks like a flat roof had holes. Just when you plugged one, another popped through.

She snuggled deeper into the soft couch cushions, deeper into her fuzzy blue comfort pajamas. Errol purred against her side. Harriet sniffled. She was pathetic and whiny, and she hated it.

She could just hear Mike, Anthony and Bill.

Hey, Zach, was it like fucking a water buffalo?

How did you even find the right hole?

You didn't let her get on top, did you? Must not have, since your spine isn't crushed.

So unfair. The sniffle became a full-fledged sob. She had no one to blame but herself. She was the one who spilled the beans. And for what? Ten minutes of purging her emotions. Money, if she was lucky. Degradation, for sure.

If Zachary had really wanted her that night, she'd totally blown it now. He'd never want her again. Not after she'd dragged him down into the muck with her.

The doorbell chimed. Too late for neighbors, or salesmen or…Zachary?

She scrambled to her feet. Errol protested with a few choice cat murmurs. She looked like crap. Her hair was ratty, her makeup had smeared beneath her eyes, and oh God, she was sure there was a small hole in the crotch of her pajamas.

The bell rang again. She could pretend she wasn't home. Or she was asleep in bed. He'd give up. Then again, she ought to make sure it was really him.

His face was longer and thinner through the peephole. She whirled, flattened her back to the door and hyperventilated.

Another peal. She wouldn't panic. She'd act calm, cool and totally in control.

After one more deep breath, she flung the door wide, her cheeks all hot and her upper lip sweaty. "Zachary." She stopped, swallowed. "What a surprise."

He opened his mouth, then snapped it shut. His skin shone with a fresh shave and a dash of spicy cologne. He looked so dear in a pink polo shirt and rumpled khaki pants. Some men couldn't get away with pink.

Zachary looked gorgeous in it. Her eyes smarted. Why did she have to want a thin man?

Zachary started again. "Can I talk to you, Harriet?" From his fingers dangled a flowered bag stuffed with brightly colored tissue paper.

He'd brought her a present. "All right."

Once inside he shuffled nervously to the couch, set the bag on the coffee table, then hiked his pant legs at the knee as he sat. Gulping air, he started talking so fast his words tripped over each other. "I'm sorry, Harriet. I never meant any of this to happen. I didn't want to hurt you. I care about you. Please can we move past this incident and get back to normal?"

It sounded rehearsed, as if he'd stood in front of the mirror speaking in different inflections to view the various effects. Harriet remained standing.

"You don't have to say anything, Harriet. I know it's all my fault. I take full responsibility and blame."

Even Harriet knew it wasn't all his fault. She could be a little difficult sometimes. Zachary was a very shy person; she might have expected too much from him. But his words sounded more than practiced, they sounded coached.

"What's in the bag, Zachary?" She was almost afraid to know.

"Tokens of my affection." He'd never bought her gifts. They'd had only the one night, or rather part of it, but she knew Zachary well enough to find the whole "token of his affection" speech suspect.

Her heart beat a little faster, and tears pricked her eyes again. "What?" It came out sounding nastier than she meant, but the dull ache in her chest didn't allow her to take it back.

His pale hand disappeared into the froth of pink and blue tissue, emerging with a gift-wrapped box. She knew that wrapping, could see the name though the thin paper.

Candies. Chocolates. A pound of them. The weight would adhere to her thighs like an alien creature.

Zachary would never buy her chocolates on his own. He wouldn't stop her from eating them, but he wouldn't put the temptation in front of her. At work, if a client sent a treat in appreciation, Zachary would carry the box around, making sure it was empty but one by the time he got to Harriet.

He hadn't had a mere coach, he'd had a bad coach.

Pissed because he'd been talking to someone about her, because he should have known better, she laid into him with her hands on her hateful fat hips. "So you want me to stay fat."

"No, I—"

"You want someone to whom you can feel superior."

"That's not—"

"What else is in there?" She stabbed at the bag.

A box the size of a jewelry case. Jewelry. A little of her misery seeped out her nostrils with a sigh. Oh, Zachary. In her hands, it was heavier than a ring box. A flowery aroma floated into the air. She fumbled with the wrapping and the box lid, unearthing a bottle of cologne. Cheap cologne.

"This isn't what I wear."

"I didn't know you wore any. You always smell so—"

"Bad? So you thought you'd give me a hint that I stink?"

"I don't think—"

"You never think," she screeched, and with that she

threw the bottle at him, the atomizer popping off when it hit his shoulder. Perfume splashed his hair and neck and stained his shirt.

God, that was bitchy. And out of control. The stench made her eyes itch and water.

Zachary merely picked up the bottle from his lap, snapped the atomizer back in and set it on her coffee table.

She felt so bad, she couldn't stop. "Anything else in there?"

"One more."

"Well, then you've got one more chance, don't you? This better be good." Harriet the Harridan. She knew exactly why they called her that. But she couldn't have shut it down now any more than she could give Zachary the benefit of the doubt. Not now, not when she knew in her bones that someone had told Zachary to ply her with presents. Someone who didn't know her at all.

Someone like T. Larry who was only concerned about getting rid of her pesky little lawsuit.

With a timid hand, Zachary reached in once more. Another box, eight by eight. It didn't rattle as he held it in shaky hands. Please don't let it be. *Please* don't let it be.

She unwrapped it. A miniscule slinky pink teddy with white lace foaming at the high-cut legs. It wouldn't cover her breasts. It wouldn't hide one butt cheek, let alone disguise her thighs. She'd look like Miss Piggy in a pink tutu. "So you think you'd get a big laugh out of telling everyone what I look like in this."

"I'd never—"

"Well, I wouldn't put this on for you if it cost a million dollars." She'd burn it first. In fact…

She reached down for the lighter she used on her scented candles. Zachary's eyes widened at the flame, bulging as she held it to one frothing lacy leg.

The material didn't burn, it melted, emitting an odor so foul, her eyes stung. Harriet screeched and threw it at him. "It's polyester. It's goddamn polyester. You couldn't even buy silk or real lace. You cheapskate. You asshole. You pig."

Her head throbbed, then pounded so fiercely she was sure she'd popped a vessel.

"Get out. Get out. Get out." Chanting, until she didn't have a breath left. A frying pan, she needed a frying pan to bash him over the head. Better yet, a knife to cut off his balls.

He scuttled out the door like the terrified little mouse he was, taking with him the reek of cheap perfume.

Harriet burst into tears.

For about two minutes. Then she dried her eyes, stuffed the three boxes back into the bag, massacring the delicate tissue paper, and walked to the window.

His Nissan was still parked beneath the streetlight.

Window open, she leaned out, then flung the bag as far as she could. Splat went the chocolate, crack went the dime-store cologne. The teddy ended up at the curb in a mud puddle left by Mrs. Murphy's son when he'd washed his mother's car that evening.

Screw Zachary. Screw T. Larry. And screw Madison who would have looked perfect in that stupid pink teddy.

Everybody loved Madison. Everyone thought she was sweet and perky and wonderful and cute. Everything Harriet couldn't be even if she downed a year's supply of diet pills and turned bulimic. It wasn't about their weight difference. Men would buzz around Madison like good-for-nothing drones whatever she weighed.

If Zachary had made love to Madison on the conference room table, the next day he for darn sure wouldn't have pretended nothing happened. No, he would have asked Madison out and paraded her on his arm through the office as they left. Together.

Her blood boiled and her sinuses ached. Harriet had seen him slinking over to Madison's desk for his daily dose of Reese's cups. Reese's hah! His daily dose of sweet, perky, wonderful and cute was more like it.

How would Zachary feel about Madison if she wasn't perky all the time? How would everyone at Carp, Alta and Hobbs feel about her without the perk?

Harriet smiled to herself.

She'd give Madison's perpetually perky persona a shake-up.

ZACHARY STUNK like a whorehouse.

And he'd blown it again.

He stared at the grubby teddy in the street. Harriet would have looked luscious in that pink teddy, good enough to eat. Not that she'd ever realize that herself. And he knew he wasn't man enough to show her how truly beautiful she was.

He should have told T. Larry those gifts were all wrong for Harriet. But T. Larry, being older and wiser, said chocolates, perfume and lingerie would help Zach slip right back where he wanted to be. In Harriet's bed, between Harriet's thighs, tongue in Harriet's succulent mouth.

He'd have Harriet, and he'd have his job, because surely Harriet would drop the suit.

But Harriet wasn't like Madison. She wasn't fun loving, easygoing or sweet as the dickens. She wasn't quick to laugh at herself or swift to forgive. He'd never know a moment's peace. He'd be forever patching the holes she put in the wall. She was a powder keg, and boy, she'd just blown sky-high.

Yet he still wanted her. Badly. Physically and emotionally. As if her tirades tripped a switch in him.

It was an odd game he'd watched his folks play, though at the time he hadn't understood. Zach now wondered if his dad picked fights just for the making up later, when he'd given his son ten bucks to disappear to the movies for the evening.

Come to think of it, the night he'd made love to Harriet, they'd been arguing over something on the AMI return. With the bright color flaming her cheeks, the glittering light in her eyes and her agitation, he'd been like a rock then, too.

Damn. Maybe he was one of those guys who had to beat a woman up to get off. Maybe he was into S and M. Maybe he should be locked away where he couldn't hurt anyone.

Maybe. At least he didn't feel like a total ghost anymore.

CHAPTER NINE

"*THESE* ARE THE WORKPLACE rules you want me to type up?"

"Our sexual harassment protocol."

Madison held the handwritten document gingerly in her fingers. "T. Larry, I think you might get sued over your rules."

He cocked his head. "What's wrong with them?"

"They're not well-defined."

"They're totally self-explanatory."

"You ought to hire a Human Resource professional to handle this, T. Larry."

"There's not a thing wrong with that list."

"No sex in the office," she read.

Someone, sounding suspiciously like Anthony, snorted on the other side of her cubicle wall.

"Succinct and to the point."

"You haven't defined sex."

"Sex is sex. Everyone knows what it means."

She rolled her eyes at him. "There's foreplay. There's manual manipulation. There's oral—"

He screwed up his face in distaste, at least she thought it was distaste, and held up both hands. "Madison, please."

The guffaws next door shook the fragile wall.

"The rule stands as written. Anthony, get back to work," he called over the wall. "Don't you have a client to see?"

"Yes, sir."

"Then get out of here. But be back by eleven."

"Yes, sir." But the sputtering went on.

Madison kept reading. "No remarks concerning attire."

"What's wrong with that one?"

"What if someone accidentally left their zipper undone? How can you tell them if you can't comment on their attire?"

"That's covered in the next rule. No looking at zippers. No looking at breasts. No looking period. You see, no one will even notice then."

She huffed, skipped number three since he'd already covered it, and moved to rule four. "No remarks concerning body parts."

"You can't find anything wrong with that one."

"I'm thinking."

"Which means there's nothing wrong with it. Type up the list for the eleven o'clock meeting. And I want a laminated copy to be posted on the copy room door and in both restrooms." He stopped, then added, "Please."

"What about rule number five?"

"Madison—"

"No dresses or skirts above the knee."

His shoulders sagged. He shook his head with a pained grimace on his mouth. "That was the hardest one to write."

Not to mention that the rule was sexist. "But I'll have to buy a whole new wardrobe."

"I know." Then he brightened. "But you can still wear yesterday's outfit. That reached to midcalf."

She shook her head. "T. Larry, are you going to tell us exactly what Harriet's suit is about?"

"No."

"I'll find out when I type up your letters or whatever."

"Do I have to get the dictionary to show you the meaning of the word confidentiality?"

"I won't tell anyone."

He glanced over the row of uniform cubicle walls. "You won't have to."

She tried a different tact, anything to get rid of that pained, hollow glaze in his eyes. "Is there anything I can do to help you, T. Larry?"

"Stay away from Harriet and make sure your skirts are…" He leaned over her desk and looked at her thighs in her short red skirt. "At least twenty-five inches long."

"I meant was there anything I can do to help you *personally* through this trying time?"

He went stock-still, staring at her with the most unreadable expression. Then he shook himself, and his gaze cleared. He eyed her red skirt and her tight red-and-white striped sweater. "Don't wear sweaters that are extra small or smaller."

The phone rang before she could ask why, besides the obvious. "Carpel, Tunnel and Syndrome."

"Is that you, beautiful?"

Richard. Her heart skipped a beat, and she chanced a look at T. Larry. Oops, that was a mistake. He glowered and knew, just by the fact that she'd looked at him, who it was.

She turned her back, wrapped her hand around the receiver and lowered her voice. "I really can't talk now."

"But—"

"T. Larry's got something he needs me to do right away."

"Is he standing there?"

"Yes. He needs me. Gotta go."

"But—"

"Later. Ba-bye." And she hung up. It was rude, but T. Larry was upset, and she just couldn't enjoy a phone call from Richard with T. Larry all out of sorts like this. She looked at him. Ooh, mucho big-time glower now. "Ah, you were saying?"

He clasped his hands, squeezed, his knuckles cracking. "I don't trust him, I'm going to watch every move he makes, and I'm not going to let him do a damn thing to you."

Madison had a feeling T. Larry had more than one meaning.

HARRIET ENTERED the conference room ten feet tall in her peacock-blue power suit. Then she sat, her feet barely reaching the floor, and the effect was lost. Still, her shoulders were squared, she had a don't-mess-with-me glint in her eyes, and a Harriet the Militant glare punctuated her face.

The rumors had buzzed in the halls, the bathrooms, the copy room, the file room and through the phone lines. As though the ink had somehow leaked off the pages of Harry Dump's complaint, everyone knew what Harriet claimed occurred in this very conference room.

Poor Harriet. Poor Zachary. Poor, poor T. Larry who would have to clean up the mess.

Mike, Anthony and Bill sat like peas in a pod across from Harriet. ZZ Top sat three chairs down and six inches from the table, eyes front and center, gaze awkwardly avoiding the surface of the conference table. The chairs were filled, the overflow lined the walls. Receptionist Rhonda hovered by the door, for easy escape if Harriet whipped out her Uzi and started blasting.

T. Larry took his usual spot at the head of the table, his back to the window, and his eyes on the door for latecomers. There were none. No one would dare.

Liberally applied drugstore perfume tickled Madison's nose as she passed out T. Larry's new Sexual Harassment Protocol. The odor didn't emanate from Harriet. She exuded an expensive yet subtle scent designed to cloud a man's mind rather than beat him over the head like a club. Madison kept sniffing. Leaning over Zachary to plunk down a copy of the rules on the table in front of him, Madison almost fainted from the strength of his less than manly cologne.

Paper rustled as everyone began reading.

A soft noise. T. Larry's head popped up. "Who said that?"

No one spoke. The noise came again.

A gentle "Oink-oink-oink."

Someone snickered. Someone else stifled a giggle. Madison realized she should have added another rule. No denigrating pig noises. This was exactly what she'd been trying to tell T. Larry. No list of rules could be specific enough to safeguard Harriet. Somehow every good thing a person tried to do for her backfired.

T. Larry banged his fist on the table. Everyone jumped, the pig grunts evaporated and the laughter faded. "That's enough."

Oh, she did adore a take-charge man.

"You have the rules. Obey them. Or you're dust."

He had such a way with a good colloquial expression. Surely Richard effected this same stunned silence in a courtroom.

T. Larry blanketed the group with a laser-sharp, all-inclusive, thunderous scowl. No one uttered a word. "The first infraction earns a verbal warning, the issuance of which shall be documented in your file. The second, I write you up. And the third violation—" again, his gaze blasted the assemblage "—you're fired. Except for rule number one." He glanced down at his memo, then shot Madison a glower. "I mean number five."

She'd changed the order, listing them with increasing severity, the most important, in her opinion being T. Larry's first rule, *no sex in the office,* so she'd put it last. Though she couldn't do a thing about his wording. Sex still wasn't defined properly.

"Number five, you're terminated on the spot." He narrowed his focus on ZZ Top and Harriet.

Goodness, he was tough. She'd never seen him quite so firm. A spark of awareness licked Madison's spine.

"Meeting adjourned." They all rose like automatons. Harriet's face stony; Zachary's shoulders slumped; Mike, Anthony and Bill with their hands over their mouths. Rhonda scurried out ahead of everyone.

"Zach," T. Larry barked.

ZZ Top turned, his red face stark next to the peacock-blue of Harriet's jacket.

"In my office. Now."

Power fit T. Larry like a tailored suit. Madison leaned forward, lips at his shoulder. "Does the T stand for Terminator?"

ZZ and T. Larry disappeared behind closed doors.

Voices buzzed amid the cubicles like a nest of angry hornets.

Harriet stopped at Madison's desk. Her gaze flicked from Madison's short skirt—the one she wasn't allowed to wear after today—to her sweater stretched over her breasts—the sweater she'd have to replace with something blousy—to the four-inch heels on her feet. There'd been nothing about shoes. Wonderful.

"Don't worry. He's not going to fire you no matter what you do, say or wear." Harriet's venom hit Madison full in the face.

Madison wiped it off as if it were spittle and tried to be supportive. "I'm sorry about everything, Harriet."

"Sorry? It's because of you." Harriet could be so pretty when she wasn't sneering like that.

"What do I need to change to make it better?" Madison reached out to touch Harriet's arm, retracting it at the last moment when Harriet tensed.

"You could die, that's what you could do. Eat shit and die."

Oh my. Harriet was a little angrier than she'd realized. "Maybe I could talk to Zach for you."

The sudden office hush screamed around them. Harriet's eyes narrowed viciously. "You go near Zach, and I'll—" She stopped, backing off, her face an odd shade of blue as if she'd choked on a chicken bone.

"Harriet, I want to help you."

"You won't be able to help yourself when I'm done with you."

Harriet's malevolence chilled her insides. "What have you done, Harriet?"

"Oh, you think it's just T. Larry and Zach in that suit, don't you? Well, you're in there, too. And when I'm finished with you, you won't have your pretty little clothes or your spiky little shoes or your cute little car.

You won't even have a dime to perm your hair and paint your nails."

Talk about in your face, this time Harriet did leave a spray on Madison's cheeks. Then she stalked down the hall, her legs stubby in her flat shoes—goodness, wasn't that a disturbingly catty thought—and slammed through the reception door.

The place erupted, everyone talking at once. Madison ran to the restroom to see if her flesh had been flayed from her body.

MADISON'S DISCOMFORT from her earlier run-in with Harriet the Harridan was still apparent by the time their date rolled around.

Her lips were a brilliant red on her pert, but troubled face. Damn. Lipstick. Not a good sign. Her stretchy dress hugged every curve and rode up her thighs no matter how much she pulled it down. Laurence decided then to forget about Dick the Prick's call. After all, Madison cut Dick off pronto. Besides, she was with *him* now, not Dick. Her perfume enveloped him in the confines of his immaculate Camry, overpowering the vanilla deodorizer he'd installed beneath the dash.

"I heard about your conflagration with Harriet."

Madison made a noncommittal noise.

"Are you okay?" Laurence insisted.

"Mmm." Committal this time. She was most likely emotionally all right. But was she physically safe from Harriet?

"Do you want to talk about it?"

She turned those emerald eyes on him, now filled with just a hint of hurt. "Does my hair look like it's permed?"

He hadn't a clue, except that he couldn't envision

Madison without her bright titian curls. They were as much a part of her as her green eyes and succulent lips. "No, it doesn't look permed. And what does that have to do with Harriet?"

"Nothing." She tugged down the hem of her dress. It sprang back. He snapped his eyes to the road just in time to slam on his brakes before he hit the car in front. His hand shot to Madison's shoulder, holding her in place as the car rocked forward.

"I really don't think your hand on my chest is going to stop me flying through the windshield."

His fingers had managed to find the soft upper swell of her breast instead of her shoulder. He gripped the steering wheel once more. "Sorry. Automatic response." More than she knew.

"You're such a dad, T. Larry. Very protective."

Dad. Brother. What about lover? Didn't she ever think about that? "What happened with Harriet?" The question sounded sharper than he intended.

Madison didn't flinch. "She seems a bit…upset."

"That's a mild way of putting it."

"You didn't tell me she'd named me in her suit."

He'd wanted to save her the consternation. "It doesn't matter. I'm handling the problem." Which sounded irritatingly like what he'd said to Ryman. "Don't worry."

Zach had failed miserably in the first attempt. Laurence, of course, had a backup plan, though he'd conceded to a day's cooling-off period before they acted again.

"I just don't know how to help her." Madison heaved a sigh Laurence felt throughout his body.

"Help her?" The thought was ludicrous. Harriet didn't want anyone's help.

"She's so misunderstood."

"Harriet?"

"This wouldn't have happened if we'd been more sympathetic."

"Are we talking about Harriet the Harridan here?" Against his better judgment and intentions, he started to boil. Harriet treated Madison abominably. "She's envious, Madison. You could wear sackcloth, and she'd still be jealous." He struggled to find the least nasty comment. "Harriet simply doesn't know how to…laugh."

Madison grabbed his thigh. He almost lost control of the car. Again. "Oh my God, T. Larry. That's it. I have to teach her how to laugh. Especially at herself." She bit her lip. "But first I'll have to get her to stay in the same room with me."

The woman was crazy. He peeled her fingers one by one from his leg before he wrecked the Camry. "Stay away from Harriet. You'll only make things worse."

"I don't think they can get much worse," she murmured, tucking herself into her corner by the door, an atypical Madison position.

"She really bothered you, didn't she?"

"I don't think I've ever been hated before. At least not that I know of. It's not a nice feeling."

In some ways she was so naive, so untouched. All the more reason to keep Dick the Prick from taking advantage of her. "Harriet doesn't hate you—"

She stopped him with a look.

"All right. She hates you." He wanted to protect her from Harriet's hurtful words just as he wanted to save her from whoever had slashed her tires. Unfortunately, he was sadly deficient on the Harriet front, a fact that turned him grumpy. "Let's talk about something else."

She shrugged off Harriet as if she were a coat too heavy to wear. "Where are we going?"

One couldn't stay grumpy with Madison around. Except Harriet.

"It so happens, we're here." He'd exited the freeway and entered a worn, cracked parking area while she sulked in her corner, not that sulk was really a word that applied to Madison.

Castles, windmills and a giant laughing clown mouth rose above them. Madison jumped from the car, stood transfixed, her smile wide and the skirt of her spandex dress hugging her bottom. Watching her, Laurence could have died a happy man if that was the picture he'd take to his grave. Madison's smile did nothing less than bowl him over.

"Miniature golf," she said in hushed, reverent tones. "Do you know how to play?"

He settled at her side. "I was champion of my senior class."

"Oh, T. Larry." Were those tears in her eyes? "I didn't think you had it in you. I really didn't."

He hadn't known he had it in him, either. Planning for the future, he'd thrown off those youthful games. Watching Madison gave him a tiny stitch in his side. Maybe he'd missed something in the ensuing years, something Madison knew innately.

"I'm proud of you."

Laurence's chest swelled unaccountably, though he wasn't quite clear why she was proud.

She looked down at her hands, then flipped one out. "Picnic." She flipped out the other. "Mini golf." Repeated the process. "Picnic. Mini golf."

"What are you doing?"

"I'm trying to decide which is more romantic."

He grabbed her hand and tugged her over the scarred macadam to the entrance. "Miniature golf is far more romantic," he decided for her. He'd be damned if he'd allow her to make Dick comparisons on *his* date. "Subject closed."

Nothing was ever closed with Madison unless she decided it was. "Well, I really think it depends on the man."

He snarled as he dropped her hand to grab for his wallet. She moved to her purse. He snarled again.

"But it's dutch."

Dutch over his dead body. Not when she'd gladly let Dick pay for her meal. This was a *date*. He'd want to be with Madison in this moment whether or not someone had slashed her tires and regardless of Dick the Prick entering the picture. Finally admitting the full truth to himself, relief suffused him. He no longer needed to make excuses. No more minimizing his emotions. He wanted Madison's sweet, crooked smile all to himself.

He had their tickets, scorecards, miniature pencils, and not a red cent from her. "Choose your weapon."

She viewed the range of putters, picked one with a neon-pink handle with no regards to accuracy.

"About the romantic angle…" She'd bitten into the damn question with a tenacious grip.

He selected his own putter, minus the neon bright. "You said this was an outing, not a date, so you're talking apples and oranges."

She took a practice swing, her delicious rump agitating. "*You* only called it an outing because you wanted to make sure you slipped neatly through all those rules you made up today."

Actually, she'd been the one to call it an outing. He'd always considered it a date. Not that it mattered. She was with him, and that's all that counted.

The night was balmy on the Peninsula, several degrees warmer than it had been up in blustery San Francisco. Tuesday night didn't appear to be a particularly big golfing night, two couples battling it out four holes ahead of them, and no one in line behind. Good, no one would notice the way he eyed Madison's sweet rear end in that too short, too stretchy, perfect dress.

A scalloped neckline left her collarbones bare. There was something sexy about bare collarbones, especially Madison's.

"Ladies first." He smiled, anticipating the view.

She bent daintily to place her lime-green ball on the tee. Nice muscles. Nice calves. Nice…everything.

"Now, about a picnic being more romantic."

Nice everything except her topic of conversation. "We never agreed a picnic was more romantic."

She straightened, lips pursed prettily and that damnable lipstick all moist and shiny. "Will you let me finish? I'm trying to figure this out for future reference."

"Fine. Talk while you're putting. We don't want to get behind."

"There's no one behind us."

The telltale rumblings of a family outing sounded from the parking lot, and Laurence wanted to get a good five holes ahead of them. "Putt."

She did. Her ball clattered right through the faded covered bridge and landed within four inches of the hole.

Damn.

She skirted the bridge, bent down on the other side to stare at him through the bridge's overhang, then stuck her tongue out.

His putter got stuck on a tuft of plastic turf, and the ball skewed to the right, bouncing off the cement siding and coming to rest inches before the wooden planks of the bridge.

"You did that on purpose."

She laughed. "Did what?"

Bent over. Couldn't say that aloud, though. "Take your shot."

She wiggled, she wriggled, she stuck the tip of her tongue between her teeth, then she made the four-inch putt. Laurence closed his eyes when she bent over for her ball. His heart couldn't take anymore right then.

"So anyway, what I was saying about taking the man into consideration when you're determining the level of romance."

"I'm concentrating." His ball had rolled a few inches from the concrete edging, but he still didn't have a straight shot through the bridge.

His need for concentration didn't concern her. "For one man, a champagne picnic—"

"Champagne?"

"With strawberries soaking in it."

He groaned. He'd never be able to compete with strawberries and champagne in a park. So, he took his shot with geometric calculation, banking the ball off first the right wooden wall, then the left, and watched it roll straight into the cup.

Madison clapped, bouncing on the two-inch soles of her snazzy black sandals. "I think you cheated."

"Then we're even."

She moued and preceded him to the next hole and obstacle course. "Okay, so a champagne picnic can be nothing out of the ordinary for one man. And another man—"

"Can we please stop talking about this?" Laurence didn't like the rise of these feelings of inadequacy.

Madison ignored him as she did that deliberately intoxicating wiggle-wriggle before her ball. "And another man might be wholeheartedly romantic when he takes a girl miniature golfing. Or…" She straightened, a gasp on her lips, putter in midswing behind her. "Or bowling. Like the time Marge Simpson fell in love with her bowling instructor because Homer gave her a bowling ball for her birthday."

"I've never watched *The Simpsons*. And putt, you're throwing off our schedule."

"Well, it was very romantic because in the end, Marge chose Homer over that French bowling teacher."

He balanced his putter on the toe of his canvas shoe. "Are you trying to say bowling is more romantic than a moonlit picnic?"

"No, I'm saying it depends on the woman."

"I thought you said it depended on the man."

"It depends on both."

He ground his teeth. How had he allowed himself to be trapped into this "comparison" game? The operative word was trapped. He had to know. "So which is better, a picnic or miniature golfing?"

She turned back to her ball. "Maybe you should give me champagne while we're playing so it'll be a fair comparison."

She hit. A flash of neon green zipped through the clown's laughing mouth, shot past the arc of the pendulum tongue, came out on the other side, then slid right into the cup. Hole in one.

Madison jumped, her skirt riding dangerously high. "Come on, tough guy, beat that." Then her hands spread. "Oh my God, is that what the *T* stands for? Tough Guy?"

"That would be *TG*."

She stopped then, halfway around the clown face on the way to retrieve her ball, though she was too far away for him to gauge her relative seriousness. "Is this a date, T. Larry?"

His heart seized. The distant sound of freeway traffic faded, childish laughter blew away into the night. There was only Madison. And him. "That depends on your answer to my question." His pulse pounded in the silence waiting for her answer.

"I've known you for seven years, T. Larry. I think this should be just an outing."

He wasn't hurt. Real men didn't get hurt. They didn't wear their feelings on their sleeves. He was simply angry. What did the length of time she'd worked for him matter? Unless it was that word. Work. And the fact that *she* worked for *him*. Damn and blast.

He hit his ball harder than he intended, watching with a jaundiced eye as it skidded just to the left of the swinging tongue and plopped right into the hole.

Hole in one. He didn't leap the way Madison had.

"Does this mean we're tied, T. Larry?"

Perhaps in miniature golf. In everything else, Madison was winning. "I think it means we need a bet."

"What kind of bet?"

"Over who wins the game."

"What will we bet?"

He stepped closer. "What do you want?"

"How about lunch?"

"Think bigger." Five inches separated them. Her scent matched the glossy pink-and-red flowers on her dress and filled his senses.

She chewed her lip, eating off a taste of her lipstick. "How about a week of lunches?"

"Done," he said before she could shrink the date range.

"Starting Thursday, because you have that appointment tomorrow with Davis Dullard."

"It's Dillard. And don't call him that to his face."

She flapped a hand. "Dillard, Dullard, same diff. What do you want if you win?"

He took the shortest of pauses. "A kiss."

Her eyes flared. She swallowed. "Just one?"

"That'll be enough. For now."

"Excuse me, mister, you done playing this hole?"

Madison made a sound like a small bird cheeping, tripped over the back of her sandals and caught herself on his arm.

Damn the kid. Damn the parents. Damn. "We're done."

He helped her to the next hole sporting a devil with a swinging pitchfork. He'd lost one advantage, but sought another. "Afraid of losing, Madison?"

She didn't look at him as she squared herself in front of her tee. "Of course not."

"Then why not take the bet?"

"It's the idea." Her putter slipped, nicked the ball unintentionally but sent it far enough to qualify as her turn.

Laurence gave her a beatific smile, blinked slowly and set up for his putt. "What's wrong with the idea if you're sure you're not going to lose?"

"Somehow I think you're sure *you're* going to win."

He straightened, his shot waiting. "I *am* sure."

She stared at him from two yards away, hands on her hips and eyes narrowed.

He raised an eyebrow. "You aren't afraid of a little kiss, are you? I think you even enjoyed the last one."

"You took me by surprise."

"Maybe that's why your mouth just popped open for me. All that surprise."

"That is not true."

He gave her his shark smile, one he usually reserved for staff accountants with big egos. "What's not true? That you enjoyed the kiss? Or that you opened your mouth voluntarily?"

"Oh, take your shot," she snapped. Madison never snapped. He was winning.

"I can't take a shot until we finalize the bet."

She stamped her foot. Another good sign. Madison wasn't a foot stomper. "All right, you're on."

He hit the ball, which whizzed past the devil's pitchfork, and sank another hole in one.

CHAPTER TEN

MADISON WAS WINNING! She was winning! By a lot. He-he-he. She wouldn't have to kiss him.

T. Larry had scared her the last few days. Madison had scared herself.

The worst part? Mini golf with T. Larry, king of plans, was far more romantic than a dozen champagne picnics.

But if T. Larry was The One, wouldn't she have known it a long time ago?

"I'm so looking forward to not packing a lunch for a week."

T. Larry eyed her speculatively. "I'm down four strokes. There's one hole left. What do you say, double or nothing?"

"What, two weeks of lunches versus two kisses?"

"Make it a month of lunches. If I win, I get the kiss and another date on Friday."

She leaned on her putter. "This isn't a date."

He didn't acknowledge her clarification. "Bet?"

"What if we tie?"

"Then we flip a coin. Heads I win, tails you lose."

Four strokes ahead of him, how could she lose? She wouldn't have to eat Hamburger Helper leftovers, turkey hotdogs, or bologna sandwiches for a month. On the other hand, she might get fat. "You can't take me to McDonald's all the time. Some have to be places with Chinese chicken salad or vegetable stir fry."

"I'll take you wherever you want."

A lesser woman would have thought the Top of the Mark or the Equinox overlooking Alcatraz and the Bay. Madison thought Max's Café and that hole-in-the-wall Chinese place over on Taylor. She loved food. Her mouth watered. "You're on."

Then she saw the windmill. The wood had been washed clean of its white paint and the red siding faded to brown. She hated the windmill. The space between the wings—what on earth were those long whirling arms called?—always got the best of her.

It wasn't the actual kissing or even the date that bothered her. It was the confusion. She didn't know what T. Larry expected. She didn't know what *she* wanted.

The sun had fallen behind the mountains, and bright incandescent lights shone down on the grubby indoor-outdoor. She lined up her first shot. She wasn't overly optimistic for that first try. She had to warm up. Shuffling her feet, she planted them just right, counted the seconds between the swing of each wing of the windmill, then closed her eyes and putted.

The ball hit a wooden arm with a thunk and rolled back. Stop, stop, stop, she mentally shouted at her ball. The closer her shot got to the windmill, the easier it was to time the turns. Four feet. It seemed like a mile.

"Time the ball, Madison," T. Larry murmured behind her.

She whirled on him. "I can't concentrate when you're breathing on me. And I do not need you to coach me on this."

No big deal. She could at least break even with him.

She wiggled into place. T. Larry sighed. She tried to ignore him. The ball went awry anyway and bounced back even farther than before. Perspiration gathered beneath her breasts.

"It's all right, Madison. You still have two more for the win." He was even closer now, his indefinable male scent messing with her mind.

She elbowed him. "Back off." But then she moved to the shot too fast after he did. Darn. Muffed it again.

She turned on her heel and pointed. "Stay over there."

Counting, counting. She tapped the ball because last time she'd whacked it too hard. The ball rolled. Then stopped six inches in front of the windmill.

"You can't lose now," he called, the tone definitely a taunt meant to rattle her.

He was right. How could she miss from six inches away? A month of lunches with T. Larry. Every day, sitting across from him. Or beside him. Close enough to breathe in his scent.

The putter slipped in her now sweaty palms, her count not exact, and that darn arm hit that darn ball and knocked it clear off to the side.

She raised a hand over her head and scooped her hair back from her face. T. Larry made some strange unintelligible sound. He was probably laughing. But when she looked, there was just a sort of dazed hockey-puck-to-the-head stare.

"I have one more, then we'll tie."

"Then we'll fli-ip the coin." His voice cracked oddly.

She was at a bizarre angle, with the ball off to the right of the windmill wing-things. T. Larry had moved closer, eyeing her ball on the green carpeting. She didn't have the concentration to spare to tell him to park his butt elsewhere.

She did four trials, moving her hips back and forth to find the right spot. T. Larry made some weird strangled noise.

Concentrate. Count. Putt. She did.

The ball slipped right in, sucked into mini golf heaven. Madison jumped, hopping, hooting and throwing her arms in the air.

"If I get a hole in one, we tie and resort to the coin toss," T. Larry said. She didn't trust that smile. He'd tricked her somehow. She just knew it.

"You said you were champion of your senior class."

He shrugged. "That was twenty years ago."

"Have you been giving me shots to lull me?"

"I wouldn't dare. I have to see you in the morning."

She crossed her arms, realized it pulled the hem of her dress almost to her crotch and let her hands fall to her sides.

"Go for it," she finally said.

He did. Bend. Place. Count. Putt. And the little ball was sucked away along with hers.

Darn. "That was too easy. I'm sure you cheated."

With a lazy T. Larry shit-eating grin, he said, "I didn't."

"All right. Let's flip." She could still win. She dug in her purse for a quarter and couldn't find even a penny.

"Let's do it at the car. These people want to start the last hole."

She looked for his trick in that, but could find none.

Leaving behind their putters, they stepped into the intimate gloom of the parking lot. Several overhead lamps had burned out, and T. Larry had managed to park right beneath one, beneath a whole slew of them, in fact. His car sat in a pool of darkness.

He held a coin in his hand. "Heads I win, tails you lose."

She grabbed the coin, turned it over in her fingers to make sure it was a real coin, squinting to see clearly in the lack of good lighting. Heads one side, tails the other. Fifty-fifty chance. "All right."

Silver spun in the air. T. Larry caught it with practiced ease, then pulled a palm aside. Madison leaned closer to see.

"Tails you lose," he murmured close to her ear.

That mutant tingle clamored inside her.

"Let me see that." She pulled him into a touch of moonlight. Tails. Darn. There was only one thing to do.

She closed her eyes, puckered her lips, put her hands behind her back and leaned forward.

"I don't think so." He pushed her up against the car door.

Her breath got sucked out of her, and her eyes went wide. That car of his certainly didn't retain the heat because she was cold on the backside and hot-hot-hot on the front. Then T. Larry swooped down on her. No prelim, just his tongue along the seam of her lips. His fingers tunneled through her hair, holding her in place, and then that horrible, excruciating, wonderful tingle swamped her.

It rippled in her body like sweet wine. She couldn't help but open her mouth, first to sigh, then to let him in. And her arms—of their own volition they wound round his neck, pulled him closer, forcing him to drop his hands from the back of her head.

His fingertips skimmed her shoulders, trailed the

outside of her breasts, his thumbs caressing within a centimeter of her nipples. Oh my. He squeezed her ribs, moved to her waist, then her hips, his body dipping as he diddled with the hem of her too-short dress.

All the while he mesmerized her with his lips, his tongue. Boy, T. Larry could kiss. T. Larry could make her forget who she was, who *he* was. She moaned into his mouth and pulled him deeper.

He plucked at the stretchy material covering her bottom, tugging it up past her butt cheeks. She pried his fingers off, yanked her dress down, her mouth still fastened to his, his still fascinated with hers. He moved to the front, tarrying between her hem and the bare skin of her thigh.

She simply couldn't catch her breath. Then he nipped her lip and backed off an inch or two, resting his forehead against hers while his breath sawed from his chest at an irregular rate.

"Better than Richard?" he murmured against her tingling lips.

"Richard who?" She honestly didn't know.

Until he laughed softly with a hint of smugness.

It didn't matter, not right now. All she wanted was for T. Larry to hypnotize her with his lips again. His fingers traced her collarbone, then the scalloped neck of her dress, finally dipping low against her bosom. She drew in a breath. Her chest swelled against his touch.

A child laughed, footsteps stomped, then a car alarm beeped.

Goodness, she'd forgotten they were in a parking lot. Granted, the dark hid them, but T. Larry had made her lose sight of exactly where they were. And she'd let him hike her dress so that her buns showed. Oh my God.

She pushed, managing to secure several inches of breathing space she sorely needed to yank her dress back down. Afterward, he caught her wrists and placed her hands against his palms.

Then she recalled what he'd whispered against her lips. "Is that what kissing me is all about? Besting Richard? And my lipstick is all over your mouth."

His gray eyes glittered behind his glasses as if light somehow penetrated their dark corner of the lot. "It's all over you, too. Wipe it off for me."

The touch of her fingertips against his lips was too terribly intimate. The brush of his against hers short-circuited several brain cells.

"There, all cleaned up," he whispered. "It's about choices, Madison."

"What?" She'd lost the bent of the original conversation.

"Richard. He isn't the only one you can choose."

Her heart skipped a beat. "What are you saying?" She was afraid she already knew.

"If you want to fall in love, you don't need Richard."

Her head started to spin, and every inch of her flesh prickled where she touched him. "You can't be serious. You're not suggesting…you don't mean…"

"That's exactly what I mean." With a half step back, hands still imprisoning hers, he bowed at the waist. "I'm at your service for whatever you need."

She couldn't help it. She laughed. Not at him, or about him, but at the absurdity of the situation. "You're my boss."

His eyes turned a flat, stormy gray. "The rules you typed up didn't state you couldn't fall in love with your boss."

"I've known you forever. You're like one of my brothers."

"If you'd said your father, I'd have to beat you."

"I just don't feel that way about you, T. Larry."

His eyes narrowed. "You sure as hell kissed me like you were feeling 'that way.'"

She had. Twice. And twice she'd forgotten her name the moment he'd touched her. "It would just get too complicated."

"Why?"

She shrugged. "Well, you know, when it was over...I'd still be working for you, and things would be all difficult and changed. I don't think I'd like them that way."

He cocked his head, tugged on her hands and turned his to lace his fingers through hers. "So maybe you think you're not going to die after all. Is that what you're saying?"

"I don't know. I never really did know. But I won't have children or get married just in case I do die. And by the same token, I can't get involved with my boss just in case I don't."

"You have a very strange sense of logic."

She grinned, feeling the win despite her captured fingers. "Why, thank you."

He advanced. She had nowhere to go except up against the car, which had proved to be a very bad idea the first time.

He let go of one hand, took off his glasses and laid them on the roof of the car. "It's not complicated unless you make it that way."

My, he had extraordinary eyes. She couldn't think of a thing to say in return.

"You fall in love. You get what you want."

Her throat was awfully dry. "What do you get?"

His hands slid up her arms, bracketing her collarbones. "What do you think?"

Goodness, sex. "You don't really want me like *that,* do you?"

His eyes were dark and intense without the benefit of glasses. "Exactly like that."

He stole her breath. Those mutant tingles made her knees weak. She would have fallen if he hadn't wedged her between his body and the car.

"I can't think about this now." She couldn't find the right objection when he stood so close. "Let's talk about it tomorrow."

"All right. Tomorrow."

She'd feel sane tomorrow. "T. Larry, I have a question."

"What?"

"If heads you win, and tails I lose, how was I ever supposed to win the toss?"

A corner of his mouth lifted. "Don't think about it now, Madison. Just think about this."

Then he kissed her again, and she had a bad feeling, a really bad feeling that he'd won the toss because she'd wanted him to.

"I'M NOT INVITING YOU IN."

"I can wait until you're ready." Laurence realized Madison was now running scared. He'd wanted to buy her a nice meal in a swanky restaurant, but she'd insisted on fast food, which she generally avoided. In fact, she was avoiding him, cutting their date short and turning their kiss into a distant memory instead of little over an hour ago.

"I don't think you should get your hopes up."

Laurence pulled in beneath a streetlamp outside her apartment. "Something's definitely up, and it's not just my hopes."

She blushed. Madison had the prettiest blush. Then she turned in her seat. "T. Larry, what's gotten into you? I've never heard you make a sexual innuendo. In fact, I've always thought you were *asexual.*"

Christ. If she wasn't careful, he'd show her just how asexual he was right on the front seat of his car. Or maybe he'd just beat his head against the steering wheel. He had to say something to keep from strangling her.

"When are you seeing him again?"

"Tomorrow night."

He'd been hoping she'd say never. Laurence restrained himself, but his fists ached with clenching the wheel. "So you're driving yourself in to work."

She nodded.

"Carry your car keys between your fingers so you can poke out the eyes of anyone coming close to you."

"T. Larry."

"And have Squeaky walk you to the elevators."

"T. Larry." More strongly.

"Promise."

She gave him a you-pitiful-man look and huffed. "Promise."

He'd still worry, but didn't know what else to do, besides tying her to his bed. Hmm, not a bad idea. "I'll walk you up."

"You don't need to do that."

"I always walk a lady to the door and see her safely in."

"You aren't going to kiss me, are you? It confuses me."

"I won't kiss you." He smiled to himself because

her admission seemed a point in his favor. "Unless you beg me to."

She snorted, then climbed out, her fanny outlined in the delicious dress. Just that sight, her smile and those kisses were worth everything. At the foot of the stairs, she waited.

"Ladies first," he murmured with his hand extended.

She narrowed her eyes. "I know what you're doing." But she preceded him, tugging at the bottom of her dress.

At the top of the stairs, she squatted to retrieve a key from beneath the mat, eyes on him over her shoulder. He took it from her hand when she rose.

"What the hell are you doing leaving a key under your mat?"

"My brother was going to fix my sink."

"Anyone could have found it, not just your brother."

She frowned. "Why would anyone care?"

Because she was young, beautiful and very kissable. "I'll check inside before you go in there."

She pursed those kissable lips. "I'm not inviting you in."

"I told you I wouldn't kiss you if you didn't want me to." He wondered how long it would take to make her beg. "This is about your safety. Is sex all you have on the brain?"

She snorted again, an oddly petite and dainty sound.

"Stay in the doorway while I check that everything's okay."

She rolled her eyes, said nothing, but waited for him on the doorstep.

The shade by the window where he'd kissed her was down. He crossed the room, snapping it up, letting street light swamp the room. Pink-and-green neon stripes flashed across the ceiling. She'd cleaned, her clothing was put away and the magazines straightened. A single rose unfurled in a bud vase in the center of the coffee table.

No monsters lurked behind the couch. Laurence moved down the short hallway and stopped at the bathroom door. Gleaming pink-and-gray tile adorned the walls and countertop. Her jewelry sat in a bone china cup resplendent with blossoming blue roses. Scents abounded—strawberry hand lotion, a bottle of honeysuckle shampoo, lilac bubble bath. Eyes closed, he breathed deep of her essence.

"Are you done in there yet?" she called from the front door, exactly where he'd told her to stay. A first. Madison doing what he told her to do without much of a fight.

"I'm just checking to make sure there's no psycho behind the shower curtain."

"Get out of my bathroom."

He rattled the plastic curtain. "Looks like you're okay in here. I'll just check the bedroom."

"Stay out of my bedroom."

Neon shone through her unshaded window. A thick comforter covered the bed, matching pillows scattered with artful display along the headboard. Another red rose on the dresser, in a blue bud vase, lightly scented the air. She'd stuck photos of nieces, nephews, brothers and so on along the edge of the mirror. A silver-handled comb lay in the center of a square lace doily. Pots of makeup lined the back of the vanity.

He wanted to touch her feminine things, hold the lace of her nightgown, which was laid out on the bed, to his nose, drink her in.

"Are you done?"

In a moment, he'd be the one begging. "I'm just checking the closet." He slammed the door. "No monsters in there. I guess it's safe. Wait, I forgot the kitchen."

"Don't you dare go in my kitchen."

When he made it back down the short hall, she was standing in front of louvered swinging doors, hands behind her back protectively.

"Do you mind not putting your back to the door like that? Someone could knife you between the louvers."

She pursed her lips combatively.

"I have to check it, Madison." He held out a placating hand.

She dashed through the door before he could stop her, then gasped from somewhere on the other side.

He lost a lifetime in that gasp and the "eek" that followed.

"What's wrong?" The doors hit him in the back as they swung in after him.

She stood by the sink. Light falling through the window shone across her face. Hand on the tap, she turned the water on, turned it off, back on again, then leaned to the switch and flipped on the garbage disposal.

It coughed, spat, choked and fell silent.

"Not fixed," she muttered. "He's going to kill me because *he* had to do the dishes."

"Your brother?"

"Uh-huh, Sean. He did the dishes to make me feel guilty for leaving such a mess and didn't fix the garbage disposal to punish me."

Nice to have a plumber, contractor, mechanic and dishwasher all in the family. Madison never had to pay for a service.

Now all she needed was an accountant. Christ!

T. LARRY HAD VAMOOSED like a man with a stick of dynamite where the sun don't shine. Whatever had gotten into him? Her house was clean, her dishes done and her clothes picked up. What more could a man ask for?

She put the key under the mat, closed the door, poured herself a glass of wine, then walked down the hall to her bedroom.

Sean would probably finish the garbage disposal tomorrow, and she'd make sure there wasn't one single dish in that sink.

Her bedroom smelled of roses. She flipped on the light. The bed was made, her nightgown neatly displayed, and a single rose stood on her vanity.

This really wasn't like Sean. Odd. Very odd. Unless he wanted to make her feel terribly guilty for having left a mess for him to wade through. Now *that* was like him, going overboard to make a point. Still, cleaning her entire apartment, not to mention picking up her nightgown off the floor and folding it on the bed, was a very strange form of punishment even for Sean. And the rose. With this amount of effort, he must have been livid and probably wouldn't be back to do the garbage disposal for weeks. She should have felt awfully guilty, but how could she when she now had such a lovely clean apartment?

Switching on the small lamp, she slid onto the stool in front of her vanity mirror and reached automatically for the brush that wasn't there. She picked up the silver comb instead, sliding it through her hair, pulling on one or two tangles.

She sipped from her glass, licked her lips, and tasted

T. Larry. Oh, she really was all mixed up, she thought as she pulled on her nightgown.

By the bedside, her phone rang. After ten, it couldn't be Sean, nor any of her brothers, not even her mom. Crawling onto the coverlet, cradling her wine to her breasts, she reached for the phone.

"Hello?" She answered with a hint of trepidation. It might be T. Larry to confuse her again.

"Madison?"

"Richard." She'd relented, giving him her number last night.

"I just called to say good-night."

"You called to see if I was home from my date with T. Larry."

The silence, except for cell phone static, was short but telling. "Last night you said it was just an 'outing.'"

That was before T. Larry talked about sex. "I don't know quite what it was, Richard."

A sigh. "Does this mean you don't want to see me anymore?" A pathetic note crept into his voice.

T. Larry demanded, steamrollered and teased. He did what he wanted and her desires be damned. He was anything but pathetic.

Poor Richard. Despite his beautiful face, he needed her. T. Larry didn't, unless it was to type his latest office protocol. Ah, the crux of the whole thing. Part of falling in love was feeling needed, and much as she told everyone T. Larry needed her, she knew he'd toddle on through life quite well without her.

"I want to see you again, Richard."

"Tomorrow is still on?"

"Of course it is."

His relief and his smile slid across the vast

airspace between them. "I have another surprise, better than the picnic."

Surprises eventually led to bells. "I love surprises."

"I'll meet you in the lobby of your building at five."

"Make it five-fifteen. The elevators are slow." And she'd need to touch up her makeup in the bathroom.

"Great." A pause, then, "Uh, Madison?"

"Yes, Richard?" Her mind strained toward his voice, waiting for…something.

"Is everything else all right?"

What was he fishing for? "Sure."

"You're sure you're okay?"

"Don't I sound okay?"

"Yes, but…I just worry about you."

"Whatever for? Do I sound strange or something?"

"No." He stopped. Could he hear the residual T. Larry tingle in her voice?

"I'm fine, Richard. I'm looking forward to tomorrow night." Traitorous thoughts, she was looking forward to seeing T. Larry tomorrow morning.

"Until then."

Richard hung up first.

She sipped her wine, a vague tightness in her chest. The scent of the rose, while sweet, was overpowering. Madison climbed from the bed to open her window. A touch of fresh air in, a taste of gagging flowery air out.

Quiet filled the street, though a hint of traffic, both foot and vehicle, drifted down from University Avenue. Richard was like the glow of her neighbor's neon bathing the narrow road with color. Flashy without depth. T. Larry was like the cinnamon from the bakery below wafting on a slight breeze. Understated yet tantalizing.

She had to do something to turn the tables on her

feelings. She had to do something about *herself.* She had to...

Make over her hair. Yes. Absolutely.

On the corner, a figure stood just beyond the circle of lamplight. Her lights were off, but the neon glow would frame her in the window. Not that being seen bothered her; the lace of her nightie was pretty and the cut sexy. But T. Larry would expect a bit more decorum from her. Goodness, she was thinking too much about what T. Larry wanted.

Setting her wine on her nightstand, Madison burrowed back beneath the covers.

She dialed BeeBee, who never slept—except if you counted the hours between 1:00 and 3:00 a.m. She was a whiz with color. Magic flowed from her fingers. Hair magic.

"BeeBee, I need help with a capital *H.*"

"What's wrong with your hair now?"

"I need highlights. Golden highlights."

"It's too late to do it tonight."

"I was thinking tomorrow." For Richard.

"You're working tomorrow."

"I know. But since you're off on Wednesdays, I was thinking maybe you'd like to come into the City for lunch."

"And to do your hair."

"I'll get that mu shu pork you adore," Madison coaxed in a singsong voice. "With extra pancakes."

"If I didn't love you, I'd say no."

"But you love me."

"I'm wrapped around your twisted little finger."

"You're a lifesaver."

"The candy variety or the water variety?"

"Both."

"Where can I set up?"

"T. Larry's bathroom."

"Won't he be in his office?"

"He's got a lunch appointment, and Mr. Dullard always keeps him an hour longer."

"You like living dangerously."

Nah. Everything would work out perfectly.

CHAPTER ELEVEN

"THANKS FOR CLEANING the apartment, Sean."

"Why would I clean your apartment?"

"Because you love me?"

He made a rude noise over the phone. "It was a pigsty."

"I've been busy."

"With that T. Larry guy?"

Sean's interest set her nerves jangling. She glanced around the cubicle as if someone were hiding behind the file cabinet, then leaned around her entryway to eye the hall. It was early. T. Larry hadn't come up from his workout. Keys clicked in a distant cubicle, the rest were silent. Accountants were not, by nature, an early lot.

"T. Larry is just my boss."

"Right. And I bet that's why Ma skipped over to clean your apartment after I told her what a pig you are."

"Ma did it?"

"Hell if I know, but it sure wasn't the tooth fairy. And neither James nor Patrick would be caught dead washing a dish."

Or leaving her a sweet-smelling rose, two of them. She'd noticed the other on the coffee table this morning. Duh. Of course, her mother did it. Silly to have thought Sean would leave roses and pick up her nightgown.

YOUR OPINION POLL
THANK-YOU FREE GIFTS INCLUDE

▶ **2 ROMANCE OR 2 SUSPENSE BOOKS**

▶ **A LOVELY SURPRISE GIFT**

OFFICIAL OPINION POLL

YOUR OPINION COUNTS!

Please check TRUE or FALSE below to express your opinion about the following statements:

Q1 Do you believe in "true love"?

"TRUE LOVE HAPPENS ONLY ONCE IN A LIFETIME."
○ TRUE
○ FALSE

Q2 Do you think marriage has any value in today's world?

"YOU CAN BE TOTALLY COMMITTED TO SOMEONE WITHOUT BEING MARRIED."
○ TRUE
○ FALSE

Q3 What kind of books do you enjoy?

"A GREAT NOVEL MUST HAVE A HAPPY ENDING."
○ TRUE
○ FALSE

Place the sticker next to one of the selections below to receive your 2 **FREE BOOKS** and **FREE GIFT**. I understand that I am under no obligation to purchase anything as explained on the back of this card.

Romance

193 MDL EE5Z

393 MDL EE3Q

Suspense

192 MDL EE6D

392 MDL EE32

0074823 ‖‖‖‖‖‖‖ ‖‖‖‖‖ ‖‖‖‖‖   FREE GIFT CLAIM # 3622

FIRST NAME

LAST NAME

ADDRESS

APT.#

CITY

STATE/ PROV.

ZIP/POSTAL CODE

(TF-HQN-06)

The Reader Service — Here's How It Works:

Accepting your 2 free books and gift places you under no obligation to buy anything. You may keep the books and gift and return the shipping statement marked "cancel." If you do not cancel, about a month later we'll send you 3 additional books and bill you just $5.24 each in the U.S., or $5.74 each in Canada, plus 25¢ shipping & handling per book and applicable taxes if any.* That's the complete price, and — compared to cover prices of $5.99 or more each in the U.S. and $6.99 or more each in Canada — it's quite a bargain! You may cancel at any time, but if you choose to continue, every month we'll send you 3 more books, which you may either purchase at the discount price...or return to us and cancel your subscription.

*Terms and prices subject to change without notice. Sales tax applicable in N.Y.
Canadian residents will be charged applicable provincial taxes and GST.

If offer card is missing write to: The Reader Service, 3010 Walden Ave., P.O. Box 1867, Buffalo NY 14240-1867

BUSINESS REPLY MAIL
FIRST-CLASS MAIL   PERMIT NO. 717-003   BUFFALO, NY

POSTAGE WILL BE PAID BY ADDRESSEE

THE READER SERVICE
3010 WALDEN AVE
PO BOX 1341
BUFFALO NY 14240-8571

NO POSTAGE
NECESSARY
IF MAILED
IN THE
UNITED STATES

Now Ma would definitely do it to teach Madison a lesson, the old Catholic-Episcopalian guilt trip. It was just her style.

"And since *your* mother shows you excessive amounts of favoritism, I vote she did it."

"She does not show me favoritism, Sean, and you know it."

"Hah. You always get the leftovers."

"That's because she thinks I don't know how to cook."

"Do you?"

"Of course, I do. And I can start cooking again as soon as Patrick installs that spice rack he made for me." She paused. "And you put in the new garbage disposal."

"Then you should have washed the dishes before I got there."

"They're done now," she answered sweetly.

He huffed. "All right, today. But Sherry's threatened divorce if I fix your garbage disposal before I put the new faucet in for her so you better not tell her."

"I love you."

A snort. "You always manage to get what you want with those three simple words."

"I mean every one of them whether you put in my garbage disposal or not."

"Yeah, yeah. You're spoiled."

She didn't argue. "I left a surprise in the refrigerator."

"I hate moldy bread."

"I threw that out. This is something better." A bottle of Dom Pérignon for his anniversary next week. She'd paid full price, too, because Sean was so special.

"You didn't knit me another sweater, did you?"

"Now, why would I put a sweater in the refrigerator?"

"Well, the last one you gave me was frozen."

"That's because BeeBee told me it would shrink. I made it just a little too big in the first place."

"The kids use it for a sleeping bag."

"I don't remember sewing the bottom closed."

"Madison, you scare me. By the way, I'm having a little operation next week."

Her heart stopped beating in her chest. "Operation?"

"I'm getting my tubes tied."

All the blood drained right out of her head, leaving her dizzy with relief. "Men don't get their tubes tied."

"Tubes tied, vasectomy, whatever."

"Ma's going to kill you when she finds out."

"Ma's the one who suggested it."

"God, she's getting liberal."

"She also wants to know if you're on the pill."

Madison choked.

"Because while we all like T. Larry and think you deserve every ounce of happiness you can find, we don't want any little T. Larrys running around until you're married."

Madison growled, but Sean had already hung up.

She dialed her mother to thank her for the cleaning. It was the right thing to do.

Ma, however, wasn't home. Madison left a message with lots of kissy thank-you noises, all the while, thanking the Lord for the delay. Because she knew her mother, and when she did call back, she'd give Madison "what for" for letting her apartment get that messy in the first place.

And if her mother tackled the sex issue again...well, that was just beyond the pale.

THE SCENT OF FRESHLY brewed coffee called to Laurence like a siren. Madison bought special beans from a coffeehouse down on Market Street, ground it herself and always used bottled water. Her coffee soothed the most frazzled of nerves—it was working on Laurence's, or was that just the thought of seeing her?—and tamed the wildest of beasts.

In this particular case, the beast was Harriet.

Laurence stopped just outside the copy room door and inhaled the rich coffee aroma, only to swallow a taste of Harriet's unmistakable perfume.

He eavesdropped unabashedly while his senses cleared.

"Day number one and I see you've already decided to break one of T. Larry's rules."

A pause, then Madison's soft tones. "I didn't have time to go out shopping. But this is one of my longest skirts."

"And one of your tightest sweaters."

"Well, it's the one that matches the skirt." T. Larry idly wondered which sweater and which skirt. Not the flowing one she'd worn on Monday, perhaps something pleated that whirled nicely around her thighs.

"You're so disgustingly obvious."

He sensed Madison's deep breath before she spoke. "Did I ever tell you about my first job?"

"Am I supposed to care?" Harriet was a tough nut to crack.

"Actually, it's just a funny story."

"I don't feel like listening to a funny story."

Madison apparently didn't hear her. Or didn't care. "I had to carry this huge box of reports from the computer room. We didn't have a laser printer or anything."

"Was this like twenty years ago or something?" Harriet's snarl was written all over her voice.

The slur bounced right off Madison. "We were on a limited budget. Anyway, it was a really big box, and I was wearing this full skirt, and I accidentally got it caught on the top of the box when I picked it up, and there I was walking through the whole office with my skirt hiked up to my waist." Madison laughed with an unselfconsciousness Harriet would never master.

"So everyone was staring at your panties. Bully for you. Let's just add exhibitionist to your list of admirable traits."

"I just meant that it was embarrassing at the time, sort of like walking through a restaurant with toilet paper hanging out the back of your pants. But now it's one of my funniest stories."

So that's what she'd meant last night. Madison's first lesson in teaching Harriet how to laugh at herself. Harriet's first lesson in teaching Madison that no one laughed at Harriet, especially not herself. While the idea might be profound, Madison's sense of timing, quite frankly, bit the big one. Like Daddy Bear, Laurence had the urge to rush to her rescue. She wouldn't appreciate it, especially when she was playing Miss Fix-it with Harriet's psyche. Instead he leaned against the wall, folded his arms over his chest and eavesdropped some more.

Harriet must have shot her straight through the heart with one of those famous Harriet scowls because Madison pushed on, trying a different tack this time. "You know, Harriet, I really admire the way you handle coming to work even after bringing the suit against us."

"You admire me? And what did you expect? That I'd slink home with my tail between my legs like a dog?"

Madison tried a recovery. "No, but it takes a big person—I mean a *strong* person to—"

"Nice Freudian slip, Madison." If Harriet had had a knife in her hand, the floor would be awash in blood.

Harriet *didn't* have a knife. Did she?

"I didn't mean it like that." Madison was failing fast.

"Next you'll be saying how you admire the fact that I'm back after that little oink-oink episode yesterday."

"Well, actually I—"

"Don't you worry, because I'm writing down every little remark, every bit of nasty talk I hear. And you'll all be sorry."

Steam began to percolate from his ears. Enough was enough. Even Madison couldn't expect him to let her handle this on her own. Laurence showed himself in the doorway. Wide-eyed, desperate and speechless, Madison's gaze leaped to his. *Stand back, ladies and gentlemen, let the boss handle this.*

Madison had a way of making a man feel ten feet tall, while Harriet merely cut everyone down to size.

"Don't threaten, Harriet. It won't help your suit."

"Coming to her rescue like always, aren't you, T. Larry?"

Harriet's vitriol shoved Laurence back a full step. Her face throbbed with the color of beets. A furious shade of red tinged the whites of her eyes. Her lips turned blue as if she'd failed to take a breath between any of her sentences. In short, she looked ready to rupture. What had they done to her without thinking? Sympathy grew inside him like a germ. The germ sprouted guilt. They'd all had a hand, himself included, in creating this Harriet.

But Harriet had no right to heap the punishment on Madison, the only guiltless one in the office bunch.

"I expect civility from you, Harriet, no matter what your personal problems are."

"Personal problems?"

He cut her off with a look, a hand gesture and a step forward. "If you need to vent your feelings, I expect it to be done in my office behind my closed door. You can say anything you want in there, but out here, you treat everyone with respect. Understood?"

Her mouth worked. Clearly, she didn't have the faintest desire to give in. But something, whether it was his authority or the preservation of her suit, forced the spiteful words back down her throat.

Her heels pounded the linoleum. Laurence wondered idly if she would have pushed him had he gotten in her way?

Things were deteriorating rapidly at Carp, Alta and Hobbs.

"SHE ROASTED ME, BeeBee. It was horrible. But T. Larry was magnificent." Madison closed her eyes and relished a deep satisfied breath, only to break out in a hacking cough when the caustic fumes of BeeBee's dye hit her nostrils.

Her mascara dripped, and her nose watered. T. Larry's bathroom during the lunch hour probably wasn't the best place in the world to spread a load of toxic chemicals on her hair. His desk chair had barely fit through the door, the tile crunching ominously beneath the casters. But the bathroom had water and a sink, a mirror for Madison to watch the procedure and a counter for BeeBee's dyes, foils, combs, scissors and clips. Madison only prayed BeeBee wouldn't drop any of the goop on T. Larry's leather chair.

BeeBee took the clip from her mouth to pin another bit of tinfoil in place against Madison's scalp. "Definitely an Uzi-in-the-workplace type of gal. I'd watch out if I were you."

"Going postal is a male-dominated act of aggression."

"There's always a first time." BeeBee stroked a goo-tipped brush across another lock.

"Well, I'm not giving up. T. Larry says maybe in addition to learning to laugh at herself, she needs to learn how to build people up rather than strip them down."

"Sounds like something her mother should have taught her," BeeBee muttered, her teeth clenched on another clip.

Her chin barely topping Madison's head, she went on tiptoe to pat the foils in place. Two white stripes flashed from her temples through her short, black hair like wings. Cat's-eye reading glasses—which she wore more for effect than use—slipped down her nose. Madison wasn't at all sure that the speckles on the fuchsia frames didn't come from all the goo BeeBee applied rather than by design.

"What time did you say T. Larry's coming back?"

Madison waved a negligent hand from beneath the black poncho BeeBee had brought to protect her clothes. "At least not until two o'clock. Davis—

"I know. Davis Dullard *always* keeps him out an hour longer. I still think we lost valuable time eating the mu shu first."

"But you were hungry." Madison coughed again, the small bathroom having failed to provide adequate ventilation. Hopefully the smell would be gone by the time T. Larry got back.

BeeBee pushed her hair back with a bent wrist, her hands covered with latex gloves and the strange orange goop. "Have you noticed how changing the inflection on a word changes the meaning of the whole sentence?"

"Huh?" Madison answered.

"Well, if it's Davis *always* keeps him out an hour longer, then we're safe because he'll be gone another forty-five minutes."

"It's *always*."

"But," BeeBee went on as if Madison hadn't replied, "if it's Davis always keeps him out an *hour* longer, it almost becomes a question, like are you sure it's an hour, Madison?"

"Of course, it's an hour." It was always an hour, it really was. "How long before we're done?"

BeeBee clucked and lifted and eyed. "Oh, forty-three minutes, I'd say."

"You're trying to scare me." Not that T. Larry would care. He never cared about anything she did as long as her work was accurate and finished on time. He hadn't even cared that her closet had been bare of skirts longer than twenty inches when she'd promised to go shopping this weekend.

"Phase one complete." BeeBee smiled, patted the layers of foil, then bent down to lay her cheek against Madison's. "You look like *My Favorite Martian*."

"BeeBee," Madison warned. "How long is this really going to take?" Honest Injun, it wasn't that she cared if T. Larry found her in his office having her hair done. It was more that she cared about him seeing her with fifty pounds of foil on her head.

"Well, since I don't have a dryer, it'll take a little

longer than normal. Because we don't want to turn it orange, you know."

"You didn't bring a hair dryer?"

BeeBee shrugged. "I forgot it."

"My hair takes forever to dry."

"Yes," BeeBee agreed despite the melodramatic exaggeration, then snapped off her gloves to inspect her nails. She'd painted them red, white and blue in honor of the fourth of July, though Madison wasn't sure they'd make it even two weeks with all the chemicals BeeBee loved.

"So how am I going to be finished in forty-five minutes?"

"I might have a little something up my sleeve. If…" BeeBee fluffed her dark locks in the mirror.

"If what?"

"If you introduce me to T. Larry."

Madison thought she detected an avid gleam in BeeBee's unmarried eyes. "Why?" she asked, just to be sure.

"You always talk about him."

"I do not."

"Yes, you do. And—" she tapped her cat's-eye glasses "—curiosity killed the cat."

"He probably won't be back in time."

BeeBee flicked through the settling foils on Madison's head. "Davis *always* keeps him out an hour longer?"

"I sniff a blackmail here."

"Come on, let me meet him, and I'll make sure he doesn't find a single foil wrapper in his trash can. He sounds like a paragon."

T. Larry? A paragon? Interest—could it be prurient?—bathed BeeBee's porcelain skin.

BeeBee was five years older than Madison, bore the proportions of Marilyn Monroe minus a few inches in height, enjoyed a fantastically interesting career and she could do T. Larry's hair for free. Oops. T. Larry didn't have much hair to do. There were other compensations. BeeBee loved finance.

They'd hit it off tremendously. Madison felt a little sick.

Then she looked at her head covered in foil and knew she didn't have a choice. "All right. You can meet him. If you get me out of this foil, shampooed and dry by five minutes to two."

"Deal."

The locked office doorknob wiggled.

Madison froze with a round O pursing her lips.

"Who locked my door?"

Oh my God. T. Larry's muffled, irritated voice.

The office reeked of color solution, blobs of dye dotted the tile countertop of his bathroom, Madison's head looked like something out of a fifties monster B-movie—her black mascara had smudged beneath her eyes, and her lips were bare of lipstick or gloss.

The faint tinkle of keys slipped beneath the half-inch gap at the bottom of the door. The knob rattled. BeeBee frantically scooped the tricks of her trade into her immense plastic carryall.

The door opened. Madison swiveled in the leather office chair. T. Larry advanced three giant steps and stopped.

Resplendent in a gray three-piece suit, white shirt and silver-and-blue tie, he stood stock-still and rigid for a full ten seconds. Madison's heart went into atrial fibrillation.

Light reflected off the lenses of his wire-rimmed glasses. "What's on your head?"

"Tinfoil." Miraculously, not a tremor marred Madison's voice.

He used another three seconds to assimilate that. "Why?"

"My hair—" she started.

BeeBee finished. "Madison's been receiving radio signals from outer space through her fillings. The tinfoil keeps them out."

He ran his tongue over his teeth beneath closed lips, then said, "Oh."

After another moment, he turned on his heel and left, closing the door behind him.

BeeBee rested her hand on Madison's shoulder as they stared at the closed door. "He's gorgeous," she murmured on little more than a breath.

"But he has no hair."

"I know. I'm thinking *The King and I, Kojak.*"

"Skinner on the *X-Files.*"

"Jesse 'The Body' Ventura."

Madison put her hands to her flaming cheeks. "Oh, I love the ex-gov."

"Mr. T without the Mohawk."

Madison gasped. "Oh my God, I never thought of him." Mr. T Larry. Perfect, so absolutely perfect.

"Does he have a hairy tangum?"

"A hairy *what?*"

"Tangum. You know the part of the ear right here in front. Some men get this horrible tuft of hair growing there."

God, it had sounded like something too, too private. "No. His ears don't stick out, either."

"Thank God. Do you think he'll fire you?"

"He looked too confused to consider termination. Maybe later."

BeeBee bent over her head to fumble with various bits of foil. "Uh-oh."

Adrenaline shot through her blood. "What?"

"Nothing, nothing."

"What's wrong, BeeBee?" She couldn't eradicate a plaintive note from her voice.

"Pumpkin is such a lovely shade next to your natural red."

She grabbed BeeBee's hand and shook with all her might. "Tell me you're fooling."

The speckles on the cat's-eyes sparkled. "I'm fooling. But you're not cooked yet. Red's the hardest color to get in, and it's also the hardest color to get out. A few more minutes."

Madison sighed her relief. "Remind me to never try slipping in a quick highlight at work again."

Thirty minutes later, she was foil free, golden, not pumpkin, shampooed, cut, hair dried by the dryer BeeBee just happened to "discover" at the bottom of her bag and out from beneath the humid black poncho. T. Larry had not reappeared. Maybe terror had rendered him incapable of movement.

"I don't suppose this is the best time for an introduction." BeeBee stuffed the last of her kit-n-caboodle into her bag.

"I think we should forget the whole introduction thing period."

BeeBee eyed her in the mirror. "Why?"

"Why is everyone asking me *why?*"

"You okay?" BeeBee removed her camouflaging glasses.

She wasn't sure. T. Larry catching her with foil in her hair? The thought of him having a cozy tête-à-tête with BeeBee? "Do you think Richard will like my hair?"

BeeBee stood beside her, patting a **stray** lock in place, her eyes on Madison's in the mirror. "He's going to love it."

But how much did she really care anymore?

DAVIS DILLARD always enjoyed a long lunch. Laurence had always let him. Until today. He'd rushed the man, answered his questions at the speed of light and signaled the waiter for the check before Davis had even finished his bread pudding.

And why? Because he'd had some antiquated notion of racing back to the office to protect Madison from any more attacks by Harriet the fire-breathing Harridan.

Instead he'd found her capped in foil, getting her hair highlighted, and God knew what else. On a Wednesday. A workday. Not even Madison had done something like this before. There was only one explanation. She was primping for Dick the Prick.

Nor was she done yet. He'd gone to the men's room. He'd prowled the maze of cubicles to catch any slackers. He hadn't discovered any, not in his well-run firm. He'd made coffee with Madison's special blend. Standing alone in the copy room, Florsheims tapping impatiently on the linoleum, he'd drunk two cups.

Still Madison wasn't done. He wanted to strangle her.

Next to the copy room, his office door opened. A girlish giggle, a murmured shush, footsteps receding on the carpet, then the snick of a door closing again.

Madison wasn't at her desk. His office door was closed. Laurence's ire boiled over. He burst into his office—*his* office, mind you—slammed the door behind him and locked it. He took his suit jacket off, fitted it over the hanger on the coatrack, then mentally rolled up his sleeves.

"Madison, we're going to have this out right now."

Mascara wand in hand, she leaned over the bathroom counter. "Can I fix my makeup first?"

Her breasts strained against the tight summer-weight sweater. The pleated skirt he'd admired outlined her bottom. Her hair glowed like golden fire in the vanity lamps framing the mirror.

"No. We'll talk *now*."

She eyed him in the mirror as he came within a foot of her. Her sweet scent took the bite out of the lingering chemical odor. "All right. Then I'll just finish while you're yelling at me."

Without conscious action, his fists flexed at his sides.

She touched the wand to first one set of luxurious lashes, then the other. "Actually, before you start yelling, I have to apologize. It was an incredibly stupid idea to have BeeBee highlight my hair today. I don't know what came over me."

Impressing Dick the Prick came over her. Through his eyes, a tinge of red haloed her face. The small rational part of his mind left realized he'd never been this angry with her before. He'd never been this angry, *ever.*

She put down her mascara, fumbled with a tube of

some female gunk, then looked at him. "By the way, what did you think of BeeBee?"

His lip twitched into a snarl, one he manfully regained control of. "Nothing. I didn't think a damn thing." She was *not* setting him up with anyone.

Unscrewing the cap, she pulled out the long stick of gloss and held it close to her mouth. "Is that a good or a bad thing?"

Eyes on the wand so close to her lips, his own barely moved. "She's looks like the Bride of Frankenstein."

"That's just bleach. It'll grow out." She turned her eyes back to her reflection and waved the wand across her lower lip.

"What's that?"

"Lip gloss," she answered before sliding it over her upper lip.

All he could see was the wet stuff glistening on her full mouth. "Why not lipstick?"

She shrugged, rolled her lips together, then puckered. "I don't know."

He knew. Dick the Prick. No lipstick to smear when she kissed him.

His hand reached out. He found himself grabbing the gloss tube from her fingers and tossing it on the counter where it rolled and clattered to the floor between them.

"Stop that goddamn primping."

"T. Larry." Her green eyes widened, and her mouth puckered, almost in invitation.

"I am not interested in your friend BeeBee."

"But—"

"And you are not seeing Dick tonight."

"His name is Richard."

"And you sure as hell are not kissing him."

Then he grabbed her arm, dragged her to his leather sofa, pulled her down on top of him and cut off any further protests with his mouth.

CHAPTER TWELVE

T. LARRY'S ARMS surrounded Madison, crushing the air from her lungs. Trapped by him on his couch, she opened her mouth to breathe, and he took control of that, too.

She forgot all about falling in love with Richard. T. Larry needed her. It was there in the way his tongue swooped in, the hot taste of him, the flex of his hands against her sweater as he gentled his hold.

He didn't kiss like a T. Larry. He kissed like a T. Rex—hungry, dangerous, territorial. Madison responded to the need, the anger and the passion she'd never dreamed T. Larry capable of.

Her hands smoothed from his arms to his shoulders to his neck. The rigidity of his muscles eased, but not the hardness. The faint scent of the mothballs his suit had been packed in tickled her nose. Leather squeaked beneath their bodies as she lay across his lap.

Wrapping her arms around his neck, Madison blossomed. Angling her head to receive him better, she moaned softly. He backed off to taste her lips with his tongue, moving one hand to the side of her breast while the other held her pressed to him. His thumb caressed subtly.

She wanted more, stroking his tongue with hers in imitation of the way she wanted him to stroke her breasts.

His lips slipped from hers, his gray eyes smoky. Yanking his glasses off, he tossed them onto the table. Madison prayed he wouldn't say a word. If he did, she might ask him to stop. She might start to think, and the bells would never ring if she was thinking.

His gray eyes were flecked with green and gold, his lashes longer than she'd ever noticed. He met her gaze with a question, brushing the hair back from her face with a soft caress. Madison covered his hand with hers and placed his palm over her breast. If he never touched her again, she still wanted his touch now.

With trembling fingers, he undid the first button of her sweater. Eyes still on her, roving from her hair to her cheeks to her lips, he popped three more. Then his gaze dropped to the swell of her breasts above the lace of her black bra. His swallow was audible, sending a thousand sparks shooting over her skin.

His fingers trailed the lace, barely slipping beneath. Her breath caught in her chest. Fire blazed through her. Her nipples hardened, catching his attention. He rubbed the flat of his hand over first one, then the other. Her head fell back across his arm. She closed her eyes and swallowed to wet her throat.

God, this was T. Larry. T. Larry dipping into the lace, pushing it aside, palming her, breath puffing in time with hers. Oh God, T. Larry, plumping her breast, then bending to take her in his mouth, sucking her nipple until a spot between her legs ached. He nipped. Her hand flew to the back of his head, holding him tight against her. He shifted, letting her slip farther over his arm so that he could tongue her other nipple. Her legs twisted restlessly. She kicked off one shoe, then the other. They landed with a soft thud against the carpet.

The scent of his aftershave edged with the rich aroma of fresh coffee beans swirled around her. He planted kisses along her collarbone, tracing it with his tongue. One hand drifted down her side, caressed her hip, cupped her bottom, then pulled at the hem of her skirt. He found her thigh, his hand slid up, then down, and finally to the top of her stockings.

Mouth buried against her neck, warm breath heating the flesh of her throat, he murmured, "What are you wearing?"

"Stockings and a garter belt."

He stilled. "Did you wear them for him?"

There was only T. Larry at this moment, T. Larry's hands, T. Larry's mouth and T. Larry's hardness beneath her hip. "Who?"

He struggled with a breath, then answered, "Richard."

"I wore them for me." To make herself feel sexy. Because Richard's gaze didn't do that for her.

But oh my God, T. Larry's did. Sinfully sexy. Terrifying. Impossible. Delicious. "Don't stop."

His fingers moved, tested the clip holding the stockings, then found her bare, burning skin. He stroked, easing his thumb closer to the juncture, slid back, teased. Then he found the elastic of her thong panties, followed the length of it to the top of her hip and groaned for the first time. He leaned his forehead against hers and gulped air.

Madison tightened her arm at his neck. She couldn't ask for what she wanted, not from T. Larry. Because there was tomorrow. And the day after. And the day after that. Body on fire, knees weak, breath puffing, the sensations could be fear as much as anything else. If only there were bells ringing somewhere.

In the space of a heartbeat, T. Larry made the decision for her. Cupping her with his hand, then slipping a finger beneath the edge of her panties, he stroked the curls.

Oh. Oh. Her thighs parted. His fingers slid into her cleft, across her clitoris. She moaned. He stroked back the other way, carrying her own wetness over her. Her fingers dug into his shoulder, his neck. Then he went deep inside with two fingers, his thumb nestled against her, rubbing. Oh, please. She wanted to beg with her mouth as her hips began to move in time with his caresses.

Eyes squeezed tight, stars shot through the darkness behind her lids. All that existed in the world was the glide of his fingers against her, back and forth, around, driving her crazy, burning her up. He whispered against her throat, her ear: temptation, encouragement, need, appeal.

He wanted it. She couldn't stop it. Oh my goodness dear God, T. Larry was making her—

The stars exploded into fireworks. She shook and clung, started to cry out only to find his lips on hers, his taste filling her mouth, his hand tireless, ceaseless, taking her to the last tremor, the last lightning bolt, the last frontier.

She came down to earth to discover herself snuggled against his chest, skirt smoothed, sweater buttoned, hair tamed, and his warm male scent in her nose as heady as the touch of his hands and the taste of his tongue.

Were exploding stars just as good as ringing bells? Yes, my stars, they were. Even better.

"What about you?" She didn't open her eyes to look at him.

"What about me?"

"I…" She cleared her throat, tried again. "I…you know."

"You came."

"Umm…yes. And you…well…"

"I didn't come."

"Uh…right."

ACTUALLY, HOLDING MADISON while she bucked against him, feeling her detonate in his arms with just a touch, Laurence had almost embarrassed himself. "This wasn't about me."

"What was it about?" Her soft murmur caressed his chest.

He massaged her back, fingers flexing lightly. "I don't know." He couldn't remember. He'd been angry, jealous, then out of control, trying to prove something to her.

After that, there'd only been the feel of her skin, the taste of her breasts and the headiness of her desire. His desire.

"T. Larry, we're in your office."

On his leather sofa, arms tangled, and her shoes on the floor. "The door's locked."

She sat up suddenly, levered herself with one hand on his chest, the other on the arm of the couch. "When did you lock it?"

"When I came in."

"You mean, you intended to…do what you did?"

His gaze skipped from her naked lips, red and plump from his kisses, to her troubled eyes and her magnificent fire-lit hair. Then he looked at the corner of his office where the molding met. "I intended to tell you…"

What? That she had to stop seeing Richard? That she had to start seeing *him*, really seeing him, T. Laurence Hobbs, not as an accountant, not as her boss, not as someone she went on "outings" with, but as a man. Just a man. One who wanted her.

She'd shell-shocked him instead. He didn't even know how to distinguish between the morass of emotions coagulating his blood, infesting his organs and dizzying his mind.

She tugged on the knot of his tie. When he looked down, he couldn't believe the material of his vest appeared untouched and his shirtsleeves unwrinkled.

He couldn't say as much for his control, or even his heart.

When he still didn't speak, she rolled from his lap, reached down to slip on her shoes and stood.

There, he could identify an emotion. Bereft at the loss of her warmth.

Without his glasses, her features blurred, and he couldn't read her eyes at all. But Laurence didn't put on his glasses.

She glanced out the window, her head tilted to the side. "I don't suppose it matters that someone might have seen us."

Hopefully no one else was wearing their glasses, either. The thought had never even crossed his mind. More aptly, his mind hadn't been capable of thought. Now, he simply didn't care.

"We just broke your rule number five. No sex in the office."

Actually, it had been rule number one before she'd changed the order of things. "That wasn't sex, Madison."

She waved a hand in the air, whether with agitation

or carelessness, he couldn't tell. "Right. I forgot. It's not sex if there's no genital to genital contact."

He winced. That was *not* what he'd meant.

She inched closer, tipping her head to look down at him. "I'm not mad at you, T. Larry."

The words had been mad, but the tone something indefinable. "You should be. My carelessness is unforgivable."

She closed the remaining distance between them, until he could see her face clearly.

"Well, I'm not mad or sorry." Her eyes glowed that special brilliant emerald. "No one's ever made me feel what you made me feel."

His right ventricle burst.

"It was kind of scary. A good scary." She bit her lip. "And I liked it. A lot. I liked especially that you didn't make me do anything for it. Like it was a gift just for me."

His left ventricle went the way of the first, and he was surprised to find he still had a pulse beating at his temple. "Make you do what?"

Her smile grew on the lopsided half. "You know…the same thing…" She spread her fingers. "Or something else."

He knew exactly. Her hands. Her mouth. Even the whole nine yards. He was still hard. She'd just made him harder.

"I'd better unlock the door before anyone realizes it's locked." Then she leaned down, one knee on the sofa beside his leg, and kissed him with lips and tongue. "Thank you, T. Larry."

Jesus H. Christ.

Heart thudding, he watched her sashay to the

bathroom, gather her makeup and stuff it all in a min-iscule case. When she left, she closed the door behind her. He stayed on the couch, not reaching for his glasses, not moving a muscle, just feeling, enjoying the weight in his groin and the lightness in his head.

MADISON MADE the decision somewhere between the dazed look on T. Larry's face and the door. She wasn't a virgin, but she wasn't loose, either. After what she'd let T. Larry do, she couldn't, in all conscience, go off with Richard as if nothing had happened.

She could have called him, but she wasn't a Dear Richard kind of girl. She let a man down face-to-face. He deserved that, at least. She'd meet him tonight as she'd said, but she'd tell him before the surprise he'd promised her.

She wasn't dazed like T. Larry. In fact, she saw more clearly than she ever had.

Jeremiah Carp commented on the smile she wore. "You look like a contented pussycat."

She surely did.

Anthony and Mike for once not in tow, Bill offered to buy her a triple white chocolate mocha from the espresso bar in the building's lobby. "You need some-thing to slow you down."

Rhonda asked if she'd overdosed on happy pills.

Overdosed? Oh no, she hadn't gotten anywhere near enough of T. Larry. Waiting for the clock to hit five, she typed three memos, two lengthy letters, answered fifteen e-mails and watched T. Larry open his door twice. He looked at her, glasses now firmly set on his nose, shook his head, then went back inside.

Madison smiled. T. Larry, her Frog Prince. She'd

kissed him, and before her eyes, he'd changed into a prince. A perfect candidate for The One. He turned her insides squishy. He made her tingle. And she couldn't forget the exploding stars.

T. Larry was the best choice. He'd rebound nicely when it was all over—*however* it ended. He'd return to his Financial Plan and his Family Plan, create a Madison-is-gone Plan, and he'd be fine. What a load off her mind. She'd worried about the mental fortitude of her prince once she…passed on.

Three…two…one. Five o'clock. T. Larry didn't pop his head out to mentally punch her time clock the way he usually did. Still stunned, she assumed. Or he'd looked out his window and realized they'd been on display like Fourth of July fireworks.

Actually, *she'd* been the one displayed. It had been worth every second. Not that she intended to keep exposing herself. There were T. Larry's rules, after all. T. Rex. Mr. T. She smiled, gathered her purse, forewent the makeup check and stepped into the lobby five minutes later.

She paused a moment to admire the view. Eager beaver Richard waited by the espresso bar, which was doing as brisk a business in the late afternoon as it did in the morning. Hand in his pocket, jacket pushed aside to reveal a crisp white shirt and fashionable suspenders, Richard nursed a coffee and surveyed the throng buzzing about the faux marble floor. His head slightly down, a lock of dark hair fell agreeably across his forehead.

He watched shoes, women's high-heeled shoes especially, his gaze following the wearer, ear tilted slightly to the tap-tap on the tile. When the door revolved them out, he found another. Watch-watch, tap-tap.

He turned at the sound of her heels on marble and said her name before his eyes rose the length of her body to her face.

"You're early," he said, face bland, eyes remote. Did he know what she was going to tell him? Then the look vanished, replaced with an expectant gleam. He switched his coffee from his left to his right and held out his hand. She took it, finding his skin still warm from the cup.

"You had your hair done."

"Yes." She didn't ask if he liked it.

He complimented her anyway. "It's gorgeous."

"Thank you." She was starting to feel lower than low.

"Ready for your surprise?"

Was he ready for hers? She didn't know how to bring it up.

Richard didn't let go of her hand as he threw his coffee away and tucked her hand through his arm.

"You didn't have to toss it. I'd have waited for you to finish."

"I was done."

He'd been drinking a large, which meant he'd been waiting longer than five minutes. Her heart sank at his enthusiasm. He didn't have any idea. She hated hurting people. She hated scenes. Maybe there was a little white lie she could tell that would save them both. She had pancreatic cancer with less than a month to live. Sort of close to the truth.

No, she had to be honest. Well, honest while preserving his feelings as best she could.

He dragged her into the revolving door. She stepped on his heel, tripped, but picked herself up before the door mowed her down. When they exited onto the sidewalk, her breath came in little pants.

"You okay, Madison?"

"I'm fine." She put her sunglasses on against the glare of the overcast sky. *Tell him.* The right words just wouldn't come. She opted for buttering him up first. "Richard, I really can't let you go to such an expense like you did with your last wonderful surprise."

Her heels click-clacked as he pulled her along. "Is this some feminist thing?"

"No." It was the lower-than-dirt-because-I'm-dumping-you thing. "I like my doors opened for me. I like flowers on my desk. I like four-inch spiked pumps, too." She paused for a breath and a reaction, then rushed on. "But sometimes I like to treat a man the way he deserves to be treated."

Richard stopped smack-dab in the middle of the sidewalk, grumpy businesspeople buffeting Madison from left to right. "That's the nicest thing anyone's ever said to me."

About the shoes or the treat? Richard hadn't specified. She patted his cheek. "You're a nice man."

His face beamed. A golden flame danced in each of his beautiful browns. He squeezed her hand. And she couldn't wait, not another minute. It was too cruel.

"Richard, we have to talk." She tugged him through the danger zone of rushing commuters into a sheltered doorway.

A flicker of fear doused the flames in his eyes. "About what?"

She clutched his hand in hers. Be firm, be straight, be unequivocal. "I can't see you anymore."

A taxi driver laid on his horn and shook his fist in the air, screaming obscenities no one bothered to listen to.

Richard leaned closer. "What? I didn't hear you."

She sucked in a breath carrying his very ordinary scent, which was nothing like T. Larry's musky, heady, mesmerizing aroma. "I said I can't see you anymore."

He stiffened, squeezed her fingers almost painfully and pinned his very puppylike eyes on her. "Why?"

Time for the little white lie. She didn't go for the cancer thing. "Remember when I called you Matthew on the phone."

"No."

Shoot. She'd been going for the least amount of explanation. "He was the guy I used to date?"

His head tilted like that selfsame puppy. "Yeah?"

"I realized I'm not over him." She bit her lip and decided to lay it on a little thicker for the sake of Richard's feelings. "If only I'd met you first..." She cut herself off almost wistfully. "But I didn't."

He stared at her a moment, something brimming in the depths of his gaze. "It's your boss, isn't it?"

Busted. "Of course not."

He dropped her hand to grip her shoulders. "I can take care of you better than he can. I know I can if you'll let me."

"I don't need to be taken care of, Richard."

"But I can be there for you, Madison, whenever you need me. I can massage your feet when you're tired. I can cook for you. I'm a great cook, did I tell you that? I can clean house and I do yard work. I even retiled my own bathroom."

"I'm not looking for a maid or a handyman, Richard."

"Please."

She almost broke down, he looked so desperate, so lost.

But T. Larry had touched her, and when he did, he seemed to touch far more than her body. She needed to know why, what it meant, what *he* meant. And how she felt about it. She sacrificed Richard to her need to know.

"I can't."

His fingers flexed, tightened, then he whispered, "Madison."

"I'm sorry."

His Adam's apple shot up and down. His lips thinned to a white line, and his eyes glossed. Then he let go. The sound of street traffic, voices and the steady cascade of feet against concrete separated them. "If it doesn't work out, call me."

"Thank you." She wouldn't. For a lot of reasons, the least of which was fairness.

He took three steps back, pushing against the stream of passers-by. They flowed around him, grabbed him and dragged him away in their midst.

Gee, that hadn't felt good. In fact, it felt kind of crappy. Tears pricked her eyes. While she wouldn't take back what she'd done, not any of it from the moment Richard called, she wished she could recall the hurt. She even wished she could erase that dazed look from T. Larry's face.

He would still be up there, still secreted in his office. She wanted to run back up there, tell him what she'd done and ask him to hold her.

What kept her from doing it was the fear he'd tell her he'd changed his mind.

This afternoon's elation died a nasty death in the fading light. Harriet had ripped her to pieces with her knife-sharp words. While her own instrument of de-struction had been blunt, Madison had nevertheless dealt Richard's heart a blow. And T. Larry? He hadn't popped his head out of his office to say good-night. It *sounded* silly to be bothered by the omission, but this was T. Larry, creature of habit. She knew, just *knew,* if she went to him now, he'd tell her he'd made a big mistake.

She melted back into the tide of walking traffic, her heels tap-tap-tapping on the concrete as she returned to her car in the garage to head home.

LAURENCE IMAGINED Madison down there on the street, one of the dots, scurrying to meet her Richard. He hadn't asked her not to, after that first outburst which really didn't count. She hadn't offered not to, even the two times he'd opened his door and stood waiting for her to state her intentions.

Dusk was falling, muted oranges and reds streaking across the sky above the building opposite. Lights now on in many of the offices clearly delineated tables, computers, chairs, people, even individual books on shelves, though certainly not their titles.

He'd exposed Madison to that, prying eyes, a voyeuristic populace. True, he'd turned his lights off when he'd left for lunch, and Madison hadn't turned them back on except in the bathroom where BeeBee had done her hair. Visibility in the other offices had grown exponentially only with the waning sun in the over three hours he'd been staring at them through his window.

It didn't matter. He'd lost control. He'd taken advantage of her. He hadn't thought. He'd only wanted. That wasn't like him.

Until Madison.

He was in over his head.

He'd lost sight of the goal, couldn't remember what it had been in the first place. He still trembled with the memory of her going off in his arms. More, he wanted more. Where would it end?

She didn't want love, she wanted fantasy. She didn't want a man, she wanted an emotion, an illusion, a delusion. She thought of the moment, not the future. She was like a tornado he couldn't avert. She'd pick him up in her whirlwind, toss him around, then spit him out like a broken bit of furniture.

What he'd thought was a mere case of Secretary Lust was turning out to be life-threatening.

Laurence had fallen in love.

CHAPTER THIRTEEN

HARRIET SORTED her basket of laundry into two piles, one light, one dark. She'd survived another day in that hellhole. Harry Dump had called to say in his over-exerted voice that he was enthusiastic about the results of the case. When she'd pressed him for those results, he'd tsk-tsked and said he wanted all his ducks in a row before he shot them.

The muted scents of fresh detergent and dryer sheets tickled her nose. She usually did her laundry on Friday and Saturday nights when the machines were the least in demand. Still, it was Wednesday dinnertime for most, and she was quite happily alone in the laundry room. Pumping in quarters, she poured liquid soap, let the water run three inches deep, then loaded her whites.

Harriet was proud of herself. She'd done her work. She'd taken the stares, the whispers and the muffled laughter with little more emotion than she would an IRS seminar on 1031 exchanges. She'd made herself a fluffy omelet with red peppers, diced tomato and spinach. She'd savored it, every bite, every swallow.

Perhaps her mellow mood stemmed from her ability to make Madison cry. The girl had closeted herself in T. Larry's office during lunch. When he'd arrived back, he'd sequestered himself in there with her. Hand raised ready to knock, Harriet was sure she heard Madison crying on the other side of the door.

Harriet knew she shouldn't feel happy about it. It was a low-down, dirty rotten thing to feel. She smiled to herself anyway as the bubbles in the washer rose to the top and she closed the lid, the swish-swish of the agitator soothing. Madison's tears afforded her a small measure of vindication. The girl had given her an apology, Harriet had given her tears.

Harriet didn't like to give in easily. She was used to fighting. But maybe Madison's misery could be enough to appease her. Maybe it was time to forgive and forget.

Footsteps sounded on the linoleum along the hall outside. Quiet time was over. Putting the pile of darks in her basket, she hefted it to her hip.

Zachary appeared in the door as if her thoughts had conjured him. His appearance wasn't unexpected. T. Larry was bound to send him on another mission. "Harriet, we're going to talk whether you like it or not."

Such a commanding tone. His suit jacket lay open, the knot of his tie loosened. Her pulse tripped over itself. "How did you know I was down here?"

"Your neighbor came out when I was banging on your door."

Mrs. Murphy had smiled at her in the hall on her way down. "You'll get me evicted if you keep bothering me like this."

But he was here, for the third time in less than a week, with or without T. Larry's intervention. That fact sang through her heart. Madison. And now this.

"Hear me out. Then I'll go away."

She didn't like that, the going away part. For a

moment, she'd hoped…but he was simply here for another bribe or a threat. "Tell it to my lawyer."

She tried to push past. He blocked her. "I'll say it to *you.*"

She dropped her basket and childishly stuck her fingers in her ears.

"Stop it."

She started humming. His mouth moved. She missed the words. Then he shouted. Switching to a cadence of la-la-la, she closed her eyes. Then, in her chest, she felt the slam of the door. His hands clapped over hers and pulled them from her ears.

"Damn, Harriet, I'm tired of this. You will listen to me."

The domination in his voice sent a thrill through her. "Nothing you say will change a thing." Unless it was what she wanted him to say.

"I didn't tell anyone about what happened that night because it was too special to let them—"

She cut him off, couldn't bear to hear him say what he'd been afraid of, easier to say it all herself. "To what? To let them make fun of you? You could have just told them to go fuck themselves. Or maybe it was just me you fucked."

He shook her by the shoulders. "I did not fuck you."

She wanted to curl up in the corner and die, wished to God she'd never brought the damn suit because she couldn't go through this again. Her mouth wouldn't shut up. "Then what did you do?"

"I made love to you."

She rolled her eyes, part sarcasm, part desperate attempt to stem the tears. "Oh right, that's why you never asked me out, why you didn't tell anyone, and why you didn't try to do it again. Because we made love." She twisted the words with her voice.

"I tried, Harriet. I took you out to lunch, I—"

"Those were work lunches, not dates."

"I asked you to the Christmas party."

"You offered to drive me along with Madison and Rhonda."

His jaw worked. "I didn't tell anyone about what happened that night because it wasn't any of their business."

That was as bad as his other reasons. "You were ashamed."

He stopped, cocked his head, then looked deep, deeper than she thought he ever could. "I'm tired of shouldering all the blame. It wasn't my shame, Harriet, it was yours."

"Don't be stupid."

"It was yours, Harriet. Remember what you called me? A gutless, pathetic wonder. You didn't want them all to think you had to scrape the bottom of the barrel to get laid."

His words squeezed her chest. "That's not true. I only called you that because I was mad."

"So you never said I was the runt of the litter in the office?"

"Of course not."

"Then why did Rhonda tell me you said it to her?"

That big mouth. "That was before I got to know you."

He didn't seem to care. "I have no guts, no backbone, I'm a nothing who'll always be a nothing, isn't that what you said?"

"I told her all that before I knew you better."

"But it's still why *you* didn't want anyone to know."

She put her hands to his chest and pushed. He didn't budge. "If that were true, why would I use a lawsuit to tell them what we did?"

"You tell me, Harriet. Maybe you're getting lonely. Maybe you're starting to think the bottom of the barrel isn't so bad."

"You don't know what you're talking about. You don't know what I'm feeling." Confused and scared. "Get out of here before I call the cops."

"You want to get laid, Harriet, I'll lay you. I'm a glutton for punishment. I thrive on it. Is that what you want, Harriet? I can come over here every night and fuck you senseless, and it can be our little secret. What do you say?"

She slapped him full across the face, the imprint of her hand turning his skin crimson. She wanted to cry. She wanted to deny. She could do neither. He might be right in everything he'd said.

He turned around and walked away from her.

ZACH STOPPED DRIVING when he reached the beach. The sidewalks teemed with flocks of teenagers, skateboarders, guitar players, dope smokers and beggars.

Threading through the crowd, he headed into the Boardwalk along the beach. The day had been hot with little humidity, a last lingering breath of still warm air forcing him to take his jacket off. He kept the sunglasses despite the fact that dark had fallen over an hour ago.

Zach liked the flashing lights of the Boardwalk, the grind of the roller coaster, its timbers creaking, the screaming and laughter, the scents of mustard, popcorn, chicken poppers, commingled with the salty aroma of the ocean. A child pulled cotton candy from a stick. His mouth watered. A couple of teens shared an ice-cream cone, licking and kissing each other clean like animals.

He hadn't wanted Harriet that way tonight, not with innocence or gentleness. He'd wanted to throw her on the washing machine.

It was the anger that made him feel this way. Just like his old man. His parents would have a whopper of a fight, then his mother would drag his father into the bedroom, slam the door, and...well, he'd always thought the screams were the sounds of her frustration and the banging was her throwing things at his father's head.

He was fifteen when he opened the door to see if she'd killed the old man. He didn't need sex education after that.

Christ. He didn't know what he needed now. He'd always known there were two sides to every story. The number of sides Harriet displayed boggled him. His own behavior frightened him. Even odds that he'd screw her on the washer or he wouldn't. For a moment there, fingers flexing, he almost had.

He didn't want nice, quiet and sweet like Madison. He didn't want perpetual laughter, spontaneous gaiety or eternal optimism.

He wanted war. A flashing firefight, an exhilarating, heart-pumping skirmish. He wanted it in Harriet's bed. On her washing machine. In her car.

But first he had to put a stop to the battle Harriet waged with Madison in any way he could.

"MA, DO YOU THINK I'm going to die like Daddy did?"

The question had always been an avoided topic. At

least since Madison decided that she might suffer her father's fate. She didn't like to upset Ma with the death-and-dying conversation, and she wouldn't if she hadn't started having all these scary, crappy feelings. First, Harriet, then Richard. Not to mention what she'd done in T. Larry's office. She suddenly felt so mixed up, even though what T. Larry had done was so very nice.

She didn't want him to be hurt. If something happened to her. If. When.

Her mother put another butter tart on Madison's plate, then poured two cups of tea. Finally, she said, "I pray every day that you won't die until I'm long gone. That's the way it should be."

"Is that why you go to church?"

"I go to church because I believe in God."

Madison loved the warmth and scents of her mother's kitchen at night, even on a warm June evening. The tart sweetened her mouth. The tea warmed her belly. There really was no place like home. Her mother had lived in the same house since the day she was married. The new couple had paid next to nothing for it in today's terms; it was now worth a fortune. Her mother would never sell. Every five years her brothers painted inside and out. They'd refinished the cabinets and retiled the bathrooms. They'd added the sunporch at the back, planted perennials and annuals, trimmed the bushes and topped the trees. It was everyone's home. None of them would ever truly leave.

"Do you believe you're going to die, Madison?"

Madison savored another bite in the same way she did everything, as if it were the last time. She knew her mother hated this kind of talk, and she hated to bring it up. Yet she didn't have anyone else she could turn to with this odd feeling bubbling up inside. "I don't feel like I'm going to go today."

"Then I hope you feel that way every day."

"But if I do die, you still promise to cremate me?"

"I rue the day your brothers started that worm thing." She hated the thought of worms eating her. "Promise?"

"I'll do whatever you ask."

"Thanks, Ma." Madison spooned a taste more sugar into her half-empty cup and stirred. "Do you think I'm selfish?"

They sipped their tea, took bites of the luscious tart, then her mother answered. "You're the most unselfish person I know."

Madison flexed her fingers, the bad hand tighter than normal as if all her tension and indecision resided in that side of her body. "I don't like to hurt people. Especially you."

Her mother patted her hand flat. "I know you don't. And I think you've done a super job so far."

Madison swallowed her last bite of tart, got to her feet and bent to her mother, cheek to cheek, hands on her shoulders. "Thanks, Ma. That's why I like coming here. You always tell me exactly what I want to hear. You'd tell me I was the kindest person you ever met while I was ripping the head off the neighbor's cat. I appreciate that kind of unconditional love."

Her mother held on to one of her hands when Madison would have straightened. "What's really bothering you, sweetheart?"

If she didn't die right after her twenty-eighth birthday, she'd have to live with the consequences of what she'd done today, both with Richard and T. Larry.

Whatever those consequences might be. She was terribly afraid the consequences wouldn't be to her liking.

"Nothing's wrong, Ma. It'll all work out. It always does." She'd lived by that philosophy since the day she came out of the coma after her stroke. No reason to doubt it now. Even if she'd never felt quite this confused. "I gotta run or I'll never be able to get up in the morning." She kissed her mom's cheek. "Thanks for the tea, tarts and talk."

"Say hello to that nice T. Larry for me," Ma called as Madison headed out the door.

Her mother always had to have the last word.

When she reached her apartment, she saw that her porch light had burned out, leaving her stairs and stoop in the dark. Digging in the special purse pocket for her keys, she came up empty-handed. With no light on the scene, she'd never find them in the hodge-podge filling her bag. Bending, she pulled the mat back. The extra key was gone. Darn that Sean. He'd probably left it on her coffee table with an admonishing note. Very T. Larryish. Her brother, all her brothers, in fact, had been cut from the same mold. It took five minutes of finger-searching to locate her regular set of keys.

Dumping her purse on the counter, she checked the garbage disposal first. On, off, water running. The device whirred with a beautiful high-pitched wail. She fed it a crusty old piece of bread she found hiding in the fridge. It took it like a dog devouring a bone. The bottle of champagne had miraculously disappeared, replaced by a smiley-face note. But no key.

Nor was the key on the coffee table. The miserable

cur threw out her rose. Darn. In all her gloom and life contemplation, she'd forgotten to thank her mother for yesterday's cleanup and the beautiful rosebuds.

Unfastening her sweater, she threw it across the sofa. Undoing the button and zip of her skirt along the way, she ambled down the short hall to her bedroom. The skirt caressed her legs as she slipped it off her hips, reminding her of T. Larry's hands. She flipped on the light and stopped, arm in a midair toss.

The closet door stood ajar, her clothes strewn across the floor and bed in a jumble of color. Rose petals had been crumbled and thrown atop the mess, their scent pungent and overpowering.

Her skirt fell to the floor from her numb fingers. Needles shot through the flesh as if her hand had fallen asleep. She stared at her ruined clothing, the slashed material.

The six-dollar fully lined, Evan Picone black dress with the princess neckline from the church thrift. The black-and-white silk Ann Taylor blouse her mother had uncovered for fifty cents. Two sizes too small, that had never mattered since Madison loved tight and the feel of silk against her. The fitted velvet jacket BeeBee had given her when she was cleaning out her closet last year. The blue leather skirt from the same clean out. They were priceless, irreplaceable. Money had nothing to do with it. Stories went along with each piece. Comforting scents of the previous wearer never really faded away.

She bent for a favorite Liz Claiborne sweater, holding it to her nose. Years of collecting, hours spent with friends and family picking through thrift shop racks and garage sale tables. Each garment had a beautiful memory attached to it like a broach or a pin. Some people had photos. Madison kept clothes.

Thank God she'd taken some pieces to the cleaners the other day. She couldn't remember quite what, but some had been saved.

She stood in the middle of her bedroom in her high heels, panties, garter and bra, the lights on, the shade not pulled. Kinda stupid. She shut off the overhead light, the shade rasped on its roller, then she fumbled for the switch on her bedside lamp. Rummaging through the carnage on the floor, she found the pink robe her friend Barbie Doll had brought back from the Royal Hawaiian last year.

When she stuck her hand in the pocket, her fingers fell through a hole to her thigh.

She sniffed but didn't cry. Scooping an armload from the floor, she tossed them to join those on the bed. Turning to her violated closet, she swiped at her cheeks.

Who would want to hurt her like this?

The flowing black wrinkle skirt she'd worn on Monday hung from the rack. Survived. Unblemished. Still on its hanger. It was not short. It was not tight.

The length of it brought to mind only one person.

But Harriet couldn't have done this. She didn't even know where Madison lived. Or did she? The key was missing. Harriet had been so angry. She hated short skirts and tight sweaters. She'd specifically named Madison in her suit.

This went beyond anger. It entered the realm of hate.

Her shoes flashed from the floor of the cupboard. Neatly lined up, colors coordinated, she had two pairs of each of the basics. By no means Imelda Marcos, she still loved her shoes. She saw Richard watching women's shoes clicking across the marble lobby. Her shoes hadn't been touched.

She'd just dumped him, ugly word but true. If angry, would he destroy shoes, leave them alone, or take a pair for a trophy?

But he didn't know where her apartment was. Harriet could have sneaked the address from personnel files, but Richard wouldn't have a clue. Reverse directory from her phone number? She was sure you had to be listed for that, and her brothers had *insisted* she be unlisted almost as a condition of letting her move out of Ma's house.

Had she done something to piss off one of her friends?

Oh my goodness God, none of her friends would do something like this. Neither would Richard or Harriet. Nobody could hate her like this. Nobody. She hadn't hurt anyone enough to deserve something like this. Had she?

She ran back down the hallway, made sure the front door was locked and propped a chair beneath the knob. Oh my God. What about the animals Ma knit? Miraculously, they were fine, nestled against the couch cushions. Oh, oh, if they'd been harmed...that would have been the worst. She checked the windows in the living room, then gathered the pink pig, the cowardly lion and the white rabbit in her arms and carried them all to her bedroom. She'd sleep with them. Finally she snapped the latch on her bedroom window, too. All locked up tight now. When it was too late.

Robe cinched around her, she crawled into her bed, the pile of clothes heavy on top of her, the stuffed animals comforting on her pillow, and picked up the phone.

She should have dialed 911. Instead her fingers

picked out T. Larry's number. She knew the office number, his cell phone, his home phone, even the number for his favorite restaurant three blocks from his house. She'd call them all if she had to, but he answered at home just before the message machine picked up.

"T. Larry?"

"It's past my bedtime, Madison." No inflection, no hint of the erotic, just T. Larry her boss.

Her tummy tumbled over. To him, this afternoon had been nothing more than an irate mistake. Madison, however, didn't ask for verification on that. "It's only ten o'clock."

"I retire at nine-thirty."

"T. Larry—"

"How was your date tonight?"

"Short."

"How short?"

"Less than ten minutes."

A lengthy pause, then, "Why?"

"I'm not in the mood for twenty questions, T. Larry."

"Then tell me all at once instead of piecemeal. Did you tell him you're not seeing him anymore?"

"Of course that's what I told him. What else would I have done after what happened this afternoon?" Even if the experience hadn't changed things for T. Larry, it certainly had for her.

T. Larry paused as if she'd taken his breath away with the list of things she'd now want from *him*. Then, "I don't think we should talk about that."

She wondered if her words to Richard had hurt him as badly as T. Larry's hurt her. "That's not why I called."

"Then why'd you call?"

She couldn't lie, not in the security of her bed, with

her ruined clothes like blankets on top of her. "To hear your voice."

"This is getting too serious."

She wouldn't cry. She would *not*. "Just wanting to hear your voice is too serious?"

"Yes. It's a sign of attachment and the need for comfort."

She needed his comfort, and not for what happened today but for what she'd found in her apartment tonight. "Didn't you say you wanted me to fall in love with you?"

"I've changed my mind."

Her fears confirmed, she sighed and climbed from the bed, the portable phone still at her ear.

"You're breathing heavy. What are you doing?"

She twisted her lips. "I'm going to the kitchen."

"Why?"

"Because I'm upset."

"Because of what happened between us today." Not a question, a statement.

She couldn't bear to hear another word on the subject. "I'm going to cook."

"Why?"

"I always cook when I'm upset." She reached into the cupboard for her selection of gourmet ice cube trays.

"What are you making?"

"Jell-O Jigglers."

"That's not cooking. It's heating up water."

"Yes, but it doesn't need a recipe. That makes it inventive cooking. Do you want raspberry or blueberry?"

"Raspberry."

She held up two ice trays to inspect. "Do you want creepy crawlers or body parts."

"Don't you have anything ordinary, like balls or cubes?"

"I'm not ordinary, T. Larry."

"I know." She thought she heard him groan. "I'll talk about what happened if you need me to, Madison."

She put a kettle on the stove to boil for the Jigglers, then pulled out a box of raspberry Jell-O. "I've changed my mind. I don't need to talk anymore." She'd die *before* her birthday if she had to listen to him call what they'd done a horrible mistake. "I'll see you tomorrow."

"Madison—"

She pushed the off button in the middle of his voice. She wouldn't tell him about the clothes. She wouldn't tell him about the missing key, the lost hairbrush, the hang ups, the rose buds or her clean house. Her mother had nothing to do with that.

T. Larry would say it was Richard. Madison feared it was Harriet. She simply could not call the police. In good conscience, she had to talk to Harriet first before she released the bloodhounds on her.

For now, she called her brother and told him she needed new locks since he'd lost the key she'd left him. Sean had very big shoulders. He handled the guilt trip quite well.

She gave in to her tears when she was again nestled in her bed, the Cowardly Lion pressed to her cheek and her closet full of ruined memories.

LAURENCE SAT ON HIS COUCH, lights off, phone clutched to his chest, a glass of whiskey resting on the sofa arm.

Though he kept a stocked liquor cabinet for entertaining, he didn't usually drink. He drank tonight to blot

out the feel of Madison in his arms. It hadn't worked.
Her call made it worse.

If he touched her again, he was doomed.

CHAPTER FOURTEEN

MADISON WOKE Thursday morning with a plan, two plans, in fact—goodness, she sounded like T. Larry. What a wonderful thing sleep was, bringing about a complete attitude adjustment as if by a miracle. On the way to the train, Sean once again promised to change her locks out that day as she handed him her only remaining apartment key. She was positive he wouldn't look in her bedroom closet. The lock crisis settled, a great weight off her mind, she made the commute into work with accomplishment on her mind. First, Harriet, guilty or not guilty. It would take digging to figure it out. Then T. Larry. Talk wouldn't do. He required action. In his office. Despite his rules. Only eight days until her birthday, she wouldn't take no for an answer.

She stowed her purse in her desk drawer, then, trays of Jigglers in her hand, rounded her desk en route to the coffee machine. Just as she stepped into the hall, the reception door opened to admit Richard's charming visage. So good-looking. But she'd made her decision. He needed to respect that.

"Richard, what are you doing here?" She set the Jigglers on the desk beside her.

The flowers in a plain brown paper bag said it all.

He shouldn't be bringing her flowers. He shouldn't be here, period.

"I brought you these." He jostled the bag at her.

She tried to ignore the flowers. "Rhonda shouldn't have let you in unescorted."

He eased closer. She backed up to the cubicle opening.

"Don't blame Rhonda. I told her I wanted to surprise you."

He was too sweet, too eager to please, too unsure. Guilt tied her stomach in knots. She'd sensed he was fragile during their first date, and she never should have continued. Still, she had to end it. "Richard, I thought you understood last night."

He pushed at that endearing lock of hair falling over his forehead. "I was hoping you'd changed your mind."

She really disliked uncomfortable situations. "I'm sorry."

His mouth drooped at the corners, then just as quickly he smiled again. "Nothing ventured, nothing gained."

Madison tried to keep the relief off her face, but she wasn't good at hiding things.

Richard read her thoughts. "It's all right. Our timing was off. I do understand."

Or T. Larry's timing was right on. "I really am sorry."

He sighed heavily. "Will you promise me one thing?"

"If I can." Which left her an out once she heard what he wanted.

"If you figure out he's not the right one for you, call me?"

She'd never confirmed T. Larry was the "he" she'd

chosen over Richard, but there was a tension in the air that said he knew. But what was the point in denying it? "I can promise that." She dipped her head. "Do I still get the flowers?"

That was a bit rude. It was equally rude to refuse them.

Richard smiled, and the smile dazzled. It just didn't make her tingle the way T. Larry did.

"They're yours. Do you have a vase to put them in? I'm sorry I didn't have time to get one."

"A vase?" She looked around her office awash in file folders and correspondence.

"How about your coffee room? Maybe someone left one behind."

He was amazingly sure of himself, suggesting, leading, not quite the Richard of Friday or Monday night. Or even a few moments ago. "I'll look."

Madison sidled by him and headed down the hall to the copy-coffee room where she was sure she'd seen a vase in the cupboard under the sink. Glancing at her watch to find it almost eight o'clock, she realized T. Larry would be up from his workout any minute. Best to get rid of Richard *ASAP*. She ran water in the green glass vase and hurried back to her cube.

Richard had set the bag on her desk and was busy removing the wrapping from the flowers, a profusion of pink, blue and red carnations. Their sweet fragrance overwhelmed the cubicle, a little too sweet, almost sickly. The reception door opened. Madison held her breath, but the footsteps, muffled by carpeting, headed in the other direction.

Richard handed her the plastic wrapping. She dropped it.

"Are you all right, Madison?"

She was terribly nervous about T. Larry's reaction. Which was silly because he'd never made her nervous before. But then he'd never touched her that way before, either. "I'm fine. But I'm running a little late this morning."

"I'm sorry." A little boy's hurt crept into Richard's voice.

"I'm not rushing you or anything—"

"But you don't want *him* to walk in and find me here."

Her fingers arranging the flowers, she looked up to find his smile gone and his lips tense. She went for honesty since anything else might give Richard the idea he still had a chance. "It does make me a tad uncomfortable."

He contemplated his feet. "Yeah. Sure. I better go."

"I'll walk you out."

"You better not. Wouldn't want *him* to see us together." He folded the paper bag and tucked it beneath his arm instead of throwing it away in her trash can.

The door opened again. She knew T. Larry by the sound of his footfall, heavy on the heel, a determined step, unfaltering. Then he was in the doorway of her office.

His nostrils flared and his gray eyes smoked, the only signs of emotion. He stared at Richard. Richard stared back at him. Like two gunslingers. Then without a word, T. Larry went into his own office and shut the door. Extra quietly.

Still staring at T. Larry's closed door, the slight disturbance of air currents warned her Richard had moved around her. He stood at her cubicle entrance, his face impassive and unreadable. "Goodbye, Madison."

"Thank you, Richard." She didn't walk him out, just watched him disappear into the lobby, sure she'd missed something in the little episode.

LAURENCE COULD HAVE beaten the younger man to a pulp. Then he could have dragged Madison into his office.

Thank God he had more control. All he had to do was keep his door closed and tell himself he didn't care what was going on outside.

It was a good thing he was already bald; he didn't have any hair to tear out.

BILL TAPPED HER DESK. "Hey, beautiful."

"Hey, handsome." She didn't look up from the pile of yesterday's correspondence she was editing.

Bill didn't move on as he usually did. "Where'd you get the flowers?"

"Secret admirer," she quipped, still without looking up.

Bill made a noise, perhaps a snort, sniffed once, then three more times in rapid succession.

"Yes, the coffee's ready," she told him.

"What's that smell?"

"What smell?" She sniffed, too. Something sweet, yet laced with a hint of…meat slightly off? Could it be her meat loaf sandwich? Nah, that had been less than a week old. She'd noticed the smell when Richard brought his flowers. She hated the thought of throwing them out. "Maybe it's the Jell-O Jigglers I left on the counter in the copy room."

"Jigglers?"

"In the shape of body parts. And creepy crawlers. When you move the wax paper they're sitting on, they jiggle," she said with a smile.

"Has anyone ever told you that even as cute as you are, you're a very scary person?"

"Just you, Bill." And her brothers. Her mother. T. Larry. Just about everyone.

He laughed and headed for the coffee, his voice floating back to her. "I like scary."

She didn't want to know what Bill liked. T. Larry had kept his office door closed against her and hadn't asked her for a single explanation about Richard or the flowers. *Well, we'll see about that, Mr. T. Laurence Hobbs.* But first, there was Harriet.

She beeped Rhonda. "Have you seen Harriet?"

"She came in half an hour ago."

Madison went prowling the cubicles. There weren't enough to go round and no assigned work spaces, partners and managers excluded, primarily due to the fact that many days the accountants themselves were out at the clients. When in the office, he or she took what she could get.

Harriet had secured the corner cube, outside Ryman's office, on the opposite side from Madison and T. Larry. Her fingers flying over the calculator, she didn't hear Madison's approach.

"Harriet, can I talk to you?"

She finished adding the column of numbers twice before turning. She'd been crying recently, evidenced by puffy eyes and too much makeup to cover them. "No."

She'd replied. That was a good sign. Well, not exactly good, but a step above hopeless. Madison persevered. "I really, truly want to apologize for whatever I did that offended you."

With little emotion, Harriet's gaze flicked over Madison's long black skirt and turtleneck. Thank God for air-conditioning or she just might boil over on another warm June day, the long-sleeved turtleneck was one of the few things she had left.

Lips thinning, Harriet muttered, "Apology accepted," and returned to her numbers.

Now *that* was good, even though Madison didn't believe it. She needed more if she was to be sure Harriet hadn't been in her apartment with a knife. "Will you tell me what I did wrong? I'm still not clear on that."

"You were born."

Okay. That definitely fell on the not-good side. Madison took the direct approach. "Do you hate me?"

Harriet swiveled on her chair, venom in her eyes, her nostrils flared and her lips parted.

Madison smelled Bill's coffee before she saw him. Darn. He stopped beside her in the cubicle opening. "Slumming, Madison?"

Knowing precisely who the cutting remark was aimed at and that it didn't fall under T. Larry's office protocol, Harriet's face flushed.

Bill really was an ass.

Madison leaned over to look in his coffee cup. Very white, a lot of cream. "Is that really hot?"

He gulped, looking at her the whole time. "No." Then he smiled, all slimy and sexual. "But not due to a lack of effort on your part."

"Good." She elbowed him out of Harriet's cube, hitting his hand holding the foam cup and sending coffee flying across the front of his white shirt.

She cupped her hand to her mouth. "Oh, look what I've done."

He backed up, holding both arms out to survey the damage. His already swarthy complexion turned beetish. "You did that on purpose."

Harriet stared, her mouth open.

Madison smiled, clasped her hands beneath her chin and said sweetly. "Why yes, I think I did." She batted her eyelashes. "And if you apologize to Harriet, I'll apologize to you."

Wide-eyed, he sputtered, "Apologize to her for what?"

"That 'slumming' remark."

"I didn't mean anything by it." His head shook as he spoke.

Madison tipped her nose. "Yes, you did."

His chin went down. A line formed between his brows. "I was just kidding around."

"We didn't think it was funny."

His gaze flipped from Madison to Harriet and back. "I…well, I guess I'm sorry then."

Madison looked to Harriet, whose answer was merely a tight nod of acceptance.

"I'm sorry I dumped your coffee all over you. I was just kidding around, too. Do you want me to wash your shirt out?"

He held his hands up, empty coffee cup in his right. "No, no, don't touch me." He left down the center hall, hands still surrendering in the air.

Harriet sat in silence.

"Now what were we saying?" Madison prompted.

"You asked if I hated you."

"Yeah." Madison nodded. "Do you?"

Harriet stared for the longest time, head tilting left, right, then she gave a slight shake. "I don't know."

WELL, THAT WAS SUCCESSFUL. At least Madison *thought* it was. Harriet hadn't reacted with glee, or even a smug knowing smile, when she saw Madison's skirt and turtleneck. By the end, she'd seemed stunned. Madison knew body language, and Harriet's wasn't that of someone who'd just torn through a closet full of clothes.

Nope, Harriet hadn't done it. Madison held her I'd Rather Be Skydiving coffee mug in her hands for warmth against the sudden chill. So who had? Maybe it was time to call the police. Except that they'd scream and yell because Madison had shoved all the clothes into the bottom of her closet, touched practically every doorknob and almost certainly destroyed any finger-prints that might have been there.

For now, she was safe at work. She'd worry about the rest when it was time to go home. "Procrastination is my middle name," she chimed under her breath. Besides, she had to brave T. Larry in his office.

Putting her coffee down, she squared her shoulders, knocked on his door and opened it.

"I don't recall saying come in."

With the light streaming in through the window behind him, his arms folded over his chest and his hands dark against his white shirt, he reminded her of Buddha. He wasn't granting her an audience. She closed the door behind her, then leaning against it, she flicked the lock in place.

He heard the faint sound. "What are you doing?"

Madison looked at the couch, and the slow pump of her blood increased fractionally. With a few steps forward, she stood opposite him with her hands on the back of his leather guest seat. She pointedly ignored the fact that Richard had been in her office. "We have to talk about yesterday."

"We already decided last night that it was a mistake."

"You decided it was. That's not the same thing."

His lips bleached. The overhead lights reflected off his glasses. "All right. Unlock the door and we can discuss it."

She moved around his desk, trailing her finger along the dark wood, turning until she stood on his side of the desk, right in front of him. His breath quickened in the silence. Her flesh went all goose pimply. Her hands were suddenly cold, and her rings slipped around on her fingers. She didn't know if she could do or say the things she'd concocted in her mind.

As she inched closer, T. Larry rolled back. She leaned down to grab the arms of his chair. "Let's leave the door locked so we won't be interrupted."

He swallowed with effort. "I'm glad to see you're wearing more appropriate clothing, but didn't you wear that skirt Monday?"

She looked down, her hair falling forward, the ends brushing his belt. "It's the only one I had left...I mean, that was long enough."

The pulse thrummed visibly at his throat. He was barely hanging on, despite the almost neutral quality of his words. "Perhaps you should shop this weekend."

She pulled her gaze to his and pursed her lips in a pouty little smile. "Don't you want me, T. Larry?"

Behind his glasses, his eyes went wide and dark. His mouth worked, but she'd robbed him of speech.

Very good. "You said you wanted me the other night at mini golf."

"I got over it."

She lifted one leg and set her knee beside his on the chair. He jerked. "Are you sure? It didn't feel like you'd gotten over it yesterday when you had me on your lap."

His hands went to her arms, but he neither pulled her

in nor pushed her away. "Yesterday I was insane. I apologize. It won't happen again."

She might have believed him except for the tremble in his touch and the uniquely hot male scent rising off him like a mind-altering vapor. Madison pulled at her skirt, slid her knee along the chair, then straddled him before he had a chance to act.

"Jesus Christ, Madison, what are you doing?"

She wriggled on top of him, adjusting her legs and skirt in the tight fit between the arms of his chair and his thighs. He groaned. "T. Larry, it feels like you want me." She pressed down on the issue for proper punctuation.

His hands flexed convulsively on her arms. "Madison," rasped past his vocal cords.

"You said I should forget about Richard. I have."

"Then why was he here?"

Ah, she had him. "He just showed up. I told him to leave."

His eyes got all smoky hot. "What about the flowers?"

Wonderful reaction. She smiled. "I'll throw them out."

"It doesn't matter to me."

She knew by the set of his lips that it did. But enough about Richard and his flowers. This was about T. Larry and her. "You said I should give you a chance. I will."

"It's impossible. This is the office. We're breaking all the rules."

She smiled brightly, shaking off his touch to loop her arms around his neck and lean closer. His hands fell to her hips and settled there, clutching, kneading, stroking.

"I've only got a week until my birthday. T. Larry, you're my only hope."

"Couldn't you fall in love with Bill?"

She wrinkled her nose. "Yuck. He torments Harriet. I couldn't love a person like that."

"What about Zach?"

She rolled her eyes. "He can't even look me in the face when he asks for a peanut butter cup. I scare him."

"You scare me, too." His hands worked the flesh of her hips, sliding down to cup her bottom, then up her sides to the swell of her breasts, setting off the most delicious little tingles. "Don't you know anyone else who can help you? A friend of one of your brothers?"

She smiled, then swooped in to rub her nose against his. "Nope. Just you. And it's your duty since you made me tell Richard I couldn't see him anymore."

"I can't." He sounded half-strangled. "I really can't."

"Maybe you should try kissing me."

His grip fell once more to her hips, his eyes closed, and the lower half of his body surged against her, perhaps involuntarily. Oh yes. Oh goodness. Her panties and the material of her skirt were barely any barrier against the hard ridge of his penis.

"God, Madison Avenue. Jesus." The words nothing more than a groan on his exhale.

She put her hands to his cheeks. "What did you call me?"

"I…" Eyes the color of smoke, he stared as if for a moment he couldn't remember who she was, who *he* was.

"You called me Madison Avenue. You gave me a nickname."

Jumbled words croaked from his lips. He swallowed, then tried again. "I did?" He blinked, a little of the muddle fading. "I mean, yes, I did."

"Oh, T. Larry. I can't tell you how much that means

to me." It meant he wasn't immune. It meant he didn't think yesterday was a mistake after all. She kissed him full on the lips, leaving behind a red smear, then climbed off his lap.

"Where are you going?"

"To my desk. If I stay on your lap, we're definitely going to violate rule number five all the way."

He spluttered.

"Besides, I didn't bring any protection."

He choked and turned an apoplectic shade.

She peeked in the bathroom, rolled her lips to smooth her lipstick. "You better wipe my lipstick off your mouth before anyone sees it." She blew him a kiss. "And if you want, you can drive me home tonight and we can discuss it some more."

LAURENCE'S MOUTH still hung open two minutes after she'd closed the door. Maybe it was longer, maybe less, he couldn't think enough to be sure.

She was forward. She was outrageous. Those characteristics had never bothered him. He'd never been her victim before.

There was no way on God's green earth he was driving Madison Avenue home. Why had he called her that anyway? Because he'd been dreaming about her last night, and he'd called her quite a few things, Madison Avenue being only one of them.

His intercom chirped.

"Did you take care of that…problem yet?"

Her voice managed to scramble his brains again. "What?"

"My lipstick on your dipstick. I mean, mouth."

Ah God, that image. He scrubbed at his lips. "Why?"

"Harry Dump's here to see you."

"Christ. Why didn't you tell me we had an appointment?"

"You didn't. He just showed up."

Not now. His mind was not in functioning order. "Then tell him I'm not here."

"T. Larry, you better see him." He didn't like the sound of her voice. She lowered it to a whisper. "He's not alone."

"Who's with him?"

She didn't answer for at least ten seconds. "Mr. Dilly-Dally."

Laurence sighed. Did the timing really matter? He'd have to face Dump at some point. What was Zach doing with that Appeasing Harriet Plan? And why the hell wasn't Laurence himself putting this problem down as his number one priority instead of getting up Madison's skirt?

Who the hell was Dilly-Dally anyway?

"Give me five minutes." He rolled from his chair like a man twice his age and dragged himself into the bathroom.

Madison was all over him, from the red lipstick on his mouth, to the sexual flush on the top of his head, down to the noticeable bulge in his trousers. She'd been right about one thing; if she hadn't climbed from his lap when she did, he'd have abandoned every rule in the management handbook.

Laurence wiped her off as best he could, but her flowery scent clung to his clothes.

He opened his office door.

Mr. Dilly-Dally was as tall as Harry Dump was short and as thin as the lawyer was wide. The cut and quality of his pin-striped suit was far above that of Harry's. A diamond pinkie ring in the shape of a horseshoe winked on his finger. His cologne reeked of an expensive department store. Harry was drugstore bought and paid for from the cardboard belt to the two-dollar spice of his aftershave. So what were two such disparate characters doing in his office?

Harry Dump's hand, when Laurence shook it, left his palm coated with a slime of perspiration.

"Mr. Dilly-Dally."

In sharp contrast, the other man's grip was dry and cool, his voice cultured, a hint of Brit. "It's William Daily, sir." Looking down his long angular nose, he perused his palm, then wiped his hands together as if to erase the bit of Harry's DNA that had transferred in Laurence's handshake.

"Please excuse the mistake. Madison's hard of hearing."

"Perhaps that would explain it." A hint of distaste still populated his tone.

"Won't you both sit down?" He started to raise his hand to the two chairs opposite his desk, then remembered Harry's bulk and pointed to the couch instead.

"Don't mind if I do." Harry perspired his way to the sofa, and sank down, with slow side-to-side movements, into the corner.

The same corner seat where Laurence had held Madison just yesterday. Harry Dump, through no fault of his own, defiled it.

Laurence had done all the defiling himself, to his everlasting shame.

Daily took the matching chair, forcing Laurence to sit on the couch at the opposite end to Harry. Neither carried a briefcase, standard lawyer garb. Harry's eyes danced. Around his chin, the flesh bubbled with excitement.

Laurence had a very bad feeling, and it wasn't indigestion. "What can I do for you, gentlemen?"

Daily, after hiking his pants and crossing his legs at the knees, let Harry do the talking.

"We've come to suggest a settlement."

Laurence stretched his arm along the back of the sofa to appear relaxed, cool and calm. "Then you should have made an appointment so that my lawyer could attend."

"Oh, I don't think we need your lawyer for this, Larry."

"The name is Laurence, and I don't make deals without my legal advisors."

Harry's lips twitched. "Perhaps you'll want to think about making this one after you hear what Mr. Daily has to say." He extended a plump hand to the other man.

Daily retrieved a small notebook and a pair of gold reading glasses from his expensively tailored suit pocket. He made a production of perching the glasses on the tip of his nose, opening the notebook and finding just the right page.

"At approximately two o'clock yesterday afternoon, as I was eating my cheese and tomato sandwich—" he raised his eyes to meet Laurence's "—thin-sliced wheat bread, of course—" then lowered his gaze once more to the page "—I happened to glance out my window on the twenty-second floor to the neighboring building."

The feeling that suddenly gripped Laurence certainly wasn't indigestion. A mixture of fear, anger and disbelief overcame him, a need to do violence to someone, anyone, yet a strange immobilization of his muscles. As if his body hoped and prayed his ears wouldn't hear what his mind knew was coming.

"I observed a couple rather flagrantly displayed on a black leather chesterfield—" he glanced at the sofa beneath Laurence's buttocks "—quite similar to this one, I believe." His mustached lip twitched like a mouse's whiskers. "It appeared to me they were involved in some sort of sexual congress as the man's hand was up the young lady's—"

"That's enough." Laurence stood. How the hell had the man seen? The angle of the sun had been all wrong, the—did it matter? The real question was how the hell he and Harry Dump had found each other in less than twenty-four hours. "What is it you want, Dump?"

"It's Doomp."

Laurence leveled him with a malevolent gaze. "I repeat, what do you want?"

"Five hundred thousand dollars in settlement of Miss Hartman's suit—"

"Of which you get two-thirds."

"One-third." Harry struggled forward until his feet firmly found the floor. "It will cost you far more in legal fees and embarrassment, not to mention the… uh…young lady involved."

Monday, he'd liked the man and admired his empathy for Harriet. Today, he'd have gladly wrung the wretch's neck.

"Get out of my office."

"We can pinpoint the exact location of the activity described, and after meeting your secretary, Mr. Daily is prepared to testify as to the identity of the female participant."

Laurence battled the urge to throttle the man. His chest tightened, the air he dragged in unsatisfactory.

"I know it'll take time to get the money." Harry struggled to his feet, the top of his comb-over not reaching farther than Laurence's biceps. "I'll give you seventy-two hours."

"I suggest that if you don't want the police breathing down your neck for blackmail, you both get out of my office now."

"Seventy-two hours or Mr. Daily gives me a deposition attesting to everything he saw going on," he said, patting the leather, "on this cushy little piece of office furniture."

Laurence bared his teeth. "Get. Out."

"Seventy-two hours, Larry." Harry waddled to the door, Daily gliding on his heels. "We'll show ourselves out."

Laurence congratulated himself on his ability to close the door gently behind them. He was not a violent man, but he wanted to slam his fist through something, most especially Harry Dump's head. He wasn't a sex-in-the-office type. Madison drove him to things he'd never contemplated.

Christ. *Admit it, Laurence, you lost control and inflicted irreversible damage.* Nothing had been Madison's fault.

He recognized her tentative knock. "Come in."

"What did they want?"

He couldn't trust himself to speak. The veins at his temples throbbed, and his face burned with a rush of blood to the surface of his skin. His eyes bathed the office in angry shades of red. It picked up the fire and gold in her hair.

She put out a hand, but at whatever she saw in his eyes, stopped just short of touching. "T. Larry, you look like my father did the day he had his stroke."

"You weren't more than a few weeks old when he died."

"It's some sort of universal knowledge I share with my brothers and mother."

He couldn't deal with her craziness, not now, not when he had to figure out how to protect her from his incredibly stupid folly. "Get Harriet."

She opened her mouth to ask yet another inane question.

"Now, Madison!"

She rushed to do his bidding as if he'd lit a fire under her bottom.

What had he brought down on their heads? What had he been doing for the entire last week? Where was his usual command of the situation, all his plans?

Standing in the doorway, Harriet looked like hell. Laurence motioned her to a seat, closed the door and sat facing her across the wide expanse of his desk.

Harriet, except for the shade of her dyed hair, had always taken care with her appearance. Today her hair hung in strings. The makeup smudged beneath her eyes looked suspiciously like yesterday's application.

Laurence couldn't afford to feel sorry for her, baby her or wait her out. "Call off your lawyer, Harriet."

He knew it was the inflammatory thing to say, had when he'd planned his speech in the spare moments it took Madison to get Harriet into his office. Harriet wanted Mr. Nice Guy. Laurence was done playing the game her way.

She pulled at her knee-length skirt, which at least

conformed to the new company standard, and her narrowed eyes took on that Harriet the Harridan glare. "I have every right to—"

"You will *not* disrupt this company with your romantic problems. If you want Zach, fight for him. Lie, cheat, make him jealous, anything, I don't care. But don't involve this firm." Laurence realized he could take some of his own advice. "You'll never recover from this debacle. It will follow you to every job you take. If you can get a job. Accounting is a small world."

"Are you threatening to sabotage my career?"

"You've already done that yourself, Harriet." He leaned forward, his arms on his desk. "But it's not public yet. You can still save yourself."

"I think you want me to save *you*."

He wanted to save Madison. And he did not have five hundred thousand dollars to pay off Dump and Dilly-Dally. "Save us both. Talk to Zach the way you should have eight months ago. Air your problems with him, but take it outside company time and property, the way you should have in the first place."

"My problem is with you, not Zachary."

"Then find another job."

"You *are* threatening me."

"I'm suggesting a more palatable method of dealing with it than destroying this company with a frivolous lawsuit."

She smiled then, a cunning, mean smile. "So, I *am* having the desired effect."

There was no sense in denying his total failure. "You are. And you might revel in it now, but two, five, nine months from now you're going to wish to God you'd made a different choice." Laurence was wishing he had, too, like taking Madison home and spending days with her in his bed rather than expose her, literally, to the world. "What is it you really want, Harriet? Money? An apology?"

"I don't want anything from you."

"You do, Harriet. Or you wouldn't bring this suit." He sat back, folding his hands over his stomach. "Tell me what you want."

Her chin went up defiantly, her trembling lip mitigating the effect, until she spoke. "I want you to fire Madison."

Fire Madison? He couldn't imagine Carp, Alta and Hobbs without her. Why, there'd be nothing to look forward to, no reason to hurry in every day, no reason to come in at all. No Reese's Peanut Butter Cups in a drawer, no special coffee brewing, no hair bleach in his bathroom, no appointments out of place, no impediments to his plans, no candy necklaces, no flirting, no teasing. No joy.

"I'll drop the suit if you get rid of her," Harriet repeated.

And maybe no choice if he wanted to protect Madison from the consequences of his reprehensible action yesterday afternoon.

He punched the intercom button. "Madison, come in here."

CHAPTER FIFTEEN

"PLEASE SHUT THE DOOR and have a seat, Madison."

T. Larry kept his eyes on hers. Not on her breasts or her lips, not even her hair. He'd erased all emotion from his features, muting even the expression in his gaze.

Harriet stared at her hands.

Madison began to get worried.

T. Larry cleared his throat. "Harriet says she'll drop the suit if I fire you."

Her heart skipped her stomach and plunged right down to her toes. She loved Carp, Alta and Hobbs. She loved the people she worked with. She loved her job. She loved T. Larry.

Some of her shock must have shown on her face. T. Larry looked to the corner of the ceiling, then back at her. "I won't do it unless you agree."

"Agree to be fired?" Somehow that seemed an oxymoron.

"Agree to pack your things and go." How could he say that with so little emotion? "Of course, I'll give you severance pay and a reference."

Harriet shifted in her seat, the leather chair creaking. Her fingers plucked at cat hairs on her dress.

"I have a lint roller at my desk you can get that stuff off with," Madison offered.

Harriet's fingers stilled, but her gaze didn't rise. "I've got one, thank you."

The room fell silent. T. Larry leaned his elbows on his desk, steepled his fingers and rested his chin on the top. Harriet fidgeted, swinging her legs an inch short of the carpet, chewing the inside of her cheek.

They were like schoolgirls sitting in front of the headmaster. Backlit by the windows, T. Larry's bald head gleamed, his gaze now focused on Harriet. The tick of the clock on the wall exploded in the silence. Traffic commotion slipped through the double-pane windows. Madison had never realized you could hear it. The sound of the phones ringing, the chunking of the copier and voices drifted beneath T. Larry's closed door.

Had anyone heard her cries yesterday afternoon? No, T. Larry's mouth had taken care of them.

Give up Carp, Alta and Hobbs? Could she? What about T. Larry? Her leaving didn't mean she wouldn't have a chance to fall *in* love with him. T. Larry always had another plan. She was only sorry she wouldn't be there to protect Harriet from Bill, Anthony and Mike. But, if she'd done a proper job of that in the first place, none of this would have happened. She should have dumped Bill's coffee on him years ago.

"For the sake of the company…" And for T. Larry. Especially T. Larry. "I'll do it."

Harriet gasped, abandoned her perusal of her hands and stared at Madison. T. Larry's eyes clouded, his jaw clenched, then he closed his lids for the briefest of moments.

"Will three months severance do?"

"Three months?" Her birthday was a little over a week away. She didn't have three months. She wouldn't need to find a job or make new friends. But T. Larry had a plan gleaming behind his glasses, and she'd play along in any way he wanted. "Do you think it'll take me that long to find a job?"

He glanced at Harriet, the smoke in his eyes now a true flame. "I'm sure you'll have one by tomorrow. But you'll still get three months severance."

"Wow." Except for Harriet, she would have asked him if they were still on for their date on Friday. He couldn't have a single objection now. He wasn't her boss anymore. She rose. "Okay, well, I guess I'll pack up my stuff." Her plants, her photos, her cards, her daily calendar with the cats on it. "Do you want me to leave the Reese's cups?"

"Yes." No inflection and no play of muscle around his mouth. Maybe he was seeing all the possibilities, too.

She got halfway to the door. "Do I get a going-away cake and a lunch?" She glanced at her watch. "It's too late for today, but I can drive in tomorrow."

T. Larry stared hard at Harriet, but all Madison could see was the back of her bent head. "Tomorrow'll be fine Madison. Where do you want to go?"

"How about…" She tapped her finger on her lips.

Harriet jumped up before Madison could think of the best place in all of San Francisco for her going-away lunch.

Her gaze darted between the two of them. "I've changed my mind. Just forget it, okay? I—" Harriet put her hand to her mouth, edged toward the door, then suddenly turned and fled.

T. Larry remained motionless and emotionless behind his desk.

"Does this mean I'm not fired?"

"I think it does."

Madison puffed out a breath of air. "Well, that's good."

"I agree. Breaking in a secretary is an overwhelming task."

"Yeah, it sucks." She furrowed her brow. "Would you really have let me go, T. Larry?"

"If I thought it was best for you."

Which didn't answer the question, but he was playing Mr. Enigmatic, and she was sure she wouldn't get another answer out of him. "You were bluffing, weren't you?"

He rubbed the top of his head, saying nothing.

"Does this mean she's dropping her suit?"

His mouth lifted slightly in one corner. "I guess we'll have to wait and find out."

"I guess we will." She turned to him with the brightest smile she could fit on her face. "Can I still have a cake and lunch anyway? We can say it's my welcome-back lunch since I was fired for at least five minutes."

HALLELUJAH, she was staying.

Laurence basked in the afterglow of Madison's lopsided smile as she exited his office. He hadn't been bluffing, Harriet had. What made her back down? Madison's ready acceptance? Guilt? He didn't care. He'd wanted only one outcome.

The scene would play across Harriet's mind over and over again until she did indeed call off Harry Dump. And in turn, Harry would call off William Dilly-Dally.

This nonsense with Madison, however, would have to stop. For her own protection. A boss had no right crossing that line with his employee. She would henceforth be off-limits, even in his fantasies.

He could do it.

After all, back in college, he'd once gone without making a plan for an entire six weeks because his girlfriend, Constance, told him he was inflexible. Six weeks, cold turkey. Until he realized the folly of it, sent Constance on her merry, flexible way, and started on the dual Financial-Family Plan.

He'd learned his lesson then. Remain in control. He wasn't about to repeat the failure with Madison.

MADISON'S FINGERS clicked happily over the keys as she typed time sheets into her hours worksheet. Harriet was gone, running out, purse in hand. The fuss was over. Dear Lord, she even thought she'd heard T. Larry humming in his office.

The reception door banged against the wall. Madison's fingers skipped across a number of keys and deleted half the cells she'd just entered. Undo didn't work. Double darn. Who—

Sean's boots thumped on the carpet in front of her desk.

"What are you doing here?"

"What the hell happened to your clothes?"

Oops. "What were you doing looking in my closet?" She pushed past him to glance outside her cubicle.

Rhonda peeked through the glass separating the reception area. Bill, then Anthony and Mike poked their heads out of the coffee room—didn't they ever work? ZZ Top turned a corner and stopped smack-dab in the middle of the aisleway. T. Larry appeared at his door.

Madison sat in the proverbial fishbowl, and this time she wasn't sure she liked it.

"What's going on here?"

Sean turned to T. Larry. "Your secretary here had her entire wardrobe slashed to bits and didn't see fit to tell her brothers."

T. Larry's cheeks stiffened, and he came to stand shoulder to shoulder with Sean, two big ugly lugs staring down on her.

Time for a lie to save her neck. "I called the police."

"Liar." She wasn't sure whose mouth that came out of.

Okay, so a little lie hadn't worked. She tried minimization. "I had to get rid of them anyway. All my skirts are too short."

Sean's green eyes, a mirror of her own, flashed with an angry conflagration. "Your tires were slashed last week. Now someone breaks into your bloody apartment to slash your clothes. And all you can say is you needed new stuff anyway."

Now for deflection. She had an arsenal of sneaky weapons. "They didn't break in. They used the key under the mat."

Sean bellowed, "How many times do I have to tell you not to leave the key under the mat all the time?"

"How would you get in if I didn't leave the key?"

Sean narrowed his eyes. "Stop trying to distract me."

He *was* distracted. She took another shot—shifting the blame—to throw him off completely. "You didn't answer my question. What were you doing searching my closet?"

"I was looking for the damn key because *I* knew I

sure as hell hadn't lost it." He dipped into his jeans pocket. "And speaking of it, here's your damn new key for your damn new lock."

"Thanks, you sweet guy." Madison slipped the key from the desk and into her drawer. "But you shouldn't say *damn*, Sean."

T. Larry burst in with, "What the hell is going on, Madison?"

She took T. Larry and Sean in with the same glare, straightened to her mighty height of five foot two and jammed her hands on her hips. "There's just a bit too much swearing going on around here. This a place of business, you know. You should both conduct your-selves accordingly."

"The tough stuff's not going to work, little sister."

T. Larry ignored her huff. "Sean, tell me."

Sean did, without taking his eyes off Madison. "She tells me *I* lost the key she leaves under the mat when I have to fix something, and asks me to put on new locks. I thought she lost the key herself."

T. Larry eyed her. "Sounds like what your sister would do."

She wanted to take a swat at him, but Sean mowed her over.

"But I left the damn key where I always leave the damn key, and my memory's a damn sight better than hers."

Madison wagged her finger. "I'll tell Ma you were swearing."

"I figured she set it down somewhere and forgot. So I *looked*, not searched, and what did I find?" Sean, a handsome guy even if he was her brother, was not handsome with that sneer on his face. "Go ahead, Madison, tell T. Larry what I found."

She took a moment to wonder if any one of the rubberneckers standing in the hall was wondering how her brother knew T. Larry.

"Madison."

They were *all* waiting. Then Sean sniffed. "What's that smell?"

She'd thrown her meat loaf sandwich in the copy room trash, but the slightly rancid odor lingered in the cubicle. And thank you very much God for finding something to take their minds off her little apartment problem. "It was just my lunch. I think I left the meat loaf in the refrigerator too long."

Sean wrinkled his nose. "You had *that* in your refrigerator?"

She rolled her eyes. "At least I didn't eat it. And I did learn my lesson. You shouldn't let your meat loaf."

Much to her dismay, no one laughed. Meat? As in the male organ? Don't let it loaf around? Well, if she had to explain it, the joke lost its punch.

"Now that we've dispensed with your lunch, Madison, why don't you tell me what your brother found?"

Darn T. Larry. She'd almost had Sean sidetracked. There was still a chance. "Then again, maybe it wasn't the meat loaf. Maybe it's the flowers." They did smell a bit funny, not like any carnations she'd ever whiffed. "Maybe you should throw them in the hall garbage on your way out, Sean."

"Madison."

Ooh, everyone was saying her name that way. "All right. Someone cut up all the clothes in my closet. Sean already told you that. Everything was destroyed but this." She spread the folds of her lacy black skirt. The little bells at her waist tinkled.

T. Larry studied the skirt. "That was left untouched?"

"Yes."

"Isn't that your only long skirt?"

Goodness, he was going right where she didn't want him to go, to Harriet. Maybe the rest of the truth would deflect him. "And actually, it's been a bit more than the tires and the clothes."

"What?" they growled in identical voices.

She hemmed and hawed, pursed her lips, then said, "I've had a few hang up calls."

Sean gave her a narrow-eyed scowl. "How many?"

"Three or four a night."

More glares and scowls from everyone, but T. Larry was the one who spoke. "What else?"

Trust T. Larry, with that sharp accounting mind, to know there was more. "Someone stole my hairbrush, and they cleaned up the apartment and left me two roses."

"I knew Ma hadn't done that."

T. Larry picked up something in her tone. "Blood red roses."

She held her chin high. "Actually, yes."

"And you didn't tell anyone?"

"It was all very harmless."

"Madison, it's the pattern, not the individual acts themselves." There he was, on that serial killer kick again. T. Larry watched too many of those detective shows.

"We're calling the police," Sean thundered.

"What are they going to do except yell at me for not calling in the first place?"

"We want it on record," T. Larry said as if he and

Sean had one brain and one mouth. Maybe they did, they were men after all.

"The next time something happens, they'll have to take action."

"But you just changed the locks, Sean."

"And you're not taking the train anymore," her brother ordered. She could just kick dictatorial brothers.

"I'll drive her to and from work," T. Larry added.

And dictatorial bosses.

"But T. Larry, that's miles out of your way."

Sean held out his hand. "Give me the phone book. I'm reporting this, then T. Larry's taking you to the police station."

"But he's got appointments all afternoon."

"Cancel them," her despotic employer ordered.

Madison was outnumbered, outflanked and outranked.

RYMAN CORNERED Laurence in his office while Madison canceled the appointments he had for the afternoon. "What the hell is going on, Hobbs?"

How many people were going to ask the very same question, himself included? Madison just seemed to bring that out in people. Along with fear and protectiveness and a host of other unmanageable emotions. Why wasn't she more concerned for her safety? If anything happened to her…

"Madison had a break-in at her house."

"What has that got to do with *us*?"

Laurence tilted his head, using his height and his youth to intimidate Ryman, an action which was somehow becoming almost habit now. "She works for me. I'm concerned for her welfare."

Ryman wasn't intimidated. Nor did he come close to

being human. "It's personal business. If she keeps bringing her personal business to work, tell her we'll fire her."

"Her tires were slashed while her car was parked in the garage we recommend to employees. That's not personal business."

Ryman waved a dismissive hand. "One incident has nothing to do with the other. Besides, *we* didn't recommend that garage, Hobbs, you did."

"What are you saying, Ryman?"

"I'm saying you're stretching your tether a little too far. Remember who the senior partners are. We can terminate you as easily as we can any of the other little peons here." Ryman wiggled his bushy white eyebrows. "I'm sure there's some provision of the partnership agreement you're violating. Now what's happening with that termagant's suit? And have you met with Stephen Tortelli the way I told you to?"

Ryman Alta was threatening him. Stephen Tortelli was a mobster. Harry Dump was a blackmailer. Madison's life was in danger. His day couldn't get worse. Laurence went for broke.

"For right now, shove the Tortelli account up your ass, Ryman, along with anything else you choose to put up there."

Laurence didn't usually conjure such images, let alone say them aloud, but he left Ryman Alta standing in his office, the man's jaw almost touching the floor.

THEY WERE ALMOST to her apartment building, and Laurence hadn't let up on her since they'd left the police department.

He was still going strong—and rightfully so—as he

negotiated busy rush hour on University Avenue. "Perhaps they'd have been more excited if you'd called them when it happened. And perhaps if you hadn't put all the clothes away and destroyed all possibility of finding any evidence—"

Madison fluttered her fingers at him. "Perhaps, perhaps. But I didn't. It's over now. The police can't do anything. I missed the window of opportunity. It's not a big deal."

"I don't see how you can be so blithely unconcerned for your safety."

"Well, I wasn't hurt. And I got my house cleaned for free. Besides, God doesn't have a serial killer in his plan for me."

He punched the brakes too hard as he jerked into a parking space in front of her apartment. Madison slapped her hand against the dashboard to keep herself from slamming into it.

He should have felt repentant. "That's the most ridiculous thing I think I've ever heard you say."

"Oh," she said, as if she had nothing to add.

"You should stay with your mother until this thing is over."

"This thing?" The question implied she didn't even know what "this thing" was, although they'd gone over it and over it. She simply wouldn't accept that it could involve someone she knew.

"The Danger." He said it with a capital *D*.

She shrugged. "If you're really all that worried, maybe you should spend the night to protect me."

He rolled his eyes, then shot her a glare and a scowl. Nothing worked with her.

"I'll make you dinner," she cajoled.

"I had enough of your Jell-O Jigglers today."

"I can cook things besides Jell-O Jigglers."

"And no meat loaf."

"I promise." She held up her fingers in a Boy Scout salute. "So you're spending the night."

He stared at her, lips flat so she couldn't pretend he was anything close to a smile. "I didn't say that."

She huffed through slightly parted lips. "Dinner?"

"I didn't say that, either."

The sun baked through the windshield. Madison opened her door. "Well, good night then. Thanks for the ride. And thanks for going to the police station with me."

What the hell? "Where are you going?"

"Up those stairs," she said, pointing, "and inside my apartment." She put one leg onto the pavement.

Laurence's eyes shadowed the movement and glued themselves to her black-clad ankle peeking from beneath the hem of her skirt.

He cleared his throat. "You are not."

"Then why did you park here?" She skimmed her purse strap up her arm and over her shoulder, then pulled it taut down her cleavage, outlining her breasts.

His vision seemed slightly out of focus. "I'm not sure. I should have taken you directly to your mother's."

"My mother couldn't do a thing to protect me. I'd have to protect her."

"One of your brothers then."

"They have too many kids and too few bedrooms to put me up."

"You could sleep on their couch."

"*You* could sleep on *my* couch."

He choked, the flesh of his face started to burn and his eyes to bulge. "Not likely."

"Afraid you wouldn't be able to *stay* on the couch?"

"Are you suggesting I couldn't help but crawl into your bed?" God help him, it was exactly what *he* was afraid of.

"I'm just trying to figure out why you're so scared."

"Scared? Hardly." His voice broke irritatingly on the words.

"What happened between yesterday in your office and today?"

He wanted to close his eyes and rest his neck on the headrest.

"Didn't you like touching me?"

His throat rumbled, his lips fumbled, but no words came out. Was this what they called tongue-tied? He'd never experienced the like in his life. Until Madison. Until this week.

"Don't you want to touch me again?"

He looked everywhere but at her, his fingers slithering all over the steering wheel as if they were disconnected from his brain commands. Finally he managed to get out, "That's really not a good idea."

"Why?"

He did turn to her then, his hands rigid on the wheel so he wouldn't, couldn't, touch her, which was all he really wanted to do. "Why do you always ask why? Most people wouldn't have said anything at all. They would have just dropped the subject."

"I'm not most people."

He snorted in agreement. "I'm your boss. It shouldn't have happened in the first place."

"But it did. Why did it?"

He executed a series of throat clearings and wheel tappings, and suddenly a light seemed to go out in her eyes.

"Richard made you jealous. Now he's gone. You're in control again." She spread her hands. "So it's over. Just like that."

Her eyes shimmered. He felt lower than a garden slug.

"You should have just fired me this morning in front of Harriet. Then the suit would be over. And *we* could be over."

"There never was a 'we,' Madison. And we can forget about what happened yesterday, go back to the way it was before our little…" What could he call it? Whatever it was, it certainly wasn't little. He tried anyway. "Our little lapse."

"We can never go back to the way it was."

Hurt gleamed in her moist eyes, trembled on her lips and sniffled in her nose.

Hell.

She climbed from her open car door.

"You are not staying alone."

"And I'm not going to my mother or my brothers."

He wondered if it was a calculated challenge. The brief idea vanished as quickly as it came. Madison didn't know the meaning of underhanded. "All right, I'll spend the night."

A facsimile of her slightly lopsided smile appeared on her lips. "You will?"

"But I'm sleeping on the couch."

"Of course you are."

He shook a finger at her. "And there will be no sex."

She graced him with the full wattage of her smile. "Of course there won't be any sex."

Laurence had the sense he'd set himself up for total failure.

CHAPTER SIXTEEN

THEY WOULDN'T HAVE SEX. They'd be making love.

Steam from her bath rose to mist the mirror. A bath ball fizzed in the water, the scent of tangerines filling the moist air. She sipped a glass of sweet German wine. Liebfraumilch. She couldn't say the word, but the taste garnered a sigh and a lick of her lips. She'd given T. Larry a glass of wine, too.

She'd made T. Larry dinner. Not Jigglers or meat loaf, but Hamburger Helper. She didn't tell him that, though. Men didn't understand that Hamburger Helper was like making from scratch, without the hassle. T. Larry had eaten it and asked for seconds.

Thank goodness there'd been no hang up calls, which would have made T. Larry only more jittery. And Sean must have cleaned up any mess the police technicians made dusting for fingerprints or whatever it was they did. One wouldn't have even known they'd been there. She knew she should be more worried. A normal girl would be. But…she had T. Larry to protect her. And her brothers. Besides, as she'd told T. Larry, God simply wouldn't follow through on a threat of bodily harm when he'd given her a stroke at fifteen and just might give her another at twenty-eight. See, that wouldn't make sense in a cosmic sort of way.

Okay, so that explanation was a lot more agreeable than actually thinking that some Jack the Ripper was going to rip her. She shivered despite the steamy water.

Enough. She was scaring herself. Much better to think about T. Larry. She only had eight days until her birthday. Well, seven, since today was almost over.

The last few drops of wine trickled down her throat. Her flesh had sizzled long enough in the slightly too-hot tub. She rose, water sluicing down her limbs. She had such plans for T. Larry. She towel dried, wiped condensation from the mirror and surveyed her pink cheeks. She'd scrubbed her makeup off and decided against applying any more. Pulling her nightie over her head, she tugged it down to midthigh. Maybe blue sheep weren't the thing for seducing a man, but she loved her sheep. T. Larry wouldn't want her to be anything other than what she was.

Adding just a touch of gloss to her lips, she opened the bathroom door, steamy, humid air rushing out and filling the apartment with a light tangerine scent. She found extra sheets, a pillow and a light blanket for him in the hall closet, and armed with her offering, she entered the living room.

"We can make up the couch with these."

T. Larry stared at her bare thighs, then his gaze trailed her legs down to her feet and back up again to the center of her chest. "What are you wearing?"

"My jammies."

He'd been standing. He flopped down heavily on the sofa without another word.

She flashed him a brilliant smile. "Do you want me to tuck you in and kiss you goodnight?"

"No kissing."

She pursed her lips. He was being very difficult. "It was just a joke. My mother always used to tuck me in." She plopped the bedding down next to him and opened her mouth.

"And I'm not tucking you in, either," he said before she could get a word out.

"I was going to ask if you wanted me to put the sheets on?"

He raised his eyes to the ceiling. "I can handle it," then belatedly added, "thanks."

She put her hands behind her back and rocked heel to toe. "Do you want me to wake you up at a certain time in the morning?"

"I'm sure I'll wake up on my own."

"Do you want to take a shower here?"

"I'll take one after my workout."

"Are we going to stop at your house for a change of clothes?"

He eyed her as if she'd suggested they have a little nookie in his bed at the same time. "I've got a change in my locker at the gym." Again, that belated, "Thanks."

This wasn't going the way she planned. Not that she'd had a real plan, not like one of T. Larry's meticulous-down-to-the-last-detail plans. She'd thought the sight of her in her jammies might drive him wild with desire. Had the sheep been a mistake?

"All right, well, umm, good night." She backed up, waiting for him to say something, waiting for him to beg her to stay.

He didn't. All he said was, "Good night."

She was forced to go down the hall to her bedroom. Before slipping beneath the covers, she'd left the door open a few scant inches. The sound of his movements drifted through the cracked door, the snap of sheets, the pounding of a pillow, the soft snick of the bathroom door. She'd left an extra toothbrush out for him. The door opened, a zipper rasped. Her cheeks heated, imagining him undressing. He'd fold his slacks just so and hang his shirt over a chair to keep it from wrinkling. T. Larry wouldn't sleep naked.

Well, what to do now? Madison didn't like to give up. She closed her eyes, hovered on the edge of sleep despite herself, until he groaned and punched his pillow.

The solution came to her as if it had been there all the time. What she needed was a nightmare, one that would bring him rushing to her bed like a hero in a romance novel.

SHE'D DRIVEN HIM CRAZY with that bath. The citrus scent hung in the humid air. Laurence had salivated over every slosh of water, every sigh, every chink of her wineglass against the porcelain tub. He'd imagined her naked in bubbles, the tips of her breasts peeking through. He'd imagined licking the water from her thighs.

Then she'd come out to say good-night in her terrifyingly short blue-and-white nightie, her legs bare, her nipples perked.

He couldn't sleep for the life of him. He'd tried counting sheep, but then he saw her nightie instead, and began stripping it off in his mind. Sheep definitely did not work.

Laurence tossed. He turned. Listened to the occasional drone of a car engine as it passed, the tick of the kitchen clock, the high-pitched bark of a dog. A soft sleepy moan from her room.

Oh God.

Not a moan. More like a cry. A frightened cry. The sound galvanized him. He threw off the blanket and sheet, grabbed his glasses from the coffee table, rushed down the hall, and pushed her door open. Her head twisted on the pillow, and she made another distressed little noise.

"Madison?"

She didn't answer, continuing to thrash beneath the covers. One hand swatted at something he couldn't see. She was dreaming.

He whispered into the night, loath to cross the threshold. "Hey, Madison Avenue, wake up. You're having a nightmare."

Her citrus scent called to him, as did her frantic motions. Christ. She was probably dreaming about the person who'd broken into her apartment, endlessly running from the perpetrator.

He took three steps into the room, called her name again and realized he was clad only in briefs and a T-shirt. Moonlight fell in through the window. Her hair, spread across the pillow, begged to be touched. A soft sigh and her still stepped-from-the-bath fragrance seeped inside his head. His groin tightened impossibly.

"T. Larry?" Her voice quavered as if the nightmare hadn't quite receded despite the fact that he'd managed to wake her. Had she heard the nickname?

"It's me." God, he wanted to climb beneath those covers, lift that little nightie, touch…taste…stroke.

"Thank goodness. I was having a bad dream. I thought someone was in my room." Her voice was tiny and weak.

"It's over now. You can go back to sleep." Not that he'd be able to.

"I'm scared, T. Larry. Could you sit with me for a while?"

He wanted so much more. Looking around, he found the only seat was a round stool in front of her dresser. He skirted the bed to sit, hiding his erection in case she should look.

"That's too far away. It doesn't help." She patted the bed. "Come here."

Inside her skin was the closest he could get. His fingers clenched, but his legs moved despite the screaming protest from his brain. Setting his glasses on the bedside table, then nestling down on the covers next to her, he itched all over to crawl beneath.

She turned on the pillow, her eyes reflecting moonlight.

He searched for anything to take his mind out of his shorts. "What was the dream about?"

She shrugged, hair rustling against cotton. "Don't remember."

Of its own accord, his hand reached for the silky tresses. His fingers tangled in the locks. It was just hair, he could touch his fill and no harm done.

She murmured deep in her throat, as if she had nerve endings in the strands. "That's nice."

So many nice things he could do to her. She'd pushed the bedspread down to her waist. His touch followed the length of one long curl, the backs of his fingers lingering against the swell of her breast.

"My mother used to stroke my hair."

The things he thought of doing weren't the slightest bit motherly. She purred like a cat under his ministrations.

"I think my bath was too hot. I'm burning up."

He was burning up.

Then she flipped back the spread and clambered out to lie beside him.

His heart stopped, his fingers slid to the flesh at her throat, and his gonads snapped. She sighed, and he felt it to the tip of his penis.

"There, that's better." She closed her eyes as if she hadn't a clue what she was doing to him.

Lying flat, her nightshirt drifted down against her full breasts, outlining her peaked nipples. The hem rode up to the tops of her thighs, seducing him.

"I'm not sleepy anymore," she said, letting him play with her hair and his fantasies. "Are you?"

Sleep? It was the furthest thing from his mind. "What are you wearing under that?"

"Under this?" Her fingers plucked at the flannel material covering her hip.

He nodded, incapable of speech.

"Nothing."

He shut his eyes and clamped down on a groan. Her fruity perfume made stars dance before his closed lids.

"I never wear anything. Is that bad?"

Run, a voice shrieked inside. His muscles neither listened nor obeyed. Instead his fingertips trailed between her breasts, followed the slope of her abdomen and twitched above her hip bone.

"Madison." His voice rasped in his parched throat. He hadn't even kissed her, but gone straight for the goodies like an eager schoolboy.

"It's all right, T. Larry."

What was all right? "I want to kiss you," he managed, dragging his eyes to her face.

She smiled. Then, oddly, the smile faded. "T. Larry, I just can't do it."

Something began to pound behind his eyeballs, inside his chest. "What do you mean?"

"I lied to you."

"It doesn't matter." Nothing mattered but touching her.

"But I tricked you. And it wouldn't be fair."

"Of course, it's fair." What? He didn't care about *what*.

"I can't make love with you when I lied."

He wanted to cry, but shut his eyes once more and drew in a deep breath of her. "Tell me about the lie."

"I didn't have a bad dream."

"That's good." What the hell dream was she talking about?

"I just pretended to have a nightmare so you'd come in here."

Oh, that dream. He was beyond anger. "That's okay."

"But it was such a childish thing to do. I don't know what came over me."

He opened his eyes to find hers seriously gazing at him. "You shouldn't have done it," he said to placate her. "Now kiss me."

"But it isn't right."

He cupped her head, pulled her against him, then took her lips. Oh, the taste. Sweet wine, toothpaste and Madison. She parted her lips, took his tongue, then glued her body to his, arms wrapped around his neck. Her nipples were hard little nubs against his chest, her leg smooth as it curled around his. His hand slid down her back to tug at the flannel until soft flesh sizzled beneath his fingers.

God, if this was having sex, he wanted it as he never had before. If this was making love, then he didn't think he could live without it. He pulled his lips from hers, trailed his mouth down the side of her neck, licked, suckled.

"Do you forgive me, T. Larry?" she whispered next to his ear.

"I'll get mad at you in the morning." He'd think about his control failure tomorrow. Then he pulled her nightshirt over her head and pushed her to her back.

God, he'd never seen such beautiful skin, soft, delicate. And her breasts, round, beckoning. He sucked the plump flesh, then pulled a nipple into his mouth.

She gasped, put her hands to both sides of his head and held him there, one smooth leg caressing his.

"Do you like that?" he murmured after a swipe of his tongue.

"Yes."

He heard her swallow, felt her chest move beneath his mouth. He switched to her other nipple. She tasted like oranges. She arched against him, moaned. It drove him crazy. So many spots he wanted to taste, to touch, but his body called him to that place between her legs. He tested with his finger, felt her spasm and her wetness.

God, she wanted him. Madison really wanted him. It was almost too much to believe, and he removed his hand, pulling back to stare into her face. "Are you sure about this?"

"I'm sure." She ran her hand over the top of his head. "I love your head, T. Larry. Did I ever tell you that?"

"Uhhh, no." She loved bald? "I thought you always said it made me look old and stuffy."

She grabbed his chin in her fingers and squished his lips together until he felt like a bloated fish. "I *never* thought that, T. Larry. Didn't I tell you bald is sexy?"

"Yes, but—"

She put her thumb on the seam of his lips. "No buts. I love it. And I only said you were stuffy when you were talking about your silly plans. And don't say they're not silly!"

He couldn't say a word, first because the pad of her thumb caressing his lips did odd things to him and second because the thought of her loving his bald head was...nothing short of a miracle.

"I'm not lying, T. Larry."

He hadn't said a word.

"But I can hear what you're thinking."

He blinked.

She removed her thumb and brushed his lips with hers. "You've got hot eyes, too, all smoky and stuff, and they do funny things to me. Are you going to make love to me now?"

He swallowed, and knew if he were in his right mind, he wouldn't simply accept everything she said. He'd return to his station on her couch. "I don't have any protection."

"There's something in the nightstand."

He wouldn't ask why even as the thought stabbed him. Instead he rose, stripped off his T-shirt and briefs, then opened the drawer to find a full box of condoms. She lay on the bed looking beautiful, trusting and vulnerable.

He put one on while she watched, her eyes glittering with fascination, and then he moved between her legs. He pulsed against her, but something held him back from simply entering, taking. He wished suddenly he hadn't rushed with the condom. Rising above her on his elbows, he nibbled her bottom lip.

"Put me inside you."

She reached between them, found his length. His fingers joined hers, enjoying the feel of her hand wrapped around him. Then he slid away to touch her, finding the same sweet spot he'd known so lovingly yesterday. She sighed, arched and caressed him with her hand, her touch only slightly diminished by the rubber.

He delved more intimately. God, she was so wet, so ready, as ready as he. Still he couldn't quite believe it. He entered her with two fingers. She squeezed him, then reached down to cup him.

"Do you want me, Madison?" he whispered into her hair.

"Yes. Please." Her breathy voice made him jerk in her hand.

He withdrew his fingers, sliding them once more over her clitoris, then joined with her hand to guide himself inside. She held his buttocks as he entered fully. God, she was tight. He buried his face in her neck, her hair, and eased deeper. She slid damp fingers to his back, his shoulders, then hugged him close.

Raising her hips to meet him, she rode each thrust.

"Are you going to tell me what the *T* stands for after this?" she whispered as if it were a sweet nothing in his ear.

Jesus. He'd tell her anything she wanted to hear. She was hot and slippery and unlike any woman he'd ever known. And this, this was unlike any act he'd ever known. Her soft cries echoed in his ears as he pumped, and when she started her orgasm, she bit into the flesh of his shoulder. The love bite sent him over the edge, and he dived headlong off the cliff he'd been standing on.

The cliff was called Loving Madison Avenue.

MADISON HAD BEEN AWAKE for some time. T. Larry snored gently against her arm. All was right with her world. At least it should have been. He made love to her, the most fantastic glorious love, along with all the other delicious little adjectives she couldn't think of at the moment. T. Larry had taken her beyond anything she'd ever felt in her entire life. Yet...something was missing.

One-sided love just wasn't enough.

With anyone else, she could have deluded herself, but love would never hit T. Larry unexpectedly. She wasn't in his plan.

She rolled to her side, pressing against him, to look at the clock. T. Larry grunted softly but didn't wake. The alarm would go off in two or three minutes. He slept like a child, his face smooth and unlined, almost young.

Looking at him, she ached inside, which wasn't something she was used to. Being in love with T. Larry, she was destined to feel this particular ache a lot. Still, a tiny smile grew on her lips. The man was adorable.

Beep, beep, beep. She didn't use a music alarm. Music lulled her back to sleep.

T. Larry jerked. "What?"

She clambered over him, reached for the switch, then lay still against him, chest to chest. She was hoping for a good-morning kiss. "It's time to get up."

He didn't put his arms around her. She rolled back to her side of the bed. "I'll take my shower first if you want to lie in bed a little longer."

"All right."

Yep, she was destined for that ache.

She'd set her clothes out the night before, jeans and a T-shirt being her only choices since she couldn't stand another turtleneck. She climbed from the bed, made sure her nightshirt—which she'd put back on last night when T. Larry donned his briefs—covered her butt, and gathered her apparel.

"Madison."

She whirled, ready to throw her baggage to the floor and jump back into bed. "Hmm?"

"Why did you have a box of condoms in your drawer?"

Oh. She'd noticed his hesitation last night. "I bought them for you. Just in case."

He didn't say anything.

"Are you mad?" Now he could yell about the dream, too.

"No."

She should go. This was sort of humiliating. "Are you sorry about last night?"

"No."

Then what? "Do you want to tell me what you're feeling?" Fat chance. He was a man. Men never said what they were feeling.

"Not right now."

She gathered her bundle close to her chest, but the ache didn't stop. She wanted to tell him she loved him, wanted to ask if he might give up his plans and love her. For the first time in her life, she didn't say a thing that was on her mind.

"I'll take my shower then. Do you want some breakfast?"

"I have some fruit at work." Then a second later, "Thanks."

The whole scene was beyond mere humiliation. Making love was supposed to bring two people together.

Instead, she couldn't blurt out one teeny-tiny feeling. She padded down the hall to the bathroom and left him alone.

Maybe the *T* stood for Temporary. Temporary Larry, temporary in her life.

Loving him wasn't supposed to hurt like this.

CHAPTER SEVENTEEN

LAURENCE HAD JUST pulled into the parking garage after the longest, quietest forty-five minutes he'd ever spent in Madison's company when she broke her silence.

"All right, I'm done."

His usual parking space was empty, waiting for him. "Done? With what?" Him?

"Pouting."

"Pouting?"

"T. Larry, why are you repeating everything I say?"

"I'm trying to understand." He'd never seen her pout. He'd assumed her silence meant she was hurt because he hadn't declared his undying love nor encouraged her to declare hers. Pouting, on the other hand, was an emotion that didn't run deep.

"It's unbecoming. So I'm done. We can get back to normal."

"Normal?" The night before they'd experienced the most incredible sex of their lives, and now she wanted normal? Maybe the "they" was the problem. *He'd* experienced the most incredible sex of *his* life. He didn't have a clue about Madison.

"Stop that."

"Stop what?"

"Repeating what I say," she almost shouted.

"I think we should talk about last night."

"I think we shouldn't." She opened her door, stepped out, then closed it on him.

Then he understood. He'd blown it that morning, when he'd given her monosyllabic answers, terrified if he allowed anything else, he'd humiliate himself by telling her exactly how he felt.

He caught up with her at the elevators in their building. Normal. If normal was what she wanted, that's what she'd get.

They faced the elevator doors. The light dinged, the doors opened. He held them as she boarded, then pushed the button.

Their reflections in the silver door screeched at him. She barely reached his shoulder, especially without her usual high heels. In the wavy image, she was all glorious red hair, he was all bald head and seriousness. What the hell had he been thinking last night? That was the problem, *he* hadn't been doing any thinking at all. His male member had been doing it all.

Just then, Madison slipped her hand in his, tugged on his fingers until his gaze met hers in the silvered door.

"You know, T. Larry, no matter what else happens after this, I want you to know last night was the best night of my life."

The doors whooshed open, she dropped his hand, graced him with a killer smile and left him to make his own way back down to the gym on the eleventh floor.

She couldn't see it, but an answering smile curved his lips. While everything certainly wasn't right with the world, Laurence was sure it wasn't all completely wrong, either. Madison had said she loved his bald head.

LAURENCE FOUND HER an hour later on her hands and knees under her desk making sniffing noises. The sight of her delectable rump in the air, encased in tight jeans, gave him heart palpitations.

"What the hell are you doing?"

"Don't swear at me," came from beneath the desk. She backed out, sat on her haunches and stared at him. "Can't you smell it?"

He sniffed just as she had. He hadn't noticed a thing, assailed as he was by prurient images of Madison on all fours. But now that she mentioned it… "What is that odor?"

She plopped her hands down on her thighs. "I smelled it yesterday, but it's way worse today. I checked the trash cans and behind the filing cabinet. I even threw away Richard's flowers."

Good riddance. "It smells like something died in here. Call Maintenance. Maybe there's a mouse in the air-conditioning."

"It's only around my desk. I checked the other cubes and the copy room."

Bill walked by behind Laurence. "New cologne, Madison?"

She stuck her tongue out at him.

"That was rude." Laurence had never heard Bill say anything so downright mean to Madison. The place was going crazy. Had the moon been full last night? That would explain a lot. "What's wrong with him?"

"He's miffed because I spilled coffee on his shirt yesterday." Madison climbed to her feet and dusted off her hands.

"Didn't you tell him it was an accident?"

"It wasn't."

He was afraid to ask. "Call Maintenance."

She did, amidst a chorus of gags and gasps as his crew began to arrive. It was pretty bad. Definitely a mouse. Or a lost and forgotten bit of Madison's meat loaf.

Before the words could leave his mouth, Laurence backed into his office and closed the door. He dropped his briefcase on the desk, hung his jacket, then sat in his chair. A myriad of letters needed signing, client documents needed reviewing, and there were checks to be authorized. He ignored them all, thinking instead about the smoothness of Madison's skin.

He was definitely a basket case.

The door opened behind him. Jeremiah; he recognized the throat clearing. Laurence turned slowly in his chair.

Jeremiah Carp's face had grown to resemble his name the way some people grow to resemble their dogs. His cheeks looked puffed up with air, and his lips seemed to be in a perpetual pucker.

Laurence folded his hands in his lap to hide his state of arousal. "What can I do for you, Jeremiah?"

"It's about that smell."

"Why are you whispering?"

Jeremiah shrugged, then raised his voice. "I'm not sure." Entering, he closed the door behind him.

"You were saying?" Laurence prompted.

"The smell. Ryman has a client coming in this afternoon, and he'll pitch a fit if…" Jeremiah's voice trailed off, and he held his hands up in defeat or acceptance.

"We'll have the mess cleaned up by noon. Besides,

Ryman can walk his client around the other side of the cubicles. The distance to his office is the same."

"Actually, he's bringing the client to see you."

Laurence groaned. "Not Stephen Tortellini." He snapped his mouth shut, realizing belatedly he'd used a Madison nickname.

"Tortelli," Jeremiah corrected. "And uh…yes, he's bringing him to see you." Jeremiah didn't meet his eyes.

"When did you stop backing me on this Tortellini thing?" Laurence already knew. Ryman had gotten to Jeremiah. The man was a pushover, an excellent accountant, but a pushover nonetheless.

"You know Ryman."

"You were the one who said any man who wore a Rolex watch, drove a new Porsche Boxster and had just purchased a home in Saratoga couldn't be making less than a hundred thousand a year the way Tortellini claims." Laurence would have given his eyeteeth to live in that quiet little suburb. But he couldn't afford it, and he had brought in over a hundred K last year.

Jeremiah spread his hands and waffled. "Well, on the face of it, I suppose it is a bit suspicious."

"But you want *me* to handle Ryman."

Jeremiah puffed his cheeks like a blowfish, then smiled in an almost boyish fashion. "Yes," he said as he darted for the door, exited, then leaned back in for a parting shot. "Right after you get rid of the smell."

The situation was becoming farcical.

The phone rang. He let it go four times before he realized Madison wasn't going to pick it up for him.

"Hobbs here."

"I'm still waiting for an answer." The slightly stuffy tones of Harry Dump.

"My seventy-two hours aren't up."

"You just want time to put pressure on Miss Hartman."

He raised a brow though no one would notice. "Yes. You're exactly right. And I think she's caving, Dump." He was sure to give the name its phonetic pronunciation.

"I won't put up with any shenanigans, Hobbs."

"So sue me."

He rammed the receiver back in its cradle, hoping the noise would split the man's eardrums. Damn, that felt good. He should have been worried about Madison's reputation, about his position in the firm.

Primarily, he felt like a warrior in battle. He was going to win. Ryman would drop that damn client like a hot potato. Harriet would drop her suit. And Madison...

What did he want from Madison?

STAN THE MAN—Madison wasn't sure of his last name—stretched on his ladder, screwing the air-conditioning plate back in place, his plumber's crack staring her in the face.

"I really don't think there's anything up there, Madison. You'd smell it all over the office, maybe even the whole building, if something died up there."

"I've looked everywhere down here. It has to be up there."

Stan climbed down, hitched his pants up as far as they would go, scratched two inches short of his privates and took a deep, considering breath. "Did you check out your desk?"

"How could a mouse have gotten in my desk?"

"They're sneaky little bastards."

"Stan," she warned.

He gave her a pudgy grin. "Sneaky little sons-a-bitches?"

"That's even worse. I think."

He erased his smile. "All right. The 'little darlings' can get into anything. Open your drawers."

She wanted to laugh, but then she'd have to explain the image to Stan. So she did as he asked while he watched over her shoulder, sniffing close to her ear.

"See, I told you there isn't anything in there."

He did some more sniffing and snuffling, his nose wrinkling. Shuffling across the carpet, he bent at the waist. Madison had the awful thought that he looked and sounded a bit like a pig.

"It's over here somewhere," Stan pointed, "and closer to the floor. What about that file cabinet?"

"I don't usually go into the bottom drawer. It's just got some old diskettes and stuff." Plus it was her secret hideaway for T. Larry's body parts, when she had a mind to tell people she'd cut him up with her chain saw.

Stan, still leaning over and shocking her with an enormous amount of his crack, put one hand on his knee and slid the drawer open with the other. The smell intensified.

"Ewwwwe." Madison put her hand over her nose and mouth.

"Jesus H. Christ."

"What for God's sake is that?" Voices punctuated Stan's.

"I'm gonna puke."

She didn't have to turn to know it was Mike, Anthony and Bill. They stood at her cubicle opening like a grazing herd.

Seemingly undisturbed by his audience, Stan rummaged around in the contents of the drawer. "You know what's in that box?"

"What box?" She didn't want to get close enough to see.

"The one that says 'Happy Birthday, Madison' on it."

A present? Hidden in her drawer? Ooh, how fun. She stepped forward, stopped. "That's not what stinks, is it?"

Hands on both knees, Stan looked over his shoulder. "Don't know. But one of us has to open it. I just didn't want to spoil your birthday surprise."

"Smells like it's already spoiled," quipped one of the herd.

Someone else snickered. A crowd was gathering. Even Harriet had come out to play. Standing next to the wall, ZZ Top's gaze moved from Harriet to Madison and back over the massed heads.

As a matter of pride and bravado, Madison took the box. Multicolored balloon paper wrapped what seemed to be a shoe box. Written in each of the balloons on top, in different-colored inks, "Happy Birthday, Madison" shouted at her.

The stench was everywhere now, clinging to her nostrils, making it impossible to tell the origin. Certainly not this festive shoe box. She slid a fingernail along the underside of the lid, slicing the paper neatly.

"Don't you need to blow out a candle before you open your present?" Bill needling her.

"That's before you cut the cake."

"Smells like someone cut the cheese." Anthony? Mike? She couldn't tell.

Fear suddenly wet her palms. Something terrible lay in wait for her. Maybe it was the tire slashings, the calls, her clothes, everything catching up with her; her hands started to shake.

"You want I should open it for you, Madison?"

Stan. What a man. She wished T. Larry would come out of his office and rescue her. But it was best not to admit weakness when you were actually freaking out. "I can do it."

She set the box down on the desk because she couldn't stand to hold the present against her while she opened it. Slicing through the paper the rest of the way, she slipped a finger beneath the lid, hesitating.

"Come on, Madison, we can't stand the suspense." Laughter.

She wondered if they knew how scared she was.

She gave it a flip, sent the lid tumbling and screamed. Stumbling back, she tripped over her chair, shooting it into Stan's knees. Falling hard on her butt, her head whacked her bookcase, and this time she saw stars for a very different reason.

They were on her, squirming, writhing maggots, hundreds of them, swarming right out of the box, streaming over her legs and her arms, crawling up her nose. Ohmygod. Ohmygod.

Voices. All around her. "Jesus, it's a dead rat."

"Gross."

"How long's it been there?"

"Must have been days."

"Christ, who would put something like that in her drawer?"

"Madison, are you all right?" ZZ Top crouched at her side, touching her arm. She almost started screaming again, but she did at least realize the maggots weren't actually crawling on her.

"What's going on?" T. Larry. Someone must have pointed at the box, because he said, "Get it the freaking hell out of here."

"You better call 911." ZZ's voice rumbled in her ear. "I think she hurt her head when she fell."

Madison sat up. "I'm fine." Except that she had the silly urge to throw herself into T. Larry's arms no matter who was watching. "I hit the books, not the case itself." Which was a lie, but she wasn't going to any hospital and she wasn't letting any 911 people touch her. No way. They probably dealt with maggoty dead people all the time. "Make them go away, T. Larry."

He squatted beside her, touched the back of her head and knew exactly what she meant. "Go back to your desks," he barked. "Fun's over." Then, when only Stan and ZZ remained, he said in a quieter voice to her, "You've got a bit of a bump."

"It just scared me, and I fell."

Something lit his eyes, she couldn't tell what. "What happened?"

"Stan found it in the file drawer. It said Happy Birthday."

He glanced at the discarded paper. "And you had to open it."

"They were all watching. I couldn't wimp out."

"Of course not." His hand stroking her arm now, he glanced at Stan by the desk. "Why don't you take that into my office?"

Nodding his thanks as the big man shuffled away, box in hand, T. Larry tapped ZZ on the knee. "Zach, call the police." He rattled off the name and number of the detective handling Madison's case. "Tell him we've got another incident."

"The police," she squeaked.

"That paper has your name written all over it. Someone put a dead rat in your drawer and waited for you to find it."

"I think it was a squirrel, sir," ZZ said as the phone ostensibly rang in his ear.

And it was covered with maggots. She hated maggots. She hated to think of them crawling all over her when she was dead. She wanted to be cremated, she'd told Ma. No maggots, no worms.

They wrap you up in a clean white sheet and throw you down about six feet deep. The worms crawl in, the worms crawl out...

Her brothers had taunted her with that little ditty for years. At least until she'd had her stroke. But she never forgot, never stopped being scared of the worms and the maggots.

She whimpered. Who would do this? It couldn't be someone she knew. Yet it could be any one of them. Richard who brought her flowers. Harriet, Richard, Mike, Anthony or Bill. Even ZZ. No. A voice inside her head screamed for her to stop. It had to be a stranger. That thought was far less scary. She would not accuse a single one of her friends.

T. Larry wrapped her in his big strong arms. "It's all right, baby."

ZZ Top murmured on the phone, but his eyes were wide as saucers taking in T. Larry's tone and the grip he had on Madison.

T. Larry helped her to her feet. "Let's go into the conference room, and I'll get you some coffee."

The rank odor followed them down the hall. She'd never stop smelling it. It had seared itself into her nostril hairs. But she liked T. Larry's arms around her, the gentleness of his voice, and she gave another weak whimper to make sure he didn't stop.

"I WANT TO TALK TO YOU."

Zachary grabbed Harriet by the arm, pulled her through the lobby, along the hallway, and into the rarely used stairwell.

"What for Christ's sake did you think you were doing?"

He towered over her despite her attractively tall heels like something Madison would wear. Harriet liked this new Zachary even if he did spend most of his time yelling at her. He was standing up to her. He was coming out of his shell. Maybe it was time she came out of hers, a little at least. "I've been thinking about what you said the other night."

He drew back several inches. "Yeah?" A question and a derisive comment at the same time, as if he didn't believe she could actually consider his opinion, or change hers. "And what have you come up with?"

"Maybe you aren't to blame for everything." There, she'd said it. She expected a little softening.

Instead, he stuck his finger in his ear and wiggled it around. "I don't think I'm hearing right. You, admitting you might be wrong?"

Definitely, the Zachary she'd known was losing the battle to a newer, more outspoken man. She felt a little shiver in the center of her abdomen. "I might have been a little wary of what people would think if they knew about…" She dipped her head, wanting him to think she was hesitant to say the words. "If anyone knew what we did that night in the conference room."

"You were ashamed."

Not ashamed. She just didn't want to defend dating him. Then she'd gotten mad because she'd realized he didn't want to defend dating *her*. She looked up, trying one of Madison's please-forgive-me-I-didn't-mean-it looks. It always worked for Madison. "Can't we start over, Zachary?"

His face hardened, like a mask of clay slipping over his features. "It's too late after what you did today."

For the first time she began to doubt he'd dragged her out here just to talk about their relationship. The shiver in the pit of her stomach turned to a knot. "What do you mean?"

"Why did you put that box in Madison's drawer?"

All the blood in her body drained down to her knees, leaving her light-headed. "You think *I* did that?"

"Yes." He didn't even hesitate, that hard mask still in place, even his eyes glinting like obsidian. "And it follows that you ruined her clothes, too."

Zachary had hurt her before, but the pain of it had been mild compared to the way his words slashed her heart to ribbons. "How can you say that?"

"I've seen you hate, Harriet. I've seen you vindictive. I've seen you rip people to shreds with a few words."

The way she'd tried to shred him, but only because he'd hurt her. It was a way to fight back. "Sometimes I say things...."

He seemed to read it all on her face, every transgression, every thought. "And sometimes you *do* things."

Like the lawsuit.

He read that in her expression, also. "You named her in the suit as well as me. Stands to reason you hate her just as much."

"I never hated you, Zachary," she whispered.

"Then just what do you feel? If it isn't hate, then what made you do this to all of us?"

She wanted to squeeze her eyes against the pain of his words. "Us, Zachary? Who's the us you're talking about?"

"Harriet against the world, that's always been your motto. All of *us* against you. Killing that squirrel and putting it in Madison's drawer is the end. I don't care what I did to you, how I hurt you, how you think everyone's hurt you, you had no fucking right to do that."

Goose bumps rose on her arms. She sat heavily on the first concrete step, gripped the iron rail in tight, pained fingers. "I didn't put that box in her drawer. I couldn't kill anything. I didn't tear up her clothes."

"I don't believe you."

She looked up at him, eyes brimming, his impassive face wavery through the moisture. She wanted to be angry with him. Anger had always been her best outlet. She wished she could scratch him like a shrieking cat, like the Harriet she'd been two days ago. Instead, her heart wanted to burst from her chest.

"Do you really think I'm capable of doing those things?"

"You aren't the same girl I made love to eight months ago, Harriet." His eyes burned her. "So the answer is yes, the woman you've become *could* do it."

She let the tears fall. Maybe this time she deserved what she got.

CHAPTER EIGHTEEN

THE POLICE CAME, photographed, dusted, noted, questioned, frowned, sighed and questioned more. They sent the foul birthday package to their lab. Laurence made sure they had Richard Lyon's name again. Since he'd paid Madison a visit the day before. He was grateful to know a check had been run on the man but disappointed to learn it had revealed nothing incriminating. The detectives' diligence and thoroughness amazed and pleased Laurence, especially considering that it was a different jurisdiction from Madison's apartment. The fact that they were no closer to finding the culprit when they vacated the premises, however, did not please him. Nor did the mysterious absences of Harriet or Zach. He promised himself and the detectives that they would be available for questioning the next day.

By midafternoon, Madison's effervescent smile sagged on both sides of her mouth. Screw Tortelli's visit. Ryman could meet the man without him. Laurence had far more important things to attend to, such as taking Madison to the Emergency Room, insisting on it actually. There, the doctors characterized her injury as a bump, no stitches necessary, no concussion evident. The diagnosis mollified him.

The ensuing argument about where she would spend the night did not. Against his better judgment, he drove her to her apartment, accompanied her inside, searched the abode for any signs of forced entry or devastation and found none. Thank God.

"I am not going to my mother's."

"I can't spend the night with you." Nevertheless, he removed his suit jacket and laid it across the back of a chair.

"Why not?"

He hadn't expected such resistance, even from Madison. Short of telling her about William Daily's threat to her reputation, he didn't have a good answer. He used the only weapon he had left. "Madison, a relationship between us is out of the question."

So was leaving her alone.

"I don't want a relationship, I just want you to hold me."

The downturn of her mouth and the moisture in her eyes almost undid him. Almost. He groaned silently, turned to pace in front of the window over her garage. "I know you're afraid—"

"I'm terrified. How could anyone do that to a poor little squirrel?"

"They did it to *you*."

She bit her lip, sniffled.

"Not everyone is good and sweet, Madison. There are bad people out there."

She wrapped her arms around her middle and dipped her head. "Please don't, T. Larry."

He had to make her see she was in danger. "I know you don't want to hear—"

"Stop it. I'm scared. And I do know." She scrubbed

at her cheeks. "Please just hold me. I'm not asking for anything else."

He'd never seen her scared. He'd never seen her anything but up, up, up. He didn't doubt for a second that her emotion was real, not something she'd manufactured to get him to crawl between her sheets. His fear, for her and of what she made him feel, was no less. "I don't think we should start this all over again."

"I know," she sighed, toeing her tennis shoes off, and curling into a corner of the couch. "We don't suit each other. It will all end badly. Our relationship is doomed to failure."

He couldn't remember saying the like to her, only thinking it. Her melancholy made him ache. "I don't want to hurt you." It went without saying that he would, just as she would hurt him. "I only want to protect you."

She shook her head slowly, her eyes following his movement as he wore holes in her carpet. "I don't need protecting, T. Larry. I need..." She never finished, as if admitting her deepest needs aloud was too much even for Madison.

"I'm sorry." For touching her, for wanting her, for exposing her to the likes of Harry Dump and William Dilly-Dally.

"You're afraid I'm too fickle to truly fall in love."

"I never said that."

"I'm good at reading between the lines. You think I have no concept of the future, of living past this moment. But I do, T. Larry." Her chin trembled, her voice stuffy with tears not shed.

He couldn't stop the movement of his feet as he rounded the coffee table and hunkered down in front of her, his hand inches from her knee. "Don't cry."

She wrapped her arms around her legs, hugging them to her chest. "I'm so afraid, T. Larry. It's not just that poor little squirrel or my clothes or my tires." She sucked in a shivery breath. "I'm so scared of dying, T. Larry." Her voice dropped to a whisper. "I fill up every moment, savor them all, just so I won't have to think about what might happen."

Jesus, oh Jesus. "You're not going to die."

"The worms crawl in, the worms crawl out," she singsonged softly. "My mother promised to have me cremated, you know."

"Dammit, Madison, stop—"

A single tear breached the rim of her eye and trailed down her cheek. "I'm afraid. I want someone to love me so that I can pretend everything will be all right."

His finger followed the track of that tear. He'd never dreamed what she really felt…he was sure no one had.

Laurence, for the first time in his life, put aside his own fears, and for this one moment, lived only for the present.

It was easy to pull her down off the sofa and into his arms. Leaning back against the stuffed edge, he cradled her, whispering meaningless words as he nestled his nose against her hair. He stroked tendrils of hair at her temple, the silkiness of her skin, the rough denim against her hips and thighs.

"I'm tired," she murmured against his chest.

"It's been a bad day."

"I'm not going to cry, though."

"I know you're not." He assumed one or two tears weren't considered crying.

Her fingers tangled with his tie and wrinkled his shirt. "This is nice." She tilted her head back, lips luscious and inviting even without her usual crimson color. "Are you mad?"

"No." She frustrated him, teased him, inflamed him and drove him insane, but anger him? Not for anything she'd done today. "I'll tuck you into bed."

He intended tucking himself in beside her, the decision made between the tear in her eyes and the feel of her in his arms.

In her bedroom, late-afternoon sun streaked the blue carpet and bathed the bedspread in light. He threw back the covers, coaxed her down on the mattress, then moved to close the blinds.

She looked at him from her pillow, luxurious hair strewn across the pale cotton. "Promise not to leave until I wake up?"

"I'll stay." He came to sit on the bed beside her, tugged his tie from his neck, threw it across the bottom of the bed, then leaned down to untie his shoes. Once done, he removed his glasses, put one hand on the bed beside her and tossed them onto the table. Ah, made it with no damage done. "Move over."

Her eyes widened, irises the deepest green. "You mean you're going to get in bed?"

"That's exactly what I mean." He rolled to his side, tucking his bare feet under the covers next to hers.

"You don't have to do that."

So close he could almost taste her peppermint toothpaste, he pulled her flush against him. "I want to."

"I'm not trying to trick you."

"It doesn't matter if you are." He insinuated his knee between hers, then tugged her leg until her calf rested on his thigh. God, she felt good, warm and soft. "I want to kiss you."

She bit her lip. His groin tightened. "You sure, T. Larry?"

"I've never been more sure of anything."

"And you won't blame me later?"

"Let's just go with what we feel, Madison."

It was on the tip of her tongue to ask him what he felt, then Madison realized she didn't want to know. He might stop if she asked. With his arms around her, the heat of his body warming her, the hardness of his thigh between hers, she wasn't afraid.

She kissed him, with her lips, her tongue, her soul. Lifting his head so she could wrap her arms around his neck, he moved so that he lay half on her. She relished his weight, her nipples peaking against her lace bra. His chest grazed the sensitive tips. Heat built low in her belly, and her thighs gripped his leg. Her body shifted involuntarily, rubbing his hardened ridge.

"T. Larry, I have this awful feeling I want to make love," she murmured against his lips.

"Madison, I have this perfect feeling that's exactly what we're going to do." His gray eyes sparkled with humor, not ire. She couldn't resist him when he was laughing with her.

"I like you without your glasses on, T. Larry."

"I like you without your clothes on."

"Are you going to take them off for me?"

He dipped his head to her neck, touched his tongue to the hollow of her throat. "In a minute."

With deft fingers, he pulled her T-shirt from the waistband of her jeans and pushed it up to her armpits. His tongue grazed skin at the edge of her bra, sneaking just beneath the lace, tantalizing her nipples.

"Are you going to regret this tomorrow?" She had to ask though she was scared he'd stop.

He pushed the cup aside with the pad of his thumb and spoke with his lips against her breast, his breath unbearably seductive. "I don't know what I'll feel tomorrow, but it won't be regret."

He licked her nipple, blew on it. Her back arched, a moan slipping from her lips. "T. Larry—"

"I want to taste you, Madison." He flicked her with his tongue. "I want to touch you. I want to be inside of you. So please shut up."

She tried, she really did, but she had to tell him. "I'm not afraid of dying right now."

He tucked his fingers beneath her waistband. "I'm not afraid of making love to you right now."

Her body hummed with his hot touch. A pulse beat at her center. Maybe he could learn to love her eventually. "I didn't throw out the rest of the condoms."

He unsnapped the front closure of her bra. "We don't need them yet. I'm not done touching and tasting."

"Do you want me to take off my jeans?"

"I want to take them off." But he didn't. Instead, he moved fully between her thighs, and slid deliciously down until he braced himself on his elbows, his mouth mere centimeters from her breasts. "Do you want me to suck your nipple?"

One tiny part of her brain, the only sane part left, couldn't believe this was her T. Larry saying these things. Just hearing the question drove her excitement higher.

"Yes," she whispered, and guided his mouth to her nipple.

He suckled. She moaned. He ground his hips. She

rose to meet him. She reached between them to unsnap her jeans. His fingers stilled hers. "Not yet."

"Please."

He rose above her, smiling like a triumphant warrior. "You're not ready."

"Yes, I am." More than ready.

"We have all night."

She stilled. "You're going to stay the night?"

"I couldn't leave if I tried."

"Is this just sex?" *Please say it's not.*

He framed her face with masculine hands, slightly rough, smelling of soap. "I've never had casual sex in my life."

Jealousy knifed her stomach. She didn't want to think about all the women he'd made love to in his quest for the future Mrs. Hobbs. She wriggled beneath him, planting her hands on his chest to push.

He pinned her. "I've never had casual sex. But I've never made love, either. Until last night."

She wanted to cry buckets of tears.

"Lie still, let me make love to you," he murmured, then shook his head. "No, don't lie still. I want you to wiggle and squirm and scream if you like what I'm doing. Just don't stop me."

Oh goodness, there were depths to T. Larry she'd never dreamed of. And she wanted to see what happened tomorrow, in the morning light, wanted to give it a chance more than she'd ever wanted anything in her life. "Okay."

"Okay?" His lips softened with a smile. "Okay what?"

"Okay, I want you to taste me and touch me and be inside me."

His hips surged against her, and she reveled in the power.

He undid her jeans. She lifted her hips to help as he slid them and her panties down her legs. Her socks came off in the leg holes of her jeans and landed on the floor with everything else. He came down on his elbows between her legs.

Her breath almost gone, she managed, "Aren't you going to take off your clothes?"

"I like it better with them all on and you completely naked. Get rid of that T-shirt."

She did, along with her bra, his intense eyes tracking the movement. This T. Larry *was* unknown. And terribly exciting.

He lay poised between her legs, his mouth only inches from the place her body ached, his quickened breath fanning her flames. She wanted to wriggle, squirm and scream. He didn't touch her.

"Aren't you going to?" she finally got out.

"Going to what?" The edge of his teeth showed like a hungry predator.

"You know."

"Say what you want *me* to do."

He challenged, yet an indefinable need laced his voice.

She swallowed. He wanted her to say it aloud, ask for it, beg for it. Oh, he needed her. "Taste me, T. Larry."

He groaned, then touched his tongue to her.

Electricity jumped through her body. Her head fell back against the pillow. Oh, T. Larry. Oh goodness. She squirmed and wriggled the way he'd wanted her to, but managed not to scream. T. Larry, fingers kneading her bottom, held her tight to his mouth.

Her hand found the edge of the mattress, the other gripped her pillow, pulling it over her mouth.

He lifted from her long enough to whisper hoarsely, "Scream. I want to hear you scream my name."

Then he was back. She bucked, lost her hold on the pillow, lost her hold over herself, arched her back and gave him exactly what he wanted. She screamed her orgasm, screamed low and long and heartfelt, said his name over and over. And still he kept his mouth on her, prolonged the climax until she thought she'd fallen off the edge of the Milky Way.

She came back to his kiss on her belly, his tongue on her breast, his mouth finally against her neck. He lay for a moment breathing her in, his nose in her hair.

"Thank you."

She barely heard his words. "Shouldn't I be thanking you?"

He was silent a long time, his weight heavy but comforting. "That's what I meant."

He'd meant something else but changed his mind about telling her. She wanted to ask, but his cotton shirt rubbed her sensitive skin as he moved, and her vulnerability suddenly overcame her.

"Are you going to take your clothes off *now?*" She feared he'd roll from the bed and walk away.

He did just that, but instead of leaving, he towered over her at the side of the bed. She pulled the covers to her armpits.

She loved him in the waning light. "T. Larry? Can I do that to you?"

"What?" His voice rose on the word.

"Taste you."

The silence was longer this time. He was too far above her to read his eyes or his expression. "You don't need to do that to get me to stay. I'm not leaving, Madison."

The idea should have stung, but she recognized his vulnerability. "I *want* to do it."

Long seconds passed. "I don't think I could take it if you did that right now."

Power rushed along her arms, leaving goose bumps in its wake. She rolled over, cool air on her exposed backside as she opened the sidetable drawer for a condom. "Then can I put it on?"

His Adam's apple bobbed visibly. He bulged the front of his slacks. "I'm not sure I can stand that, either."

"Let me." She held the packet up, the foil glinting. "Take off your clothes," she whispered when he merely stood there.

After a moment's hesitation, he unfastened his shirt buttons with slightly trembling fingers, threw his shirt and undershirt to the carpet, then lowered his hand to his pants.

She stilled him with a light touch. "I'll do this part."

He swallowed again. Was this anything akin to what he'd felt when she'd asked him to taste her? Power lay in words and shaking hands and labored breath. Could love exist on the same plane?

She rose, bent her legs beneath her, the sheet falling to her lap, exposing her breasts. Her knuckles brushed his penis as she unzipped. His body jerked. His fingers gripped hers.

"Don't play. I can't take it."

"I'll just help you put on the condom." She'd never actually done that before. She wanted him to help her, the idea of their hands doing it together somehow more exciting.

The corner of his mouth tilted. "You like this, don't you? The fact that I'm almost out of control."

"I like it as much as you liked hearing me scream."

"Tit for tat. Jesus, Madison, have it your way." Then he shucked his pants and underwear and for once didn't bother to fold his clothes or hang his slacks.

The sight of him overwhelmed her. "Oh my goodness."

He sat on the bed beside her. "You saw it last night."

"No, I only felt it. It's huge."

He groaned. "When was the last time I told you how crazy you make me?"

"I'm sure it was earlier today. Can I put it on now?" His penis bobbed as she reached for it. Oh my. She reached for it again. It moved again. "Are you doing that?"

"You're doing that. It's overexcited."

She stared with awe. "Can you really move it without touching it?"

He grabbed her hand and pulled her to the carpet between his legs. "Jesus, Madison, just put it on."

He looked even bigger from this new angle. She tried opening the packet, but her fingers kept slipping. He reached for it, opened it with his teeth like a pro and handed it back.

She held the rubber between her thumb and forefinger. "What do I do, T. Larry?"

"Don't you know?" Their voices dropped to a whisper with bizarre reverence for the task.

She looked up. She knew the mechanics of it, but with T. Larry, everything was new. How he felt in her hand, his body inside her, what he liked, what he loved, what made him see the same stars she did. "I want you to show me."

Something passed through his gaze, then he guided her hand. "Put it here like this," he demonstrated, moving her other hand lightly from his base to the crown, then back. He gusted out a long sigh. "Hold the tip, then roll it down."

He took his hand away. Before she gave herself a chance to think or him a moment to stop her, she leaned forward and took him in her mouth.

"Christ." His hands fisted in her hair, holding her tight.

She swallowed the salty taste, then slid him fully inside her mouth. She loved the taste and the breadth of T. Larry. She loved the growl in his throat, the harshness of his breath out of his lungs, the near pain of his hold on her.

She pulled back, ran her tongue around the velvet tip, then let him pop out.

"I almost came." He sounded surprised.

"You did not."

"Do it again and I will."

"But I want you to come inside me."

He ran a finger down her cheek, along the side of her neck, into the vee between her breasts. "Then put the condom on."

In the end, he did it himself because she couldn't seem to stop stroking and caressing and making him breathe harder. The task done, he pulled her onto his lap, raising her above him, spreading her legs and bringing her down onto the head. He slid inside. Filling her, he held her still a moment, his head back.

Then he looked in her eyes. "Come when I come, Madison."

She pumped with the help of his grip on her buttocks, then he put a hand between them, between her legs, rubbing her, and she came because she couldn't help it. She came seeing stars and yes, she was pretty sure she heard bells, too. He followed close on the heels of it, because *he* couldn't help it. At least, that's what she wanted to think.

LYING BESIDE HER, Laurence watched Madison in the full darkness, the red glow of her digital clock falling across the pillow to illuminate her. She lay on her stomach, her head turned to him, her hair over her face, bare shoulders inviting his lips.

She'd screamed *his* name, came with *his* mouth on her, *his* penis inside her, her fingers caressing *his* scalp.

It wasn't enough.

The darkness played tricks with his mind. He imagined soft echoes of her voice crying other men's names. She knew how to make a man come with little more than a stroke of her mouth.

Laurence couldn't stand the thought.

A week ago, he'd have said he could never be a jealous man. That was before touching Madison. Now he didn't know who he was. He didn't know who had begged her to say all those things aloud, didn't know what part of himself had to hear them or die.

But he hadn't heard the one thing he truly wanted. That she loved him. Yet even if he had, he wouldn't have believed it.

He was afraid she'd leave him when she realized *he* was the one who couldn't change. He was afraid to stay with her long enough for that to happen.

He woke her to savor making love one more time as the sun came up.

CHAPTER NINETEEN

LAURENCE SETTLED into his car next to a steaming Madison Avenue. The steam had nothing to do with making love in the early hours of Saturday morning. It was due to his ordering her to her mother's house.

She fought him every step of the way. He'd told her to pack. She couldn't find her favorite slippers—Laurence had the erotic image of Madison wearing nothing but fuzzy slippers. Then she couldn't decide which scented shampoo to bring. Or which hand lotion. Laurence dumped the entire contents of her countertop into a plastic bag and handed it to her. "Take it all, dammit."

Finally, they had packed an overnight bag with her remaining clothes, Laurence got her into the car by nine o'clock.

He would find the culprit—and he'd find him today—since the police hadn't and Madison couldn't, and he'd go through his own people to do it. Harriet disappeared yesterday. So had Zach. He'd start with them, and he'd end up with Dick the Prick because he was sure something funny was going on with the man. He would browbeat answers out of Dick in a way he knew the police couldn't.

He'd clue Madison in after his intentions were fait accompli.

"If you don't stop fidgeting with that bag, it'll

break." Laurence adjusted his rearview mirror. Odd, that black BMW he'd seen on University Avenue was still behind them.

"I'm not fidgeting, I'm making sure my tangerine lotion is here." Madison twisted the bag closed. "Thank you for making love to me. Both times. That was beyond the call of duty."

He glanced at her. There was no sign of tears in her eyes. "Are you being sarcastic?"

"Absolutely not."

He couldn't figure out what she was being, except too nice about the whole thing after her display while getting ready. He went on the defensive. "I'm not dumping you at your mother's."

"I agree it's the best place for me right now."

"Right." That made him think the best place for her was at his side so he could keep an eye on her. He moved to the mirror again. Damn, the black car was still there, and it bothered him. He'd have asked Madison if she knew the make of Richard Lyon's car, but he knew the question would only spark another argument. She'd been none too pleased that Laurence had insisted she add Dick to the list of names she gave the police. She hadn't been pleased about creating the list period.

She glanced behind her. "T. Larry, what are you looking at back there? You just missed my mother's street."

"So I did. I'll go down the next street and come in from the other way. And you don't have to thank me for making love to you." He should be getting down on his knees and thanking her for how she'd made him feel. But now it was morning. He had to put the night to bed. Though he was no longer exactly sure why.

"I'm thanking you because you made me feel special."

God, she hadn't a clue how special she really was. To him. To everyone. His heart contracted. "You're welcome." An inadequate reply, but the most he could muster.

He turned at the next street. The black car followed and stuck with him as he turned once more, onto the road where Madison's mother lived. It was beyond odd, had moved into the realm of suspicious. Dare he drop Madison off at her mother's?

A plan bloomed full grown in his mind. If the driver of the black car was Madison's stalker, then he would trick the sneaky bastard. He'd let Madison out of the car, drive away, then double back to see if the Beemer was nearby, watching, waiting. He'd catch him in the act and get the cops down here PDQ.

Brilliant. Absolutely brilliant. If he found her stalker, Madison would see that his constant planning actually had merit.

"T. Larry, are you all right?"

"I'm fine. Why do you ask?"

"Because you didn't tell me I was blathering too much."

He realized she must have been speaking the whole time he was formulating his splendid plan. Christ. How much trouble had he gotten himself into by not paying attention?

"You weren't listening, were you?"

It must have been something really important. "Of course, I was listening. There's your mother waiting. And your brothers. Wonderful." Thank God for distractions.

The whole O'Donnell clan stood on the porch, dribbled down onto the front walk and out onto the lawn.

Sean barreled down the walk with furrowed brow, his sandy eyebrows almost meeting in the middle. James came next, then Patrick. They rounded the front of his car like one great behemoth. The Beemer, its windows tinted and disguised, pulled into a driveway two houses down, executed a three-point turn and went back the way it had come.

Laurence wasn't fooled.

He turned to deal with the brothers. Who were most likely going to ask him why the hell he hadn't brought Madison to her mother's last night, followed quickly by where the hell had she spent the night, and dammit, had she been alone.

Laurence prepared a lie to save her reputation.

MADISON TASTED HIM in her mouth when she licked her lips, felt his skin against her, roughened with hair. His scent covered her like a sun-dried blanket and erased the stench of that poor animal. Waking with T. Larry beside her, she'd wanted to bask in the afterglow. She wanted to believe bad people didn't exist, though yesterday had proved that they did. She'd wanted to keep all her fears at bay. Mostly she wanted to believe she'd make it years, even decades, past her twenty-eighth birthday.

T. Larry had ruined it all by taking her to her mother's.

He'd had some lame excuse about keeping her safe and talking to the police again and speeding up the discovery of the squirrel killer. The truth was he'd made love to her because she'd cried. It was the only way to shut her up.

She knew how Harriet felt. People did what she

wanted so they didn't have to listen to her gripe. De-
moralizing to realize T. Larry had treated her just like
Harriet as he dumped her on her mother's doorstep and
stood at the curb arguing with her brothers. Madison's
bag of bathroom goodies bounced against her knees.

"We were so worried when you called this morning."

"I'm fine, Ma. Honest."

"I wish you'd called me last night."

She took in her mother's troubled eyes. "I didn't
want to worry you." She glanced back to her brothers.
"Any of you."

"We were frantic anyway."

She squeezed Ma's hand. "I should have told you."

"But you didn't because…" Her mother looked to
the street, as well, but her focus was on T. Larry.

Madison watched him gesturing wildly by the side
of his car. Very unlike him. Tears burned at the backs
of her eyes. Silly girl. "I think I'm in love with him."

Her mother's arm drifted across her shoulders, then
tugged her in close to her cinnamon-scented warmth.
"And he hasn't figured out he's in love with you yet?"

"He's putting up a valiant fight."

"Men do that. They're like scared little boys. Your
father caved after six months."

Madison's chest tightened, afraid to think six months
into the future. "I can't wait that long."

"It'll pass more quickly than you think." Her mother
held her chin. "And you have a lifetime."

"Yes, Ma." Her mother needed to hear her agreement, and Madison needed to start believing it. She
didn't want a week with T. Larry. She wanted a lifetime.

Out on the street, Sean's face had turned hopping-
mad red. Patrick looked close to throwing a punch.

James's head was covered by a cloud of steam. Though he was no taller, T. Larry seemed to tower over them all. Like an avenging angel. Her guardian. "Do you think someone's really trying to hurt me, Ma?"

"Yes." Her mother's hug tightened. "That's why T. Larry was right to bring you home." Tilting Madison's face to hers, she added, "He's doing it for me, too."

Madison let the tears mist her eyes. "I'm sorry, Ma, I'm so selfish. I never even thought about how you must feel."

Ma cupped her cheek. "Stay and keep me company until T. Larry finds out who's doing this and puts a stop to it. I'd feel so much safer."

"Of course." What if T. Larry couldn't figure it out?

Tiny fingers tugged at her right hand. "Don't cry, Auntie Madithon."

Little Kirsten stared up at her with pleading eyes and dirty face. Madison dropped her bag to the porch and squatted to touch her niece's cheek. "Auntie's not crying, sweetie."

A single tear slid through the grime on that angelic face. The last of Madison's self-pity slid away with the dirt in that solitary drop of moisture. "Why don't we clean up your face? Then you can make me another candy necklace. I ate the last one."

Rising, she took Kirsten's hand and turned for a last glance at the street. Over the roof of his car, T. Larry watched her from behind his sunglasses.

She was still afraid. She'd been afraid so long she was sure it wouldn't go away overnight, not even if that night had been as wonderful as last night with T. Larry. But she had her mother, her brothers, her nieces and nephews. Her family gave her hope.

So did the way T. Larry removed his sunglasses to look at her. As if he didn't want her to think he was hiding from her. As if he were trying to communicate something. Then he raised his hand in a wave before climbing into his car and pulling away.

Madison decided to trust him with her heart as much as she trusted God and her family with her soul.

THE O'DONNELL BROTHERS had been ready to murder. Fortunately Laurence hadn't been the intended victim, Madison's madman was. Which made it doubly troubling when they'd acquiesced so quickly upon his proclamation that he would solve Madison's problem himself. It couldn't have been a lack of caring on their part. It wasn't that they failed to grasp the gravity of the situation. It wasn't a lack of emotion, either. Even Laurence felt buffeted by their consolidated overabundance of testosterone.

He had a terrible feeling they were matchmaking by letting him be Madison's savior. He wasn't sure he deserved that level of trust.

So here he was, disguised by his tinted windows and dark sunglasses, parked on the other side of Ramona Avenue, watching for the black Beemer to pass ominously by the O'Donnell house. He would not fail the O'Donnells or Madison. He simply could not.

Fifteen minutes ticked over to half an hour. The June sunshine percolated the inside of the car. His polo shirt itched around his neck. He pulled the wool blend away from his skin and rolled down the driver's side window. Where had the bastard disappeared? Laurence tapped a finger on the steering wheel.

Lace curtains flicked at an upstairs window of the

house he'd parked in front of. A breeze rustled through the branches of overhanging trees. The neighborhood was too damn quiet, no children in the streets, no teenagers with non-existent mufflers. And no black BMWs cruising the macadam. Dammit.

Forty-five minutes. The sun threatened to fry his brain. His lids drooped. The breeze carried Madison's flowery scent to his nostrils. The faint taste of raspberry lip gloss blossomed on his tongue. His chest expanded, his gut tensed, and his trousers tightened over his erection.

The soft rumble of an engine broke his reverie. Exhaust fumes obliterated Madison's flowers. His eyelids snapped open just as the Beemer's brake lights came on for a full stop. Heart racing, Laurence reached for the keys in his ignition. Dammit, dreaming of Madison, he'd almost missed his quarry.

The black car slowed in front of the O'Donnell house just as Laurence did a roll stop through the intersection.

It *was* tracking Madison. And Laurence was tracking it. Hot on its tail, he made the same right turn, then another right, and a left. Heading back to Madison's apartment? By God, Laurence would catch the bastard in the act, stealing something, leaving something, pawing through Madison's things.

He did consider calling the police, but rejected the idea as quickly as it came. With sirens blaring, they'd scare the culprit away. Or he'd wriggle off the end of their hook. But he wouldn't wriggle away from Laurence.

Exhilaration turned him almost giddy.

Until the Beemer passed Madison's apartment building with nothing more than a tap on its brake.

Dammit. Damn. It. Thank God he hadn't called the police. They didn't need a false alarm distracting them, making them reconsider Madison's level of danger. Some knight in shining armor he would have appeared.

They entered downtown Palo Alto. At the left turn on University, two vehicles managed to slip between Laurence and the black car. His pulse quickened, but he maintained control. He'd follow until the bastard proved his evil intent.

His prey wandered through interminable lights, causing Laurence's fingers to tighten on the wheel as he feared the yellow. The crush of traffic grew. A bead of sweat trickled past his eye. Right turns, left turns, El Camino, through the mall parking lot and out the back side, up toward the 280 freeway.

He could almost believe the man was leading him a merry chase. Laurence didn't doubt for a moment that it was a man. It wasn't Harriet—he'd have known if she drove an expensive BMW—nor was it Zach. For the same reason. Some inner sense, maybe a sixth one, if he believed in that kind of thing, told him there was something more malevolent at work here than petty anger over a tiff at work.

Thank God it was a Saturday, and 280, trafficwise, was never as much of a problem as Highway 101. The Beemer kept a safe, steady sixty-five miles an hour. Laurence slipped in easily three cars behind, ready for any lane changes.

He'd begun to doubt he'd stumble upon any red-handed activity with which the police could nail the perpetrator to the wall. But when the little black bomb finally stopped and the driver exited his vehicle, Laurence would have an identity. He smiled. This was far more than Madison would have expected from him. She'd be delighted. She'd be grateful. She'd drag him off to—

The black Beemer exited the freeway, another mall exit, dammit, dammit. Didn't the man know how difficult it was to follow in all that ridiculous shopping traffic? Of course, he did. Laurence's jaw turned to steel.

The bastard found a nifty little spot right near the mall entrance, with nowhere even remotely close for Laurence to park. He couldn't just idle in the lane waiting to see who emerged from the vehicle, especially since somebody behind him laid on the horn when he didn't turn into the next aisle fast enough. Talk about attention getting. He circled, tromped on the accelerator and zipped back down the aisle his quarry had parked in.

Empty car. Empty aisle. Empty sidewalks at the entrance to the mall. Laurence hit the steering wheel with his fist. Now all he could do was find a convenient spot—of which there appeared to be none—and wait for the bastard driver to come back.

He circled twice, found a slot one aisle over but facing, the view unobstructed. He'd wait until his quarry returned.

He wouldn't daydream about Madison's firm breasts, would not close his eyes and imagine her tightness as he entered her or the sweet suction of her glorious mouth. He'd pay attention, focus on that car until his head hurt and his eyes dried out. He'd concentrate so hard his brain would—

The passenger door opened. He turned to stare into the barrel of a gun, then lifted his eyes to the face.

Dick the Prick.

Shit. He'd known it in his gut.

Still, he'd failed to solve Madison's problem, failed to protect her. Her danger was far from over. It was only beginning.

CHAPTER TWENTY

"MA, DID I LEAVE my slippers the last time I was here?"

"Which ones?"

"Cat in the Hat."

"No self-respecting female is going to catch a man when she's wearing the Cat in the Hat," Sean grumbled from a filled mouth.

Ma had piled the kitchen table high with meat, cheese, bread and fresh-cut vegetables for her family's health. Silverware and china clattered as they gathered round on chairs and stools.

"Since when is any man going to see me in them?" Madison slapped deli-sliced turkey on buttered bread.

Sean harrumphed, mouth now closed. James raised his eyebrows and looked to Thomas crawling between his feet.

Patrick snorted. "He's not going to understand what we're talking about."

Ma pursed her lips. "The rest of the big ears will."

Indeed, childish eyes rounded and ears seemed to wiggle.

"Let's drop the subject," Madison decided, a faint unease setting butterflies free in her stomach. Her brother couldn't be matchmaking. Could he?

Sean swallowed. "You could do worse than T. Larry."

My God, he *was* matchmaking. Despite being Episcopalian by training, they were still Catholic and Irish by birth. Their heritage was in their genes. Catholic brothers simply shouldn't approve of their unmarried sisters spending the night with a man. Not even T. Larry.

"I haven't seen your slippers," her mother said neutrally.

"Bet T. Larry has." Patrick waggled his eyebrows, then took a bite of his sandwich before she could be sure the words had come out of his mouth.

"Bet he's seen more than her slippers," Sean murmured, gaze on her face.

"If he has, she has to marry him." James scooped Thomas onto his lap, cradling his huge sandwich in his other hand.

Madison made a study of pasting cranberry jelly onto her turkey. "He hasn't. And we...haven't."

Three snorts accompanied that disclaimer.

"If ever there's a man that looked like he'd just—"

Being closest, James's wife, Carol, slapped Patrick on the arm and pointed to all the big ears.

"You'll have to marry him," Sean remarked, this time his eyes on his wife, Sherry.

"Too late to plan a June wedding," James added.

"Sean asked in June, and we still managed to get married in September," Sherry said. "We'll all help."

"T. Larry hasn't asked me."

"James never asked me, either." Carol retrieved Thomas from her husband's lap and used a wipe on the boy's sticky face.

"All I asked about was my slippers," Madison muttered, concentrating on her sandwich creation which seemed to grow larger the longer the conversation went on around her.

A small hand tugged on the hem of her shirt. Madison looked down to find little Kirsten beaming at her. "I like Uncle Larwy."

Madison's chest got tight and her eyes blurred. "He's not your uncle, Kirsten."

"Yet." She wasn't sure who had said that. It could have been any of her brothers.

And then they bombarded her.

"He's got a steady job."

"Great earning potential."

"He's old enough to take care of you properly."

"To keep you in line when you need it."

She drummed her fingers on the table. The sound reminded her of something, she couldn't think what. Probably the beating of her heart last night when T. Larry touched her.

"He's not in love with me." As much as she wished and prayed and hoped, sitting at the kitchen table, her family doing all the talking, she just couldn't seem to share their faith.

"What man ever believes it when you first tell him he's in love," Patrick's wife, Sophie, expounded.

"He thinks I'm all wrong for him." Except for last night when she did actually seem to do everything right. But that wasn't love. It was something else, at least on T. Larry's part. Sandwich ignored, Madison's fingertips drummed faster, quick, staccato beats.

"Don't be silly. He adores you." This from her mother, the one person she'd assumed sane in the now too-tiny kitchen.

"What about my slippers, Ma?" Her voice held an

edge of hysteria. Tap, tap, tap went her fingers on the Formica tabletop. Tap, tap, tap, like high heels on tile.

"I told you I haven't seen them, sweetie."

Tap, tap. Yes, high heels. Someone watching women in high heels. Tap, tap, tap. Richard watching. Avidly. Eyes glazed. Oblivious to anything else but...footwear.

Amongst her slashed clothing, she'd found one untouched skirt, the one she'd worn on her date with Richard. She'd even thought of him when she saw her shoes had made it through the devastation unscathed, and Richard loved shoes. The smell that permeated her cubicle began with the arrival of Richard's flowers. He was alone in her office while she went for the vase. Hadn't he suggested she go to the coffee room? Yes, he had, providing time to put the box in her file drawer.

She'd discounted Richard because she thought he didn't know where she lived. And more importantly because she didn't want to think someone she knew would do these things. Believing in her friends was good, but not everyone who came into her life was a friend. What she thought was loyalty and trust was really just blind stupidity.

"I know who did in that poor little squirrel," she whispered. An ache beat in her chest right along with her heart.

LAURENCE WOKE with a blinding headache and the knowledge that he'd failed Madison miserably. That fact hurt worse than his head and his predicament. Which he took stock of through slitted eyes.

He was tied to a metal chair like the ones he'd sat on in school when he was a boy—hard, unrelenting and cold. The ropes didn't have an ounce of give as he tried to wiggle his arms. A bare bulb hung from the low concrete ceiling. An array of vicious-looking tools adorned a heavy workbench against the concrete wall to his right. Or his left. His head pounded so badly he couldn't tell left from right. On his other side were shelves filled with cans, bottles and jars whose labels he couldn't read. A series of gray metal cabinets hugged the wall in front of him. The cold of the cement seeped through the soles of his shoes.

A door opened, above and behind him. Footsteps on wood, stairs, he presumed.

Dick the Prick appeared in front of him.

Laurence managed a growl. The man had forced him at gunpoint to drive out of the mall, through narrow, cluttered streets, and into the driveway of an unprepossessing house in a first-time buyers' neighborhood. When he'd realized he'd left his garage door opener in his own car, Dick had hit Laurence over the head with the butt of the gun and knocked him clean out.

"How did you get me down here without the neighbors noticing?" His bruised and aching body was certainly a testament to being dragged down the stairs.

Pretty Boy Dick just stared at him, the gun in his hand wavering slightly. Considering his blurred vision, aching head, queasy stomach and the fact that he was tied to a fucking chair, Laurence debated the wisdom of pushing the man too far too fast.

Dick looked the worse for wear. He'd torn the pocket of his neat cotton cardigan meant for the golf course, oil stains marred the knees of his slacks, scuff marks peppered his leather shoes, and his hair, neatly combed and professionally styled on the two occasions

Laurence had seen him, now stood on end in some places and matted down in others.

He looked like a wild man. For the first time since he'd seen the gun in his face, Laurence felt a tickle of fear. Good God, the man might actually kill him. His only choice was to take the bull by the horns and hope to talk the little bastard out of it with strong dialogue.

"I suppose you've worked out how to dispose of my body once you kill me."

Dick cocked his head but said nothing.

"Or are you going to just leave it here to rot? The neighbors might notice the smell, you know." Unlikely, since he was obviously in a basement and the smell wouldn't travel through concrete, but still he wrinkled his nose for effect.

"You're a pain in the ass, you know that?"

"Ah, he speaks. Why exactly do you consider me a pain in your ass?" The question seemed a good diversionary tactic. A man with a gun in his hand who could easily have killed Laurence in the car and dumped the body in some field yet had chosen not to…well, that meant he wasn't too sure about what he was doing. Keep him talking, and he might talk himself out of it.

Dick dropped the gun to his side and paced the width of the small basement. "She was supposed to turn to me." He stabbed his finger at his chest. "But there was always *you*."

The finger then stabbed at Laurence, who miraculously managed to keep his head still. "Why on earth would she turn to you?" He was afraid he knew.

"Because of her tires. Her apartment. The squirrel."

"You did all that just so she'd cry on your shoulder?"

He snorted. "Pretty lame, man. You should have waited until she knew you better."

Dick's shoes slapped against the concrete. "It's worked before." He shrugged. "Well, almost."

What clues were there in that story? What had not been uncovered in the police background check? "What happened?"

Dick looked at his shoes and grimaced. "I don't want to talk about it."

Imagining the details the man *couldn't* talk about, Laurence's blood had never run colder in his veins. He probed on Madison's behalf. "Let me get this straight. You talk to her once on the phone, then slash her tires, trash her clothes and put a dead squirrel in her drawer." He shrugged his shoulders as best he could with his hands tied to the chair. "To what purpose?"

Dick wagged his head dejectedly. "You don't understand." He certainly had that right. "I saw her all the time on the train. Way before I called her. I tried to talk to her. But…I couldn't. So I followed her around. Just to see where she lived and worked and stuff." The bulb glinted off his spiky hair as he looked to Laurence for…something.

Laurence offered nothing.

"Then I thought about calling and pretending I thought she was someone else." Dick's eyes suddenly brightened. "It worked. It was marvelous."

"But you blew it with the tires." It may never have come down to a choice between them if Madison hadn't been in danger.

Dick grimaced.

"How'd you get her key?" Most likely from under the mat.

The little bastard surprised him, though, with his ingenuity. "That first night, when I went back into the restaurant to get her purse, I made an imprint of her key. It was easy to have it copied." Hell, he'd probably done it before, too, one of those other times his plan had "almost worked."

"I just wanted to see inside her apartment, that's all. And I only borrowed her hairbrush, I was going to return it."

Her hairbrush? That's the first he'd heard her hairbrush was missing. Then again, would Madison notice in the mess?

"And I cleaned up for her, too. I left her roses." Dick raised his arms, questioning. "She didn't even say anything to me about it." His head dipped to his chest. "Then she dumped me."

Laurence quickly quashed a spark of sympathy. After all, Madison hadn't fully appreciated Laurence's manly attributes for seven years, and he hadn't taken to slashing tires and trashing clothes. "So, now you've decided you need to get me out of the way so she'll finally turn to you?"

Dick backed up until his butt hit the metal cabinets with a clang, then slid down until he'd seated himself on the floor, his forearms draped over his knees, the gun dangling between them. "I didn't exactly decide. I just saw you following me. And I had this brilliant idea."

Laurence knew all about *brilliant* plans. Look where his had gotten him. Trussed like a turkey in a crazy man's basement. "So…how are you going to do it?"

"Do what?"

"Kill me."

Dick's lips worked. His head wagged. "I don't know.

It'll be such a mess. It was bad enough getting you in here. With you still sitting in the driver's seat, I had to roll the car into the garage, drag you up the steps to the kitchen, then down here. I had a helluva time. Jesus, you're heavy."

"I work out regularly. It's all muscle." He bantered while his mind worked furiously. He could talk Dick out of it. He was sure he could. Maybe he could even work these bonds loose. With a little help from God or a few angels.

"What am I going to do?" Dick moaned, putting his head in his hands, the gun perilously close to his skull.

For one thing, Laurence decided, the man could pull the trigger right now and thankfully blow his brains out. Not the best tack, though. With Dick's gaze on the floor, Laurence wiggled his arms. Yes, they were looser, he was sure of it. "Have you got a tarp or a nice big piece of plastic?"

Dick raised his head and looked at him with baleful eyes. "No. Why?"

"You could put it under me, then shoot me so the blood and gore doesn't get everywhere. The cops can find evidence of blood even if you think you've washed it away."

Dick grimaced. "I really hate blood. It makes me queasy."

Being on the wrong side of that gun, Laurence knew all about feeling queasy. He played Dick's squeamishness for all it was worth. "Killing someone's a messy business, you know."

"I hate messes."

Laurence hated messes, too, especially when it involved his own blood. He debated whether it was time for his punch line, but figured the boy wasn't quite there yet. "The mess aside, once you've killed me, you have to figure out how to get rid of my body. Do you have a chain saw?"

"No. I usually hire the gardener to cut the trees."

"How about a good butcher knife and some acid?"

Dick rolled his eyes. "That's disgusting."

"Well, you can't just drag a body out without someone noticing. It needs to be in pieces."

Dick groaned. "Oh, I'm going to be sick. How did I get myself into this?"

Laurence flicked his thumb down to see if he could find the knot. Barely, just barely. If he wiggled a little more... "All right. Let's think. You've got my car, which you'll have to get rid of anyway. So, you can take me back upstairs..." And being free to walk up the stairs, Laurence would have a fighting chance. "...kill me in the garage, put my body in the trunk, then dump the car at the airport and take a taxi to yours at the mall. It could be weeks before anyone notices I'm in there." He narrowed his eyes. "Except for the smell. Make sure you park in Long-term."

Dick moaned, his head once again between his knees, and Laurence wondered if he'd gone too far with the scenario. Or not far enough.

Laurence grabbed the advantage and jerked on his bonds, but hell, they weren't going to just fall off. "But then someone would probably hear the gunshot. Do you have a silencer?"

Dick shuddered, huffed in a big breath, blew it out, then started to talk. "I hunted high and low for a house with a basement, for a moment just like this." He waved the gun. "You don't know how hard it is to find basements in California. Especially in such a good neighborhood."

Dick couldn't have known he'd need a basement to hide Laurence in. He'd needed it for the women who'd refused his so-called comfort. Like Madison. Laurence pictured her trussed up in the chair, and his head throbbed even worse. If he didn't stop Dick now, Madison might very well end up as the next victim. He gave his bonds another desperate tug.

"I think it must have been a bomb shelter. The house was built in the fifties." Richard paused, bit his lip. "I just don't know if I can do it."

Laurence almost sagged with relief. Until he felt the bite of the rope that still wouldn't give.

"I've never killed anything, you know."

Laurence remembered the squirrel.

Dick read his mind. "I found it already dead. And the idea just came to me." For a moment, he almost looked pleased with himself, a slight smile on his face, the lightbulb casting a long shadow of nose. "Maybe I *can* do it. But you're right, someone would hear the gunshot if I do it in the garage."

Oh shit. Him and his bloody mouth. Now what to say? He was sure he could work himself out of these damn ropes given a little time alone. Laurence went for the gusto. "All right, so you'll do it down here. The walls will muffle the shot." Maybe not, but Dick seemed to buy into that with a nod of his head. "But you'll need some stuff first. Got some coveralls?" This time Dick shook his head. "Blood spatters. You'll need coveralls. And a tarp." With a quick glance around the small room, he added, "Make that three tarps so you can cover everything. Are you going to go the chain saw route or the acid route?"

Dick turned green again. "Why are you helping me?"

Laurence almost laughed, stopped short of crying. The kid was kind of pathetic. And just a little stupid. He wasn't even a man; he thought like a boy. Even though he was in his thirties, he acted like a boy. Laurence could win with his superior intellect. The timing wasn't going to get any better. "You want the truth?" Dick nodded almost eagerly. Laurence went for his punch line. "I don't think you're a killer, kid. You might be able to shoot me if you close your eyes and put the gun right up here next to my head, but you won't like dealing with the aftermath, cleaning up the blood and the brains. Because you can bet you'd splatter my brains all over."

"Please don't talk about it."

"See? If you can't talk about it, you can't do it."

"What other choice do I have?" A whine crept into his voice.

"You can untie me and let me go."

"But you'll tell the police."

"I won't—" which was a lie "—if you promise to leave Madison alone." He couldn't allow the boy the chance to try again.

"How can I believe you?"

"You have my word of honor." Honor didn't count for much when there was a gun stuck in your face. Besides, the kid needed help. This way he'd get it.

"I don't know."

"It's the coveralls, tarps and chain saw if you don't. The choice is yours."

Dick took one baby step toward him. Then Laurence's cell phone went off in the pocket of his jacket.

Dick jumped back. "What's that?" he cried as Laurence's phone toned the first few bars of Beethoven's *Fifth*.

"My phone. It's okay. I can't answer it."

Dick waved the gun at him. "Who is it?"

Laurence groaned. "How would I know if I can't answer it?" The tune played irritatingly and finally cut off. "There, it's gone to voice mail. Everything's okay."

Dick's eyes darted. "No, no, we have to know who it was."

"Why?"

The gun shook in the boy's hands. "What if it's Madison, and she's looking for you?"

"She's not going to find me here. Just untie me, and you won't have to worry."

"No, no, it's all changed if Madison knows about me."

"I'm not going to tell her. I won't tell anybody." Laurence began to work harder at the ropes, reaching under with his thumbs, regardless of what the kid might see.

"I want to hear the voice mail."

"Jesus." It would be Madison, he knew it. What if she said something about last night? The kid would go ballistic. God, now that was a very bad word choice. But Madison wouldn't say anything like that, not with her family all around. No, it would be something harmless, then he could get back to the task of getting Dick the Pathetic to untie him.

"It's in my pocket. Go ahead and listen."

Dick's playing in his pockets unnerved him more than the gun in his face had. But he gave over the codes and listened as the kid held the phone out for them both.

Madison's sweet voice had taken on a mechanical caste. "T. Larry, call me right away. I know who it is." Oh shit. He didn't have a chance to look at Dick's face. "You're going to be mad because you were right. It's Richard. I don't want to believe it, but it's him. Call me when you get this message."

Dick punched the end button with his thumb. "She knows."

Shit.

"What did you say I'd need? Coveralls, tarps and acid?"

And shit again.

"HE ALWAYS ANSWERS HIS PHONE."

"Maybe he was in the bathroom."

Madison had a bad feeling, a very bad feeling. Richard drove a black Beemer, and it bore a striking resemblance to the one T. Larry kept staring at in his rearview mirror as he drove her to her mother's. She should have known then. Jeez, how dumb could a girl be? She'd wanted to believe in the goodness of people, so she'd ignored all the warning signs that bad things were afoot. Now T. Larry was in danger. It was all her fault.

"Then he should have called back. Sean, I'm scared." She didn't like admitting it; she'd been admitting far too much out loud lately, but this...well, this was about T. Larry.

"Ma, clear the kids out, would you?" James, being the oldest, took charge.

The noise level dropped to tolerable as Sherry, Sophie and Carol took their respective broods to the backyard.

"We should call the police, James." She should have called the police an hour ago when she realized Richard had stolen her slippers when he trashed her apartment.

"T. Larry is fine."

She narrowed her eyes on Patrick and his disclaimer. "What were all of you talking about out front of the house when he dropped me off?"

"Guy stuff."

That earned Sean a narrow-eyed glare. "You know where he went, don't you?"

James answered for all of them. "He was just going to ask some questions. You're getting all het up. He'll call you back."

"Who was he going to question?"

"That Harriet girl, and the kid at the office, Zach or ZZ or whatever." And Richard. That would have been part of his plan even if he hadn't said so.

Madison left her brothers to whisper among themselves while she made some phone calls. Harriet hadn't seen T. Larry; the concern in her voice tilted Madison sideways. ZZ Top was a no go, too. T. Larry's not being where he said he'd be wasn't like him.

She just knew he was in trouble.

CHAPTER TWENTY-ONE

"WHAT DID THE COPS SAY?"

Family meeting in the living room: couches and chairs full, three brothers, two wives, mother and sister present, children outside. Problem of the big ears again.

Madison suppressed a small hiccup that might have been a precursor to tears. "They said he couldn't be considered missing for twenty-four hours, and that neither Richard's shoe fetish nor my missing slippers were enough to get a search warrant for his house." This time the hiccup bubbled out. They'd also run a search on him yesterday and nothing came up. "They did say they'd drop by his house today and ask him a few questions, maybe shake him up a little." That simply wasn't good enough.

"T. Larry may still answer your call."

It had been two hours. T. Larry would never wait this long. Unless he was avoiding her because of last night. But that didn't make sense; she'd left him such a detailed message about Richard. Even if he wanted to avoid *her*, he wouldn't avoid that message.

"He's not *able* to answer, James."

"You're blowing this way out of proportion, Madison." Sean shook his head, disapproval pulling down his mouth at the corners. "Give the guy some credit. He wouldn't go doing something stupid like pissing off your stalker and getting himself killed."

"How can you even say that?" It was exactly what she'd been thinking. Not the stupid part but that T. Larry, in trying to protect her, could actually get hurt. Or worse. Madison stood, suddenly as resolute as her brothers appeared. "I'm going to Richard's."

"You don't even know where he lives." There was almost a question in Sean's voice.

"Yes, I do." She didn't go into how insistent he'd been that she take down his address, that she call him if she ever needed anything, *ANYTHING*, underlined and in capitals, a fact which now took on a whole new meaning. For some weird reason, Richard had become obsessed with her. "And no," she answered Patrick's raised brow, "I've never been there. But I can find it." She stuck out her chin for emphasis.

"That's a stupid idea, Madison."

Ma, silent up to this point, set her glass of iced tea down on the coffee table with a definite clunk. "You can't let your baby sister look for T. Larry on her own. You'll all go with her."

"But Ma, she should wait for the police."

"Don't 'but Ma' me. Your sister is right. So go with her."

That was that. Ma was Queen Bee of her household even though her sons—and daughter—were all over the age of twenty-one.

LAURENCE SAT IN THE DARK, bound and now gagged. He'd ripped his fingernails to shreds, but the bonds, though looser, were not falling off. Dick had left with his list of supplies. Laurence could only pray that buying tarps, a chain saw and acid would call attention to the purchaser of such items. Police attention. He wouldn't, however, bet his life on it.

He might be betting Madison's life, though. If Dick carried out his nefarious plan, there would be no one to protect Madison from what the evil pipsqueak would do.

Christ. Madison. Laurence had loved her in one breath and failed her in the next. He wasn't deserving of her trust or her love. He'd screwed up. Royally.

Only one thing lay in his favor. He wasn't dead yet. If he did get out of this alive, he'd squash Dick like the worm he was. And he'd set Madison free to find a man worthy of her. One who would love, honor *and* protect her.

Then he heard the door above open.

"GIVE IT UP, MADISON. No one's answering. The guy isn't home, and T. Larry isn't here."

Frustrated tears stung her eyes. She couldn't bear it if anything happened to T. Larry. "We'll canvas the neighborhood to see if anyone's seen or heard anything."

"You're not a cop. No one's going to talk to you."

She'd been listening to her brothers' negativity for forty-five minutes, the entire drive from Palo Alto. She was ready to scream, cry or stamp her feet. She was ready to break into Richard's house. She was ready to admit that T. Larry was right, falling in love *wasn't* one-sided. She needed him to be all right so that he could return her love.

"I want to look in the garage."

"Someone's going to call the cops on *us*."

"Good. Then they'll have to talk to Richard, too." And find T. Larry. Safe.

She determinedly marched along the neatly trimmed front path to the driveway, went up on her tiptoes and stuck her face to the garage door windows.

"Oh my God." The words came out as a shriek.

"What?" Her brothers stumbled over themselves getting to her side.

"That's T. Larry's Camry in there."

James peered through the glass. "You don't know that for sure. You can't even see the license plate."

"Richard doesn't drive a Camry. He drives a BMW. That's not his car. It's T. Larry's." Panic rose in her throat. In the space of a few hours, T. Larry might have been ripped right out of her life. Panic wouldn't do. Later, but not now.

James backed off and paced the drive. Two children on bicycles rode past slowly, but when he raised a hand—presumably to ask them if they'd seen anything funny—they sped off as fast as their legs could pump. "All right. We'll call the cops."

"We don't have time."

Patrick jammed his fists on his hips and stuck his face down into hers. "And just what do you propose we do?"

"We have to break in. T. Larry's in danger." *She* was in danger of losing him. Strokes weren't the only way people died. Car accidents and serial stalkers happened, too. Oh yes, she now knew all about bad things that happened.

"We'll get arrested."

"Fine. You go sit in the car, and I'll break in. Then they can just arrest me."

"You know we can't do that. Ma would kill us."

She grazed them with her most scathing look. "You're all a bunch of babies." Then she brushed them aside and went to the front door one more time. She wouldn't lose T. Larry, not now, not ever. Even if it meant making sure she lived long past her twenty-eighth birthday. Across the street, a red SUV pulled into the drive. A man got out and stared.

Madison raised her hand, pounded on the door and yelled as loud as she could. "Richard, if you're in there, you better answer right now. And I mean *right now.*"

Her brothers stared at her with mortified faces. They didn't believe. They honestly didn't believe she was right.

No sound from inside penetrated the door. She peered through a side window, but every curtain was pulled against her. Richard could be out. His BMW was gone.

She pounded on the door again. "Open. Up." With the next breath, she yelled, "All right. I'm breaking in."

She stepped backward off the front porch, turned on her heel to head for the backyard with some vague idea of finding a tool back there, something to smash a window or jimmy a lock.

The front door opened.

Her jaw dropped. She hadn't expected Richard to open the door.

"Why are you yelling, Madison?" He raked a hand through incredibly spiked hair, the antithesis of his usual neat, fashionable style. His clothes appeared Saturday work-in-the-yard raggedy, yet the quality of wool in his sweater and the dry-clean-only look of his pants contradicted that.

Her brothers moved up, gathered round, protected.

"What are you doing here, Madison? And who are these men?"

"My brothers. Where's T. Larry?"

Something flickered in his eyes. "Your boss?" He was stalling, she knew.

"I saw his car in your garage. We've called the police. They're going to be here soon." Even as she said it, distant sirens sounded. She hadn't called. Maybe Mr. Red SUV had. Or the frightened mothers of those two scared children. Then she saw the cell phone in Sean's hand. Adrenaline rushed through her veins. Thank God help was on the way.

"You're acting like a crazy person, Madison." Richard eyed her brothers surrounding her. "I think I'm feeling a little threatened here. Maybe it's a good thing you called the police." His mouth lifted in a smug smile.

She realized then that he didn't have to let the cops in his house. They wouldn't have a search warrant forcing him to. And three strapping men, all over six foot, well that was quite daunting. They might even be considered a threatening gang. The ones in danger of being arrested were her brothers and herself. And then how would she help T. Larry?

She acted without thinking. Or rather, she thought extremely quickly and decided there was nothing else she could do. With what she hoped was a terrifyingly primal scream, she launched herself at Richard, knocked him flat on his back, scrambled over his prone body and started yelling for T. Larry.

Noise all around, sirens and shouting and the distinct thud of body against body. Madison plunged into the darkened house. She'd find him, and she'd never leave him alone again. Not ever. She opened doors to closets and rooms, a bathroom, the garage, then almost plunged down a deep set of stairs.

"T. Larry." The name came out as a whisper, something that certainly couldn't be heard over the commotion going on behind her. "T. Larry," she called louder.

The dark turned her inside out. A light switch beckoned just inside the door, but she couldn't bring her hand to move to it. What was down there? What if it was—oh please no—T. Larry's body? She choked back a sob, then reached to the switch and exposed the room below with dim light.

She would have recognized the back of that beautiful bald head anywhere. Stumbling down the stairs, catching her footing, then hurling herself to the floor beside him, she said his name.

Only his eyes could move. But thank you so much God, he wasn't dead. He didn't even look hurt. She would never ever ignore bad things that happened. Her blinders were off for good, this her solemn vow.

Gray duct tape covered his mouth. Heavy rope tied him to the arms of a metal chair. A blue plastic tarp lay spread at his feet. On the workbench lay a gun and at the foot of it, a chain saw, a can of gas, two gallons of some sort of acid and—no it couldn't be—her hairbrush.

She fumbled at the knots underneath the chair arms, poorly tied but still causing her numbed fingers problems. Plus she seemed to be crying buckets, crying so hard she could barely breathe. He was safe, but if she'd been a few minutes later, if she hadn't forced her way in…well, he wouldn't be safe at all.

"What the hell is going on here?" A uniformed cop stood at the head of the stairs.

T. Larry started to mumble behind the tape. She reached a hand to tear it off. The cop barreled down the stairs. "You're under arrest. Don't touch a thing."

She ripped the tape away, and T. Larry yelled. She was sure he didn't hear her say she loved him over the sound.

"YOU DIDN'T HAVE TO TEAR my skin off." T. Larry touched the still-tender flesh of his lips.

"I'm sorry. I thought you were trying to speak." He was safe. Madison wanted to hug him to her and never let him go.

The police had, in the end, arrested Richard, not Madison. They'd impounded T. Larry's car, had him checked out for any injuries, found none, then taken everyone down to the police station for statements and rounds of endless questions.

The sun having gone down on the whole episode hours ago, they now stood at the bottom of the stairs to her apartment. James had dropped them off. There'd been no question as to whether T. Larry was going to spend the night with her.

"I've got some lip balm upstairs."

He looked at her a moment longer than necessary to say yes. Her stomach sank.

"I should have had your brother drive me home."

"I can drive you." No, she wouldn't. "After the lip balm." She started up the stairs.

He stopped her with a hand on her arm. "I don't need any lip balm, Madison." *I'm not spending the night, Madison.* That's what he was really saying.

"Why?"

"Because my lip isn't that badly damaged. I can take

care of it myself." He didn't need her help. Not for that, not for anything else.

Her heart started sinking right along with her stomach. "What are you really saying?" Gee, wasn't she just a glutton for punishment?

"I realized something very important down in that basement."

She was terribly afraid he wasn't going to say it was that he'd discovered he loved her. She asked anyway. "What?"

His gaze roamed over her face, and she hoped he wouldn't say a single hurtful word, wouldn't waste a moment of their time together. But he did. "I'm not ready for what you're offering."

"You're afraid of what I'm offering." Did he really even know what "it" was?

His eyes fell to the step behind her. "I like my life the way it is. I like my plans."

He was lying; she knew it, and he couldn't even look at her as he broke her heart. "I love you, T. Larry. And I'm actually willing to live like I don't believe I might die of a stroke after my birthday." She dropped her voice to a deferential whisper. "I want to start planning for the future."

His jaw tensed, teeth clenching on the inside. After last night, when she'd confessed her terrible fear of the future, he had to know how much her words meant.

Still, he took a step back. "We're too different. I can't keep up with you. I can't give you what you need."

She bit the inside of her cheek. "That's presuming you know what I need, T. Larry. I don't think you really do."

"All the more reason not to let this go any further."

She moved up one step so that her eyes were level

with his. Her heart crunched inside her chest, and her skin turned cold despite the mild summer evening. "What's 'this'? You mean making love together. Working together? What exactly is 'this'?"

"All of it."

She felt her eyes grow wide. "Are you firing me?"

"It's for the best. I think we've pretty much proved we're failures at this."

This again. She could have pursued it, instead she latched onto the one word that was so important to T. Larry. "You think you failed me, don't you? That's why you're cutting me off. You think you failed by getting caught in Richard's trap."

"This isn't about Dick."

It was, she knew by the disparaging tone, the hint of spit when he said the name, the way his lips parted almost savagely.

"He's in jail. I'm fine. You didn't fail. And it was all my fault anyway." Tears pricked her eyes, but she held them at bay. "You told me that he was trying to hurt me." She didn't want to start seeing the bogeyman around every corner, but neither could she slough off what Richard and his evil plan had taught her. "You told me that all the bad things that were happening weren't coincidence, and I'll never doubt something like that again. I promise." She'd never let anyone hurt him again because of her.

He answered without thinking. That could be the only explanation for his vehemence and the fact that he ignored everything else she'd said. "*You* had to rescue me."

For just a moment, she thought hate sparked in his eyes, something she'd never seen in T. Larry before, certainly never directed at her.

"You're never going to be able to see past your failures and your plans, are you, T. Larry?" She might be able to learn from her mistake, but not T. Larry.

"Madison—"

She didn't let him deny it. "I know what the T stands for."

He remained immobile, silent.

"Terrified."

He blinked, then he turned, and finally he walked away. She didn't cry until she'd locked her front door.

She'd faced the truth, bad people did exist and bad things did happen. She'd learned what T. Larry had been trying to tell her all along.

In the process, she'd lost him.

LAURENCE WASN'T A FOOL; he was a realist. While he'd been sitting alone, waiting for death, he'd seen the truth clearly.

Madison was young. She was volatile—not flighty as he'd always assumed. She was caring. She didn't need a balding accountant who planned every minute of every day, but still couldn't manage to keep her safe. He'd let her down. He was terrified he'd do it over and over again in big and little ways.

He'd do what was best for her and get out of her life.

CHAPTER TWENTY-TWO

"IT'S ME, HARRIET. They caught the man who left the squirrel for Madison."

Harriet gripped the receiver tightly to her ear. Zachary had called to apologize. She had to remain calm, lead him naturally into it. "Madison called me to say they'd found T. Larry. They got the guy."

"Okay, well…" She could almost see him shuffling his feet as he spoke. "I just wanted to let you know."

"Thank you, Zachary."

"Well, bye then."

Goodbye? What was he talking about? He hadn't said he was sorry. "Zachary—" What could she say?

"Yes, Harriet?"

What now? She couldn't beg. "Nothing." She paused, giving him one last opportunity. He waited long enough that she was forced to speak. "Well, I'll see you Monday, I mean, tomorrow."

"Yeah." A beat. "Bye."

The dial tone buzzed in her ear. He hadn't apologized. She'd been so sure he'd realized what a big mistake he made in assuming she was capable of that horrible business.

Harriet put the phone down and stared at the muted TV set. She loved Sunday afternoon classics. This one in particular. Gene Tierney in *Leave Her to Heaven*. There'd been some terrible remake of it in the eighties, or was that the nineties? Anyway, no one compared with the devious, coldhearted bitch as played by Gene Tierney. Cornel Wilde was such a dope, believing in her right up until the end, until it was almost too late.

Eyes narrowed and lips pinched, Gene gave a masterful performance. Harriet prided herself on being able to manufacture that same exact look when she needed it, a look that could wither the recipient right before her very eyes, woman or man, boss or boss's secretary. And lover. Or ex-lover.

Her stomach flip-flopped. Something nipped her heart.

She wasn't really like that evil woman in the movie. It was an act, something to cover her fragile feelings so they didn't get bruised. Zachary hadn't apologized because he was an unfeeling lout. He knew she wasn't guilty of leaving dead squirrels.

He did think she was capable of going through with her suit. A suit he believed was mean. Vindictive.

She plopped down on the couch and watched Gene Tierney's muted mouth move.

Harriet wasn't vindictive. Why, she'd been sincerely worried when Madison told her T. Larry was missing. She'd been glad when Madison called her late last night to say T. Larry was all right. The fact that she'd been in bed asleep hadn't even bothered her.

That had to prove something. Didn't it? Didn't it mean she wasn't the cold, hard, unfeeling bitch everyone thought she was?

It might have meant something if anyone knew what she was thinking.

But they didn't.

LAURENCE SUFFERED through the rotten weekend. Thirty-six hours later, his head still ached, though the doctors had assured him he didn't have a concussion. His body was bruised and his eyes bloodshot from lack of sleep. Madison had not shown up for work. Now, Harriet Hartman sat before him, perched primly on the chair opposite. He had the vague notion of pinching his nose. One pain should stop the other. Or at least take his mind off it.

"Yes, Harriet."

"I told my lawyer, Harold Doomp, to withdraw the suit."

Laurence's coffee mug clattered against his desk. "What?"

"I dropped my suit."

He didn't know what to say. She looked neither vicious nor victorious, cunning nor duplicitous. Instead, her eyes were a bit sad. Her navy dress covered her knees. Her pumps lifted her heels only an inch off the floor. There was nothing outrageous about her, nothing on her face to indicate she had some sneaky plan going on in her mind. Her lips were not even creased with bitterness, but instead sported a becoming shade of pink.

"I'm sorry I started this, T. Larry. Can you forgive me?"

He was sure his heart seized up in shock. He'd never, ever, not since years ago when she'd accidentally added two decimal places to a client's income line, heard Harriet apologize. There had to be a reason. "Are you worried about your job?"

"I wouldn't blame you if you fired me."

"You know I can't do that." For fear of another suit. She opened her lips, paused, then took a deep breath.

"If you think it's best, I'll leave the company." She looked at him, solicitous but not cowed. "But I'd need a reference. I have done a good job for you, T. Larry, despite...everything."

Everything being instigating mutiny, slapping a suit on him and demeaning Madison. In all fairness, Harriet had received more than her fair share of demeaning. He leaned back in his chair and folded his hands over his abdomen. "What's your goal here, Harriet?"

She pursed her lips in true Harriet the Harridan style. Then she let them soften. "Zachary told me you almost got killed."

What difference could that possibly make to her? "So you think you owe me one on the suit?"

She tugged her lip between her teeth, worrying it. "There's three people in this world I owe an apology to." She swallowed almost nervously, then plunged on. "First there's you. For the suit. You didn't deserve that. And I'm sorry."

He didn't push, let her find her own pace.

"Then there's Zachary. For naming him and telling everyone what...happened between us in that horrible way." Her eyes darted to his speakerphone. "And Madison. She's the only one who never said anything mean—except for when she called me Chicken Little— but the rest of the time..." She filled the pause with another deep breath. "Well, she's been sort of nice to me. Defended me." Her hands suddenly fidgeted in her lap. "So when she gets in, I'll apologize to her, too."

"She's not coming in." Laurence wasn't sure what stunned him more, the fact that he'd walked out on Madison, or that Harriet seemed to have been taken over by a benign pod person. Though that was a tad unfair. She was an excellent accountant and a patient teacher—when she wasn't being heckled by the terrible trio. Her attitude could very well have been brought on solely by Laurence's own negligence in handling her tormentors.

"Is Madison sick?"

"I fired her."

Harriet's jaw went down, up, down, up. Finally she coughed and said, "But T. Larry, you're in love with her."

"I am not."

"But everyone's known for years you're in love with her."

"They most certainly have not." Was he so patently obvious?

"But…but…you can't just fire Madison. You know that, don't you? You can't get rid of her that easily."

He'd never get rid of Madison, not out of his head, not from his heart, but he had no intention of discussing that with Harriet. "I accept your apology. There's no need for you to resign." He might regret that decision later, but he didn't take it back. "Everything will be fine. You can go back to work now." He stood, waved his hand imperiously and was amazed to see that Harriet did exactly as he said. Then he sat back down and stared at the closed door for an eternity. Or at least a full five minutes.

The sky was truly falling, or he'd simply slipped down Alice's rabbit hole and this was his own private Wonderland. Or Hell, if one chose to look at it that way.

His phone chirped. His heart leaped, and he punched the button expecting to hear her voice. "Yes, Madison."

"This is Rhonda. Madison's not here yet."

He cleared his throat and hoped through the magic

of electronics that Rhonda didn't hear the hitch in his voice. "Then what can I do for you?"

"You've got a Mr. Daily here to see you."

So, this was where the other shoe dropped. Of course. Harriet was skipping Harry and the suit and going straight for the blackmail. She and Dilly-Dally could split the five hundred thousand two ways now, instead of three. Who needed the lawyer anyway? He should have known better than to take Harriet at face value. "Send him in, Rhonda."

You didn't face death by gunshot, dismemberment by chain saw, or Madison O'Donnell without learning a big lesson. Laurence would squash this new threat like a pesky IRS agent.

MADISON WAS LATE through no fault of her own. It was all Sean. He'd insisted on driving her himself. He was fifteen minutes late picking her up, then he had to stop for gas, and by the time they got on the freeway, it was a parking lot.

Her lateness didn't for one second relate to the fact that T. Larry had fired her or that she was afraid of him. He hadn't meant it. She'd never be afraid of him. He was a pussycat. He wouldn't hurt her. Not forever anyway.

She trembled suddenly as she pulled open the lobby door. Richard wouldn't have hurt her, either, not really. At the police station, T. Larry had explained how all the things Richard did had been to get her attention, how he'd been watching her on the train for months. She'd sensed something familiar about him on that first date, but she'd written it off as a fantasy come true. Now wasn't that the dumbest thing she'd done! Never again.

She'd be careful. Really, she would. Still, she did have to feel a little sorry for Richard. T. Larry had explained that he was really a pathetic loser. T. Larry had used some other names, as well, but he said he hadn't believed for one minute that Richard would have done anything to *her*, nor that Richard was capable of using all that stuff he had down in the basement against T. Larry.

She slipped in through the closing elevator doors. The quick rise made her dizzy. Or maybe it was that Madison still had the horrible feeling she'd almost lost T. Larry, and that God had somehow given her a second chance, in many more ways than one. Somewhere in the whole silly long weekend away from him, almost right away, actually, she'd decided she was going to use that chance to prove that she would be the best thing that ever happened to him.

She pushed through the double doors of Carp, Alta and Hobbs, once again feeling her usual perky self. Rhonda stared at her openmouthed.

"What?"

The woman's lips slapped shut, then moved in a whisper. "Harriet said you'd been fired."

"Harriet?" T. Larry had told Harriet? Of all people? Well, of course, he had. Harriet's lawsuit still hung over their heads. There'd obviously been another showdown, and he'd tried the trump card again. Despite what had happened when he'd used it before.

T. Larry's door was closed. The halls were empty, but the incessant buzz of whispers filled the air. Bill turned a corner, stopped, then smiled maliciously. "Here to get your stuff?"

She didn't let him faze her. Perky, remember perky. "Bill, that smile isn't very nice. It suggests you want me to leave."

He sidled closer as she bounced into her cubicle, setting her purse on her desk.

"I do want you to leave."

She raised one brow.

"Now I can ask you out."

Goodness. She'd thought all his innuendos were a big puff of air. "Why didn't you ask before?"

"I couldn't, not with T. Larry breathing down my neck."

She tipped her head to one side and looked over his shoulder. "He's still breathing down your neck."

Bill turned and found T. Larry less than an arm's length behind. T. Larry was breathing fire. Madison smiled. Maybe he wouldn't be too terribly hard to convince on the subject of how right they were for each other.

Piercing eyes glued to Bill's deeply reddened face, T. Larry barked at her, "I thought you were fired."

The whispers died an instant death. Heads popped out of cubicle openings and over walls to stare.

All right, so it wasn't going to be that easy, especially with an audience. "I thought you were kidding."

"I wasn't."

His glower still flayed the flesh from poor Bill's cheeks. "But since you're here, find Ryman and send him to my office."

She smiled prettily. "Say please."

He growled. "Please." Then he walked back into his office and closed the door.

She couldn't gauge a thing by that reaction. There was also something in the way he said Ryman Alta's name. Almost as if he couldn't restrain his anger, maybe even hated his senior partner.

With Bill's shuffling, cowed footsteps receding down the corridor, she paged Ryman and asked politely if he could spare a moment to see T. Larry in his office. Ryman grunted. Madison hung up and made her way to the copy-coffee room for her long overdue first cup of the day.

"Harriet."

The other girl stood at the counter stirring creamer into her coffee, her ankles quite lovely as they extended out of her attractive pumps, her navy dress chic as the dickens.

"I love your dress." Madison steeled herself for a caustic retort.

"Do you really?" Harriet's brow furrowed with concern, not anger, not malice.

Madison nodded in answer.

"Thanks."

Noise drifted in from the corridor, shoes on carpet, the hiss of voices not quite able to restrain themselves. Madison did her best to ignore them.

"Is it new?" The words were innocent, yet, not wanting to spook a skittish Harriet, Madison searched carefully for each one.

"Yes."

Oookay. Now what? She had no idea what to say to this seemingly new Harriet in front of her. So she rinsed her cup, dried it with a paper towel, poured a full mug, with Harriet all the while stirring and stirring at the counter beside her.

Poor Harriet. This must be what it felt like always expecting the other shoe to drop. "New shoes? They're pretty."

Harriet's lips curved in a shy smile. "Thanks for noticing."

Madison almost knocked her coffee cup off the counter.

This was getting frightening. Madison was used to placating, defending, smoothing over and making allowances. This...this was something completely different. "Harriet, is something wrong?"

She waited for the explosion. Of course, Harriet would come back with, "Why does everyone think there's something wrong if I smile or buy a new dress or new shoes or act like I'm a nice person instead of a bitch."

Harriet said nothing of the kind. "I'm sorry you got fired."

Madison felt herself the closest she'd been to having a stroke since she was fifteen years old. Harriet apologizing? Still a little gun-shy, Madison told herself to give Harriet the benefit of the doubt. Through Richard, she had learned that not all people deserved it, but she'd give it to Harriet this one last time.

"I'll try to talk him out of it, Harriet."

"I told him I thought he was wrong."

Little stars floated in front of Madison's eyes. Goodness. A ring of sincerity softened Harriet's usually stinging tone.

"But Harriet..." She didn't know what to say to that.

"I know you think I hate you after I...well, after everything. But I don't. I'm sorry I named you in the suit. I told T. Larry I'd apologize to you. I also told him I've dropped the suit altogether."

She was feeling quite faint now. There was a buzzing in her ears. Or that could have come from the excited eavesdroppers just beyond the doorjamb. She kept her back to the sounds. "You dropped the suit? Why?"

Still, this Harriet, the one she was sure she'd never

met before, didn't explode. Her eyes flicked beyond Madison's shoulder, then she said, "Because it wasn't fair to bring it in the first place."

A hush fell outside in the hall, probably the whole darn building. Madison held her breath, thought about hugging Harriet, but just as quickly decided that was going a bit too far. She did accept the earnestness shining on Harriet's cheeks.

"Thank you, Harriet. From all of us."

A commotion started behind her, first a couple of murmurs, feet shuffling, clothes brushing, shoes planted on the linoleum. Madison didn't have to have a sixth sense to know ZZ Top had stepped forward. The shine on Harriet's cheek moved to her eyes.

Madison had the foresight to step to her left and turn around before she risked being trampled. ZZ stood his ground in the doorway. Behind him stood Mike, Anthony and Bill, and behind them, a sea of mesmerized faces.

"Harriet dropped the suit, ZZ."

"I heard," he answered Madison, his look all for Harriet. Madison's little matchmaker heart went all gooey.

"Step away from your coffee, Harriet," he told her. She did.

"Put down the spoon."

She did that, too. Then ZZ Top moved like a whirlwind, took her face in his hands and gave her such a kiss. Openmouthed, slippery-tongued, lips just eating her up.

Madison's bones melted. T. Larry, oh T. Larry, where was he when she needed him?

The kiss finally ended. They all breathed again, some quite heavily, Madison was sure. ZZ, however, wasn't done. He took Harriet's hand in his, turned with her to the crowd filling the doorway and said with considerable pride, "Harriet and I are going to the movies tonight."

Harriet didn't say a word, but Madison was sure moisture gleamed in her eyes.

ZZ raised her knuckles to his mouth, brushed his lips across them and asked, "What do you want to see, sweetheart?"

"I'm gonna puke."

"He's lost his fricking mind."

"Do I even know him anymore?"

"I mean it, I think I'm gonna throw up."

Of course, those were male voices. But no one actually dared malign Harriet herself. From the females came a collective sigh.

Yet Zachary Zenker wasn't done. His gaze once again flashing across the assemblage like a flame-thrower, he dared anyone to make another disparaging comment. A tall specimen already, ZZ suddenly seemed taller. He stood straighter. Why, ZZ Top fairly exuded manly presence.

He caught Madison's eye, then winked, as if he felt his own presence oozing, or he'd read her thoughts. Then, with an adoring gaze on Harriet, he said, "One last thing. Harriet, we're taking the rest of the day off." Eyes darting to her face he added, "Shall we go to your place or mine?"

Harriet started to cry.

Madison did, too.

CHAPTER TWENTY-THREE

LAURENCE STARED the pipsqueak down. "Cat got your tongue, Ryman? I asked how Daily here knew that my partnership was at stake. I surmise you can answer that question."

Ryman sputtered, then finally found his voice. "I don't like your tone, boy. And you missed that meeting with Stephen Tortelli last week."

"Screw the meeting, Ryman. And *I* don't like your methods. You hired him to spy on me, didn't you?" He pointed at Dilly-Dally who wore a large smile and sat comfortably on the leather sofa, a deliberate reminder of what had taken place there, Laurence was sure.

He wasn't beaten, even if Ryman planned the whole thing, even if Dilly-Dally told the world what Laurence the boss had done with his secretary. He wasn't ashamed of it. He was only ashamed that he'd exposed her.

As the tall, thin man had tried to intimidate him, demanding an even larger sum and threatening his job as well as Madison's reputation, the Madison-induced fog had lifted from Laurence's brain. He'd seen the light.

"Harriet drops the suit, but Mr. Daily here doesn't go away. No, he's back. And this time he threatens to go to you with his story. Not Jeremiah. But you."

Laurence stabbed a finger an inch from Ryman's skinny chest. The man shrank away.

"What are you talking about? I don't even know this man." He avoided William Daily's eyes.

Dilly-Dally said nothing, but the corner of one lip lifted. He obviously enjoyed seeing Ryman on the receiving end, which made Laurence wonder about the tone of their dealings.

None of that mattered. His, or rather Madison's, predicament did. He had one card to play. "This was never about Harriet's suit or my moral conduct. This is all about Tortelli, isn't it?"

"What could Tortelli possibly have to do with Harriet's suit?" Smoothly, Ryman failed to incriminate himself by betraying that he knew even an inkling of what Laurence meant.

"You want me out so you can bring in more clients like Tortelli. Jeremiah wouldn't stop you, but you know I won't stand for your lack of ethics."

Ryman erupted. "What do you know about ethics? All you've done is keep your eye glued to a certain person's rear end, while *failing* to keep the firm's best interests at heart."

The emphasis on the hated word didn't pass Laurence's notice. He steeled himself against reacting. "Best interests doesn't mean simply bringing in more money."

"You're an accountant, for God's sake. That statement is sacrilege."

Dilly-Dally stifled a sound suspiciously like laughter. Ryman was a fool. He'd probably given the man cash up front for his part in the whole scheme. Now Daily could simply sit back to watch the fireworks. And laugh.

"I won't agree to sign Tortelli as a client."

Ryman's gaze flicked to Dilly-Dally on the sofa. Then he threw caution to the winds. "I have a witness to your immoral behavior taking place right here in this room." He flung his arm out. "On that very couch upon which that witness sits."

Laurence crossed his arms over his chest.

Ryman's voice rose half an octave. "I can and will use that to terminate the partnership agreement."

"What about Jeremiah?"

"He'll vote with me."

Laurence stared at him. Ryman wasn't bluffing. Jeremiah always voted with him. He would again.

Inside, Laurence felt all the hours, all the years, all the blood, sweat and tears he'd given Carp, Alta, and finally Hobbs. It was his life. The only place he'd ever worked, the only place he'd *wanted* to work. He loved his accountants, *his* accountants. He loved laying down the law when he had to. He loved the staff meetings, the petty squabbles, the clients, Jeremiah. He even loved occasionally punching numbers into his calculator when he could have had a staff member do the grunt work for him.

And he loved his secretary. But he wouldn't let his love for his work stand in the way of protecting her.

"Ryman." He left a pause long enough to make Ryman shift his feet. "Take this partnership and shove it."

The words fell into dead silence that lasted five heartbeats.

A staggering sense of perpetual free fall invaded his limbs.

"What else do you think you're going to do, Laurence?" This came from a very quiet and suddenly undisturbed Ryman Alta.

He took a deep breath. "I'll start my own firm. I

feel no compunction about taking my clients with me."

"That's unethical."

"Leaving them to be serviced by you and your ilk is worse."

Ryman curled his lip. "Do you really think they'll follow you like sheep, Laurence? We offer them a full package of services. Your only expertise is tax."

"I can hire the necessary professionals."

"They'll expect reduced rates going with someone untried."

Laurence clenched his teeth. "I'm not untried. They know my value. You underestimate their willingness. In fact, I've had several clients intimate they'd follow wherever I went."

"You haven't got it in you. You were born a junior partner. You'll always be a junior partner. You need someone to lean on."

The truth hit him like a fist in the gut. He wasn't a risk taker. He was a planner. He believed change took years to effect. Though he truly loved so many things about this place, this office, this very firm, he'd also stayed because he'd believed he couldn't succeed without them. Carp, Alta and Hobbs had been his crutch, fear of failure his convenient excuse.

"You're wrong, Ryman. I don't need you. Or the firm." If he *didn't* try this, he'd be a failure. If he knuckled under to Ryman's threats, he'd never stop being a failure. "My tenure here is over."

Ryman's eyes were wide, disbelieving. "You'll never work in this town again." A more melodramatic statement could only be heard in the movies.

A loud guffaw issued from the couch. Laurence had forgotten all about Daily sitting there.

But Ryman wasn't done with his threats and added, with an evil hiss, "Don't forget how all this will look for our dear Miss Madison O'Donnell."

Filthy bastard.

It wasn't just Tortelli, or Harriet's suit. For Ryman it had become personal.

His threat made it personal for Laurence. "If you hurt Madison in any way, Alta, I will break every bone in your emaciated body." What a violent man he'd become since falling for Madison.

"Your threats don't scare me."

"Face it, Alta, you're outdone." William Daily's knees creaked as he rose from the couch.

Ryman stared at him, anger and fear mixing on his features until his skin stretched thinly over his skull.

"I'm paying you for your testimony, not your opinions."

"There's nowhere to testify. The woman dropped her suit. He's not fighting the dissolution of your partnership." Daily's British accent had died an unnatural death. "I'm not shitting around with this anymore. The deal's off."

Ryman danced on his toes like a puppet. "But my money—"

"I earned your money. *You* fucked this whole thing up. I'm outta here." With that, Daily yanked the office door open to wade through a puddle of astonished, eavesdropping accountants cluttering up the hall.

Ryman turned. "You're finished here, Hobbs."

"Yes, Ryman, I am. Finished with you. My resignation will be on your desk within the hour." Laurence moved behind his desk, negligently opened a desk drawer, then another. There wasn't much there that he wanted to take with him.

Ryman pounded impotently out the door, the sea parting for him.

The sun beat through the window on Laurence's back. He'd just thrown his Financial Plan right out that very same window. With it had gone the Family Plan.

In fact, Laurence had no plans. None. Nothing more than vague ideas. Very risky business facing life without plans. One could fail. However, without risk taking, one couldn't have Madison O'Donnell.

"Where the hell is my secretary?" he asked the dumbfounded gathering at his doorway.

"Executive Assistant," she piped up, stepping from amidst the avaricious group. She truly was the most gorgeous thing he'd ever seen in his life. Gorgeous, spontaneous, full of life and laughter. And well worth risking failure.

He looked at the crowd trying to flow through the entry along with her. "Close the door, Madison."

"Yes, T. Larry," and she did just that, excessively obedient, but with a sparkle in her lovely eyes.

He valiantly managed to remain seated in his chair. "Is the conference room scheduled from—" he looked at his watch "—now until eleven? No, make that twelve?"

"Why no, I don't believe it's taken."

"Starting in three minutes, you and I have a meeting, a very long meeting. And we'll have to lock the door."

"Do I need a pad of paper?"

He rose, rounded the side of his desk, leaning a hip against the edge. "No."

"A pencil?"

"No."

"Then what do I need, T. Larry?"

"One of those candy necklaces from your niece." He smiled, stripped her naked with a glance, then added, "And you'll need me. Almost as much as I need you."

She launched herself into his arms. "T. Larry, I love you."

"I love you, too, Madison Avenue."

"Oh, T. Larry." She wriggled in his arms and hugged him tighter, as if she'd never let him go again. "Do you forgive me for letting Richard kidnap you and bonk you on the head and almost kill you?"

Her flowery scent filled his head. "Do you forgive me for being an ass where you were concerned?"

"You were never an ass."

"A staid, bald accountant then?"

She pulled him down to kiss the top of his head. "I adore bald men, especially accountants. I swoon when you quote the tax code."

He laughed and believed every word she said. "Well, then I definitely forgive you for siccing Dick the Prick on me."

She gasped. "T. Larry, that's terrible." Then she smiled. "But I sort of like that name. You're getting very good at making up names." Nuzzling her nose in his ear, she added, "We overheard everything you said to mean old Ryman. I'm so proud of you for taking the leap and throwing your job in his face. Can I be your secretary in your new company?"

"You're going to be a helluva lot more. How about my partner in every way?"

She beamed with that gorgeous, lopsided smile. "For the rest of my long, long life, T. Larry."

He pulled back enough to gaze into her eyes. "Do you really believe that or are you just saying it for me?"

"I might still get scared once in a while, but you'll be there to whup me upside the head when I need it." She worried her bottom lip. "Won't you?"

"Hell, yes, I'll be there." His heart soared, then nose-dived. "What about your birthday?"

She took a deep breath. "Birthdays don't have to be scary, either." She stopped to take his hand and hold it to her cheek. "In fact, I'm looking forward to having many more after this one."

Warmth spread from his touch on her cheek. Twenty-eight wasn't a number either of them had to fear anymore. And if she did have the occasional fright, he'd be there to help her through. "Since that's the case, don't you think you ought to know my first name before you see it written on our marriage certificate?"

She pulled back, stared at him with wide, disbelieving eyes. "You're going to tell me what the *T* stands for?"

He pulled her once more into his arms and leaned down to whisper into her ear. He had other games he wanted to play with Madison. This particular one was over.

"Oh, T. Larry," she murmured with such awe, such joy. "Can I tell everyone?"

He shuddered at the closeness, then gave her everything he had. "Go ahead."

She took his hand, dragging him to the door, and opened it to face the throng milling in the hallway outside.

"I'd like to introduce…" Madison looked up at him, eyes shining with almost tears. He slipped his hand to her waist and tucked her beneath his arm to a deafening round of applause.

Turning her high-wattage smile on her audience, Madison shushed them with a fluttering of her hand. "I'd like to introduce Tuttle Laurence Hobbs. And, because you're all so special and you're all going to follow him to his new firm, you can call him King Tut."

* * * * *

*Be sure to watch for Jennifer Skully's next romance,
coming to HQN in October 2006.
And now for a sneak preview,
please turn the page.*

CHAPTER ONE

JACK DAVIS FOUGHT DOWN the air bag and scrambled from the cab of his truck. The woman he'd rammed into was already out of her sporty red mini-SUV and on her hands and knees looking beneath the vehicle.

"What are you doing?" Jack swallowed the epithet he'd been about to use. His mama taught him politeness regardless of the circumstances.

Traffic flowed slowly through the lanes on either side of them. For once, he could appreciate the slowness of a Silicon Valley rush hour. Jack turned to the gold Cadillac that had rear-ended him when he'd slammed on his brakes. The Caddy's driver hadn't moved yet, though his air bag had deflated.

Jack ran back. An old guy, with numerous fragile bones. Squatting by the closed window, he shouted through. "You okay?"

No answer, but at least the old man's eyes were open, and he'd turned his head. Jack whipped his cell phone off his belt and punched in 911.

With the call made, he opened the door slowly, and held the man back against the seat when he tried to move. "Just stay put until the ambulance gets here. They need to check you out. Feel like anything's broken?"

The old man shook his head, but would he really know? His eyes couldn't seem to focus on Jack's face. Jack stood.

That's when he saw her. The woman, the other driver. Her butt in the air, short skirt barely covering her essentials, she looked as if she was trying to crawl under his truck. "What are you doing now?"

Stalking back, he grabbed her arm and pulled her out.

Still on her knees, she stared up at him with the bluest, most freaked-out eyes he'd ever seen.

"Didn't you see it?"

"See what?" he asked as calmly as possible. She'd started to worry him.

"The body. It fell off the overpass right in front of me. I ran over it."

She was young, midtwenties or so. Blond hair, blue eyes, and, from his vantage point as she knelt beside his truck, nice...nice everything.

Despite being batty.

"I didn't see a body flying off that overpass, ma'am." Jack struggled to retain that ingrained politeness.

She bit her lip, then looked through his legs at the Cadillac. "Maybe it's under there."

Jumping up, she tipped sideways on her high heels, recovered and rushed around him to peer beneath the old man's gold car.

She leaned into the open door of the Caddy. "Did you see that man fall off the overpass?"

The old man shook his head. He still hadn't spoken, and Jack was anxious about him. "You could have killed someone slamming on your brakes like that."

She sucked in a breath, her breasts expanding in her tight black sweater. "Oh my God, I didn't...are you all right?"

"Fine. Thanks for asking." He didn't point out she should have shown the concern before she crawled under his truck.

She put a hand on the old guy's shoulder. "What about you?"

He smiled up at her blissfully. And nodded.

"I'm so sorry. But the body just fell right in front of me."

Jack closed his eyes and shook his head. "There is no body."

She stared at him with guileless blue eyes. "But I saw it."

He didn't know why he was trying to convince her, but he walked to the front of her car, leaned down to look under it, did the same with his own truck—ah, Jesus, the crushed bumpers and tailgate made him wince—and finally the Cadillac. Then he spread his hand. "Nothing here."

Sirens sounded in the distance. Behind them, traffic was stacking up.

"Nothing back there, either," he said when she looked at the stream of cars with blinkers on, trying to merge around them.

She stared back at the overpass. She'd skidded several feet beyond it. "But I saw it. It was a vision. A premonition."

Oh man. She was schizo, a type with which he'd had far too much experience. "Don't tell the cops about any *visions* you had."

She tipped her head to the side. "But how am I going to explain about slamming on my brakes?"

"Tell them you saw a dog in the median lane, probably got trapped out there, then made a run for it."

"But that would be a lie. Dogs don't fall out of the sky."

Neither did bodies. He'd always considered himself a patient man, but he had his limits. "Have you been drinking?"

Her pretty blue eyes widened with horror. "It isn't even nine o'clock in the morning."

"If you tell the cops you had a vision, they're going to test you for every illegal substance known to man. You have that much time?"

She passed a look from the now-crushed rear of her little red SUV to the crumpled front of the gold Cadillac to the old man still sitting dazed in the front seat. "All right. A dog." She tipped her head again. "Did you see it? Just in case they ask."

"I didn't see anything but your rear end." Especially when she was kneeling down by the side of her car. Now that was a vision.

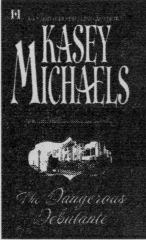

Jennifer
Skully

77027	SEX AND THE SERIAL			
	KILLER	___	$6.50 U.S.	___ $7.99 CAN.
77081	FOOL'S GOLD	___	$5.99 U.S.	___ $6.99 CAN.

(limited quantities available)

TOTAL AMOUNT	$ _____
POSTAGE & HANDLING	$ _____
($1.00 FOR 1 BOOK, 50¢ for each additional)	
APPLICABLE TAXES*	$ _____
TOTAL PAYABLE	$ _____

(check or money order—please do not send cash)

To order, complete this form and send it, along with a check or money order for the total above, payable to HQN Books, to: **In the U.S.:** 3010 Walden Avenue, P.O. Box 9077, Buffalo, NY 14269-9077; **In Canada:** P.O. Box 636, Fort Erie, Ontario, L2A 5X3.

Name: _____
Address: _____ City: _____
State/Prov.: _____ Zip/Postal Code: _____
Account Number (if applicable): _____
075 CSAS

*New York residents remit applicable sales taxes.
*Canadian residents remit applicable GST and provincial taxes.

HQN™
We *are* romance™

www.HQNBooks.com   PHJS0406BL